King's Shadow

A Novel

By
Dayna J Cash

This book is dedicated to Mark.
My inspiration
My support
My friend.

© Copyright 2006 Dayna J. Cash.
All rights reserved. No part of this publication may be reproduced, stored in a retrieval system, or transmitted, in any form or by any means, electronic, mechanical, photocopying, recording, or otherwise, without the written prior permission of the author.

Note for Librarians: A cataloguing record for this book is available from Library and Archives Canada at www.collectionscanada.ca/amicus/index-e.html
ISBN 1-4251-0999-3

Printed in Victoria, BC, Canada. Printed on paper with minimum 30% recycled fibre.
Trafford's print shop runs on "green energy" from solar, wind and other environmentally-friendly power sources.

TRAFFORD
PUBLISHING
Offices in Canada, USA, Ireland and UK

Book sales for North America and international:
Trafford Publishing, 6E–2333 Government St.,
Victoria, BC V8T 4P4 CANADA
phone 250 383 6864 (toll-free 1 888 232 4444)
fax 250 383 6804; email to orders@trafford.com

Book sales in Europe:
Trafford Publishing (UK) Limited, 9 Park End Street, 2nd Floor
Oxford, UK OX1 1HH UNITED KINGDOM
phone 44 (0)1865 722 113 (local rate 0845 230 9601)
facsimile 44 (0)1865 722 868; info.uk@trafford.com

Order online at:
trafford.com/06-2758

10 9 8 7 6 5 4 3 2 1

Prologue

Anglo-Saxon history is littered with brave and distinguished monarchs, some of them good and some of them bad. Of the bad monarchs there were some who became bad over time, corrupted by their position but others were born rotten to the core. Some of them were immensely strong and driven by the thrill of war; others were weak, happy to be led by men who lived in the shadows but wielded the real power.

Edward the Confessor ruled until his death in 1066. In his declining years he became increasingly pious and devoted to the church. Unlike his father, Edward was essentially a peaceful man, a man of conscience and embracing his faith had made him a happy man and later a saint. The real power though, did not belong to Edward. He owed his position entirely to the support of three powerful Earls who controlled the country in his name.

When Edward died early in 1066 he left behind a loveless and, more importantly, a childless marriage. William the Conqueror, (then William of Normandy) saw England as his by right but then so did Harold, Edward's brother-in-law.

Harold had the fortune, or forethought, to be present at Edward's death and declared that in the King's last words he had been named successor to the throne. He was supported in his assertion by the Earls, having already run the country for some years and in the heat of the moment nobody else cared to argue with him. As history shows, that would not always be the case.

In September 1066 Harold was forced to march his army from London to York to fend off an attack lead by his own brother, in league with the King of Norway. Harold won this battle in fine and bloody style but was immediately obliged to march his army south to Sussex, in record time, to meet William's invasion force.

In October 1066 the two armies met in a pitch battle, the exhausted Englishmen on foot and the trained Norman soldiers on horseback. Six bloody and brutal hours later, Harold lay dead on the field of battle and William was finally King of the island he had coveted for so long.

William had won a land where communities are divided into Hundreds, groups of one hundred homes, which may be made up of several villages. The people of a Hundred are to a large extent self–governing when it comes to the law of the land. Every male over the age of twelve will take the Frank–Pledge, an oath to abide by the law and to be responsible for his neighbour's actions also. This basically meant rule by peer pressure and it seemed to work. When one person stepped out of line the whole community was punished. Each hundred was largely self–sufficient, having its own mill and Miller for their grain, a tanner and a smith. They would also have a Reeve to maintain order and collect taxes for the local Lord, and should a higher authority be needed the Keeper of the King's Peace would be called. He would be responsible for a much larger area and would deal with more serious crimes, issuing fines and other punishments.

Homes are little more than single room wood and mud huts where the whole family live, eat and sleep. Most of these peasants are serfs, owned by or tied to one master, others are free men and may even have bought the right to farm land for themselves on their Lord's estate. These men are cottagers and will be required to work at least one day a week working for their Lord in part payment for their right to farm for themselves.

The wealthy nobility would have wood and stone to build with, some had built themselves quite luxurious homes with an upper storey and the extremely rich may even have glass in their windows and on occasion fresh food on their table. These noblemen and women may have had a more comfortable life on a day to day basis but they had to contend with politics and power struggles, and the occasional demands of their own master, the King.

The year is now 1086 and William the Conqueror, a grand 59 years of age, has been king of the English for 20 long years.

In an ingenious plan to reduce his overheads, William has his soldiers billeted across the country, drawing on the meagre resources of the many estates granted to his loyal subjects, and ultimately their peasant populations. Taxes have been both numerous and increasingly harsh. There has been too much pillaging and death has become a way of life. Whist not all evils could be directly attributed to William it may have felt like the land had been cursed since his arrival. There have been terrible famines, successive crop failures, occasional plagues sweeping through the livestock and once William's army have taken their share there is precious little left to feed the children with.

Infant mortality is tragically high and some of those who live are sold into slavery by their parents in an incomprehensibly desperate bid to secure the child's welfare whilst providing some little short term sustenance for the rest of the family and reducing the number of mouths to feed on a daily basis.

The latest suffering under William's rule is this year's census, designed solely to catalogue his wealth. Every home was searched and almost every pot, pig and pie was listed. In William's eyes what was theirs was now his to claim whenever he chose, after all England was his, what land they worked was only borrowed and at his discretion. It also meant that he knew where there was still money to be squeezed from the people. He could now levy his taxes far more efficiently.

William has proven himself to be a wicked man who cares little for the people he rules, but much for the wealth that brought him to this land. So much so that he has chosen to make England the centre of his cross channel kingdom.

Some say William was born of a devil, others that he sold his soul. Few know the truth.

Chapter 1
Gloucester – December 1086 AD

The darkness was almost complete, shrouding the land like a velvet cloak. Dirty grey clouds had blotted out the sunlight throughout the chilly day and now it shielded the land from the weak light of the pale and distant moon. The only light came from within the homes of the peasants where open fires burned, and from the generous hearth at the inn. Where no fires burned at all the darkness was seamless, an endless void.

As night had fallen over the market town the temperature had plummeted too. Anyone who could be indoors had been inside for hours doing what they could to stay warm and keep out the long, wicked fingers of Jack Frost. Those truly unfortunate souls who could not find shelter indoors that night had already found somewhere to hide where the wind would at least bite a little less. Jack was definitely abroad this night, leaving behind a thin veil of ice over everything he touched. Pigs and cows had seen the signs of his coming and had taken shelter where they could, huddling together for warmth. Even the smaller animals passed up the safety of an undisturbed night of foraging in favour of a warm bed.

Consequently not a single soul noticed the two cloaked and hooded figures creeping through the pockets of blackness towards the inn. The tiny sound of their stealthy footsteps was drowned out by the sounds of singing and jeering from the Royal party lodged at the inn that night. The King and his travelling court had arrived in Gloucester two days previously. Over the years the King had become a creature of habit, choosing to spend Easter in Winchester and Whitson in London. Gloucester was where he preferred to celebrate Christmas and of course it was an extra opportunity to levy some more seasonal taxes to bolster the Royal coffers.

Slowly but surely the two hooded figures crept along the rough road, clinging to the darkest corners, the blackest shadows, pausing at the smallest noise but still intent on moving forwards. About one hundred paces away from the raucous inn the two figures stopped in the inky shadows between two houses and leaned towards each other.

"It must be done and it must be tonight. The King's party prepares to move on tomorrow and we may not get another chance. Do you understand what you must do?" said the shorter of the two companions in a hoarse whisper.

"I do. Once the sleeping draught in the mead takes effect I will go directly to the King's chamber." This second voice was younger, softer and significantly less confident than the first. Threaded throughout his words was a ribbon of thinly disguised fear blended uneasily with one of determination, almost resignation. The deed must be done, no matter the cost.

The older figure spoke again.

"It will not be long now. They will sleep but I do not know how long for, it may only be a few minutes, you must hurry. There is too much at stake for us to fail." Laying a hand on the taller man's arm he paused and took a steadying breath before continuing in a gentler, more confident manner. "I will wait for you here, once it is done, come straight back to me."

The taller man bowed his head in obedient silence and turned back towards the inn. It looked bright and alive, quite forbidding. Too easily he pictured a room full of soldiers, armed to the teeth and for a second his courage faltered. He took several deep breaths and reminded himself why he was here, what he had to do and most importantly, why he must do it. The sounds of singing grew gradually quieter, fading until at last all was silent. He took one last deep breath, fixed a grim, determined expression on his face and then began to creep stealthily forwards towards the door of the inn.

The door stood ajar and he crept inside as quietly as he could, holding his breath. His heart pounded so mightily in his chest he felt that it would burst any second. He was sure the sound would wake the whole town. His eyes flew about watching for the smallest movement before edging forwards into the room. He took one faltering step away from the door and then paused, then another step. It seemed an eternity had passed by the time he made it to the centre of the room. The door seemed so far away now and each step further from it seemed so much more dangerous than the last, so much harder to take.

There was a sudden crashing noise, close behind him as something fell to the floor. His heart leapt into his throat and he whirled around in time to see a cup clatter over the bones and other debris scattered on the floor where it had fallen from a limp hand. He expected the whole room to stir, guess his plan and kill him where he stood. He froze to the spot, sweating, shaking; not daring to breathe until he could see that not a sole was moving. He took another deep shuddering breath, wiped the stinging sweat from his eyes and tried to calm himself. He knew he did not have long before the sleeping draught wore off, his deed must be done and he must be gone before then. He did not dare imagine what terrors would precede his death if he were caught in the act.

With images of being strung up by his feet and smoked over a roaring fire dancing before his eyes, he fought the powerful urge to run away and propelled himself towards the rear chambers. The largest of these would be the King's chamber during his stay. The man, still hooded, made his way directly to it.

He hesitated at the door, straining to hear the slightest hint of movement. When he was sure that all was quiet he slowly, cautiously pushed the wooden door open. It dragged on the floor, catching on straw and small stones, each creating a symphony of sound in the otherwise silent room. The King lay sprawled face down on the bed, a cup lying on the floor near him where it had fallen, mead spilled in a muddy puddle. A pale, half dressed young woman lay asleep beside him.

The hooded figure approached the bed and stood over the King's body, hesitating, wrestling with his conscience. 'The King is a wicked man, he thinks nothing of torturing peasants and noblemen alike, those he does not kill he bleeds dry with his taxes and uses their women to satisfy his lustful urges. His soldiers indiscriminately tear through towns and villages like a plague of locusts. But is it morally right to take a life, even one so evil?'

In the deep shadows outside, the older man anxiously waited. It felt like he had been waiting here for almost an hour but knew it could only be minutes. He knew that time was running out for his companion, they would start to stir very soon and if he were caught all would be lost. Where was he? Had something gone wrong?

'I must help him, this cannot fail.' Mustering all the courage within him the man took a tiny step forward but halted when he saw a tall cloaked figure stumble through the inn door and hurry towards him. Relief washed over him in large, rushing waves and he broke his cover to rush forward and meet his companion.

"I was so worried," he whispered hoarsely, "what took so long? Did you do it?"

The taller man drew several shaky breaths before replying, "Yes, I have it."

With these words he cast a nervous glance behind him at the inn door and then took a small bundle from his cloak and handed it to the older man.

"We must hurry, they are starting to wake up, it will not be long before they discover it is missing, I promise you that."

Together they hurried silently away into the shadows towards the edge of the town. They continued for many paces beyond the last home before they felt safe enough to pause in their flight.

"I must go, this must reach the Guardian before morning. You should return to Worcester, you will be safe there." The older man hesitated and laid a hand on the taller man's shoulder before continuing in a low whisper.

"You have done a great service to mankind today. I only hope we are in time. Now go, I will follow you soon. God be with you, Brother Aelfric."

Aelfric bowed his head once more and hurried away into the endless blackness of the cold night. His companion stood there a moment longer, considering the bundle in his hands. He shuddered visibly, before quickly burying it under his cloak, and then he turned and followed the cart track out of Gloucester and away into the night.

Gradually the men at the inn started to regain consciousness, holding their sore heads and groaning. The room was filled with the sounds of yawns and grunts, men rubbed their eyes and looked around them, unable to recall at what point everyone had stopped drinking and fallen asleep. It was some minutes before they realised that this was not the result of a drunken binge, something was amiss and the captain immediately sent two men to check on the King.

William had just been rousing himself, sure that he had not drunk enough to pass out. The girl slept on looking peaceful with hair fanning out under her. When the two guards burst through the door and tried to explain what had happened, William's natural suspicion exploded into paranoia. His first instinct was that someone had planned this in order to kill him and take his throne, but here he was alive and apparently well.

"Witchcraft," he muttered "but why leave us all alive?" he continued to himself. Theft must then be the motive. He glanced around, all seemed undisturbed. He suddenly lunged for the end of the pallet on which he sat, pulling at it roughly. The two soldiers watched in confusion. The colour drained quickly from William's hard, battle scarred face as the enormity of what had occurred dawned on him.

"It is gone," he roared "it has been taken. I want this whole town searched until it has been found, burn it to the ground if you have to – well? What are you waiting for?" His face flushed suddenly red, veins throbbed in his forehead and as he shouted spittle flew from his mouth. The guards hurried from the room to raise a search party.

William was frantic with fear. He must get it back; failure here was not an option. Without it he was as good as dead. It had made him powerful and strong, he had been almost indestructible for 25 years. Now, for the first time he felt vulnerable and exposed, despite all the soldiers around him.

He endured four hours of personal torture before his nervous captain came to him.

"Sire, we have searched every hut, hay barn and building and no-one is missing, but it is not here. We have looked everywhere and I have sent riders out on every road to search for strangers."

William stared at the man in stunned silence for a full minute.

"Get out. Get out, GET OUT!" His voice was hoarse and gravelly, his throat felt tight and small, as if someone were pressing their hands around his neck, his mouth was felt like dried, scraped parchment and desperate tears welled in his eyes. For the first time, William felt his own weakness and he did not like it.

Two days later the travelling court moved on. Every day William feared an ending worse than any he had yet dealt, but as time passed without incident his fear gradually lessened until one day he awoke and felt a little less scared, he allowed himself to believe that, however small, there may be a chance that he had been overlooked, that it had found a new home, a new purpose and that he might escape its wrath.

Time wore on, days became weeks, which drifted into months and slowly William relaxed. Spring in Winchester had been very profitable and life continued, as it had done for the last 25 years. That following summer, in 1087 the town of Mantes, on the River Seine, sent a daring raid into Norman territory. William's retribution had to be swift and complete. Taking little or no action against the townsfolk would show weakness to his empire on both sides of the Channel and that was something he could ill afford. William marched his soldiers into the town, torching anything that would burn and tearing down everything else, many souls perished in the flames.

William himself rode behind his soldiers, his magnificent Destrier striding through the smoke as he surveyed the destruction with immense satisfaction, revelled in his power. Flames licked and leapt around buildings, roofs collapsed, loudly and violently. He had missed this, for the first time in a long while he felt alive and powerful. As he watched the road ahead of him he could make out a bright, burning white glow distinct amongst the flickering redness all around. For some seconds it held his gaze, transfixed as it grew larger, moving directly towards him. Suddenly it raced at him and before he knew what was happening it was upon him, all around him, humming and screaming, stinging and biting at him, yet he could see nothing but the light. His horse reared up in terror, taking him by surprise. The high, blunt pommel of his battle saddle lunged backwards into his soft belly.

The phenomenon vanished as quickly as it had appeared. Wracked with pain and bleeding profusely, William tumbled from his agitated horse, hitting the ground hard. The internal damage was beyond his physician and William met his own bitter end shortly after.

Chapter 2
Worcester Cathedral – 1092 AD

The English crown passed to William the Conqueror's second son, William Rufus, and being his father's son, life for the English did not improve under his rule. He sneered openly at the Church and its leaders, acquired their property and incomes for his own and designated large areas of land as Royal hunting preserves. Available crop land diminished and what was left often fell prey to the Royal deer. From these there was no relief. 'Poaching' carried the penalty of blinding or mutilation. So, life went on as it had done for as long as many could remember. New King, new times, new means, same old suffering.

Bright sunshine bathed the lush green countryside. The summer equinox had passed but the days were still long and balmy. Men and women toiled about their chores in the fields around Worcester. A young boy herded pigs along the road, narrowly missing an old woman, who struggled with a large basket of ripening apples.

The elegant and ambitious cathedral stood on the banks of the river, bathed in strong sunlight, throwing a long shadow across the grounds. Bishop Wulfstan had had a grand vision and it was centred on this building, this focus of worship for many miles around. The influence of this diocese had started more than 400 years ago and spread as far as Dudley and Gloucester. His vision foresaw an immense creation, an inspirational place in which to praise and worship, a place people would flock to. And so, in 1084, he embarked upon his mission to rebuild the present cathedral. That was just eight years ago but already it had become an impressive and imposing landmark. It was a self–sufficient community, the grounds enclosing its own granary and bakehouse, brewery, stables and an infirmary to care for the poor and the sick.

Inside, the cathedral was spartan, with high vaulted ceilings and wide spaces. Etched and moulded grey stone created a large airy space for worship, a place where the chanting of the monks echoed richly, a heavenly chorus to lift the heart and the spirit. The mercy seats used by the monks during the long services, made up the vast majority of the furniture, but the eye was immediately drawn towards the alter, which sat majestically at the rear of the building.

Prime, the first service of the day, had finished, and the monks were making their way almost silently across the Quire to the Cloister, where they filed through the open door into the refectory to break their fast on freshly baked bread and cheese. The only sound was the hushed whisper of their rough habits as they brushed across the stone floor.

Edric was the last to finish his prayers and rise to his feet. There had been precious few worshippers there today. He prayed silently that this had more to do with the early hour and the coming harvest than the stories of heresy that had reached him recently. People seemed to be losing faith in the Church in their droves and returning to their pagan ways, worse there were rumours of people actually practising witchcraft.

Brother Edric found it hard to believe this could be true but the stories were becoming more numerous with every traveller who passed through and each week the number of worshipers seemed to lessen. Could it really be possible that these tales were true? Paganism he could believe, people had followed these ways for so many years, old habits were hard to break and he had been finding it harder and harder to convince them of the error of their ways, but witchcraft? Actual magic? Surely not. He shrugged his shoulders and a gentle sigh escaped him.

Edric's father was a wealthy, educated man, who had found his faith early and raised Edric with the religion he now cherished above all else. He had never been a pagan, had never known what it was to believe in other gods, to follow the old ways. He had always found it strange and confusing that these people could not see his God as the right and only one to follow.

As he made his way across the stone floor of the Quire towards the Cloister for his breakfast he heard the heavy wooden door in the Nave open ahead of him. Eric stopped, his stomach grumbled but breakfast would have to wait just a little longer. He turned towards the sound, remembering to smile despite wanting to join the other monks in their meal.

At the end of the Nave stood a tall man in a long, heavy cloak, a hood covering his face. Edric was puzzled, this stranger was dressed oddly. True it was still early but already the hot sun was beating down on the world.

"Good morning, friend, can I help you or have you come to pray alone?"

The stranger did not answer but started walking towards Edric, his stride long and purposeful, yet Edric thought it graceful, as if the man were almost floating. When he was a mere six paces away he stopped and stood still and silent for several seconds.

"I believe you have something I want, monk." Although this last word was almost spat out in contempt for the man before him, the voice was uncommonly rich and deep with a commanding, masterful tone. It sent a chill through Edric and his smile faded quickly.

"I do not understand. Have we met?" Edric's voice shook a little as he spoke. He did not know what had unnerved him so much but more than anything he wanted this strange man to leave, as soon as possible and yet he could not bring himself to turn and walk away, instead he felt himself fixed to the spot, waiting for the stranger to speak again.

"No, we have never met but I have spent years tracking you down, you have been a hard man to find." Now the stranger's voice had taken on a tone almost of admiration, but Edric missed it. There was something sinister about this man that made Edric's blood run cold, but he could not put his finger on exactly what that was. He struggled to compose himself.

"I am sure I do not know what you are talking about, now please excuse me, I have to go, the other monks are waiting." With enormous difficulty Edric forced himself to move, to turn away from the man and start to walk away, all the time wanting to run, and never stop running.

As a cold mist creeps across marshy land, the stranger's voice floated to him across the stone floor as if caught on a gentle breeze. It was only a whisper but Edric heard every word as clearly as if the stranger was standing at his side.

"I know you were in Gloucester that night, I know you took it and I need you to give it to me."

Edric stopped in his tracks re–living a fear he had not felt since that night outside the inn six years ago. How could this man possibly know about that? Edric's mind raced trying to think how he could have been betrayed as he turned to face the stranger once more in stunned silence.

"Where is it, old man?" hissed the hooded man.

Drawing on all his faith to find strength, Edric finally found a voice and it surprised even him when the defiant words escaped him.

"It is safe; evil will not use it again." Edric could hear his blood rushing in his ears, his hands were white and shook with fear as he fumbled for his cross and held it up before him.

"Out demon! You will not get the tool of the devil from me."

The stranger took a long slow step forward and threw back the front of his cloak. Edric saw only the briefest flash of silver and then felt the burning, tearing pain as the blade of the dagger plunged into his round stomach. He cried out weakly as he fell to his knees, clutching at the blood pouring from his belly, desperately trying to hold it in. He looked up, searching for a fellow monk, anyone who could help him, but his vision was entirely dominated by the stranger standing tall and large before him. The man was still cloaked but appeared to be dimmer than before, there but not as solid, almost as if he were fading away.

A curtain of grey drew down before Edric's eyes and he collapsed in a heap on the cold hard floor.

The dark stranger stood over the dying monk, hard and remorseless, his gaze searching the cathedral's aisles for any movement. Satisfied that he had not been seen he stepped over Edric's body and made his way towards the monk's dormitories to continue his search.

In the shadows of the stairs that led down to the Crypt, Aelfric crouched, afraid for his life, watching until the tall man had disappeared, then hurried to his old friend's side.

It was clear that Brother Edric had passed by the time Aelfric reached him. Not even in the infirmary had the young monk seen so much blood and it shook him to the core. In these times death and disease were no stranger but he had never seen such unprovoked violence, and never against a monk, a man of the church. It was a horror that would stay with him for the rest of his days, doomed to re–live this scene each time he closed his eyes.

From the little he had caught of Edric's words Aelfric was sure he knew what the stranger had been looking for.

He also knew that this…..this…..demon, would not find it here. In the midst of his sorrow for his friend, Aelfric was relieved that Edric had had the wisdom to take it to the Guardian to keep it safe. That meant that the foul creature would leave as soon as he realised it was not here. Unless the demon knew that Edric had had help on that awful night. Aelfric's blood ran cold at the thought until a fresh one occurred to him. When he did not find it here, he would leave, but not necessarily give up. He had said that he had been searching for years just to find Edric. Suddenly Aelfric knew he must warn the Guardian. If the stranger had found them here, he would surely find the Guardian, in time. He must leave as soon as possible but first he must tend to Brother Edric.

He hurried towards the Cloister to fetch the other monks.

Chapter 3

A thick blanket of cloud covered the night sky, hanging still and heavy over the land as if waiting for a sign before moving on to pastures new. The smothering stillness was broken only by an owl searching for prey in the long grass, his eagle eyes searching for the slightest twitch of a blade, ears listening intently for the tiniest sounds of a mouse creeping across the cold earth.

Autumn had taken its hold on nature, leaving a glorious red–gold carpet of dead and dried leaves on the ground that had been hardened by early frosts. Smaller animals were busy gathering the last of their stores to see them through the winter.

Startled by a sharp noise behind him the owl screeched as he swooped from his perch, making for the safety of the trees.

Gradually a feint orange glow appeared nearby. After several minutes the fire was crackling energetically, gleaming brightly, the wood spat and snapped as it was consumed in the heat of the fire. A horse grazed peacefully just a few paces away, seemingly unaware of the cloaked figure kneeling by the fire. After several minutes of absolute stillness and silence the figure began to chant in a low tone, using strange unearthly words. As he chanted his rich, deep voice rose and fell with an almost musical quality with a smooth practiced cadence. The flames of the fire rose and fell with the tone of his voice, matching its height and power as if it were enchanted.

On the floor near the fire was a small plain wooden bowl. As the chanting reached a crescendo the hooded figure took up the bowl in his hands and slowly raised it above the red flames of the dancing fire.

Suddenly the chanting stopped and as he stopped the man tipped the contents of the bowl on the ground before him. With a small, hollow rattle a number of items tumbled to the ground. There were several tiny animal bones and some small highly polished stones that had been purposely marked with strange angular symbols.

The figure lowered his head to examine the runes where they had fallen, taking care not to disturb a single one. Each rune, the way it had fallen and where it lay in relation to the others meant something, told him something.

For many minutes he did not move but then he slowly lifted his head. The fire had died back down to its original size, flickering gently and casting a soft glow across the bottom of the man's face. For the briefest second the delicate light revealed a strong chin and a wry, satisfied smile. He had the answer he was looking for.

Chapter 4
Withington – Autumn 1092 AD

The air was warm, carrying a gentle touch, one of peace and tranquillity. The breeze softly ruffled the grass as it wandered by on its endless journey and as the lush green carpet rippled it showed the first signs of decay. Soon the air would have a new passenger, one whose icy fingertips would touch every living thing. With every passing day more birds made their way south and the people of Withington went about the business of stocking barrels, shelves and woodsheds ready for the day when autumn would hand the reigns of time to winter once more.

Autumn had begun shrouding Withington in a cloak of brown, gold and red, had laid down a gradually thickening carpet of leaves and was breathing the last sighs of summer through the village's and its winding tracks. To the south of the village a large area of woodland marked a natural boundary. It was a majestic place, pre–dating the village by who knows how long. The wood provided building materials, fuel, food and skins. It was home to many creatures, from insect to the graceful deer. For others it was a place of rest, a peaceful place where they could sit and listen to nature going about its business.

Catherine's gown made a path in the leaves of the forest floor. Autumn was her favourite time of the year, the colours were so vibrant. It was a time when life had reached a peak; everything had reached a point where it had grown as much as it could, ripened to perfection. The world around her seemed to be clinging to life before it slipped into a fast decline, but for now, to Catherine, it all looked, smelled and tasted so full of zest. It inspired her, she felt energised by the nature around her and yet so at peace. Large Oaks towered above her as she wandered. They had seen so much since they first thrust from the ground, they would no doubt see much more after Catherine as gone. How many secrets did they hold within their ancient bark? Is that what they whispered to each other on the breeze that gently lifted her hair? Catherine was sure that if they could speak to her they would be very wise. She stopped beneath a giant, surrounded by a carpet of yellowing moss and sank to the ground, resting on the soft earth. Above her the sky was blue, the sun not quite directly overhead. Birds sang and chattered as they went about their business and somewhere nearby she could hear the sounds of deer grazing. She took a deep breath and closed her eyes.

"I could stay in here forever" she murmured, "I wish I was the breeze, then I could go anywhere, be with anyone and hear all the secrets the trees have to tell."

A young man stepped from behind the tree and moved closer to her, his hand on the hilt of a sword.

"No doubt they would be tedious and boring. After all, what can a leaf get up to that could be interesting?"

"You are probably right Michael, but it is nice to dream."

Catherine was the only daughter of a Knight. Her father had been granted a moderate estate with good lands and was as well-liked and respected as a knight, a deputy of the Baron, could be in the community. He was fair in his dealings with his people, generous in times of need, and there had been many of those over the past years. Too much pillaging to satisfy a royal lust for wealth, too many good men lost in the wars. But the life of a Knight was a tough one in these brutal times. The battles both on and off the field had left him scarred and a little jaded. He could not remember a time when he had been able to fully relax, there was always someone wanting more power, someone who needed bringing back into line.

Henry answered to the Baron of Gloucester who ran the Country with the other great Barons in the name of the King, but he was small enough to be below their notice most of the time, until there were taxes to be collected or there was another war to wage. There were certain advantages to being less powerful, but there were drawbacks too. There were any number of young, strong, ambitious men out there who coveted a title, lands, power, wealth and they saw him as their route to success. He had had to fight off many challenges in his time but none in the last couple of years. It was as though they could smell the odour of death on him and chose to wait in safety rather than fight and risk injury. Physicians were learning more all the time but the chances of survival after a blow from an axe or sword was still alarmingly low and Henry had a reputation for being strong and quick with a sword.

His greatest pride was Catherine, his only child. She had a good heart and she was strong and proud. She would inherit the manor after he was gone, he had seen to that. As a freewoman, of noble birth, the property could legally be hers alone. The law was on her side but there were people who would not stop to worry about that, the risk would be worth the consequences. There was also a chance that the Baron would rescind her right to hold the estate if she could no longer provide the required number of soldiers when required. He had striven to find a good match for her before he died but lately the winters had been cruel, they chilled his bones and tightened his lungs.

The manor sprawled around a rambling and draughty house, a blessing through the warm summers but when winter crept around again the heavy tapestries came out of storage, holes would be plugged and the old house would be warm once more. The walls of the house were deep and strong, supporting the huge oak beams which had been brought from the forest to build the roof. Henry had spared no expense when building; he had used the most modern methods, the best materials. Glass for the window spaces had been beyond his means but he had seen to it that the great house would last. He had even gone to the expense of adding a second level for the bedchambers. There were beds carved from Oak, as was each door, all lovingly crafted into a part of the whole home.

Mostly it was a happy enough household; often ringing with laughter or the sound of the cook singing badly in the kitchen or the maid humming as she went about her chores. Lately though the house had also rung with the sound of Henry's cough. At first it was a quiet, dry sound that only bothered him when he found himself out of breath. More recently it had become hoarse, a cough that seemed to rise from his boots leaving him pale and weak. He stayed in his bed later in the morning and retired earlier in the evening. On several occasions Catherine had voiced her concern for his health, but each time he had roughly waved her away, assuring her it would soon pass. It pained him to lie to her; he had been her only family since her mother had died in childbirth.

The old man knew he was dying and suspected he only had a short time left. Then she would be alone, she would have a house, lands and people to worry about and care for but no husband to support her, protect her. Despite the law of the land the estate could still be taken from her by the King, leaving her homeless or worse, subjugated to him. At the very least she would fall prey to greedy, grabbing nobles in the surrounding area. Some were already circling like vultures around a carcass.

As Catherine leaned against the tree her thoughts drifted to her father. She was concerned for him, she knew his health was much worse than he would admit and she knew she may have to emerge from the coming winter alone but that was a thought too dark for today and she pushed it away taking another deep breath to clear her head. After a few more moments of silence she opened her eyes.

"You are so quiet and patient, Michael. I find it hard to believe that you actually enjoy sitting out here with me." She glanced at her companion, a healthy glow touching her delicate features.

"Ah, the secret of a good soldier is being able to hear your enemy coming, to be able to set a trap and wait for the precise moment to spring it. Patience and silence are the attributes I need to excel at my work."

Michael and Arthur were two of the guards employed to protect the manor. The Knight had hired them six years ago when he realised he could no longer protect everything by himself. Now his health was failing and if he could not find a husband for his daughter he would at least protect her from the greedy landowners who would do anything to increase their own estates. Marrying Catherine was the easiest way of taking everything. If she refused, who knew what they might resort to?

It was Michael who escorted her today, who saw every branch move, heard every twig break. There had already been one attempt to kidnap Catherine and he was determined to be more than ready for another. Michael watched her carefully, not wanting to be caught staring. Her hair was a rich, warm, chestnut brown and hung straight and bright around her shoulders. Her eyes were the softest brown and her smile, which lifted the corners of her mouth in a delicate way and put a sparkle in her eyes, never failed to brighten even the greyest day for him.

It was Catherine's latest potential suitor, if he could be given such a title, who was causing current concern. Matthew Preece. He was nothing more than a rich farmer, not nobility, he was not even a gentleman as far as Michael could see, but he was determined. That was reason enough for Michael to consider him a threat. It was Preece who had tried to have Catherine kidnapped last month, Michael was sure of it. Now, today, she insisted on walking in the woods, a headstrong woman who refused to be frightened, at least visibly. He admired her for her courage, but he knew inside she must be scared. Preece was an evil little man who would stop at nothing; it seemed, to win the Knight's lands.

It was Preece that Michael watched for. He prayed that she would want to leave soon so that they could be back within the walls of the house with Arthur to ease the burden of watching. Catherine watched Michael from the corner of her eye, he was restless. He did not want to be here and wanted her safely back at the house. She was brave and headstrong but she had known him for years and she recognised his mood. She gave in, or perhaps she was scared and did not quite know how to say it.

"All right Michael, we can go now, I have had enough of this draughty old wood anyway. It is far too noisy for my liking today."

"Yes my Lady" he replied.

Michael set the pace, and they walked quickly toward the house. He would be happier once they were back out in the open, here there was too much scope for ambush, and too much was hidden, out of view. For some time now Michael had been sure he had sensed someone else, someone watching them. It could be one of Preece's men. But then why not attack? They were two people, a woman and one soldier. Why only send one man? Michael was sure there were no more. Preece would surely send more than one man; subtlety did not seem to be his style. Michael's pulse began to slow as his soldier's instincts took over and his nerves calmed. Why watch? A local man would have shown himself, greeted them. Was it a new suitor perhaps? Questions and dead ends whirled through Michael's mind as he kept Catherine on a steady and brisk course back toward the manor.

Catherine was becoming alarmed at the pace but she was determined not to let Michael down. He seemed unusually anxious and it worried her. He was always so sure and confident, much of her strength depended on that. They were almost to the wood's edge now and she fought the desire to run, if she panicked she would make things far harder for Michael, she knew that. She had been watching their three soldiers for years, she had listened and she had learned from them. For a large portion of their six years together those men had been her friends. She wanted so badly to be at home now.

"Michael?" It was a whisper that she barely managed.

"One moment my Lady" he replied, his voice equally quiet but calm and firm, betraying no trace of the anxiety she had seen in his eyes.

Suddenly they burst into the clear, beyond the trees with a hundred strides to cross before they were as safe as Michael would like but here in the open he would at least see his enemy coming. His mood relaxed greatly and he turned to Catherine.

"You had a question my Lady?" a broad smile graced his handsome features and it did more for her nerves than any spoken word could have done at that moment.

"Is everything all right? I mean, are we in any danger?"

"Not at all, you see we are almost at the gates now?"

Having noted their hasty approach Arthur was waiting at the gates for them.

"Was your walk refreshing my Lady?" said Arthur, his face a picture of peace and confidence. She was beginning to feel quite foolish. She told herself that Michael had probably been more anxious about missing the midday meal than about the monsters she had begun to conjure as they left the woods.

"It was wonderful, thank you Arthur, but a little cool, I think. I may start walking in the grounds from now on, where the wind cannot reach me." She gave him the bravest smile she could summon, thanked Michael for his patience and hurried to her private room. Her bedchamber was large and airy and has always been a source of peace for her. It was a place where she could sit and be with alone her thoughts. Once she had closed the door she moved to stand by the small window space which overlooked the courtyard she had just left. She could feel tears welling in her eyes and took several deep breaths to hold them at bay. As she searched for some distraction she caught sight of Michael and Arthur talking earnestly.

Just lately she felt she was forced to be a prisoner in her own home. A month ago, after that awful incident when a strange man had grabbed at her and tried to throw her in the back of a smelly old cart, her father had sat her down and explained it to her. He had told her about their neighbour, Mr Preece, told her how he seemed keen to marry her, with or without her consent and told her why. She recalled that she had seen him once or twice, whilst out with her father back in the spring. She remembered that she had felt uncomfortable in his presence but forgotten he existed, until just recently, when he had forced his way back into her attention. She no longer felt she could even make her favourite walk to the woodland edge without threat. She thanked the stars that she had her father, Arthur, Michael and John. Without them she would be lost. Perhaps there were worse things than being a prisoner here.

Suddenly the door flew open and Catherine's maid crashed into her room making her jump. Her face was white, her breathing laboured and her eyes wide.

"Rachel, whatever is wrong?" Catherine went quickly to the maid ready to help the poor girl. Her first thought was that she had got herself into trouble with John, one of their soldiers.

They had been close for a long time and clearly felt very deeply about each other. Catherine was not sure why they had not married yet. If she had fallen pregnant her parents would certainly disown her. Catherine had known them for a long time and they were very pious, principled people. Rachel would be forced to raise the child alone, cause enough for the girl's obvious distress. But Catherine was far from prepared for what she had to say.

"My Lady, come quickly, the Master, oh please you have to hurry Miss!"

"My father?"

With her heart racing Catherine chased after the maid towards her father's private chamber on the ground floor. She threw the door wide and found her father lying on the floor, staring at the ceiling. A small table had been overturned and an earthenware mug lay overturned and broken nearby. Arthur was already on his knees by her father's side with a deeply troubled look in his eyes. Throwing herself down beside him she clasped his cold hand in hers. His face was white and beads of sweat had formed on his forehead and cheeks, his eyes were glassy and lifeless.

"Father, it is me. Father, talk to me."

Her voice quivered and her body shook with a fear that she had never imagined possible until now. The Knight remained silent except for his shallow, rasping breath. Tears began to slide down Catherine's face and her fear grew with each breath.

"Father, talk to me, you must talk to me. Arthur, fetch the physician, please."

She raised her eyes to Arthur's face, beseeching him to do something, to make this better. Behind her, unseen, Michael stepped into the room.

Sobbing now, she begged.

"Please, you have to help him." She turned back to her father.

"Father, do not leave me. Please do not leave me. I love you. I do not want you to go. I will not let you go. Father!"

Slowly, shaking, she reached out her hand and touched his face, her tears falling on his chest. As her fingers brushed across his cheek he gently squeezed her hand. His skin felt cool to the touch and although deep inside she knew it was too late to help him she refused to accept the hard truth. His chest rose gently one last time, his grip on her hand relaxed and as the breath escaped his blue lips she knew he was gone.

Still clinging to his hand she lifted her face to the ceiling and cried out.

"NO!"

Her body shook with her sobs and one more strangled, hushed cry escaped her lips.

"NO!"

Michael stepped forward and knelt beside her. She turned to him, her eyes were grief stricken, full of shocked tears and immense sadness. Her skin was so pale and her body trembled. His heart lurched to see her this way.

Her lips struggled to speak but she managed two words.

"Oh ... Michael" then her sobs gave way to merciless grief and she let her body sag against the strength of his. The servants quietly left the room, allowing Catherine to grieve in private, the women with tears of their own. A great, dark cloud descended over the house that day.

Michael raised his eyes to Arthur's. They recognised each other's sadness and acknowledged something far greater. They both knew that with the passing of the Knight, Catherine would be in greater danger than ever before. They were resolved to protect her, whatever it took. No words needed to pass between the two men, they understood each other completely.

Chapter 5
Chedworth – Autumn 1092 AD

"My cup is empty, fetch me more ale wench."

There was much to celebrate since the old Knight at Withington had died, two days earlier. His main obstacle was now out of the way, making life substantially easier for him.

The serving girl hurried from the room gently rubbing what would shortly become a bruise on her buttock. Why could he not slap her like other desperate old men? Why did he have to pinch, and why so hard? Why was she still here? It was not because Preece paid her well, he did not. Perhaps it was Tom the stable boy that kept her here running after the old man. A smile crept across her features as she hurried for the buttery and more ale.

Matthew Preece had recently reached 46 years of age; he had never married and as far as he knew had sired no heirs. He had few of his own teeth left, those he did have were crooked, yellowed and almost at the end of their usefulness. His belly strained at the seams of his spacious tunic giving him the appearance of being bigger still. His legs were short, his warts numerous and large. What remained of his hair was lovingly distributed across his bald scalp, an effort, he firmly believed, made him appear younger. The man's face was bloated and often purple from small exertions, his eyes hid behind drooping lids but he saw none of this in his appearance. With his land and stature he believed himself quite a catch and was at a loss to understand why a 19 year old woman with hair like silk and eyes like a deer would not want to share his bed and his future. No matter, he would have her and her land; it was simply a matter of time and good planning. He would have the Withington Estate in its entirety soon enough and now the

Knight was gone he had one less obstacle to plan around, in fact, the Knight had been his biggest problem, still being the legal owner of the estate.

He scratched absently as he sat in his lavishly Oak panelled room, dreaming of his wedding night. It would be glorious, he was sure.

Bright sunlight poured through the window slits giving the wood a wonderfully warm glow and, making the tapestry on the wall come alive with colour. The quill on the table fluttered in its pot in the gentle breeze and the parchment went untouched as he moved to return to his bedchamber to daydream some more.

Beyond the window was a stable yard, busy in its daily chores, beyond that a large wall of cold and forbidding stone. Beyond the stone was lush green as the grass reached its peak before dying down for winter. On a small rise not far from that wall was a magnificent animal, a horse as black as night, with a flowing mane, long graceful legs and well defined muscles. On that horse was a tall, dark stranger. A stranger who had heard tales as he travelled, a stranger who could not resist seeing for himself the ogre who believed he was worthy of a Lady. A stranger who had to see for himself if the rumours of that Lady's attributes were true. He had satisfied this curiosity the other morning in the woods, the rumours were not exaggerated. And now, two days later he was here watching this pig of a man and finding that he believed all he had heard about Matthew Preece.

The horse shifted restlessly and the man reached forward to pat the animal's neck. He bent his dark head of tousled hair towards the horse's ears and began to whisper. Ears pricked, the horse listened intently and visibly relaxed. As the dark stranger sat up once more the sunlight washed across his face. He had tanned skin covering finely chiselled bones. His cheeks were graced with a vibrant flush. His jaw was strong and square, dark eyes glowed in their sockets, deep and wise, their blackness seeming to shroud secrets within. He had large hands, weatherworn and rough yet gentle enough to calm his skittish horse.

For now, he had seen enough. He imagined Preece reaching out to touch the Knight's daughter and his stomach lurched. She was indeed a bewitching creature, he mused. He had watched her for several minutes in the wood, as the sun had gleamed in her hair and made her eyes the most velvety brown he had ever seen. The man with her was good. He had the keen senses of a soldier and a self assured manner. This man looked at the Lady with nothing less than devotion and yet was the dutiful servant. The stranger wondered if she knew it and wondered how much more harassment she could take from Preece. As the man had led her from the trees that morning there had been fear in her face and he suspected it had been there with her in every step.

As he crouched by his campfire that night, the dark stranger thought back over the last few days, since his arrival in the area.

"What do you think Saracen?" he said to the horse as it munched steadily at the grass nearby.

"What do you think I should do? Move on? After all I have satisfied my curiosity, I have seen all I came to see, why delay? Perhaps there is money to be had here. This Mr Preece may require my assistance in attaining his goal, but then she might pay more to prevent that. I imagine they would both pay well enough. His trust would be easier to win; he has the most to gain. She is beautiful though and I am sure she would be very grateful of the rescue." Saracen continued with his meal, if he was listening at all he did not show it.

"We do not need to rush off just yet, and we will always have need of money. It is settled then Saracen. First thing in the morning we shall offer our services to Mr Preece. At the right price of course!"

* * * * *

As the sun rose on the day of her father's funeral Catherine awoke, numb with sadness, trying not to think of the familial duties she would have to perform today. Her whole life her father had been the only family she had ever known. He had comforted her when as a child she had fallen and grazed her knee. He had been her confident, her protector and her boundary. Her childhood had been unusual, her father had travelled, often for weeks at a time and she knew that he had allowed her liberties that other children did not get because of these things. But still she knew that there were limits to her freedoms, lines that could not be crossed without consequence.

Her father had always been a huge part of her life, a parent and a friend and now he was gone. It left a large gap in her world that would never be filled. It was just beginning to dawn on her that she would never see him again, would never see him smile or hear him laugh. She would never be able to hug him or spend an evening listening to his tales of the wars he had seen all over Christendom. Catherine realised that she had spent the last day or so waiting to hear the sound of his cough cutting through the silence of the house. Today she would have to accept that he was gone but knew that a part of her would probably spend many years waiting for him to return.

She wanted to cry, needed to cry but had no more tears. Her eyes were red rimmed, more obvious against the dark circles under her eyes. Her skin was pale and dull, her shoulders sagging slightly forward, bent under the weight of her pain.

Slowly she dressed, dreading the moment she would have to go down to the hall where her father's body lay, silent and peaceful. Catherine recognised his face but he looked so different. His body remained but he was gone and seeing him today would remind her of that again.

He had arranged to be buried in monastic ground, to have the local monk pray for him. A religious man, the Knight had believed that he would pass from this world to Purgatory to pay for the sins of his life and earn his redemption, before passing on to heaven. It was certain to be a painful transition, despite doing much good in later years the Knight recognised that he had killed and maimed throughout his life, it was a part of who and what he was. Being buried in monastic ground would guarantee him prayers to ease his suffering. They would be said on the day of his burial, one week, one month and one year after.

In accordance with the rituals of the time Catherine washed her father's body, prepared and dressed it in a shroud ready for burial before it was carried in a slow procession to the cemetery. Every member of his estate had been there, along with one or two of the Knights he had fought along side in the past. Catherine had walked behind her father, silent tears dripping down her cheeks, with no strength to release the sobs that dwelt inside her, concentrating on putting one foot in front of the other to get through this day.

Mass was long and torturous for Catherine, she found it incredibly hard to say goodbye to her father. He had been everything to her, for as long as she could remember. He was her only family, he guide, her teacher; he had taken care of everything for her. Now she did felt lost and alone, afraid of what the future might bring, what the next hour might bring.

Since the funeral she had been numb. There were no longer any tears while the sun was in the sky. She was desperately trying to be strong in front of the people around her. She had the whole estate to worry about; she believed that if she fell apart now she would be letting so many people down. So, while there was light she busied herself with any task she could to take her mind off her pain. She discussed taxes and other business with the cleric; she met with the cottagers of the estate to discuss their farms and the duties they would have to undertake for the estate in part payment for the land. She even took on some housekeeping and gardening chores in an effort to forget how much she missed her father.

Today she had been in the garden until it was nearly dark. Arthur had found her and made her come inside and it was then that she realised how cold she was. As she had looked around the kitchen and sipped the hot milk Cook had given her, all she had seen were warm smiles and eyes full of pity and worry. It was comforting to know they cared but it did not make the pain go away, it merely reminded her of it, she felt it never would leave her. She no longer believed in a tomorrow, she looked forward to nothing, took pleasure from nothing.

Once she had said her goodnights Catherine went to her bedchamber. She was tired but doubted she would sleep. Having dismissed Rachel, she removed her clothes carefully and methodically, concentrating on each movement. She neatly folded each item and placed it on the chest at the end of the bed. She pulled her nightgown over her head and blew out the candle. The evenings were getting cooler already; winter would not be kind this year. She climbed quickly under the rough blankets and tried to make herself comfortable.

This was the time she dreaded. While she had tasks to occupy her she had a chance. Now, lying alone in her bed with nothing but a few stray beams of moonlight for company her imagination could run wild, and it did. She was so very scared and did not know how to change it. She had never been out of control before and was at a loss to know how to cope.

Silent tears made their way across her face and onto her pillows, gentle sobs shook her shoulders. It was time to get back in control. If she married well, someone close to her, she would no longer be vulnerable, her people would be protected and she knew she would be safe. She knew that other options were far from ideal, at least this way she knew she could be content, if not happy. With Preece ... a shudder shot through her ... she would rather not think of it. Michael, Arthur and John were the only ones she could trust. It was far from ideal, but she felt so cornered. What other way was there? Her mind was made up. John was already smitten with Rachel, leaving Michael and Arthur. First thing in the morning she would decide which to speak to and she would tell him that she believed it in everyone's interest to make this partnership.

Once Catherine had made her decision she rested a little easier and eventually, some time after the moon had passed overhead, she fell asleep.

In the dead of night the house was silent, dark and cold. Everyone else was asleep except for Catherine, as she walked, almost without a sound, along the landing. Her feet were cold and the wooden beams felt rough on her bare skin. The bottom hem of her nightgown snagged and tore a little on a splinter but she did not notice, she had to keep going. Catherine felt herself being drawn, with an irresistible curiosity, towards her father's room. Something waited for her there, something called to her and she had to know what it was. Without quite knowing how, she was outside his door, her desire to push it open and see what awaited her was immense but there was also a fear. Fear that if she opened the door everything would change. Unable to resist the lure Catherine slowly lifted a shaking hand up towards the door and gently reached out to lay her hand on it.

As her palm touched the wood a loud crack ripped through the stillness of the night and she jumped back a step in fright.

Catherine awoke with a start, it had been a dream. She was still in her own bed. As she looked around at the familiar shapes she started to calm down and her pulse began to slow. As the pounding in her ears receded she became aware of a low pulsing hum that seemed to come from somewhere in the house. She had never heard a noise like it and after a few more seconds curiosity got the better of her. She climbed out of bed and crept to her door, listening intently for signs of movement. It seemed the hum had not disturbed anyone else yet, so she pulled her door open and crept onto the landing. After a few steps she began to wish she had stopped to put stockings on, it was so cold out here without any rugs on the floor; her feet were freezing.

As she moved gingerly along the landing she noticed that the sound had become more intense. How could it be that nobody else had woken up yet? Should she get someone? By now she was outside her father's room, the sound was clearly coming from inside. Catherine froze where she stood, torn between an intense desire to know what was making the sound and a dread fear that she might not like what she saw. What if it was a spirit from the dead? The sound was unearthly enough. It could be her father. She missed him terribly but a visit from his spirit could not be a good thing. His soul was at best in purgatory being tortured for all the killing and bloodshed in years gone by. At worst it would be in hell and the spirit could easily be malevolent.

She knew she could not stand there all night and yet she knew she could not go back to bed and listen to it either. So she took her courage in her hands, laid her palms against the door and pushed.

After a quick glance around she saw with a huge rush of relief that there was no angry spirit in the room, but the hum continued. She stepped cautiously into the room. The sound seemed to be coming from a chest in a corner. Catherine knelt before it, hesitating to open it, fearing what she might find inside but she was unable to resist the temptation. So she gently took hold of the lid and started to lift. Abruptly the humming ceased.

What she found was beyond her wildest imaginings. What did it mean? For one thing it meant she had never really known who or what her father was. As she sat and stared at the contents of the chest the reality of what she saw enveloped her and she began to feel suffocated by it. Dropping the lid of the chest back into place, she stood and hurried back to her own room, hoping that if she put some distance between herself and the contents of the chest, it would seem less real, hoping desperately that this was a dream and that in the morning she would wake and find things back as they were.

Catherine lay in her bed, her mind racing, trying to find a reason for what she had seen, wanting a rational explanation for its presence in the house. Despite squeezing her eyes shut and trying to clear her mind, she was unable to sleep. With every hour that passed it became clear that this was not a dream and that she would have to face the reality. So, shortly before dawn she finally gave up trying to sleep. Far from going away the memory of what she had seen just seemed to be growing bigger and more powerful. With a resigned sigh she got out of bed, put on some stockings, wrapped a blanket around her shoulders, took up a candle and returned to her father's room, closing the door gently behind her.

For the second time that night she found herself kneeling in front of the old chest. With trembling hands she slowly lifted the lid all the way back and was dismayed to find the contents just as she had left them hours earlier. As Catherine stared into the chest the low pulsing hum returned, much quieter this time. Her breath was shallow and she felt a hundred things all at once, fear, betrayal, anxiety and an undeniable urge to explore the box.

There were many objects inside, most of which she recognised. There were five large candles, all with blackened wicks and wax dribbles down the sides. There was a small calfskin pouch that contained an assortment of beautiful polished crystals. The candlelight seemed to glitter on their facets and to dance within them, making them glow like nothing Catherine had ever seen before. In a large, ornately carved box she found an array of dried plants. She knew some of them to be common herbs and others to be roots that could be found in their garden or in the woods. A small stone mortar and pestle rested in one corner of the chest, both stained from use. Next to them were some jars, which appeared to contain liquids. Catherine did not dare taste them but some smelled foul and acrid and others very sweet.

Tucked in another corner, behind a large, beaten metal bowl, Catherine found a bundle of roughly made sheets of parchment. Many of them had been written on in a strong and bold script but some were blank. She remembered that as a child her father had insisted she be educated and part of her education included being taught to read and write. Literacy was the craft of the monks. In this they were masters; they had honed their skills in Latin and were now beginning to use English in their texts. It was highly unusual to teach someone outside of the Church, let alone a woman. It had taken the Knight years to find a monk who would consent to teach Catherine. She recalled her father returning from a trip to Worcester many years ago, and instead of the gift she had hoped for he had brought her a tutor, who stayed with them for almost a year.

As she held the pages in her hands, feeling their roughness on her skin, she wondered if her father had written those words. She struggled to recall her lessons and started to read from the top sheet. It seemed to be an instruction on how to blend herbs together into some kind of broth but it was hard to read in the dim candlelight and she put the pages back in the chest.

Finally, there remained only two small boxes, sitting side by side, to investigate. The humming sound must be coming from one of these. The one on the left was plain, the other carved and ornate. It was the carved box that seemed to be humming and she felt she could not put off the inevitable any longer. Ready to pull her hand away at the slightest twitch she gingerly reached into the chest and picked up the box. As she touched it the humming seemed to become more intense yet no louder. Without a thought to the rest of the house she opened the lid and peered inside.

Lying on a bed of fine hay was a necklace. The leather thong was old, brown and worn and from it hung the most exquisite stone she had ever seen. It was no larger than a bean but it almost glowed of its own accord. It was neither stone nor crystal and it had a cloudy appearance, as if a fine grey mist swirled around inside it. Catherine gazed at it, unable to tear her eyes away for some minutes. It was only then that she realised the humming had stopped. Overcome by its simple beauty Catherine felt an urge to put it around her neck but she hesitated.

Her father had been a defiantly strong willed and apparently religious man all his life. He gave money to the Church, on occasion had entertained the Bishop, he had served King William, while he lived, and all in the name of God. Now here she had discovered what she suspected were the means for sorcery in her father's room. All her life she had been raised to believe in the one Christian God, had been taught that the old Pagan ways were wrong and that witchcraft was the tool of the devil. Under English law witches were being put to death in increasingly large numbers and in the most horrific ways. Why would her father risk everything like this?

One perfect tear formed in the corner of Catherine's eye and gently rolled down her cheek. Still raw from her father's death she now felt herself plunged into utter confusion. A part of her still believed her father to be the wise and good man she had always trusted, the man whose judgement she had never doubted and she yearned to be able to believe in him now but everything before her jarred with everything she had been taught. Catherine felt as though she had lost her father all over again and quietly mourned the loss of his guidance. She imagined that had he been there with her now, he would have told her sharply to get up and stop crying like a spoilt child. He would have a rational, reasonable explanation for what she saw before her and she would believe in him completely again.

Sadness overwhelmed her for a while and needing to feel closer to him now, she unconsciously put the pendent around her neck. For a brief moment it seemed to glow and she was a little surprised that it felt warm against her chilled skin. Slowly she closed the lid of the chest and went back to bed, where she eventually fell into a troubled sleep.

Chapter 6

The sun was rising over the Preece Estate. Servants scrubbed and cleaned, stable hands brushed horses and guards polished swords. It was the most peaceful time of the day for them. This was a time when they could laugh, when they could have peace if they wished. These few hours between sunrise and breakfast were theirs.

Through the crisp morning a bell rang signalling the arrival of a visitor to the house. The maids looked up in surprise. Their master had few visitors, he was neither a social nor a popular man and at this hour it could only be a stranger, unused to the ways of Mr Preece. His manservant visibly cringed before pulling himself up straight and tall and walking to the door.

As the door swung open in his hand the servant quickly assessed the man standing before him. He was tall with dark, wavy hair that fell around his face. His skin was sun tanned and his smile broad. Behind him two guards stood with a large black horse. The animal whinnied gently and pawed the ground, clearly unhappy with its company. Slowly the man turned to the horse.

"Hush, Saracen. I shall not be long." Turning to the guards he continued "would you be so good as to water my horse? It has been a long journey."

"Can I help you Sir?" the manservant asked in clipped tones. There was something about this stranger he did not trust, the man was far too bold and confident for his liking and that smile, well, he had not seen a smile less sincere since he had kissed his wife goodbye early this morning.

"Yes, thank you. I am here to call on Mr Preece. Will that be a problem?"

"He is resting Sir and cannot be disturbed." the manservant replied. "Could you call back later perhaps?"

"Ha, still sleeping at this hour? Then the tales were true." The stranger clearly found this amusing and continued.

"I wish to meet with Mr Preece, I have a proposal for him and my time is valuable. Is there somewhere I can wait while he dresses?" With these last words the stranger deftly stepped past the manservant into the hall and stood with his hands clasped behind his back smiling broadly, appraising his surroundings.

The floor was of the stone in contrast to the house, which was mostly built of wood. The stone was the colour of sand, rich but oddly cold here. There was one rug on the floor but it covered very little and Roland found the pattern offensive. There were several tapestries on the walls, all of which appeared to be depicting Mr Preece in various poses, which would make him as vain as people said he was. Either that or the face of Matthew Preece had been handed down from generation to generation in frightening detail.

To his left was a moderately sized room, stuffed with furniture and badly decorated. To his right was a larger hall, which seemed to have suffered a similar fate.

"The master will not be pleased at this intrusion. I do not think you will be received well."

"I can look after myself, but thank you for the warning."

"It was not you I was concerned for" the manservant grumbled, clearly not happy with the idea of rousing his master from his sleep. He had only had to do it once before. He recalled there had been news of poachers on his land. Several of his guards had been injured in a confrontation. Mr Preece had been more incensed at being woken than at the news of his men and game. He had screamed and raged for hours, throwing anything to hand, hitting anyone who happened to pass within arm's reach. The manservant remembered with more clarity than he would have preferred. Turning back to the dark stranger he said;

"And who may I say is calling?"

"You may tell Mr Preece that Roland of Langley eagerly awaits his kind attention."

The manservant pointed to the room to Roland's left indicating that he may wait there. From the man's expression Roland guessed that his wait may be a long one.

A minute or so later as Roland reclined in a ridiculously uncomfortable carved chair he could hear crashing sounds from upstairs. Was the house under attack, or had Mr Preece woken up he wondered. This was going to be an interesting meeting. He rose to his feet in one graceful, fluid movement and left the room. The sounds of shouting were floating down a corridor and he followed them easily. Before long he came across the short, fat man he had observed the day before. Matthew Preece was purple with rage, his hair hung in long strands from one side of his head, eyes bulging. He was standing in the hallway in his nightshirt with a candlestick raised above his head. His manservant cowered before him visibly shaken by the tirade to which he was being subjected.

Roland coughed, announcing his presence. He had hoped to distract Preece's attention from the bruised man before him and it worked. Preece now turned his entire attention to Roland and he was doubly outraged at the impudence of this stranger to be wandering around as if he owned the place. As Preece struggled to form words through his anger, spittle flew from his mouth.

"You impudent man. You come to my house at ungodly hours, insist that I be dragged from my bed to hear your drivel and now you have the gall to wander through my home as you please. I should have you cut down where you stand and hang your head on the gates to deter the eternally stupid from repeating your mistake."

Not intimidated in the slightest, Roland stood his ground and stared at Preece with his deep, dark eyes. The man before him shook with rage and Roland suspected that with a little more provocation his heart would probably fail under the strain.

"Mr Preece, the interruption is indeed of my doing, your servant was reluctant, to say the least, to wake you. I was somewhat pushy I am afraid but I am here to offer you the assistance you appear to need."

Despite the enormous temptation to taunt Preece and push him over the edge, Roland wanted to calm this pathetic man down, to alter his state of mind from murderous impotence to at least indignant acceptance, where he might be willing to listen to Roland's offer. Instead Preece had seen it as a red rag. Incensed that Roland showed no fear and outraged at the suggestion that this glib stranger could waltz in from the fields and overrule his orders, *his*, the master. To Preece this was a slur on his ability to keep his people in check. As his temper grew a small trickle of blood appeared on Preece's upper lip, issuing from his nostril. He immediately decided Roland was a threat. Roland, sensing murder in Preece's eyes, calmly continued.

"If I were to mention Lady Catherine of Withington, would you be more interested? If I were to say that I could help you win your prize, would you at least put down the candlestick?"

Suddenly rage was replaced by an intense curiosity tempered with caution. Roland may as well have just offered Preece the throne. That girl and all she was and owned were all he dreamed of. Preece's face displayed a string of emotions in quick succession. On the surface it would appear that this stranger had appeared and offered him the world on a plate. It could not be that simple, there must be a catch somewhere. His initial distrust of Roland rose to the surface. How had he known? Where was he from, and what did he want in return? Greed bubbled up in his mind once more. What would he not give to get her and her estate? Combining the two estates with a noble marriage would put him on the map. He would be the most powerful man for miles and then the Barons would finally have to recognise him. Slowly the candlestick was lowered and dropped to the floor. He remained silent for several seconds before speaking quietly to Roland.

"You may wait for me in my hall. I will join you when I am ready." He turned to the manservant "fetch some guards to watch this peasant then fetch my clothes." He shot one more glare at Roland and strode into his bedchamber, slamming the door behind him.

Roland turned from the window as the door of the hall swung open revealing Matthew Preece in his finest coat, one that almost fitted across the wide expanse of his belly.

"This had better be good." He spat the words at Roland trying to be as intimidating as possible, hoping it was working. In his lifetime he had found the only way to get things done was to frighten people, the more frightened they were the more they did for you. This man, however, was another story; he barely seemed to notice Preece's practised efforts.

Roland drew himself up to his full height, towering above the petulant man before him. He clasped his hands behind his back and levelled a steady glare at Matthew Preece. Keeping his voice low he said;

"I am here to help you, at the right price of course. I can get you what you seek, but I suggest that you start being a little nicer to me because I also have the power to make you wish you had treated me like a brother." His tone was even and calm, but what Preece heard was low and menacing. He looked into

Roland's eyes and saw a strength that he had never seen before. It was his turn to be intimidated. Roland could see this and a smile broke across his face.

"Now that we understand each other, let us talk business. I hear that you tried to kidnap your neighbour not so long ago, I assume this means that she turned your initial offer down?"

"The girl is young and stupid. There is no point talking to her, she clearly does not know what is good for her."

Roland looked at Preece with a growing sense of disbelief and wondered if he had taken the right side. This man obviously believed he was quite a catch and could not begin to understand why she had resisted his advances. The poor woman had probably had to leave the room to be sick at the mere thought of it. Still, he was here now and he had Preece's complete attention and probably his purse strings too.

"Let me make myself very clear to you Preece. I work alone, with my own plans. I will not take orders from you or anyone else, I will not tolerate your tantrums and I do not take kindly to deceit. I will deliver the girl to you when I am ready and you will settle my fee then. Are we in agreement?"

"Uh.. yes. You are sure you can get her?"

"Undoubtedly, it is merely a matter of time."

"She is quite exquisite. I will have her, and I will have her untouched. It would do you well to remember that."

"Take care I do not take that as a threat Preece. I remind you that I do not take orders from you. You will have your girl, be content with that certainty."

Roland walked to the door. "I will contact you again soon."

It was only then that Preece realised he did not actually know what the fee was to be. Kicking himself for a novice mistake, not one a man of his stature should make. He shrugged; he was wealthy enough to pay whatever this man asked, doubly so once he was married. He could hear Roland striding to the front door. He did not trust him but could see no other way of getting Catherine. His own guards were no match for her experienced soldiers, they were far too skilled. This Roland though, he had a confidence about him, he seemed capable of doing anything he set his mind to, he had the look of a gypsy about him too. Maybe he could be the one to get past those guards. For now though, all he could do was wait and dream of the day he had her in his arms. Willing or not, she would be his, for his pleasure and advancement.

A wicked smile crossed his face, desire lit up his eyes and with a grunt he shuffled out of his hall and hurried back to his private rooms. As his excitement mounted his clothing became more constricting. He began to sweat and his hands moved unconsciously to his groin as he closed the door of his chamber behind him.

As Roland rode out of the yard he reflected on the meeting. He had been a traveller most of his life and met hundreds of people but Preece was unique among them. In a time when you were nothing without power or status a man had to be confident and clever to get it and keep it, even though it may be a birthright. Preece had neither, he was nothing more than a pompous bully and Roland smiled to think of what the Barons would do to that impudent little man. They would not be impressed by his over-inflated ego, they would not be nervous about his imagined power and they certainly would not stand his tantrums. In fact, if they noticed him at all, he would probably be lucky to keep his head while they took his lands, bride and money and installed their own deputy in his place.

Roland turned his mind to the task at hand, how to capture the girl and deliver her to Preece, without being caught himself. Then he would have the pleasure of deciding what price to extract from Preece.

Chapter 7

It was late in the morning when Catherine woke, she felt sore and drained. She could hear the muffled sounds of people moving around the house carrying out their chores. As she had slept she had made a warm nest for her curled body and now that she was waking she did not want to move. It felt warm and safe and comfortable. It would be in stark contrast to anything she would find if she got up. So she struggled to go back to sleep, here she could at least try to hide from reality, even for a little while.

When it became obvious that she could not go back to sleep Catherine opened her eyes a crack. They felt a little gritty and her head ached. As she gradually came around she realised with surprise that she was wearing stockings and was wrapped in a blanket. A few seconds later she remembered. Slowly she raised a hand to her neck and felt the stone, still warm against her fingers. So, it had not been a dream. She was no closer to any answers this morning than she had been last night. As tempting as it was to believe the evidence she had and condemn her father as a sorcerer, she wanted so much to find another reason for the presence of the chest and its contents. Perhaps he had confiscated it from someone he wanted to protect, but why keep it? The more she thought the less things made sense to her.

Catherine knew that she would have to go and look at it all again, knew that she would not be able to resist her own curiosity or her need for rational answers. She had been raised with stories of witches, people who could fly, cast spells to bewitch others, turn people into animals, and as a child, safe in her bed with her father to protect her, and she had found those stories fascinating. But she had also been taught that witches were servants of the devil, they were creatures to be feared and reviled. As she grew older she had overheard her father talking of witch trials and had been horrified by the charges and the punishments. Still she could not understand why her father might have risked that by discovery. Keeping the evidence, so easy to find in the house seemed reckless to her, a trait she had never known in her father.

Slowly she rose from her bed and dressed. She wore a dark grey gown, a sombre colour to match her dark mood. Her skin was pale, almost translucent and her eyes, turned a darker shade from her mourning, picked up and reflected the hue of the cloth. The house was no longer filled with laughter and song, now it existed in a state of perpetual hush. The servants almost crept around doing their chores and talked in lowered voices so as not to disturb their mistress.

With a sense of foreboding Catherine returned to her father's room. She closed the door quietly behind her and stood staring at the chest, a hundred questions jumbled in her head and not sure whether she wanted an answer to any of them.

She took a step forward, hesitated, suddenly desperate to leave the room and forget what she had seen, but she knew she could never forget, so she took a deep breath and crossed the floor to the chest. As she took hold of the lid she knew what she would find but still found herself hoping that the chest would turn out to be empty. On lifting the lid and opening her eyes she was flooded with disappointment to find it was all still there, but as the first wave passed away she was also aware of a small thrill of excitement growing in her belly. It was a sensation that scared her but she did not close the lid.

Reaching into the chest she picked up the parchment and started to read. She had been right, this was a recipe but the ingredients were so unusual, the method so odd. This one needed to be simmered with a dried snakeskin for a day and a night over a large candle. Breathing very lightly now Catherine read on and discovered that this was some kind of protection potion. The next piece of parchment contained a similar recipe but this one was stronger, it was called a vanquish. Catherine's blood chilled a little at the sight of that word. That meant killing. Killing what? Not daring to read on she flicked through the pile of parchment until she found what appeared to be a letter. Putting down the other sheets she started to read.

Catherine,

In life I loved you more than anything and I love you still, yet I kept a great secret from you. I hid from you what I really am, to protect you. The things you see before you were your mother's. I wish you could have known her and what a beautiful and good woman she was.

You know that in life you must experience the good things and endure the bad. You know that in nature there is light and dark. The same is true of magic, here too there is good and there is also evil. Catherine, some witches are good and they use their magic to help and protect the innocent. It is a sad fact that people in power can be blind to this, that Church leaders feel their faith is threatened by them and seek to cleanse the world of their kind.

Your mother and I both held to that same faith but we were given gifts that we could not ignore and that we used to help others in the battle against evil. In some people's eyes that made us evil too. Your mother was also a witch, a powerful witch, who fought hard for what she believed. I too fought, in a different way, my own way.

We did have friends, good people who protected our secret and will continue to do so. When news of my death reaches them one at least will come to help you too. Trust him Catherine, do not be afraid, he will guide you and teach you.

Wear the grey stone always and heed it. Beware the other.

Take care my daughter; be guarded in your speech. In time I pray you will forgive me for keeping this from you.

Your loving Father.

Catherine sat in stunned silence, unable to take in the meaning of what she had just read. It was as if her father had spoken to her from the grave. It was a bittersweet gift to have these words from him, although it reminded her how much she missed him. But this secret, the letter explained so much, some of which was a relief, yet it raised more questions than it answered. Her Mother protected the innocent, from what? How was her father involved? What part had he played in those battles? Who were these friends and when would they come? How would she know them and what would they teach her?

She had gone to the chest again to answer her questions and settle her turbulent mind, but now she just felt worse, lost in a whirling mess of questions, half truths and complete mysteries. Slowly she read the letter again.

"Wear the grey stone always and heed it" what on earth did that mean? It was a lump of rock, how was she to heed it?

"Beware the other." Suddenly Catherine remembered the second small box. She had not opened it last night and looked at it now. What was in there? Unable to resist, she reached into the chest for the box. As her fingers closed around it she felt a small jolt at her throat. The grey stone around her neck had suddenly become quite warm, its colour too had changed, it was almost white now, glowing, and it was vibrating against her skin.

"Wear the grey stone always and heed it." Her eyes widened as her gaze lifted back towards the box in her hand. A sense of terrible dread filled her as she looked at it and she quickly put it back in the chest, dropping the lid down, and moved away to the relative safety of the window. Life could never be the same again, now she too had this great secret to keep and it felt like a heavy weight about her shoulders.

Finding her father's room suddenly oppressive she headed for the garden, hoping the cold, fresh air would bring some clarity of thought and help to answer at least some of the myriad questions whizzing around in her head. As she wandered through the house, absorbed in her worries, she passed servants without even noticing them.

They had noted the strain in her face and saw how she was becoming more withdrawn day by day, but today she barely seemed to be aware of her surroundings.

"It is not right, Rachel." Cook had said that very morning. "She cannot just hold it all in, the girl has got to let it go, I tell you it just is not natural. Mark my words; she will make herself ill if she does not grieve properly."

On her way Catherine passed by one of the larger upper windows and the bright gold and red of the woods caught her eye. She stopped and found herself staring almost blankly out into the distance, her mind wandering among the trees she loved so much. Things seemed so much simpler when she sat in the woods listening to the trees whispering their secrets to each other. Mentally she tried to shake herself free of this heaviness but found she just did not have the strength. As her attention wandered towards the trees again she caught a movement from the corner of her eye. Her head jerked towards it.

There, just beyond the walls of the house was a horse the colour of blackest night. It was a magnificent creature, its movements fluid and full of grace. As she watched, it stopped tearing at the long grass and turned its attention toward the house. She could see no-one with it, no saddle or bridle even. Could it possibly be wild or just lost? Whichever it was, it was just the distraction she needed and she leapt at the chance to see and touch something normal and natural, something that was not tainted with her secrets or tragedies.

Almost without thinking she went to the stairs and descended in a hurry to get to the front door. At the bottom of the stairs she came face to face with Michael.

Stopping abruptly in mid-flight her face was flushed with colour, her eyes had signs of life and a small weak smile lifted her features. He had not seen this much animation in her for days and the sight brought a smile to his own face.

"My Lady, you look so much better."

"Michael, you must come and see." She took his hand in hers and led him back up the stairs, along the landing to the window.

"And just what is it I am looking for my Lady?"

"A horse, there, just beyond the walls. It is beautiful, is it not Michael, and all alone. Can we bring it in, care for it?" she seemed like a child now, almost breathless with excitement. She looked at him full of hope, tilting her head to one side; she narrowed her eyes and gave him a warm smile. He could see no harm in bringing the horse in and he did not want to stifle her recovery with a refusal. At this moment Michael found it hard to remember that she was no longer the child he had met six years ago.

"Michael, I am sure it is not a spy from Mr Preece." She said quietly, noting his hesitation.

"Anything that makes you this happy is welcome here. Of course the horse can come in." He laughed at her enthusiasm and wondered at her asking for his permission when she could just order it. He retreated along the corridor to fetch Robert, the stable boy, to the gates.

It did not take long to tempt the horse with hay from the stables and it was just as easy to put a rope around its neck and lead it back to the house. Michael's instincts made him a little concerned. He took Arthur to one side of the courtyard while Catherine made a fuss of the creature.

"Who would let a horse like that wander free? It seems well cared for and tame enough, I find it hard to believe it is a runaway."

"It was probably stolen and then either got away or was left behind when the robber was caught. Michael, relax, it is only a horse!" Arthur smiled at Michael, patted him on the back and went to the animal to admire it for himself.

It was not the horse that bothered Michael as much as the owner. He was sure there must be one and he was also sure the owner would come looking for such a valuable and magnificent animal demanding its return. Catherine would be heartbroken when it had to go, he could see she was already becoming attached to it but he could not bring himself to take this away from her just now. It seemed to be the tonic she needed, and when the owner did arrive, well, she was strong and they could find her another horse in time. With a deep breath he made himself relax and resolved to enjoy the moment while it lasted. She was happier than she had been in a while and lavishing attention on the animal. He watched her with warmth in his heart. As if sensing his scrutiny she turned to look his way.

"Michael, do not be rude, come and say hello to our guest."

With another deep breath he strode across the yard and joined her.

Stepping from the shadow of the trees, Roland watched the gates of the big house close. His plan was working well, Saracen had been accepted as one of the family it seemed, it was almost too easy. Tomorrow he would pay them a visit to claim back his horse. One man with a legitimate excuse should easily be able to gain access without arousing too much suspicion and if the lady had become attached to Saracen it would be even easier to win her trust. His plan was simplicity itself and so far it was running far more smoothly than he could have hoped.

That night Catherine was able to enjoy a good meal. With an effort she even managed to speak to Michael and Arthur. The arrival of this horse had temporarily helped her to push her problems to the back of her mind; it certainly seemed to be a blessed relief from it all. Tomorrow it may all be back but until then she was determined to make the most of it. Michael was greatly relieved to see something of her old self back and Arthur shared in his relief.

The following morning Catherine rose with the sun and was in the stable yard before breakfast to visit the latest addition to the household. The sun seemed a little weaker this morning and she thought she could smell dying leaves on the breeze.

She stood by the stable door petting Saracen's head, letting him nuzzle her hand in search of any treats she may have. As she stroked his strong neck she gently whispered to him.

"What is your name? Do you have a home?"

"I am beginning to worry for your sanity." Michael teased and smiled at the flush of embarrassment across her cheekbones.

"Do you have nothing better to do than sneak up on defenceless women Sir?" It was a valiant attempt at a terse rebuke to hide her embarrassment but the smile that followed betrayed her.

Michael did not have time to respond before a servant arrived.

"My Lady, there is a stranger at the gates. He says he has lost a black horse and wonders if we have seen it. What should I say?"

Slowly the smile faded from her face and her eyes lost some of their sparkle. Her first reaction was to lie, to tell the man they had seen no such horse, after all, he had been careless enough to lose the horse in the first place. They could hide the horse for a while and then perhaps say they had bought it. Catherine felt a brief flush of irritation as she imagined what Michael would say to her suggestion. It was not fair. But she reluctantly admitted that Michael would be right, as hard as it might be to let the horse go, he did not belong to her.

"We must be honest and return the horse to its rightful owner." She looked at Michael, almost pleading with him to argue with her decision but he only nodded his agreement, his face serious once more.

She turned back to the servant "Very well, invite the man in, I will see him in the hall." She smiled and the servant nodded and left. Catherine had not believed that she could feel worse than she had this morning but now she felt completely deflated. Michael's voice cut through her thoughts.

"You knew this time would come, is it not better that it came sooner rather than later?"

"You are right of course Michael, as always. Let us go and meet our guest." Her tone was quiet and resigned but Michael heard the edge of petulance within it. He briefly wondered if it had been aimed at him until she raised a brave smile and he followed her to the hall.

She walked into the room expecting to find anything but the man she found there. The sight that met her eyes took her breath away. He was tall, head and shoulders taller than herself, she guessed. His eyes were as dark as his horse, his skin was tanned and exotic, black hair fell about his face in loose, wind torn curls. This man was clearly relaxed, very confident, the lazy smile on his face and his easy stance made him look completely at home. Gathering her wits she introduced herself and continuing quickly she said;

"I understand you are looking for your horse and I believe we may have found him. If you would like to follow me, I will take you to him, I assure you he has been well cared for."

"Of that I have no doubt." Roland replied politely, bowing his head slightly to her. He looked her over with his dark, penetrating eyes. She had a pleasing figure, small and rounded with slim waist and hips. Her neck was smooth and her face clear. Her long hair was tamed in a long plait which hung down her back and accentuated her cheekbones and jaw–line. She had a soft face with bright eyes and long lashes. Roland felt a stirring in his stomach. Sticking strictly to business would be difficult this time he realised as he felt himself drawn to the innocence he saw in her eyes as a hunter is drawn to a deer.

He followed her from the hall under the watchful eyes of the man who had entered the room behind her. He would have to be cunning to stay one step ahead of this man, Roland could tell. The man had sharp and alert eyes and Roland had no doubt he could prove to be dangerous, if given the opportunity.

They soon reached the stable yard and Saracen whinnied as he detected the smell of his master.

"Saracen! How are you boy, what did you think you were up to wandering off like that?" Roland went directly to his horse and began to stroke his nose. The horse nuzzled affectionately back.

Catherine smiled at the loving reunion. "You called him Saracen?"

"Do not be deceived fair lady; he has an evil streak in him, when it suits."

Michael stepped protectively closer to Catherine. "You will want to be on your way then, we would not delay you. Robert, bring the animal out please."

Catherine was surprised and a little uncomfortable with Michael's abruptness but bowed to his instincts and let the polite invitation to leave stand.

Roland took Saracen's rope from the stable boy. "I thank you for taking such excellent care of my horse. I am in your debt my Lady. I am Roland of Langley and I am at your service." With his free hand he took her hand, bowed slightly and kissed it gently. He smiled and left, leaving an atmosphere in his wake that could be cut with a knife.

Roland guessed that he had stepped on some toes today. How deep that feeling was eluded him for now but it was there and by fawning over the Lady, Roland suspected he had ignited some jealousy. That was good, it would make him less effective. He also knew he had aroused the man's suspicions. Perhaps he should have left it longer, asked for his horse in the village, or at the surrounding farms first; perhaps it had all seemed a little too smooth. He would need to be careful how he made his next move, but he found the extra challenge exciting and welcomed it.

Michael was indeed suspicious. This dark stranger was far too calm for Michael's liking. He conveniently turned up here before anywhere else; none of the local cottagers had reported seeing him looking for the horse. Losing an expensive animal like that should have made the man a lot more anxious than he appeared. Perhaps he was just getting paranoid, seeing danger where there was none. Perhaps the tension was beginning to get to him. If it was affecting him, an experienced soldier, how would it be affecting Catherine? It could make her vulnerable and possibly far more open to the advances of the handsome stranger. Michael breathed a silent prayer that this would be the last time they laid eyes on that man and his horse but something told him that they would be seeing him again.

Catherine was touched. She had never had such attention from a man. This one was bold, confident, gallant, tall and breathtakingly handsome. He was also at her service, apparently. Could this be the man she had been waiting for, she wondered. Would he come back? She went to breakfast deep in thought. He certainly was a powerful man and left her with knots in her stomach and butterflies in her heart. Why was that? Her first instinct was to call it fear but he could never harm her. With such a kind nature she did not believe him capable of it and if harm was his goal why not attack this morning when there were only herself, Michael and the young stable boy to contend with. The more she thought about it the more she thought they were all getting paranoid. Surely not everyone they met would be intent on hurting them.

Then it occurred to her, this was the man her father had spoken of in his letter. The friend who would come, he must be. The timing was too much of a coincidence for it to be anything else. Michael clearly did not trust him but he was wrong. She raised her head to tell Michael, let him know that the man was a friend, that he was probably just being careful in not explaining himself straight away. As she opened her mouth to speak she realised that there was no way she could tell Michael without revealing her secret. That made things a lot more complicated. She lowered her head once more and continued with her meal in thoughtful silence, wondering when the man would return and could answer some questions for her. She had so many and she badly needed some resolution, if only so that she could sleep in peace for a while.

It had been a while since Mr Preece had raised his ugly little head. Perhaps it was safe to believe that he had given up on Catherine and found a new cause to pursue. It seemed the more time that passed the more likely this became. Michael and Arthur wanted to believe it was true, however, they had met ambitious men like him before and were loathe to relax until they were sure. Besides, Catherine still insisted she was happy to remain within her own walls and this suited everyone for the time being.

It had been two days since Roland had come for his horse. From time to time Catherine's thoughts drifted to him and her eyes wandered to the trees hoping to catch a glimpse of him. She also wondered about his timely arrival. She let herself begin to believe he was what she needed. She had sensed some anxiety in Michael since Roland's visit but she could not think of a safe way to put his mind at ease. This time it was not just Michael, even Arthur had his doubts and so she was careful not to talk to them about him. Their concerns bothered her in a small way but her curiosity about Roland Langley and her conviction about his reason for coming here were stronger.

The following day was bright and sunny as Catherine knelt in her vegetable garden. She had people who could do these things for her, indeed it was their work, but it was something to occupy her mind and her hands. Soon there would be little left to care for but the most seasonal of vegetables. November would bring with it the hint of frost and the worst would kill many plants in the garden.

Nestled among the potatoes and carrots was a thin carpet of weeds. She was careful to make sure she pulled the whole growth from the ground and not leave any roots behind. Lately she found herself thinking in the smallest detail of tasks she had never imagined existed. Of course it was a defence mechanism and although everyone around her recognised this, nobody gave it a voice.

Today though, as her hands worked her mind wandered. Her life had been turned upside down. As well as losing her father she now had an enormous secret to hide, her home had become a prison, her friends her protectors. She no longer had freedom and her future was in turmoil. For the last week she had even been denied the shortest of walks and yet had rescued a magnificent horse and met a most incredible man. Since that day she had difficulty concentrating on even the simplest things. Perhaps that was why Michael was so sharp with her these past three days. She should probably try to be more attentive to matters, she decided. Still Roland of Langley was a wonderful distraction from her current predicament and he may be able to take away a large portion of her troubles.

The sound of a snort stilled her hands for a second or two. She strained to hear more but when she did not she resumed her digging. There it was again. She sat up slowly. It was a horse, she was sure. But where was it? Could it be Saracen again? She got to her feet brushing earth from her skirts and listened again. Now she could clearly make out quiet sounds of grazing from beyond the wall.

Carefully she climbed the stone steps to the top of the wall and there before her, some 30 strides away was the black horse.

"Saracen" she whispered under her breath. From directly below, someone coughed and the abrupt sound startled her. She peered over the wall and down at the man below.

She already knew who to expect as her eyes locked with a pair so dark they may have been black but it still caused a shiver of pleasure to run up her spine and her stomach to tighten in anticipation. There he was, with his hips cocked. His head was tilted back to look at her making his curls fall away from his face giving it a dark frame which accentuated his strong bones.

"Sir, what brings you here?"

"I was hoping to find you here Lady". He replied.

"On my wall? Tell me, what is wrong with announcing yourself at my gate like everyone else?"

She tried to keep her voice even and devoid of emotion, not wishing to appear too keen but there was nothing she could do to stop the small smile that had formed.

"Is this not far more romantic my Lady? I return because I could not stay away from such a beauty and I wait here because I think perhaps your guard does not trust my intentions towards you. He seemed suspicious of me, I think."

Catherine blushed with pleasure. That was a new and welcome experience for her.

"Michael is very protective of me that is all." She smiled. She had hoped he would come back and now here he was. All those conversations she had practised, all the clever things she had thought she would say to impress him were all forgotten.

"Well then, may I come in or should I bend my neck until it is too sore to gaze upon your beauty?" Roland oozed charm and he knew it was working. He had had plenty of practice at getting what he wanted but this time it was easier than he had imagined. She was more innocent that he had thought possible.

Somewhere behind her a door clattered shut and firm footsteps approached. She turned and found Arthur gazing at her curiously.

"Is everything all right?" he asked.

"Yes Arthur. I was just looking at the trees, the forest is lovely this time of year and I do miss my walks." She smiled wistfully and turned back to the trees.

"If we could borrow you from your trees for a short while, one of the cottagers has called to see you."

"Oh, I will be there now."

As Arthur made his way back to the house Catherine dared to look down again. With relief she found Roland was still there watching her.

"I have to go. Can you come back tomorrow?"

"Very well, tomorrow it is fairest lady." With that he bowed deeply and flashed a winning smile.

"Oh, and Sir? Please feel free to use my gate next time!"

With a quick smile she was gone.

Chapter 8

The cold November sun was rising slowly, mist hung just above the solid earth and there was evidence of a hard frost the night before. The garden was covered with a white frosting and the leaves in the vegetable patch were crisp and brittle from the cold. Fortunately only a few vegetables were left to be dug up and stored, losses would be light. Still, for the next four of five months fresh food would be very hard, if not impossible, to come by.

Catherine woke to the rustling sound of clothes being unfolded and gently shaken out. On the far side of the room Rachel bent over a chest, preparing her clothes for the day. Despite the cold she moved quickly and quietly, not wanting to wake Catherine, especially as she looked so peaceful this morning, Rachel even thought she had a kind of glow about her.

Catherine had indeed slept better than she had done since her father's death and she was reluctant to lose the warm and cosy feeling she had inside by getting out of bed. She had been dreaming about a man on a black horse who had whisked her away on an exciting and romantic adventure. Now that she had woken she was left with a small feeling of loss and a deep desire to cling to those feelings. She closed her eyes and tried to recapture the dream.

At last Rachel left the room closing the door quietly behind her. Catherine relaxed and once again tried to fall asleep. As it finally sank in that she was too much awake, it also sank in that not all of what she remembered was a dream and that triggered the memory of Roland of Langley promising to return. Today. Suddenly she was very much awake and very conscious of the fact that he could arrive at any moment and here she was still lounging in bed.

It did not take her long to dress, the chill in the room encouraging her to move quickly. Hearing movement in the room Rachel had come back and at Catherine's request had stayed to help her with her hair. Catherine wanted to look her best for the handsome Roland and with Rachel's assistance she would do just that. Less than an hour after first leaping from her bed Catherine was ready. She fairly floated down to her breakfast. Apparently there had been a fire burning in the hall for some time. There was an aroma of pine in the air and the enveloping warmth was a pleasant sensation against her skin as she entered the room.

With breakfast over she took some needlework from her basket in an effort to distract herself knowing that time would seem to pass more quickly if she were occupied. She did not have much success though; she really could not concentrate on anything other than what might happen when Roland arrived. Every sound, every door opening or closing caught her attention and made her wonder if he was there, on his way in to see her. About an hour before noon she heard footsteps in the hall, far too heavy for one of the maids. She caught her breath, hardly daring to hope trying to remember if she heard the door. The feet stopped directly outside the door and she could just make out the sound of a man's voice speaking in low tones to someone else. Catherine's eyes widened and her heart leaped into her mouth with anticipation and nerves as she watched the door slowly swing open.

As Michael stepped into the room and looked across at Catherine he did not know which emotion to acknowledge first. He was struck by the effort she had made with her appearance today and a certain relief that she was feeling better followed, but the look of disappointment in her face hit him the hardest. She looked a vision in red today and it stirred something deep inside to see it. However, she clearly had not wanted it to be him who had just walked through that door, which begged the question, who would she have preferred?

From his expression and hesitation Catherine guessed how clearly her face must have been displaying how she felt inside and she made a belated effort to hide it and behave as normally as she could.

"Oh, hello Michael, do you need me?"

Michael, now somewhat suspicious of her odd behaviour, continued.

"Good morning my Lady, I came to let you know that Arthur and I will be away from the house for a few hours. We will be back as soon as we can and John will stay with you so you do not need to worry about your safety."

Michael was concerned at the change in her over the last couple of days and he suspected Roland was the reason. It was a relief to see her looking so much brighter, but this bright, this soon? With a small sense of triumph Michael was glad that he had sent Roland away so quickly and so curtly. With luck he would have realised that he was not welcome here and gone on his way. Michael had not seen him before or since and assumed he must have been passing through the area and would have moved on by now. Michael was a little surprised at these feelings of his but dismissed them as being jealousy and instead put it down to caution on her behalf, after all, they were still waiting for Preece's next move.

"Very well, goodbye then." She flashed him a quick, dismissive smile and went back to her sewing without giving him a further look, pretending that she had been engrossed in it until he had arrived. She was slightly relieved that Michael and Arthur were going out, she had not been looking forward to explaining Roland's presence at the house and it meant that they would have more peace, time to be alone and talk.

Lost for words Michael turned and left. This was not the Catherine he knew, he felt like he had just been dismissed. He had thought there was at least friendship there but she had just put him well and truly in his place. 'You are hired help Michael, no more. Do not get ideas above your station' he thought to himself as he marched back to the stable yard to meet Arthur. By the time he got there he was angry and indignant and it was clear in his expression.

"Is everything all right Michael? You look like you just lost a fight."

"Maybe I did. We should go, the sooner I get out of here the better. In fact, perhaps it is time I had a complete change." With that he urged his mare forward and cantered out of the grounds with Arthur standing behind, watching in stunned silence.

When he eventually caught up Arthur was concerned.

"What happened? You seemed fine a few minutes ago."

"Let us just say I have remembered my place, or was reminded of it, by my employer. I do not know why I ever imagined it could be otherwise." Michael practically spat the words out and Arthur decided it was probably best to let him stew for a while and ask him again later. It must have been bad if Michael was considering leaving for good. He was usually so calm and understanding, especially where Catherine was concerned. She had been thirteen when they had first arrived at the manor with the Knight and over the years had witnessed the best and the worst of her moods. Michael had never been fazed by them before. Arthur had to admit he was surprised by this change in Catherine and hoped that this slide in her behaviour was a result of the stress she had been under lately.

Now that he was one Catherine was heartily ashamed of herself. She had treated Michael very badly just now and wished that she could take it back. He did not deserve to be treated like that. He was so much more than casual help yet that is exactly how she had just treated him. When he and Arthur returned later she would apologise to him.

Less than an hour later Rachel arrived to announce a visitor. Roland strolled in immediately behind Rachel, announcing himself. Catherine could not contain the smile she had been holding on to all morning. Rachel grinned and quietly left the room.

"Good morning my Lady, I have to say that you are looking truly wonderful today. May I be so bold as to beg a kiss?"

Catherine blushed and lowered her eyes as she gently nodded and allowed the man before her to take her hand in his. Slowly, gently, he raised her hand to his lips and kissed it softly. Her eyelids fluttered as a gentle flush washed across her cheekbones. She certainly was beautiful, he thought. How wasted she would be on that fat pig he was working for. Perhaps he could persuade her to stay with him, perhaps not. She did not look like she could cope well with his lifestyle or being always on the road and besides, he was not looking for a commitment and he wanted Preece's money more.

Before she had opened her eyes again his grasp on her hand had tightened. She felt herself being whirled around and pulled back hard against his body. She was trapped in his strong arms, her back to his stomach. Fear flooded her entire body. There was something else, an odd sensation; it took her a second to place it. It was the stone. The grey stone around her neck was vibrating strongly against her skin but she did not have time to think about it now. From his pocket Roland took a foul smelling cloth bundle and quickly pressed it to her face.

Catherine panicked and began to struggle against his arms. She thrashed hard trying to escape his iron grip, in so doing she caught a small stool with her foot and sent it clattering across the floor. Her heart raced, pounding hard. Her mind spun in confusion. What was he doing? Did he realise that she could not breathe? Her eyes clouded and there was a rushing sound in her ears that grew steadily louder. She tried to call for help, tried to form one word but it was too late. She was too weak to fight and the drugged cloth had taken hold of her senses. Her last thought was that Michael could not hear her call his name as her world went black. It took only seconds for her body to cease its struggle and collapse.

Suddenly the door flew open and John rushed in. Before his eyes could register Catherine lying on the floor, clearly unconscious, someone stepped close behind him. He felt a sudden, sharp flash of pain through his head before everything went blank and he hit the floor. Roland pulled John's body away from the door, dragging him out of sight.

Then he lifted up Catherine's limp body and put her over his shoulder, holding her legs with his hands, almost as if she were a rag doll. Saracen was waiting in the yard outside the front door and in one fluid movement Roland laid Catherine across Saracen's shoulders and swung himself up into the saddle behind her. Before anyone even knew to raise an alarm they were gone.

A short while later there was a knock at the front door, less than a minute later there was another. Rachel heard them both and began to wonder why John had not gone to answer it. She made her way towards the door as the visitor knocked for the third time. Warily she opened it a crack and peered out through the gap. Before her stood a tall, thin monk wrapped in a cloak.

"Good day miss, is the Knight at home? I must see him, I have an urgent message."

Feeling safe in the presence of a monk Rachel opened the door.

"I am sorry, the master died. We buried him some days back."

Aelfric's face fell, losing its colour at the dreadful news. He had been too slow getting here and the Guardian was dead.

"How, how did he......die'" Aelfric stammered the words out, terribly afraid of what the answer would be.

"The weather got to his chest; he had been bad for a long time." Rachel replied, matter of factly. "The Lady is home. Do you want to see her?"

Aelfric was plagued with emotion, sorrow that the Knight was dead, relief that he had not died at the hands of evil, concern about the fate of the box and its contents. Now he was also confused, Edric had told him of the Knight's wife, but she was dead too, had been for many years. Had the Knight re-married?

"A lady? The Knight's wife?" he asked.

"No, sir, his daughter, come in, I will let her know you are here." Rachel beckoned the odd monk in and closed the door behind him before hurrying to a nearby door. He was still trying to make sense of all this when he heard a screech and rushed towards the sound.

* * * *

It was dark when Catherine finally woke. Her head felt as if it was split open and her limbs were stiff and cold. By opening her eyes a crack she could just see that she was in what looked like a cave and it was dark outside, it might be raining too, she thought. She lay on a blanket several steps from a small fire. The ground beneath her was cold, hard and uncomfortable. She could hear the sound of the wood cracking in the flames and smelt the wood smoke all around her.

She tried to raise herself up on her elbow but her head protested so much that she gave up and lay back down very slowly. Her eyes flickered shut and she fell asleep.

When she woke again it was still dark and still cold and but the fire was glowing. Her head had cleared a bit, it no longer felt full of fog and it no longer caused her as much pain to move. She had no idea how long she had been in this state or where she was. She did realise that she was no longer at home, no longer protected and in some danger.

Gently she eased herself up to take a better look at her surroundings. The entrance to the cave was about 15 paces away, she was at the back of it and she could see no other openings. On a second look she noticed something large and dark hunched near the entrance.

"Welcome back Catherine. Did you sleep well?"

Roland's voice was deep and calm with a teasing ring to it. He rose in one fluid movement and came towards the fire. Catherine flinched back at his sudden move. He took several sticks and kindling and stoked the fire back up so that it once more radiated heat to every corner of the cave.

"Do not look so frightened Catherine, think of this as a journey to your new life, it is a beginning for you, you should be happy" he said. "Besides, it is not as if you did not expect it to happen one day, is it?" He was taunting her and her anger flared.

"Happy? You take me from my home against my will and expect me to be happy. What is this new life? Where are you taking me? Why are you doing this?" She was so confused that her questions poured out without so much as a breath between them.

"My, my, you have recovered quickly. Your new life is that of a dutiful wife. I am taking you to be with your new husband in the morning and I am doing this for ...... a handsome fee." He finished with a smile and a small flourish of his hand.

"I take it that I am not to marry you, who is it then? Who on earth needs to go to these lengths to ask me to marry him?" She tried to make the question light and careless but feared she had failed miserably.

"He is not going to ask you Catherine, he is going to marry you. You see Matthew Preece does not like being told he cannot have something. He wants you, your lands and your title and I am here to help him." He stood slowly and moved around the fire to sit beside her.

Catherine felt the blood drain from her face. It was slowly sinking in that Preece was behind this, which meant that Roland had been about as sincere as Preece was physically attractive. Her stomach turned inside her and she wondered if life was ever going to be worth living again.

He reached out his hand to touch her face and said in a soft voice;

"Still, having said all that, there is no reason why we cannot enjoy each other until you have to go, at least it will give you good memories to cling to when you accept your new husband's attentions." He moved his hand to cup the side of her face.

She flinched away from his touch, physically repulsed at the idea of being touched by Preece but far more concerned about her immediate crisis. The man before her clearly expected her to give herself to him and willingly. How could she have been so stupid, she had let herself be swayed by something new and exotic, something bold and free, something she could not have at home. Now she wished with all her heart that she was back there, a prisoner once more. Above all, she wished she had not been so thoughtless to Michael. Would he even try to come after her now?

Roland's hand slid across her face, his thumb rubbed her cheekbone. With his other hand he caressed her neck before moving to her shoulder. He gently pushed aside the fabric and began to slide his hand lower to cup her breast. His eyes lighted on the skin, seemingly oblivious to everything but his carnal intentions.

Snapping to her senses Catherine slapped his hand away and glared at him.

"I am not your toy, you do not own me and you will not have me. Keep your evil hands to yourself" she hissed. She desperately hoped that a show of opposition would stop him short and make him realise that what he was doing was very wrong. She was sadly mistaken. It seemed instead to fuel his passion.

He put one hand on each shoulder and roughly pushed her back on to the blanket, pinning her there with his hands. He brought his body down beside her, trapping her legs beneath one of his. Her mind raced as he crushed his lips brutally against hers, she tasted blood for an instant and began once again to struggle beneath his massive form. This only seemed to feed his excitement and he began to clutch and squeeze with a roaming hand, bruising her skin with his force.

He grasped the fabric of her bodice and tore it from her, exposing creamy white flesh. His fingers found her nipple and rubbed it with an urgency she did not share. She could feel his erection pressing against her thigh, could feel the heat from his taught body.

He tore his lips from hers and drew her nipple into his mouth, catching it between his teeth. Pain shot through her breast and she cried out. He moaned with pleasure at the sound and began pulling at her skirts. With her free arm she began to hit at his head and body but it did not seem to have any effect. Instinct took hold of her and with all the force she could find she brought her knee swiftly up to make hard, solid contact with his groin.

As her knee hit its mark he cried out, momentarily releasing his grip on her. It was all the time she needed to take her chance. She clubbed her hands together and struck him hard on the side of his head. He groaned and she was able to push him to one side. Instinctively she rolled the other way and scrambled to her feet. It took her only a second to get her bearings and make a dash for the mouth of the cave. She had barely made it two steps when a hand caught her ankle and brought her crashing to the floor beside the fire. Completely winded Catherine lay motionless, unable to fight the man, who was covering her body with his own.

He grabbed her by the arms, pinching her skin and turned her over. Then he was on her and she was trapped. With no other obvious option Catherine put all the force she had into spitting into his face. He flinched as the spittle hit him and slowly raised his arm to wipe it away on his sleeve. His arm still raised, he smiled at her. There was no warmth there; it was a bitter and cold smile. She glared back at him defiantly, hatred burning in her eyes.

Roland brought his arm swiftly back down, aiming his fist at the side of her face. It caught her on the cheek and once again she tasted the sweetness of blood, this time filling her mouth. Her vision blurred briefly from the blow and her eyes watered with the pain.

Quickly his hand found a way through the barriers of her skirts and rested on her stomach. With a strong leg he forced her legs apart. As she cried out in fear he claimed her mouth once again forcing an exploration with his tongue.

His hand wandered quickly and roughly across her skin and between her legs, he lingered there for a second and then invaded her body with his finger, pushing and probing. She arched her body in pain and revulsion, which he assumed was pleasure. She felt a growl of carnal desire rumble in his chest and feared for her life. She was helpless, trapped beneath this monster.

Just as quickly as he had begun he removed his fingers, she prayed it was over, prayed that he had spent his lust. But she could feel his weight shift above her, felt him fumbling with his own clothes. He moved his body directly above her and whispered hoarsely in her face.

"This is what you have wanted since we met. I could see it in your face."

She heard herself whispering over and over. "No, no, no."

He lowered his body closer to hers and she felt his naked erection brush against her thigh. It was hot and demanding. He grabbed her free hand and pulled it towards his body, forcing her to touch him. She felt bile rise in her throat and was sure she would be sick if she had to endure any more. Tears flowed freely and silently from her eyes and blood trickled slowly from the corner of her mouth.

He groaned again and she turned her face towards the fire trying to force her mind to be elsewhere when he eventually violated her. From the back of her neck came a strange sensation, she had initially dismissed it as a stone but realised now that it was moving, vibrating quite wildly. The grey stone, she had completely forgotten it. Her mind snapped back into focus and she wondered if it might be glowing, as it had with the box in the chest. Quickly she reached round with her free hand and grabbed at the stone, pulling it in front of her and thrusting it towards Roland. For a second his attention was distracted by it and that was all she needed. She had noticed some of the sticks had fallen from the fire and were smouldering nearby. With a huge effort she tore her hand from his and lunged at one of them. She grasped the nearest one, felt her skin burn from the heat but clung to it for dear life. She brought it back and jabbed it into his face. With a scream of pain he clasped his face in his hands and rolled away from her. She did not lose a second scrambling to the mouth of the cave and out into the night.

Chapter 9

Michael and Arthur had finished their business at the market and with the provisions they had bought packed in their large saddlebags they swung up onto their horses and began the ride home. Michael had been quiet and sullen on the ride to the market and had only started to communicate in the last half an hour. Arthur had never seen him this way before, in all the years they had known each other. He took a deep breath and asked the question he had been avoiding all afternoon.

"Will you tell me what Catherine said to upset you so much, Michael?"

Michael sighed heavily. His anger had subsided over the hours and the distraction of their business had certainly helped. Although he was beginning to recognise that he had overreacted earlier he was still left feeling a little hurt. He was still resolved to leaving as soon as he could. It was a hard resolve to keep but he knew that he could not remain her protector while he was emotionally involved. The way she had spoken to him today had left him feeling uneasy but he knew that some of that was a reaction to Roland of Langley. He had to admit that he was a little jealous of the dark stranger. Still, he owed Arthur an explanation.

Arthur had been patient with him. Arthur had always been patient with him, since they had met as youngsters. Michael recalled a day when Arthur had been crouched at the side of the river, up to his knees in reeds. Michael had followed the boy to see what he was doing and after a few minutes he spotted the boat. Arthur had spent days making it and that day was its maiden voyage. Michael had helped Arthur finish the boat and make it sea-worthy. If the truth be told Michael nearly took over and played with it far longer than Arthur. But Arthur had been eternally patient, even at that young age. The two of them had been together nearly every day since. They had no secrets, rarely argued or even disagreed. They laughed together and drank together. Michael certainly could not keep this from Arthur.

"I think Catherine has romantic feelings for Roland, the man with the black horse. Remember?"

"I remember but I find it hard to believe. She only met him once, a few days ago and she does not talk about him. What makes you think is falling in love with him?"

"You did not see her face Arthur." Michael's voice sounded distant and empty. "I walked into that room and she looked really good, she is certainly making an effort for someone. As soon as she saw me the smile vanished, she was truly disappointed. I was the last person she wanted to see today."

"Maybe, but at least sleep on it, do not do anything until tomorrow. Unlikely as it may seem now, you might feel differently then and I would hate to see you go because you felt obliged. I do not want to see you go at all, but you know that."

With his words of wisdom imparted Arthur let the subject drop. He knew Michael better than he knew himself. He would feel differently in the morning.

They would be coming up to the house soon, Arthur wondered if Michael might even postpone his plans as soon as they got back. Catherine would probably be waiting with an apology for Michael. He was surprised at her behaviour, Michael was not given to exaggeration so either something was going on or she would be apologetic when they got back. They rode on in easy silence, looking forward to being back inside and near a fire. They sky was dark and brooding now, threatening rain and Arthur did not want to get wet today. Years ago it would not have bothered him but since he had been at Withington he had become quite attached to the comforts of a home.

As they crested the last rise the estate lay before them. It was surrounded by grass, touched with a hint of brown. The woods loomed large up on the hills to their left and there was a large empty expanse of land before them. Something was wrong. Arthur's brow creased as he desperately tried to put his finger on it. He turned to his friend.

"Michael?"

"The gates are open." The words were barely out of his mouth as he urged his mare along the long flat track towards the open gates almost at a gallop with Arthur on his heels.

Michael was off his horse before she had come to a halt and sprinted to the house. He burst through the kitchen door and ran to the front of the house, calling in a loud voice, hoping with all his heart that his instinct would be wrong this time.

"John? Catherine?"

A small voice drifted out of the hall to him.

"Mr Michael, is that you?" It was Rachel and she sounded terrified.

Michael rushed in and was confronted with the sight of Rachel on her knees cradling John's bloodied head in her lap. John was pale but Rachel was as white as new fallen snow and her hands trembled as she stroked John's face. Slowly Rachel raised her tearful eyes towards Michael, imploring him to do something, anything. Michael stood in disbelief, trying to take in the scene before him. His gaze lifted to instantly take in the rest of the room but it seemed empty. Frantic he took a step back to go and search the rest of the house but he stopped at the sound of Rachel's shaky voice.

"Michael.. I .. I am sorry. It was that man, he took Lady Catherine and.. and.." Rachel began to sob uncontrollably, her words lost their clarity and her thoughts lost cohesion. She bent her head and kissed John's forehead so softly, all the while stroking the side of his face with the gentle caress of a lover's hand.

Michael stepped closer, kneeling beside them he laid his ear to John's chest and waited, hardly daring to breathe. Those following seconds were like hours, dragging by as if weighted by all the worries in the world. Arthur rushed in, surveying the scene quickly and went straight to Rachel's side, placing his arm gently around her shoulders.

After what felt like an eternity Michael spoke,

"He is breathing, Rachel, he is alive. Arthur, let us get him to his bed."

It was only then that Michael noticed the monk standing quite still in a dim corner of the room, His habit was dark but his face was ashen. Michael rose to his feet, drawing his sword in one practised motion. As he stepped toward the monk Rachel looked up and said,

"Michael, no! He did not do it, leave him be."

Michael hesitated for a second before sheathing his sword. The monk was shaking visibly but Michael was insensible to his feelings, distracted by the fact that Catherine was missing. While Michael and Arthur had been away from the house someone had taken her. He felt responsible, angry at himself. He needed to be out there looking for her. He pointed at the monk, his face as thunderous as his mood.

"Wait here" he told the monk, and turned back to John.

Arthur coaxed Rachel away from John and the two of them carefully lifted him from the floor and carried him to his room where they laid him on his bed.

Michael turned to Rachel and spoke to her in a soft voice.

"Rachel, how long has he been this way?" He was worried sick about what Rachel had said earlier about Catherine but the poor girl was in such a state over John he feared that mentioning that name might send her into hysterics.

"A couple of hours I think. That man turned up about an hour after you left Sir. I found John a while after that. Oh, is he going to be all right?" Rachel turned her eyes back on John as she said the words. Michael watched as what little colour was left drained from her face and her mouth sagged open at the thought of her mistress.

"Oh.... Miss Catherine. He took her, Mr Michael he took her. Did you find her? Is she all right? Did you bring her back with you?"

Rachel's words were strung together with barely a breath between them. Michael laid a hand on her shoulder.

"No, Rachel, we did not find her. But we will. Rachel, who took her?" His voice was still quiet but inside he was scared. He prayed that she would say Preece dreading any other answer she may give. Rachel's brow creased as she tired to remember, then it came to her.

"Roland, of Langley."

"Do not worry. You stay here with John, take care of him and we will go and get her back." His tone had not changed and his touch on her shoulder was light but his mood had turned murderous. His instincts had told him all he needed to know about Roland but he had not listened to them as he should. He had spoken the words with such conviction and confidence, neither of which he felt. He stayed to watch Rachel settle herself at John's bedside, she clung to his hand and chewed her lip; her eyes were full of fear and love. Michael averted his eyes, this was a private time for Rachel. He felt as if he were intruding and turned to leave.

As he left he felt a chill run the length of his spine. It was indeed cold in the room but he recognised the chill as fear. All thoughts of leaving were forgotten now, Catherine was in trouble and he had to find her.

Having heard the commotion when Michael and Arthur had returned the other servants had gathered, two of the maids had followed them and hovered outside the room. Arthur took them to one side and told them to prepare a fire in the room and to make sure that both Rachel and John were taken good care of. The two young girls immediately went to work.

Arthur started issuing orders to the other servants. Robert was to close the gates behind them and make sure the house was secure. Nobody but Michael and Arthur were to be allowed back into the grounds. The cook was dispatched back to her kitchen with orders for broth and bread. Rachel and John were to be kept warm and well fed. John was alive and needed the best care they could give him. The cook replied with a solemn nod and hurried off to her duties.

In the stable yard Arthur turned to Michael. There was something in his eyes tonight that Arthur had never seen before. It was a brand of fear that carried with it a large dose of hatred and vengeance. It was a bitter look, a deadly glitter in Michael's deep, dark eyes. Arthur said a silent prayer that before the dawn Catherine would be found, healthy and well and the look in Michael's eyes would be gone forever. Arthur could not even begin to imagine what emotions must have been churning within Michael at that moment, tormenting his thoughts and feelings. He cared deeply about Catherine but he knew that Michael cared for her in a different way. Arthur suspected that what Michael felt was much stronger.

They rode out into the darkness that had quickly descended over the countryside not knowing where to start but determined to find her nevertheless.

Chapter 10

An owl hooted quietly somewhere nearby, a family of mice scurried away at the sound. Over to the left there were muted sounds of deer grazing some way off and to the right was deathly silence. Catherine cowered in her hiding place not thinking of the irony of her situation. There was gentle, harmless life all around her, she was in the woods that she loved, the woods she longed to wander through, the woods that had always made her feel so safe and free and yet she huddled in fear in a thick bush at the base of one of those majestic trees.

She was bitterly cold and her skin stung from the scratches she had collected as she had fled through the vegetation and past the trees until finding this particular bush to hide inside. Now she lay as still as she could. She was curled up as small as she could be on the cold ground, barely breathing, knowing he would be following her and knowing that if he found her ... she dared not think about it. She was already painfully aware of what he would have done to her in the cave when he had no cause to hate her. Now, he would probably be scarred for life and mad as hell but as she thought of his marked face a part of her felt a perverse pleasure. It was no more than he deserved. The rest of her wished she could turn back the clock, wished she had let him finish then maybe she would not be about to die horribly; she wished she had never invited him to return; wished she had never met him in the first place; and wished she had never said those stupid words to Michael. He had looked so angry; would he be worried about her? Would he even come back?

A stick breaking off to her right brought her swiftly back to reality. She strained to hear, perhaps it was another deer. Perhaps. Silence. She knew it was not a deer, nothing had moved down that path for some time, it was as if every living thing in the wood knew evil was coming and had fled. Only she was left, all alone, hiding in a bush praying for her life. Tears began to form in the corners of her eyes, dripping soundlessly onto her face.

Another crack. Someone or something was creeping down the path, trying hard not to make a sound. They were doing well, had she not been listening for a pin dropping she may not have heard the tiny snaps that seemed like thunder claps to her. Holding her breath she waited for him to come into sight. She dreaded seeing him again but she desperately wanted to know where he was, she hated not knowing if he was creeping up behind her. She did not dare move to look behind her for fear of making any sound herself and attracting his attention. It seemed like hours before another sound caught her attention. This was much closer than before, she had missed several steps. Moving her head as slowly and carefully as she could, she looked around the area immediately before her. Her vision was reduced by the bush and the pitch dark but she hoped to be able to see something and stared hard into the darkness. It was not until he moved again that she realised she was looking directly at him. Catherine caught her breath and froze. He was lost in the shadows of the night, dressed in black, dark hair and skin blending in with the blackness around him.

Slowly it dawned on her that he was so well hidden precisely because of his dark clothing. Here she was all dressed up in red, with white skin clearly showing. A fresh wave of icy fear swept over her and she could feel her heart pounding in her chest loud enough to wake the dead. If he did not hear her heartbeat he would surely see her dress.

Roland took another step closer to her hiding place. He was almost close enough now that he could reach out and touch her. Catherine's heart was thumping so hard it rattled her teeth, she was trapped, if he looked directly at her he would see her and there was nowhere for her to run. As he drew closer the stone around her neck began to pulse silently. Terror struck at her heart. Was it glowing too? He took another step forward, and another. He was just past her now and she wondered if he would be able to smell her fear. He stopped again, listening intently to the woodland sounds around him. He carefully took another step forward and Catherine allowed herself a small flicker of hope. Her muscles were screaming out in pain, they demanded relief and her head throbbed but she was a lifetime away from being safe yet.

A small rustle back down the path to her right caught his attention and he turned to face it. Catherine thought her heart would surely stop any second and as he took a small step back towards her she thought she would pass out. A twig under his foot snapped loudly and Catherine jumped, there was a sudden panic behind her as the deer that had been grazing quietly kicked up its heels and ran. Roland's head snapped in that direction and he charged off in pursuit.

Catherine could hardly believe it, he was gone. She could still hear the two of them crashing through the undergrowth. It would not be long before he realised what he was chasing and there was every chance he would pick up the trail back here. She felt she had a good idea where she was. If she was right the edge of the wood was about twenty minute walk away to her left. She crawled out of the bush, cringing at the noise she made, gathered up her skirts and moved as quickly and quietly as she could along the path.

After about twenty minutes packed full of terror and panic, twenty minutes of expecting a hand to catch her shoulder at any second, she finally burst from the edge of the woods. Looking to her left she could see her house. It looked quite small from here but it did not matter, it still looked safe and inviting, full of lights and fires and love. She gathered her skirts and began to run, her lungs burning, her head light and dizzy. She was almost halfway there, completely exposed on open ground when she saw the man before her. He was mounted on a dark horse, standing between her and the house.

Tears burst from her eyes and she let out a tiny desperate involuntary cry. He had doubled back on her, fetched his horse and beaten her to her house. She froze, if she moved he would see her, if he had not already seen her, she could never outrun the horse. In desperation she decided that despite the danger her safest course would be back to the cover of the trees. As she ran she thought she heard a shout and glancing over her shoulder she saw the man on the horse coming right at her. Tears of despair and terror flowed freely as she tried desperately to make it to the relative safety of the trees. She could hear pounding hooves now, could hear the horse's heavy breath bearing down on her. She felt the breeze catching at her as the horse swept past her as she ran. The man abruptly pulled up the horse, bringing it to a jolting stop, he threw himself from its back and ran at her calling her name.

"Get away from me, I hate you, leave me alone." She cried out. Realising she could never hope to fight him she stopped running. At the very least she hoped she may be able to cause him some further injury before he overpowered her. She glared at him, bracing herself and realised he too had stopped. Momentarily thrown by his hesitation she waited, why was he not coming for her? She had no chance of escape, why was he waiting?

"Catherine?"

It was her name, spoken softly, his voice was different though. It was a trick; he was trying to make her think he was not angry so she would not fight him anymore.

"My Lady? Do you recognise me?"

That soft voice again, there was something familiar about it. What game was he playing now?

"Catherine. It is Michael, do you recognise me? I am going to take a step or two towards you now, so you can see me better."

Such a soft voice. Could it really be Michael? He took one slow step forward and then another, his face was much clearer now, it was very familiar. Still she remained silent and motionless, panicked and unsure how to react.

"Catherine, it is me. I will not hurt you. Do you know who I am?"

His soft voice. A very soft voice that finally broke through. She looked into his face, into his eyes and dared to believe.

"Michael?"

"Yes, Catherine, it is me." He stepped closer, directly in front of her now. She lifted her face and stared blankly at him, slowly relief flooded into her eyes and that quickly gave way to a great wave of sadness.

"Michael." A whisper was all she could manage before the floodgates opened, she let her emotions go and fell to her knees.

Michael was numb as he looked at her, kneeling before him, barely able to recognise him. She was covered with cuts and scratches, her dress was torn to shreds, her hair was full of leaves and twigs. There was dirt on her face and he thought he could make out a trickle of blood from the corner of her mouth. He took the last step forward and wrapped her in his arms. She shook violently and her sobs were loud and pained. Hatred for Roland rose in Michael as he held her, it was a hate so strong and fierce, Michael had never felt anything like it. He did not like this feeling and hoped it would not be long before he could lay it to rest.

After some minutes, when she was able to stand, he gently lifted her onto his horse. He mounted behind her and rode back to the house, holding her tightly to him with his free arm. His heart lurched in his chest as he recalled her face, cut and bloodied, horror in her eyes. As they neared the gates Arthur appeared, his horse breathless and sweaty. He saw Catherine, heard her sobs and saw the hatred in Michael's face. Arthur helped Michael to lift Catherine from the horse' back and then Michael picked her up in his arms. She was quiet and still now.

Robert rushed forward to take the horses from the men as they headed for the kitchen door. The room was bright and warm and she flinched at the change in contrast. Michael set Catherine's feet on the floor and helped her into a seat. In the bright light they could all see the extent of her wounds.

Her feet were shoeless and had been for some time. They were blue with the cold and bloodied from cuts and grazes. They were dirty and amongst all this, pine needles protruded from her skin. Her ankles were bruised and swollen, her shins grazed and bloodied. Her arms and hands were a mess of cuts and scratches where she had tried to protect her face as she ran and Michael took special note of the finger marks that had been bruised into her flesh. Her cheek and jaw were black and blue and there was a trail of dried blood coming from her mouth, petering out at her throat. Her left eye was purple and puffy hiding the vacant stare that was clearly displayed in the other one. She shook, partly from the cold and partly from shock.

After the initial shock of Catherine's appearance cook started to bustle. She put a great pan of water over the huge fire to heat along with some broth. Then she began to issue orders.

"Arthur, fetch the tub. Rachel, fetch cloths and blankets. Mary, see to it that there are blankets in her room, cover the windows and warm the bed."

She turned to Michael, her voice suddenly soft. "For the minute you can stay. The poor child needs comfort now and I think you are the one to give it."

"How is John?" Seeing Rachel had reminded Michael of his friend and he prayed the news was good.

Cook smiled. "He is fine, woke up a little while ago with a headache he will not forget in a hurry but he is definitely still with us."

Relieved Michael turned back to Catherine.

"How are you?" He knelt before her and gently took her hands in his. She winced in pain and looking down he saw the burn on the palm of her hand. Instead he held her arms and looked into her white face.

"Talk to me Catherine, please." She looked a little like a startled deer, wide eyed and tense.

As the door swung open she jumped so much she almost left her chair. Arthur came in with the tub and seeing her fear placed it down quietly and stepped back. Her lips moved, trembling as she tried to speak. After a few seconds she managed a hoarse whisper.

"I am so sorry." Her eyes met Michael's as she said the words and shifted to Arthur's, begging forgiveness.

"Catherine, you have done nothing wrong. You were deceived by an evil man, just like the rest of us." Arthur spoke softly, slowly, hoping she would believe him. She lowered her eyelids, hanging her head.

"Michael knew and I should have listened. Michael, I am so sorry I was horrible to you this morning. I did not mean to be and I feel so guilty. You tried to warn me and I did not listen." Tears began to flow. "Please forgive me, please stay!"

He reached out and touched her face, watching as her eyes implored him to forgive her. There was nothing for him to forgive.

"Why would I leave? Stop feeling guilty, there is no need." He opened his arms and she fell into them, clinging to him.

His back against the wall Arthur felt relieved to see her back, alive, and to see the two of them so close. Michael would stay and Catherine would eventually recover, physically at least. But he had seen the state she was in physically and could only guess at what she had been through emotionally. Arthur had never hated anyone before, not even Preece, but Roland of Langley deserved the worst imaginable. Arthur tasted hate for the first time and vowed he would do whatever it took to take revenge. There could be no forgiveness this time.

It was not long before the cook ordered the men out of the room so that they could clean Catherine's wounds and get her to bed. That was when the two men remembered the monk. They strode towards the hall where they found him sitting before the fire with a cup in his hands. When he saw them he jumped out of his seat.

"Did you find her, is she OK?" His voice sounded as worried as he looked.

"We found her and she is alive, but she has been hurt" replied Michael curtly. "What are you doing here monk?"

Aelfric crossed himself and muttered quiet thanks before raising his face again.

"My name is Aelfric and I have an urgent message for the " he hesitated, "the Knight's daughter."

"What message?" asked Arthur

"I believe she is in grave danger" said the monk quietly.

"We know" snapped Michael, his temper rising and his patience almost gone. "What do you know?"

Aelfric quailed a little at the aggressive tone of the large man before him.

"I, I cannot say, I can only speak to her." He paused, as if gathering himself. "May I stay here until she is recovered? I may be able to help."

That did not satisfy Michael and he was in no mood for playing games.

"Not good enough monk, speak up or get out." Michael almost growled the words at him.

Aelfric was quite scared and it showed but when he did not speak Michael took a step forward to eject him from the house.

"No! Please, I am a monk, I harm no-one. Really, I can help, but my message was sent for the Knight alone, now he is gone I can only speak with his child."

Arthur put out a hand to stop Michael.

Michael stood still and silent, his patience all gone. Slowly he appraised the monk, looking for signs, anything that might give him away as a liar or a threat in any way. When he could not find anything he sighed, frustrated and agitated.

"Fine" he muttered, turned on his heels and left. Arthur continued to stare at Aelfric some seconds longer before he spoke.

"Come, I will show you where you can sleep tonight. We will talk more in the morning." The monk's face brightened slightly and he quietly followed Arthur from the room. As they crossed the yard Arthur caught sight of Michael walking around the inside of the wall.

Michael could not rest. He was so angry at himself. He was angry for leaving the house, angry for leaving John alone and full of venom at the thought of that monster hurting Catherine. And so, in a fog of guilt, Michael spent the night patrolling the house and gardens, alert to the tiniest sound, looking for the smallest signs of an intruder. He felt he had let everyone down today, their safety was his responsibility. His emotions had got the better of him and he was going to make sure that never happened again. He spent the rest of the night pacing the house and grounds, slowly burying his feelings for Catherine. He would always be there for her, he knew that now, but he could not put her life at risk again. He wondered if he would ever forgive himself for this, if any worse had befallen her he was not sure if he could have lived with himself.

Chapter 11

Catherine woke with a start. Adrenaline flowed in her veins as her body prepared to flee from the monster that was stalking her. Slowly she realised she was in her own bed, it had been a nightmare. She looked around the room, calmed by familiar sights. Her first needlework project hung on the wall, her favourite chair sat in the corner, covered with a blanket her mother had made. Hanging on the back of her door was a posy of dried flowers that she had collected from the woods and arranged last year.

Outside she could hear larks squawking at each other, every now and then she could hear a horse snort from the stables. There was not much light coming in through the window and what light there was, was tinged red. Catherine guessed she had been asleep only a few hours and decided that dawn was far too early to get up. Her bed was warm and comfortable, a cocoon of peace and safety. She had no wish to leave it, to be cold and sit on a hard chair, to be pitied by all the people downstairs.

Bathing the night before had helped to wash off the dirt, clean out her wounds and rinse away the smell of him. The warm water had helped to relieve her aching muscles leaving her feeling utterly drained, mentally and physically. She yawned and curled up to sleep for another few hours. When she woke again the room was much brighter, birds still sang outside and she could hear the gentle pitter–patter of rain. She lay as still as she could, eyes still closed, savouring the warmth and comfort of her bed before she got up to face the world, although she had no idea how she would do that. She felt deeply ashamed that she had encouraged that monster, guilt that she had concealed it from Michael, Arthur and John. There was also a constricting sense of shame and disgust when she thought of the struggle by the fire. Catherine was afraid to tell them what had happened, unsure of how much to reveal. They would at least want to know how he had gained access to the house. Her gut clenched at the thought but she knew it must be done.

Before she had a chance to move a sound caught her attention and she looked over in time to see her door swing open. Rachel poked her head around the door, peering towards the bed.

"Miss, you are awake. We were starting to get worried."

Catherine sat up in bed wincing as her muscles complained and pain flared in her hand.

"You must be starving, I will run and get you some food, Cook has been working hard in the kitchen, enough to feed the King's army there is." Without another word Rachel bobbed her head and left, Catherine could hear her small feet tapping quickly along the landing. Heavier footsteps replaced them, drawing nearer. She fought to control the panic rising within her. The footsteps stopped and someone knocked gently at her door. Catherine pulled her sheets up and said "come in" in a voice that was far more timid than she had intended.

Slowly the door opened and Michael stepped in.

"Rachel said you were awake. How do you feel today?"

Catherine looked at Michael and realised that this time she saw him in a different light. Two days ago, when she had been an arrogant and selfish child, Michael had been her friend and a bodyguard she had not really believed she needed. Her father had known he was dying and he had foreseen something horrible in her future and he had planned for her protection when he could no longer do it himself. Today, as she looked at him she saw a different man. She saw his deep warm eyes, saw the strength in his jaw, the power of his body; she began to see what the maids chattered about. Catherine saw her protector, a man she wanted to run to. It suddenly occurred to her that she was staring.

"I am sorry Michael" she looked away from him, feeling the need to make an excuse for staring so boldly. "I am still tired, even after all that sleep."

"It is not surprising; you have been through a lot. You did have us all a bit worried though."

"You were worried about me?" she looked up at him.

"Of course I was!" Michael was taken aback by the question and he took a step forward, his instincts telling him to reassure her. As he stepped he remembered he was in her bed chamber and quickly stepped back again, forcing himself to be more formal.

"Yes, I was worried, we all were. You are looking better though, you have more colour."

"How bad is it Michael? I must look truly awful."

"Not at all." He could still see a dark bruise around her eye, could still see the scratch marks that covered her skin, he could still see finger marks on her neck and arms and she looked very tired. The physical wounds would heal in time; he was more concerned about her mind.

"You have a couple of small bruises, a few scratches, they will all be gone in a few days. You will have to be careful with that burn though, try not to touch it too much for a while."

"Thank you Michael. I am going to get up now. I will be downstairs shortly."

"Only if you feel up to it. We will look forward to seeing you. Cook will certainly be pleased to see you." Michael sensed he was beginning to ramble and turned to leave.

"Michael?"

He stopped in the doorway and turned to face her again. Her face was full of emotion, there were questions and there was guilt, fear and vulnerability. He held his breath and waited for her to speak.

"Thank you."

Michael smiled and bowed his head slightly, and then recalling the other reason for his visit he raised his head.

"There was one other thing. A man arrived last night; he is waiting to see you."

Catherine's mind started to race and without thinking her hand went to the stone hanging around her neck. It was still and cool to the touch, no hint of movement. She was surprised at how quickly she had realised that the stone was a warning of danger and had come to trust it.

"Who is it?" she asked, her voice faltering slightly, afraid of what the answer might be but not knowing quite why.

"A monk, all we can get out of him is that he had an urgent message for your father, but now that message is for you. Should we send him away?"

The first answer on the tip of her tongue was 'yes'. She felt she already had too much to face over the coming days, but the possibility that this man was the one in the letter was too great.

"No, I will be down to see him soon." She had no idea how she would be able to tell if he was the one, she had already made one enormous blunder trusting Roland, what if this man was an impostor, what if he was here to harm her too? From what Roland had said it seemed Preece was hiring mercenaries now, but she needed answers and she could not risk missing this chance. Her faith in her judgement had been shaken lately but now she had the stone to help guide her. As long as she met him with Michael and Arthur close by she would know if she was safe.

As Michael closed the door behind him she eased her sore, aching body from her bed and slowly, carefully dressed before teasing the knots from her hair and slowly braiding it over her shoulder. As she mechanically performed the motions of dressing, her mind drifted and gingerly touched on what had happened last night. It disgusted her to think of what he had done, what he had touched, but when she thought of what could have happened, what he had planned, she felt her stomach tighten in knots. Even worse, by this time she might have been locked in a room in Preece's house, she may even have woken up next to him, as his wife. Tears welled in her eyes and her hands trembled.

Even the thought of it was too much to bear, so she shook herself mentally, realising that she had been staring blankly at the same spot for some minutes, whilst silent tears slid down her cheek and dropped softly into her lap. She badly needed distraction from last night's events but meeting with the monk would only serve to rake up all the painful questions about her father that she had hidden in the back of her mind. With a deep shuddering sigh, Catherine wiped at her wet face, suddenly aware of a sharp pain as her hand brushed over raw cuts and grazes. With an effort she stood and made her way slowly down to the hall, although she did not feel at all hungry and approached her meeting with the monk with a great deal of trepidation and anxiety.

Taking a deep breath she pushed at the door to the hall and entered. There were three people seated at the long table already, with a fourth standing nearby. With relief she noted that Michael and Arthur were seated at the table and John stood just behind them, they seemed to be talking in low voices and stopped as soon as they saw her.

The fourth man did indeed appear to be a monk, she recognised his habit and the familiar tonsure, and he certainly did look the part. He was quite tall but thin, almost bending forward from his waist. She imagined in a few years time that would develop into a stoop. His face had a slightly pinched look, being long and thin and having a narrow nose that protruded sharply from his face. His hair was dark and fine, sitting in thin strands that barely reached his forehead. His features were lined around the eyes and mouth, giving him the air of a mature and wise man who had seen much joy in his past. As he noticed her enter and move towards the table the man stood and bowed. As she reached the table she bade them all sit and eat. Her hand went to her throat, but she could feel nothing. The stone gave no hint that it sensed danger in this room.

Aelfric lifted his head and took a closer look at the lady before him. His breath caught in his throat as he took in the sight of her face, battered and scraped, swollen around the eyes and purple about the mouth. It was several seconds before he was able to tear his eyes away and force a smile onto his face, but Catherine had already noticed the revulsion in his expression, the pity in his eyes and it hurt her to see them. Just a few days ago she had been strong, proud and handsome. Nobody had ever looked at her this way before and it made her feel small and vulnerable, made her want to run and hide from them all.

She stood at the table, her hands resting on the surface as her pride wrestled with her fears and her urge to run from the room. Then she heard a deep, soft voice, soothing and calm, reaching out to her.

"Lady Catherine, I am sorry for your loss. I knew your father, he was a good man."

Catherine looked up. Apparently it had been the monk who had spoken to her and he looked directly at her now, with no trace of the pity she had seen a few moments ago. He had known her father? A thousand questions sprang to her mind, each one desperate to be spoken aloud at once. She looked from the monk to the others and then raised a weak smile.

"Thank you, please, everyone sit and eat."

The monk returned her smile, sat down and began filling his plate. There was something about this man that drew her gaze. He was very calm and self–assured but without any of the overt confidence that Roland had shown. His voice had a purity to it that she had never heard before but she was not about to trust him. The possibilities were too awful if she got it wrong. He could be another mercenary from Preece, he could be working for the King, worse, if she let slip her secret to the wrong person she could be burned at the stake as a witch. Accused as good witch or bad, she would die the same way.

As she picked at a piece of bread she considered her options. The only thing she knew for sure was that she could not sit in this awful silence any longer.

"So, Brother, where do you come from?"

"I come from Worcester, my Lady, the cathedral. My name is Aelfric and I was a friend of Brother Edric, you may remember him, I believe he visited your father here, about 6 years ago."

Catherine did recall a monk visiting. She remembered that he had arrived in the early hours of the morning, before it was even light. Her father had sent her back to bed and the two men had left together soon after breakfast but she had never known his name. She recalled that her father had returned the following day with two young soldiers that he had hired to help him around the estate and to protect the house. That was the day Michael and Arthur had arrived. John had joined them about two years later.

Feeling somewhat bolder with the three soldiers in the room with her she resolved to test the monk further.

"Michael, I thought you should know, Roland told me he was hired by Preece, there may be more like him on their way. He said that Preece was quite determined."

Michael's head snapped up and he stared at her, hardly believing that she was prepared to discuss what had happened already, but in front of this stranger? Catherine, however, was staring intently at the monk, who had not flinched at all. Michael followed her gaze and watched as the monk helped himself to more butter for his bread. Sensing that silence had filled the room, the monk stopped and looked around at the others.

"I am sorry; it has been two days since I ate." Reluctantly he put the bread down and sat back on his stool, looking apologetic and hungry.

He had not flinched at all, not a flicker of recognition in his face. In fact, he had barely seemed to be aware that she had been speaking. Perhaps he was safe after all. Her mind a little more at rest, Catherine relaxed and smiled.

"No, please, continue, eat as much as you want, there is plenty."

By the time everyone had finished eating Catherine had had a chance to steel herself and was as ready as she could be to hear what the monk had to say. She cleared her throat to ensure that her voice would be as firm as possible.

"I need to speak to Brother Aelfric, alone. Do you mind leaving us, maybe waiting outside the door?" She looked at the three soldiers. She could see the surprise in their faces and she understood it. She was not happy at being alone with a stranger herself but she had to know and this was a secret she could not share with them. Michael remained in his seat as his companions rose and made their way to the door. Catherine looked at him and met his stare.

"My Lady, I would be failing in my duty if I left you alone with this man, I will not leave."

His stare challenged hers; seemingly expecting her to quietly consent, the expression on her face spoke of a softening will, a need to be protected. Catherine was fighting a battle in her mind. Part of her was gratified and relieved to see him hold his ground and it was that same part that told her to concede and let him stay; let him share in her secret. She needed to talk to someone and at the moment there was no-one she trusted more than Michael. Another part of her, though, needed to hear what the monk had to say on her own first, she was afraid of Michael's reaction and the spectre of a bonfire still preyed on her mind.

It was a surprise for Michael when Catherine returned his stare with her own, her chin raised and her shoulders straight.

"Thank you Michael, but really, I will be fine, rest assured that I will call you if I need you. You will only be outside the door, but I need to hear what the brother has to say, in private."

Catherine shocked herself, the voice she heard was strong, clear and confident, and she found it hard to believe it had come from her. Reluctantly Michael left the room and closed the door behind him.

She was suddenly acutely aware that she was very much alone with the monk now and looked up at him in anticipation, her heart pounding in her breast. He was looking at her intently, as if trying to read something in her face.

"You do not trust me," he said, "and you are right to be cautious. What do your instincts tell you about me?"

Catherine was quite taken aback by his directness and did not know what to say.

He seemed to sense this and continued.

"Your necklace, it is quite beautiful. It is a very rare stone, you know, and it has some" he paused, trying to find the right words "special properties. What does the stone tell you about me?"

Catherine was stunned. How did he know about the necklace, the stone? She felt a little defensive now.

"It tells me nothing, but, how? How do you know about the stone?"

"I believe your father said it belonged to your mother. Did he not tell you someone would be coming?" Aelfric could see a succession of emotions pass across her face as he spoke. He needed to win her trust but he did not have much time.

She sat in stunned silence for a minute or two before she could find the words to answer him.

"He, he died suddenly, he did not have time to tell me anything."

Aelfric frowned slightly. If she really knew nothing then his job would be much harder. He had already realised that he was no longer just a messenger. When news of her father's death reached the Cathedral, Edric should have been the one to come to her, to guide her. Aelfric had thought he would find her father alive and that he would be able to teach her all she needed to know. But with them both dead it fell to Aelfric to see that the line continued, to see that things that should stay hidden never fell into evil hands again. But she had the necklace, so she must know something. Aelfric saw no option but to be direct, so he continued, softly.

"You have the necklace and so I assume that you have found other things. Were there perhaps some papers? Perhaps something from your father that explained at least a little bit?" he looked at her enquiringly.

"Yes, there was a letter." It was almost a whisper. "Are you the one?"

Aelfric thought for a second, remembering his good friend Edric, before he answered.

"Yes, I am. I can help you to understand your gift, to teach you how to use it, if you can trust me." His voice was soft, warm and inviting.

Catherine nodded silently.

Chapter 12

Rain had been falling on the woodland canopy for several hours, gently filtering down through the leafy layers until finally reaching the soft ground in small diffused droplets. Small and large animals alike had sought shelter long ago, leaving only the birds to hunt the worms and other insects lured to the surface by the quiet drumming of the raindrops on the ground above. As the water traced its way through the leaves and branches it gathered up and carried with it the sweet aroma of the trees, leaving the air fresh and fragrant.

Deep in this peaceful sanctuary, in the mouth of a small natural cave in the side of tract of raised ground, rock that had been forced up above the surrounding ground, thousands of years before. A fire burned and crackled. Smoke rose tainting the clean air as it weaved its way up through the trees, gradually dissipating before it reached the open sky. Over the small fire hung a small pot from which clouds of steam issued. The smell was sharp and repulsive and it made thick popping, bubbling sounds as it simmered. A cloaked and hooded figure sat, hunched just within the cave, his head bowed, muttering strange words in a voice laced with menace. As he chanted his body slowly rocked back and forth and on the stone floor before him was an assortment of small stones and bones bearing alien symbols. The man reached out slowly with a large hand and swept up the runes. He muttered a few more mysterious words before dropping the runes back onto the ground. He immediately fell still and silent, appearing to study the runes intently, noting how each one lay on its own and in relation to all the others. Each one gave a message and read together they were consolidated into the answer he sought.

In those minutes that followed even the birds dared make no noise and the wood seemed to hold its breath, waiting, wondering.

After many minutes the hooded figure sighed and straightened his back, lifting his head to look straight ahead.

"It seems my diversion served me well after all. It is very close now, I can almost feel it. So, it has been hidden here all these years. I will need to be careful, it is bound to be well protected maybe even with a Guardian, but it is worth the risks. I wonder if the King would have trusted me with this task if he had known its full potential like his father had. He would never appreciate it fully or use it wisely, like I can." He laughed and the horse that had been grazing nearby looked up at the sound.

He reached forward to lift the pot from the fire, his hand apparently unaffected by the intense heat. Then he slowly raised his other hand to his face and drew back the hood of his cloak. As light fell on his face it revealed fresh burns and blisters, raw and weeping down one whole side of his face. His eye was wide and staring where part of the eyelid was missing and where the eye itself was once white, it was now blood red, the pupil cloudy. There was swelling around his nose and the hair in front of his ear had been burned away. The skin in front of the ear was blackened and charred, peeling away already. The cheek showed the yellowing signs of an infection setting in. A large blister had formed at the corner of his mouth and it wept clear fluid, which seemed to forging a path down his chin.

The horse whinnied, apparently unsettled by the sight, but the man spoke in gentle tones to soothe him.

"Do not worry Saracen, I will fix it, it will be as good as new soon, you will see."

As Roland spoke he dipped his fingers into the steaming pot and brought up a sludge–like mixture, a dark, dirty red in colour and foul in odour. Roland did not appear to mind though, as he smeared the scalding hot sludge on his face. The instant it touched his wounds he cried out in pain but it did not last long, the mixture seemed to have great soothing properties. Saracen continued to watch him intently as he continued applying the balm until a thick layer of it covered the entire side of his face. Then with a weary sigh he lay down in the cave to rest.

Earlier that day Roland had woken feeling cold, stiff and sore and his face hurt like hell. It had taken him a few minutes to work out where he was, how he had got there and why. He felt so groggy. There was so much pain in his face and it was demanding so much of his attention. He raised his hand to touch his skin, apparently there was not much left of it from the little he could feel. Every hint of pressure caused a fresh wave of pain in his face but he had to know. His face felt raw to the touch, in places it was rough and dry, in others wet and smooth and extremely sore.

Slowly, he recalled the events of the previous night. He had her on the floor and the little bitch had hit him with a branch from the fire. She had been quicker than he had expected and much better at hiding than he had thought too. Once he had realised what he was chasing he was quite a long way from the path. He guessed that she would head straight back to the house and he realised he needed to get out of the woods to have a better view when she finally left the cover of the trees. By the time he had found the edge of the forest she was already out in the open. He could see her standing still as a man approached her, he had to be one of the soldiers, probably the dark one. Roland thought quickly, he could not get her back now. He was in no shape to try and he guessed that before long the soldiers would be out looking for him. He had no choice but to leave the immediate area, lie low for a few days and then come back with a new plan.

Roland knew he could not risk towns or villages, his new appearance would draw far more unwanted attention than the old one would have. Word would spread and then he would be hounded and possibly even caught. Catherine was not just beautiful, she seemed to be almost worshipped in these parts, a proper little saint by all accounts. So he had ridden deeper into the woods to put some distance between himself and Catherine. Eventually, shortly after dawn he had stumbled across another small cave. For the most part the trees were thin enough to ride comfortably through but a small area had grown thick and provided shelter from the elements for him and a hiding place for Saracen. He spent the following few hours gathering what meagre supplies he could find and creating this shelter for himself.

After a short while of painful exertion he was ready to settle in for a few days and made himself comfortable. He was so tired and now he could rest, reassured that he was still on the right track with his quest. This was the closest he had ever been and its lure was very powerful. Roland wanted some revenge for this set back but that would have to wait, he knew he needed a plan. He would have to find out exactly where it was hidden and how it was protected and to do that he knew he would have to leave the relative safety of the trees. No doubt by now those soldiers would have spread the word and every peasant from here to Gloucester would be watching for him. At least they did not appear to have raised the hue and cry; they would have combed the woods by now if they had. That gave him time to recoup and come up with a new plan. He accepted now that his little distraction had been a bad idea. He would forget Preece and his insignificant project and continue with his own destiny again. He would need a disguise, something that would help him to fit in, so he could walk freely amongst the locals. That should not be too hard to arrange.

As he thought he grew tired and drifted off to sleep. It was several hours before he woke again. The rain had stopped but large fat drops of water still fell from the trees periodically. His eyes opened and he allowed himself to come round fully before he rose to a sitting position. Roland gently touched the red balm on his face. While he had slept it had solidified into a pliable mask over his wounds and he was now able to peel it off in one large piece. The inside was littered with pieces of burned flesh and bloody smears. He placed it on the floor beside him and lifted his hand to his face to examine its condition.

The skin was flawless, there was no longer any hint of a wound where the burn had been. Now there was healthy, browned skin that perfectly matched the rest of his face. His eye was no longer red and the lid was complete. There was not a blister to be seen.

"How does it look Saracen?" he called to his horse where it stood about twenty paces from the cave opening.

The horse snorted in approval and bobbed his head before returning his attention to nuzzling at the ground for something to eat.

Chapter 13

The day was several hours old and breakfast was underway. One end of the wooden table, cracked and lined with age, was covered with plates of bread, cheese, butter and a pot of honey. To one side was a small basket of fruit. Catherine and Aelfric sat together at the table, their plates filled with food, a comfortable silence between them as they ate.

The distraction had been good for Catherine; long talks with Aelfric had helped to take her mind off of Roland and Preece.

She was feeling brighter today, less stiff, and less painful and she had slept right through the night again. She had chosen a blue dress this morning in an attempt to bring some colour into her life. She had also tied her hair back away from her injured face.

Her cuts were beginning to heal, the bruises fading to purple, in a few days more they would turn green and she would begin to look a little more like herself again. Catherine did not feel like herself though, she felt as if she had lost control of her life, that she had been tumbling from one day to the next, never quite being able to get her feet on the floor since her father had died. At a time when she felt that everyone around her was a threat, that even those closest to her could betray her to her death if they knew, she had found someone who she trusted implicitly. She had known Aelfric only a day and yet she believed he was her friend, even though he knew enough about her to see her burn if he chose. It was hard to put her finger on exactly why she felt so safe with the monk. His voice was very soothing, he seemed to understand what she was going through and, of course, he was a man of cloth. This part both comforted and confused her though. She could not quite understand how someone so religious could be so supportive of what she had been taught were pagan practices, forbidden by the Church.

Aelfric also knew about her mother and much of what her father had been. It was as if this information were a drug she could not get enough of, something she could only get from Aelfric. It was like an addiction and she hung on his words, absorbing every morsel of information he could give her. As long as he was there and was willing to speak, Catherine felt calm and safe. In the few minutes she had been awake and alone since he had arrived she felt unnerved and restless and this did nothing to ease her general state of mind.

Last night she had reluctantly gone to bed when she could keep her eyes open no longer, as if someone had attached iron weights to her lids, pulling them closed no matter how much she fought to keep them open. Aelfric had just sat and smiled at her, unable to ignore her yawns any longer, and refusing to encourage her by continuing to talk. Then Arthur had moved over to her chair, quietly suggesting that it might be time to rest. Only then had she given up and gone to bed, where she had slept, undisturbed and unmoving until the sound of bird calls had woken her this morning.

Although she felt much better today she was still a little stiff and sore in her limbs and ribs. Her lip was healing, so yawning this morning was less painful. When she had first woken her mind had been clear and at ease, it was as she tried to move that her body had reminded her why she hurt so much. She had closed her eyes and tried to blot out the images of the black horse and of a dark stranger but it had not worked, the only way to escape was to get up and seek distraction.

As she ate she wondered if Aelfric would tell her more about the contents of the chest today and wondered how much this might scare her, or upset her, or excite her, or all three at once. They had spent much of yesterday talking around what had happened in the woods the previous night. He had gently probed and she had alluded to what had happened in vague terms without wanting to go into the awful details. Even thinking of it made her feel dirty and disgusting. Just touching on the subject roused all her feelings of guilt and shame. Her feelings were so strong in this regard that she had almost convinced herself that she was to blame for all that had happened. He had been gentle in his coaxing, careful with his questions, while she had been unwilling to confront the memories head on. In this way they had spent several hours talking around the subject, examining her feelings and reactions without discussing the facts. It was an approach that allowed her to keep that little demon locked in its box but be able to look at it from a distance, to poke it and overcome her fear of it without the risk of its escaping and getting the better of her.

Rachel bustled in shortly after breakfast with a jug of ale for them both. There was something strained in Rachel's face, Aelfric noticed it and asked her what was wrong, Catherine's head snapped up, dreading the next piece of bad news.

"Oh Sir, it is just awful, a cottager has just been along and told us the Church in Chedworth was all torn up last night. Just terrible it is, bits broken and thrown around but nothing taken, the monk says. He thinks it is the Pagan's that did it, says there has been a lot of it about lately. He reckons there are monks coming from the big Cathedral in Worcester to sort them out." As Rachel said this she realised who she was talking to and looked at him enquiringly.

"Pardon me Sir, it is not any of my business, but, maybe that is why you have come?"

Aelfric smiled at the girl and shook his head. "No, my child, I am just here to visit an old friend, if there are monks coming, they left after I did, but tell me more about the Church, this sounds awful."

Rachel revelled in the opportunity to tell him everything she knew, and embellish those bits she did not know.

She told him how some of the benches had been broken and apparently thrown against the wall, how the alter had been knocked down, the contents of chests strewn across the floor but that the resident monk had confirmed that nothing had actually been taken, which was why were suspected of this heinous crime more than a passing beggar trying to steal enough to buy his next meal.

Rachel went on to tell them both how the Miller's wife had seen someone suspicious that evening and was convinced it had been a witch she had seen. This had apparently had sent half the community into a panic, desperately trying to gather the necessary herbs and make crosses to surround their homes to keep the evil witches out, begging the monks for holy water and prayers to protect them. As much as she loved her gossip, Rachel had a fairly level head on her shoulders and did not put much stock in the Miller's wife's tale. "She may well have seen someone, but a witch? Well, that was not likely, was it!" With that she curtseyed and left the room.

Catherine only then realised that she had not moved and hardly breathed since Rachel had mentioned the witch. She took a deep shuddering breath and turned to look at Aelfric, eyes wide with fear.

"You look worried child, you heard Rachel, she does not believe there was a witch, and she will not be the only one of that mind, people will not want it widely thought that there is a witch living amongst them, bad for business, not to mention the fines. I am concerned about this though. Before I left Worcester there was much talk of people returning to the Pagan ways, I would hate to think that they have got carried away and defiled a church in this way. Still, whoever did this, we must be cautious. For a time people will be suspicious of everything and everyone, anything they see or hear that is not in the usual way will be much exaggerated, in their minds."

Catherine was amazed at his calmness, her first instinct had been panic, fear that she would be discovered as the child of a witch and dragged to the nearest pyre, however, as her pulse slowed and she calmed her frayed nerves she began to see the sense in what he said. Whilst they would not tolerate a witch openly amongst them, the villagers would not want to go looking for one. Aelfric was right, they would need to be careful what they said when people could overhear. Taking a deep, steadying breath, she looked him in the eye and asked a question that had been burning at her since the day before.

"I was hoping you could tell me what you know of my mother, what was she like? What did she look like?"

"I was only a novice then, my brother monk, Edric, was her aide. Only the very wisest and most accomplished monks are rewarded with the care of a Guardian, so, you see, I never met her myself, but I was Edric's apprentice and he talked of her a great deal. She had dark hair, almost as black as the raven, he said, and a wise face, full of care and grace; a face to place your trust in. I believe Edric described her as tall and elegant, healthy and vigorous.

She was passionate but not easily excited and not easily scared either, I would imagine and she loved your father very much. Edric told me that she found it hard to be separated from him but she believed in," here Aelfric paused, searching for the right words, "her destiny."

Catherine was transfixed, her father had not often talked about her mother, saying only that she was beautiful and kind and that Catherine was her image, but Aelfric's last word captivated her. She was eager to hear more, sensing that something great was coming but noticed Aelfric's hesitation and suggested that they retire to her solar to talk further. There, on the other side of the house, in her private rooms, they would not be overheard or disturbed. Once they had settled themselves by the fire Catherine probed further.

"You mentioned my mother's destiny, what did you mean by that?" Her voice wavered slightly, betraying how important this information was to her and once again she felt vulnerable.

Aelfric paused, composing his thoughts before he began, this was such a delicate matter, he would need to introduce it to Catherine slowly so as not to overwhelm the poor girl. He could see her strength but also knew that she had been weakened by the trials of the preceding days. He would need to be careful how he began, he needed her acceptance, needed her to finish the task. He could not afford to risk delay or failure by making a stupid mistake now.

"The stone you have around your neck, it belonged to your mother. She wore it always, until she died, giving birth to you. I believe your father put it away until such time as you were ready to have it. Has it, spoken to you yet?"

Catherine recalled something he had said to her the previous day, when they had first met. He had asked her what the stone told her about him. Almost unconsciously her hand went to the stone now, where it nestled quietly and coolly at her throat. As she touched it she recalled how it had vibrated and seemed to glow around Roland. Given what had happened shortly after, she had interpreted this as some kind of warning that something bad was about to happen, but she did not understand how it knew or how it worked. Now she thought of it, in the daylight, sitting here in the warmth and civilised comfort of her solar, she began to doubt that it had done anything at all. It may all have been her imagination, or confusion, after all everything seemed to happen so quickly and then there was the knock to her head. It would have been so easy to imagine something that had not happened. Perhaps she had dreamed it up to make herself feel that he had retained some of her wits, had some control when in reality she probably had neither.

Doubt clouded her mind she had no intention of being pronounced mad or possessed by admitting that a stone had spoken to her, so she dodged the question and become defensive.

"I do not know what you mean, it is a stone, and everyone knows they cannot speak."

Aelfric nodded, his face grave, perhaps his gentle approach was not going to work. "Catherine, have I not won your trust yet? What are you afraid of? You need to tell me what scares you the most so that I can put your mind at ease otherwise we will never be able to move on to more important matters. Catherine, how can I impress upon you the need to make the most of the little time we have?"

Catherine was once again stunned by his directness. It had taken her by surprise yesterday and it had shocked her again now. Mostly this monk was quiet, measured and thoughtful, but twice now he had struck at the truth with such bluntness that she had been unable to hide from his searching eyes. This time was no different, he was correct, she did trust him, more than she trusted anyone else around her at the moment; it was herself that she did not trust.

After almost a full minute of silence during which she examined her innermost instincts, Catherine took a breath and gave him an answer.

"I trust you, but I cannot trust myself at the moment. I am afraid that if I admit what I think I have seen and felt, that it will make it real. I am scared that with everything that has happened since my father's death, my mind has broken and I have gone mad and started to see things that are not real, or worse become possessed. I am terrified that if anyone else discovers what I found in the chest in my father's room, where I found this stone, I will be burnt as a witch. I am hunted by wicked men, my parents have become strangers to me and I cannot share my biggest secret with my closest friend in case he betrays me, even without meaning to."

Once she had begun she could not stop. It was far more honest and direct than she had intended and now she felt raw inside, exposed. She watched Aelfric very closely; waiting to see how he would react; waiting to see if her trust had been misplaced. She also wondered what he had meant by his comment about what little time they had left. It seemed an odd thing to say when he had only just arrived. But in the chaos of her mind the question was lost as soon as it was raised.

Aelfric smiled, this was more honesty that he had expected but it was good, it was good to hear that she had thought about the reality of her situation as she currently perceived it, that she had already recognised that she needed to be extremely careful who she trusted with information, that she saw that this could be a brutal world and her safety was at risk. This pleased Aelfric greatly; it meant that his news may not be the tearing shock he had anticipated. It was also encouraging to see that she appreciated directness and responded in a like manner.

"Let me ask you something else. What do you believe your mother was?"

The word immediately sprang into Catherine's mind but she was still wary of speaking it aloud. After a few seconds of awkward silence took a deep breath, raised her chin and answered his question.

"A witch."

Chapter 14

Matthew Preece was not known for his patience. The following morning as he moved through his house he seized small objects and threw them at the floor, the walls and the servants who did not move quickly enough, in an attempt to exorcise his temper. When that failed, and he began to run out of pots and trinkets, he progressed to upending his chairs and occasionally a table. This did help and he started to calm down. As his temper ebbed he was able to think more clearly.

It had been almost a week since Roland had come knocking on his door with an offer he could not refuse. He had teased Preece with a promise and talked of payments and had then left to get the girl. Since then he had heard nothing but rumours. He had received no messages, seen no sign of Roland, seen no solid evidence that he had even tried to capture the girl. Preece was extremely frustrated. Why come here and make an offer if the man had no intention of making good on it? Could it be that Roland was a fugitive who had been captured? No, Preece would have heard about that. Perhaps he had met with an accident before he had an opportunity to get at Catherine. That seemed more likely and Preece had to admit he would not be sorry of this was true. Roland had been an unnerving character. Preece was disappointed that Roland had not managed to capture Catherine for him first though. Just this morning he had overheard his servants talking of some kind of problem over at the Withington house, something about Catherine being injured or seriously ill and a mysterious monk turning up out of nowhere.

Preece was very concerned. There was a lot at stake here. If she died before he married her then the estate would go to the crown and his dreams of wealth and power would be destroyed, and with them his chance to get his hands on the house. Preece had lived around here long enough to pick up a few things. The Knight for example, how had he managed to come home unscathed from all those wars and battles when others seemed to fall like flies around him? Then there was his wife. When she had been alive there had been an almost constant stream of strange folk coming and going, nobles, clergy and peasants alike. She would often disappear for days at a time with no explanation. True, things had been a lot quieter since she had died but it was still strange that during the leaner years their crops seemed to recover quicker and be more bountiful than anyone else's. Preece doubted this was entirely down to their farming skills. He had suspected something was not quite normal about that place for years but could never put his finger on what it was. Still, the fact remained that there was something there, even if it was only good soil, and he wanted it for himself.

Just then an ugly thought occurred to him. What if Roland had discovered it? What if he had decided to get it for himself mortally wounded the girl in the process and then run off with no intention of sharing? Anger flared within him again.

His first instinct had been not to trust that man, but Roland had been so persuasive and the prize was worth the risk, so he had taken it. Preece was angry with Roland for deceiving him and he vowed that if he ever met the man again he would have him run through, although, somewhere deep inside he knew he was too intimidated by him to try any such thing. It occurred to Preece that he should also be angry at his manservant for letting Roland into the house in the first place. Most of all he was angry at himself, not that he would ever admit it, because that would mean he had made an error in judgement and Matthew Preece does not make errors. So, instead he projected his anger onto everyone else.

The maids were nowhere to be found and his manservant, Sigar, spent a large portion of the day following his master at a safe distance picking up an array of items and restoring them to their proper place, he knew his master would expect nothing less.

Preece's tantrum lasted around an hour longer and as his pulse slowed his mind began to calm, his vision improved and he started to think more clearly. Roland was no longer part of his plans, even if he returned Preece could not trust him. He needed another plan. He eased his body into a wooden chair that creaked loudly in protest under his weight. His biggest problem had always been those guards of hers. They were always there and they were very good at what they did, much better than Preece's own men. Perhaps he could hire better soldiers, although he did not know where he could go for this. He supposed the best place would be in Gloucester but the men there would all be loyal to the Baron, who lived there, and Preece could not afford for the Baron to hear about what he was up to before it was too late for him to take it all away. Preece had to be married to the girl before he could come to the notice of the Baron, in his own time.

Of course, trained soldiers would also cost him a lot of money. Once he had Catherine and her estate he would be able to afford it but even then it would eat into his profits. That was an idea that galled him; it was just not an option. Scratch that idea then.

Preece stared out the window as he thought, hoping that inspiration would come to him. He could see the trees from where he sat. It was an awful place, dark, damp, mouldy and full of flea ridden beasts.

That was it! Mould.

He would have them poisoned, there were bound to be some potent toadstools in those woods. He would make Sigar go and pick them and then find a way to smuggle them into their kitchens with the other mushrooms. The soldiers would eat them, get sick and hopefully die and his path would be clear. Preece was very pleased with himself, it was a great plan, it just needed some of the edges smoothing out and it would be perfect. How would he smuggle the fungus in? Preece's own servants would be recognised and that place was like a fortress now. He did not think knocking on the door was a very promising option. Of course even if he did get the fungus in, there was always a chance Catherine would eat some and die before he could get there with a monk. He was starting to get frustrated again and hungry. It was beginning to look as if separating Catherine from her soldiers was going to be impossible. How could he get them away?

Then it struck him, his greatest plan yet. Were there any flaws? Was there any way it could go wrong and result in the death of Catherine or damage to her property? If there was he could not see it. It was the perfect plan, simple, easy; virtually untraceable and almost guaranteed to succeed and there was no time like the present to put it into action.

The chair groaned again as he stood and he shuffled off to start giving instructions. For the first time in days Preece was smiling, in fact his face wore a large satisfied grin as he shuffled past Sigar. Sigar was troubled, his master was not a naturally happy man, smiling was more often than not a sign of trouble to come. He sighed as he watched his master go, hoping he was wrong but mentally steeling himself for trouble anyway. In his experience that was always best.

Sigar had been in Matthew Preece's service for more years than he cared to remember and he had always been the same. Preece had a wicked temper and Sigar had never come across anyone else whose blood seemed to be almost constantly simmering, just below the surface. There seemed to be so much rage trapped in that body and nobody knew why. Perhaps it was precisely because of the body, after all Preece had not so much been blessed with beauty as cursed with a pox. His skin was marked and florid; he was short, fat and sweaty. Sigar was not surprised Preece had never managed to marry, but that was not for want of trying. Over the years Preece had set his sights on several women, always tall, willowy, and beautiful and of noble birth, women who had no shortage of handsome, wealthy and vigorous suitors. Yet Preece never showed any hint of recognition that he was not physically attractive, in any sense, never seemed to understand why such women would want to look elsewhere for their husbands.

This time Preece had set his sights on the lady from Withington. Sigar had never seen her but he had heard she was both rich and striking to look at. He felt a little sorry for her. It must be awful to be pursued by such a pig of a man, an ugly man who believed he was attractive, a moderately rich man who believed he was worthy of the Barons' attention, an arrogant man who had little reason to believe himself superior.

Sigar suspected that Preece was up to something new, it could not be anything good but he did not know what it was and believed himself safer if he did not know.

Two days went by in relative peace and Sigar was now very worried. His master had been in a good mood since his rage the other day had lifted, there had been no throwing, no shouting and no hitting, worst of all. Sigar was convinced Preece had almost said 'thank you' that morning. Sigar considered calling the physician, his master was undoubtedly ill, but he would see what Margaret thought first.

As he entered the kitchen he could smell meat cooking on a spit over the fire, it reminded him that the midday meal was not far off and his stomach rumbled in anticipation of scraps.

"Margaret, I am worried about the master, I think he is ill."

A woman stood behind a table covered in flour, up to her wrists in dough. She snorted. "What makes you think that? His appetite is not lessened and his sleep is not disturbed at all."

"I know, but he is different, softer, as if he has taken it into his head to be nice to people. I swear he almost thanked me this morning, and then swallowed it."

"You are the one that has gone soft Sigar, I will admit it has been very quiet about here these past couple of days but it is more likely he is up to some new plot than ill. Talking of which, did you hear another church got all torn up last night? They say nothing was taken again. The Reeve is blaming it on pagans, not that he has the slightest idea who did it this time, any more than the last."

"That is awful, was anyone hurt?" asked Sigar.

"No, but they overturned some benches and broke up the candles and then covered the place in dirt. If you ask me it was strangers on their way through. I have never known anyone round here that would do such a thing." As Margaret spoke she pounded the dough on the table, flour puffing up and covering her and everything around her in a fine, grey dust.

Sigar was appalled.

"Maybe folks do not want to believe what the monks preach but there is no need to go round breaking things and making a mess." He was upset at this news, he himself chose not to believe this new religion and kept very quietly to his old ways but he did not approve of violence and trouble making in general and he tried very hard to bring his children up the same way. If life with Matthew Preece had taught him anything it was that he would rather be a kind, poor villein than a wealthy but bitter and mean old man.

Sigar himself knew several people, who like himself, chose not to follow the new ways. There was a sense of distrust, not simply because it was new and required change, something which did not come easily, but because it was so radically different from everything they knew; everything they had grown up with; everything they were comfortable with.

The monks preached forgiveness and kindness to fellow men, to Sigar this sounded great but a little too good to be true. Then he had learned about Purgatory and Hell. There was the catch. It did not seem right to him to punish men for being men and doing what came naturally with eternal damnation. How could you expect a child to understand that? How could you expect a simple man to remember what he was supposed to have done wrong when the punishment came along maybe thirty years later? No, he would stick with what he knew, thank you very much.

A roar from along the corridor told him that his master was out of ale and he rose from his chair and made his way to the front of the house.

Matthew was pacing his hall when Sigar arrived and he was almost relieved to see irritation in his master's face. Things were getting back to normal. Sigar placed the flagon of ale on the table and took a few steps back. Preece turned and fixed him with a cold stare.

"I am expecting some men to visit, make sure you bring them straight to me when they arrive." He paused then, his face softening a little as he struggled with the words. Sigar's apprehension grew, this meant that his master was thinking and that never turned out well. He waited, expectantly.

"Have you heard any..news? What is going on in the village these days?" As Preece finished his sentence he forced a small smile on his face, almost as an afterthought.

Sigar was stunned. Preece had never taken an interest in what people did before. Maybe this new religion was worth taking a second look at. Preece had converted some time ago and it was said that people could have a complete change of character when they found their god. He recalled something one of the monks had said about a King some years back who had gone the same way.

"Well, Sir, I hear talk of another church being all torn up last night. The Reeve thinks it is pagans rebelling as nothing was taken, only broken. At least that was his guess as no-one can find any trace of the monk that tended to the church."

"A church, you say? That is awful, it is sacrilege, and these people should be hung for their insolence." Preece looked annoyed and Sigar felt a sense of sympathy with the man for the first time. He knew how it felt to have your beliefs brutally rejected and shunned, to be told what you had always felt was right is now wrong. Preece must be feeling something similar now, that his belief was being rejected, and in such a violent way.

Sigar left him to his thoughts and returned to the kitchen to assist Margaret with the meal preparations.

Chapter 15

Aelfric had been in the house less than a week but already Catherine found herself dependent on him. He was calm, intelligent, wise and most of all he knew her secret, was a part of it. Better yet, he knew a side of her parents that she never had.

Today Catherine was excited. Her bruises were fading, the cuts healing. She was feeling more like herself than she had for days. There had been no visitors, no strange discoveries, she ate, slept and talked. Life had been almost normal, although lately Catherine was having trouble defining normal. Discovering that her existence until now was only a tiny part of a much larger world had shaken her. Learning that such things existed outside of her nightmares and church sermons was shocking enough, learning that she had been separated from that world by such a thin membrane for so many years had changed her forever.

Today her emotions were a bittersweet mixture of excitement, fear and apprehension. Today she would start to learn. Aelfric felt she was ready to learn about her parent's craft and he seemed very keen to start her lessons as soon as possible.

"How good is your reading?" Aelfric asked.

"My father insisted I learn when I was young. A monk came to stay for a while to teach me" she paused, "I thought it was odd because none of the other children learned and father was always telling me it was our little secret." Catherine recalled her childhood as she spoke and began to see the smallest memories in whole new light.

From a very young age she recalled having sprigs of mixed herbs around her chamber. In the hot, still summer air the smell could get overwhelming and once or twice she had thrown them out only to be punished. Then the monk had come to stay. At the time she had resented him being there, taking up so many hours of each day with boring lessons when she should have been out playing with the other children. To begin with she believed she was being punished for something, after all, none of the other children had to learn letters.

About a year later her father had allowed her to spend more time with the adults who visited the house and she became even more confused when she discovered that women were generally expected to be ignorant. They had no need to read and write, even in the highest circles. They were expected to marry, bear children and leave the business to the men folk. Literacy was a skill that was jealously guarded by the monks and only they could teach it. Only they could approve a student worthy of instruction. Yet she had been taught, a mere child and a girl at that! She had tried asking her father but he had always been vague and evasive with his answers, to the point where she gave up asking and did her lessons. Even after the monk had left her father had insisted she practice regularly to keep it fresh in her mind. Out of habit she did it still. So, now when Aelfric put a text in front of her she was able to read it aloud and then copy a portion if it onto the parchment he gave her.

Aelfric was very impressed. He had never known anyone outside the church with such a high level of literacy, in fact, he knew only a few outside of the church with any level of literacy. His job would be that much easier, of course she would still need to commit much to memory but she would be able to use all that her Mother had left, and in time, add to it. Aelfric had not yet seen what the Lady had left. Catherine had been reluctant to discuss what there was. He only knew that there were some effects. That must be where she had found the pendent she now wore. He was unsure if he should ask yet, it may be too soon. Aelfric sensed great trepidation in her when conversation turned to the reason for his arrival. Perhaps the wisest course would be to give it more time and start with a little bit of history and some of the basics.

Aelfric inhaled deeply, pursed his lips a little, leaned back in his chair and folded his arms across his chest.

"How much do you know about magic?" he asked. He needed to know how much she knew. Had she been taught anything? Perhaps she had been told of her heritage disguised as a bedtime tale. Maybe her father had discussed with her the reason why so much of the church preached against magic, where there was a difference between magic and heresy.

Catherine met his gaze. "Nothing really, only that the monks believe it to be bad, well, other monks anyway. They say that it is devil worship and that these people do awful things, they never go into detail though."

So, Aelfric would need to go back to the start, explain a few things to her, correct some of the lies she had been taught.

"Magic has existed since the world was created. It is a part of us all, to greater and lesser degrees, but not all of us know it now. There was a time, and not as long ago as you might think, when everyone knew of magic, believed in it and practised it. You will know them as , and no doubt you will have been told they are ignorant people, non–believers who refuse to see that there is a better way to live. The people who told you this are good people, kind people. People who believe in something passionately but too literally, in my opinion."

Catherine was enthralled. She wanted to hear more but something bothered her, something about Aelfric that she could not make sense of. Seeing the confusion in her expression, Aelfric stopped speaking and raised his eyebrow, inviting her question.

She began slowly, "I do not wish to cause offence, simply to understand" she faltered, unsure of where to begin. Aelfric anticipated her question. It was one he had asked himself many times in the early days. He voiced the question for her.

"How can I be a man of the cloth, devoted to the one God and the church, a church that teaches us that magic is evil, that anyone who does not believe is a heretic, a church that burns witches at the stake, and yet still be here with you, teaching that magic is good and should be embraced? I must seem very hypocritical to you."

Catherine was embarrassed, he had summed up her confusion well and now she felt she had surely offended him, but she still needed to hear his answer.

"Yes, a little. Actually a lot. How can you continue as a monk when your beliefs differ so much from the teachings of the church?"

"I have asked myself the same question. I continue because I do believe in the teachings of God. I believe in forgiveness and charity and that all men are equal in his eyes. I also believe that God gave me freewill and this is why some men stray from the path of good to the path of evil. The church teaches that these men use magic and sorcery to do their evil deeds that they call upon evil spirits to do their bidding and make pacts with demons. The church calls this heresy. This is where my beliefs differ. I think these good people have taken the teachings far too literally. Man has freewill, yes he can choose to follow evil, but he can also choose good, a choice distinct from merely survival and obedience. He can choose to call upon evil spirits or good ones.

In my humble opinion there are three types of thinking within the church. There are those who do not believe in magic at all, they believe solely in God. These people are extremely passionate in their belief and feel that anyone who chooses to believe differently is wrong and should be forced to conform. They see it as a threat to the powerful position they find themselves in and wish to set an example, a deterrent for others who may stray.

Then there are those who see only God's way or evil magic. To them magic is wrong so they see no possibility for it to be good also. These are people who spend time in communities; they see the common people daily. They are more open-minded than the first group but will always follow the power.

I fall within the third group. I believe in God, I believe he created magic and then gave man the freewill to use it in whatever way he chose, or not to use it at all. There is only one magic, it is how it is used that makes it good or evil. There is much evil in the world today but there are also some people who possess a great gift in being able to call upon magic for good, to ..... counter the evil."

Aelfric knew he must choose his words carefully so as to introduce Catherine to her destiny slowly, gently, almost so that she did not notice.

Catherine sat in silence, staring at Aelfric for what felt like minutes before she as able to speak. Everything she knew, had been taught and believed, it was all brought into question by what he had just said. She did not know how to believe him. Was she able to throw away years of understanding and replace it with Aelfric's view? He had given her no reason to doubt him thus far but he was asking an awful lot of her now. No, she was wrong, he had only asked one thing of her since he had arrived, that she listen. Well, she had listened and she had heard and now she needed to make up her own mind on what to believe. Certainly all that he had said made sense to her. It filled the gaps that the monk's teachings had left, leaving her feeling more balanced in her understanding of the world. What she did not understand was where her parents fitted in, what role had they played in this strange new world. For that matter, what part was she to play? Aelfric had travelled here to see her father. Her father was gone and yet Aelfric remained, why? Why did he want to teach her if not to......Catherine looked up and into Aelfric's eyes.

"Aelfric, why are you teaching me, exactly? Her voice was calm and measured and she met Aelfric's gaze head on. Aelfric was a little taken aback; he had not anticipated her reaching this level of understanding so soon, had certainly not intended it. Still, there was no avoiding it now, she already suspected, any avoidance now would lose her trust. Carefully he began.

"Your mother was a wonderful and powerful woman who chose a path of good. She was blessed with a gift of magic and chose to use it for good. Your father did not have the gift of magic but he had other skills and he also chose to do good. It is right that you understand your parents better in order to understand your own place in the world. I believe you also have a gift of magic and that you should have knowledge of its meaning, its use. Only then can your choice be an informed one."

"My choice? What do you mean?"

"I mean that one day, possibly sooner than we may think, you will have to decide between good and evil and you will be glad of your knowledge when that time comes."

Catherine suspected that Aelfric knew more than he was letting on but at the moment she was happy to let him keep that secret. There was a limited amount of life changing a person could take in a day and on top of the last couple of weeks she did not believe she could handle any more. For a little distraction and time to gather her wits she rose and poured herself another cup of ale and sipped it slowly. By the time she returned to her seat she felt a little calmer.

"Tell me more about my mother, what did she do?"

"To be able to understand that , you need to know more of what she was. Let me tell you about Wicca, or magic."

Before he had a chance to go further the door opened and Rachel stepped into the room carrying some plates.

"I have just come to start serving dinner my Lady."

Catherine nodded and Rachel went about setting plates on the table ready for the food that Cook had prepared.

The door opened a second time and Michael entered the room, a dark and troubled look on his face.

"My Lady," Michael bowed slightly as he spoke, "Hugh is here, your cottager from the village. He is asking for assistance, he is raising the hue and cry."

Catherine was alarmed by this news, the hue and cry was raised only when a serious crime had been committed and the criminal had absconded. Hugh was seeking men to join the search. She rose from her seat, instantly dawn back to the present, forgetting her conversation with Aelfric.

"What happened? Is anyone hurt?"

"No, we do not think so, Hugh's farmhouse was robbed and one of his serfs has disappeared. It is thought the serf intends selling what he has taken and running away on the proceeds. I am sending Arthur and a couple of the servants to assist; John and I will stay here." Michael paused. "If that is acceptable to you, my Lady."

"Of course." She replied. "Was much taken?"

"Strangely no, certainly it would seem not enough to live on for any length of time, I think Hugh said they had only taken some candles, some bread and some jewellery that belonged to his wife, just something simple one of their children had made for her."

"How odd." Catherine replied staring at the floor. "Do you think I should visit, offer help?" Catherine was torn between wanting to go to the aid of one of her father's cottagers and staying at home, where she was safe. It occurred to her then that the cottager was no longer beholden to her father, but to her. Slowly she looked up at Michael.

"No, my Lady, there was little stolen and no damage, I believe it would be best if you stayed here."

Michael had noticed the vast improvement in her looks over the last two days and was much relieved by the difference in her spirits. Although he was a little jealous of all the time she spent with the monk, he had to admit, it did seem to be doing her good. As he bowed and left he wondered if things had changed forever.

Catherine turned to Aelfric. "If you will excuse me I would like to freshen up before the meal." She turned and left, leaving Aelfric and Rachel alone in the hall.

Aelfric looked over at Rachel, she was a local girl, and she may be able to tell him more of the robbery than Michael knew, or was letting on.

"Excuse me, Rachel, is it? I wonder, do you know anything of this robbery? Was so little really taken?"

"Yes, Sir, it is really weird, Roger just did not seem the type to steal. We grew up together, he was always the sensible one, then a couple of days ago he goes off on an errand for his master and comes back hours late and now this? I would not mind betting there are some in the village reckon he has gone mad, been possessed, Hugh certainly seemed worried." Rachel stopped to take a breath.

"Why do you think he is worried?" Aelfric pressed.

"Well, you know, after the churches being defiled and all, folks are starting to get really nervous with all the strange goings on, talking about witches some of them, they reckon one has moved into the woods and is up to no good." As a horrid thought occurred to her she took a sharp intake of breath and looked over at the monk. "You do not suppose the witch has snatched him for some kind of sacrifice do you?"

Smiling Aelfric replied, "I think that highly unlikely child."

As she finished setting the table she smiled and left Aelfric to his thoughts. He was also a little concerned. Was this another example of Pagan uprising, but how did the farm fit in? Or were these just isolated events? His thoughts were interrupted by the arrival of the food followed closely by other members of the household come for their meal.

Chapter 16

The morning dawned bright and clear. It was crisp and cool with a frost on the ground that crackled underfoot. The air carried the sound of young children playing before they started their chores. In the woods they could do anything, be anyone, kings and queens, knights and robbers. They could go anywhere their imaginations took them. One day there would be mountains to be climbed; the next a castle to lay siege to and the trees played their parts admirably.

Today the four children were knights on opposing armies, fighting with wooden swords and shields. They fought with great courage and valour, quick on their feet but clumsy in their swordplay. It did not matter, for they were the finest knights in the kingdom.

Rob parried with Cedric, first pushing forward and then being forced to retreat, defending himself from harsh blows with his shield. Cedric had the upper hand, he was a full two inches taller than Rob and used it to beat the smaller knight backwards.

"Aha, I will have your lands Sir Knight, you will surrender to my might" cried Cedric.

Rob fought bravely, holding his ground for a minute or two before being beaten back still further. There was a clatter of wooden sword meeting wooden shield off to his left and Rob was distracted by the war being waged around him long enough for Cedric to land a crushing blow on his shield that sent him stumbling backward. His foot snagged on something and losing his balance, arms flailing, Rob fell backward, dreading the fatal blow Cedric was about to deliver and waiting for his backside to meet the hard ground.

With a dull thud Rob hit the earth and was momentarily surprised at the softness of his landing. After being bested by Cedric he sat up and found himself sitting on a small mound of earth. It as a little crusty on the surface from the frost but appeared to have been disturbed recently.

Cedric stuck out a hand to help his worthy opponent back to his feet and as Rob took his hand he glanced down at his feet. It was a second or two before he realised what he had snagged his foot on earlier but when it registered he let out a cry of fear and disgust and scrambled away as quickly as he could.

"Cedric, run to the village, get the Reeve, quickly." Rob's voice shook a little as he spoke, all the colour in his face had faded away.

Cedric looked at him in utter confusion, "What is wrong with you, what are you rambling about?"

Rob was still staring at the ground, transfixed by what he had seen and Cedric followed his gaze, curious, until he saw it. Rob stayed as first finder with the other two boys, while Cedric ran as quickly as his legs and lungs could take him.

It was about half an hour later when the Reeve arrived in the woods, convinced the boys were playing another cruel prank on him. These two had more imagination than was good for them and this time was sure to be no different. Until he saw Rob, pale and shaking, sitting on a log. As the Reeve approached, Rob looked up and pointed at a small mound of earth behind him. Rob stood and backed away as the Reeve passed him.

It was hard to miss the hand that protruded from the mound, even though one or two of the fingers had clearly been nibbled at by passing animals. The Reeve had seen his share of bodies over the years and from the discolouration and bloating he reckoned this one had been dead for several days. He called to the boys.

"Get back to the village, the lot of you. Raise the hue and cry. Now!"

None of the boys needed telling twice and they fled to the village calling for men as they passed fields and houses, letting them know where to find the Reeve in the woods.

As men started to arrive the Reeve set them to work digging the body out of the ground. It was hampered by the cold and the stiffness of the body but by the time they had cleared the mud away from the face, most of the men of the village had arrived, including Michael and Arthur.

The Reeve stepped forward and knelt beside the body. "There is no doubt, it is Roger. How did you get here lad?" He let out a long breath, thinking hard for a minute or two.

"Well, that leaves us with a problem. He looks like he has been here for days, but Hugh swears he was at the farm just yesterday morning." The Reeve scratched his head and looked around at the men about him, hoping for some offerings of inspiration. There were none.

Puffing a little as he rose to his feet the Reeve turned to the crowd of men.

"Someone must go for the Keeper and someone must stay with the body. Who will go?"

Nobody seemed keen, winter was setting in, the wind was bitter and the Keeper of the King's Peace was many miles away, almost in Gloucester. It would take a couple of days to get there now that the days were so much shorter, and the Keeper may not even be there when they arrived. Besides, even though the harvest was in and most of the food stored, there was still much to do making their homes fit to survive the winter weather and storing wood to burn. No, nobody wanted to go.

Michael and Arthur looked at each other, they would normally be the first to volunteer. They had horses and could get to the Keeper much quicker than on foot but they were unwilling to volunteer knowing it would mean leaving Catherine that bit more vulnerable. It would be a bad time to show any weakness at the house, she was still not herself after her ordeal in the woods. Michael shuddered when he thought of it. He did not know any details, he did not need to know. That Roland had tried to rape her had been enough. Michael knew that he had crossed a line but there was nothing he could do about that now. The line had been crossed a long time ago and he could not go back now, he cared for her beyond the loyalty of a servant, perhaps even beyond friendship, but he knew he could never act on it and would do all he could to make sure it did not affect his judgement as a soldier. Right now his instinct told him Catherine was still in danger so he held his tongue while he and Arthur tried to blend into the background, hoping they would not be volunteered.

Slightly irritated by the wall of silence that met his request, the Reeve resigned himself to the task of choosing a volunteer, as unpopular as that would surely make him.

"Miller, you will go for the Keeper, best get started while it is still early."

With an audible grumble of discontent from the large round miller, he started back toward the village to tell his wife he would be away for a few days at least, maybe a week. She was not going to be pleased, he had promised to plug a leak in the roof. 'Still,' he thought to himself, 'it is a week of drinking as much as I please when I stop and not being nagged about it.' His mood lifted slightly as he trudged away from the woods.

The next job for the Reeve was to choose people who would stay and guard the body. There would be a heavy fine on the hundred if it should be left alone, not to mention if it disappeared or was eaten, although who would want to steal a frozen dead man was beyond the Reeve. But then he could not imagine anyone wanting to kill the man in the first place.

He chose men from the crowd to sit with the body in pairs, night and day until the Keeper arrived, making sure the first watch started immediately. Then he mustered the rest of the men to check and search the area for any missing villagers, any blood and any blood stained weapons. He wanted something good to tell the Keeper when he arrived, in an effort to keep the fines as low as possible. Leaving two men behind, lighting a small fire, the rest of the group dissipated and were soon all gone.

Michael and Arthur returned to the house several hours later, having found nothing to offer the Keeper when he arrived. Something was bothering Michael, or more precisely everything was bothering him. He had never known so much happen in such a short time, in such a small place. Now he thought of it, he did not believe there had been so much activity here in all the years he had been there put together. Churches ransacked, a house robbed, the suspect turns up dead, apparently murdered and no sign of the loot. It just did not add up but Michael could not think why. Aelfric talked much about a rise in paganism and heresy, perhaps that was the answer after all. It would certainly explain the damage to the churches but it did not seem to explain Roger, although Michael was not sure what could explain that.

Over dinner Michael and Arthur related the day's events to Catherine, Aelfric and John. Catherine seemed dismayed by this new development. Michael watched Aelfric very carefully for his reaction to the news, still not entirely trusting the man. Michael thought he saw the briefest glimpse of alarm in the monk's face but as soon as he thought it was there it was gone and Aelfric was bemoaning a general fall in morals and a lack of respect. He seemed to blame this behaviour on confusion created by the introduction of a different religion. Michael was not sure he accepted this reasoning. Christianity was not that new, although he knew it was struggling to secure a foothold in many of the more rural places. Perhaps the monk may have a point, at least it was worth further consideration, and Michael admitted that much.

Catherine was indeed shocked at this news. "Are you sure he was murdered?" she asked.

"Yes" said Michael calmly, "men do not lie down in the woods to die and then bury themselves, he certainly died at the hands of another, not that we could find any trace of who that might be."

"I suppose that will be up to the Keeper now, but it is a terrible shame, just when the people are starting to get back on their feet with food in their stores, this happens. The Keeper will certainly be heavy with the fines if the culprit cannot be found. I cannot believe it was anyone who knew Roger, besides they have all taken the Frank Pledge, they are responsible for each others actions. Who would want to make others suffer, make their neighbour's suffer?"

Catherine was concerned for her people with good reason, they would suffer a fine if they could not produce the killer and if it had been a stranger who had moved on already that had committed this foul crime they would not stand a chance. And this on top of the taxes they already struggled with. There would be more needy than usual at her door this winter, she was sure.

Aelfric was concerned too but for different reasons. It had struck him as very odd that Roger had apparently been seen days after his body said he had died. His first instinct had been to suspect sorcery but Michael and Arthur seemed to think Hugh must have been mistaken in his identification, it was indeed possible. There had even been a quiet suggestion that perhaps Hugh had a motive to lie, especially if it was he who had killed Roger for stealing from him. True, the punishment did not seem to fit the crime, murder for a few candles and a trinket, but some men did desperate things sometimes and Aelfric did need to remind himself on occasion that not everything was driven by evil, sometimes men just did awful things. This may very well be one of those times.

Putting the matter to the back of his mind for now Aelfric sought to finish the meal on lighter topics and tried to engage everyone else in a discussion about the latest in husbandry techniques. He had heard that there was quite a difference in the quality of cattle populations in isolated pockets of the country.

* * * *

The Miller set out on his journey early that day and had walked almost two miles when he heard a rumbling, rattling sound somewhere on the track behind him. It was a minute or two before the source of the racket came into view and the Miller could not believe his luck. Coming towards him was a large cart, being drawn along by two oxen. A large, plump man sat up on the cart, holding the reins, red in the face and singing softly to himself. As the cart drew level with the Miller the fat man called out "Can I offer you a ride good man?"

"That would be great, thanks" replied the Miller, "where are you headed?"

"Gloucester, I am heading for the big market there."

Now the Miller was sure someone was smiling down on him, not only did he have a few days drinking without his wife to nag him, but he would not even have to walk. Excellent. He settled in for a bumpy ride, filled with friendly chat, light signing and good ale.

The oxen were strong and the two men made good time, despite stopping for a spot of liquid lunch along the way. About an hour before it grew dark they stopped at an inn on the road, stabled the oxen and settled in for a night of drinking mulled wine and fine ale. There were already several occupants in the small inn when they entered but they did not mind having someone else to while away the hours with. Two of the men looked like servants, with tidy, nice clothes and reasonably good shoes. They seemed to answer to the third man. This one was finely dressed and well cared for, he did not seem to want for much when it came to food, as the seams of his tunic could amply testify to. All three nodded to the Miller and his companion as they took their seats.

The innkeeper welcomed them and stepped out to the buttery to fetch them each a pot of warm, spiced wine. When he returned he offered them food, which they gratefully accepted. As the innkeeper headed for his kitchen he paused and called back over his shoulder at the fine gentleman, "can I get you anything else to eat Keeper?"

The Miller was torn. So, the fine man in the room was the Keeper of the King's Peace, he was not at home just outside Gloucester at all, but travelling, and he just happened to be staying at this inn. Part of the Miller was pleased to have found the Keeper so soon, it meant he would not have to travel in the cold as long as he had feared and he could get back and fix the roof sooner. The other part of him was disappointed to have lost out on his drinking trip. Still, the sooner the Keeper did what he had to do the sooner things could get back to normal. The Miller had seen enough death over the years, surely everyone had, and now he just wanted this one sorted out, soon. He rose from his seat to introduce himself and his reason for seeking the Keeper.

Later the following day the four men rode into Withington. The Miller took his three companions straight to the home of the Reeve and left him to explain all that had happened lately, or not, depending on what the fines might be.

It was dark by the time the Reeve had settled the Keeper by his fire and served him with some of his best wine. Then he explained what had happened at Hugh's farmhouse and then the discovery of the body by the boys. The Reeve chose not to divulge what had happened to the two churches, after all, they were completely unconnected and nothing more had happened in four days, it was more than likely just travelling pagans making some kind of statement. No need to trouble the Keeper with that. It would probably just be a diversion anyway.

The Keeper rose early the next morning, keen to visit the body and release the two men who had been guarding it, they must have been nearly frozen in the night. He was also keen to solve this murder as soon as possible, he had already been travelling for several days and longed for the comfort of his home and the companionship of his wife. True his two servants were good company but it was not the same and could never be. Celia had been his best friend for years and he trusted her with everything.

Ralph had been the Keeper of the King's Peace in these parts for fourteen years now. Generally it was a peaceful place, largely rural communities where men depended on each other for their survival year round, they helped each other to make the harvest a success and keep the livestock safe and well. Murders were unusual in an area like this, certainly tempers ran high sometimes, more often than not fuelled by ale, but fights were generally limited to just that.

Focusing on the task ahead he followed the Reeve through the village and up to the woods to inspect the body. There was a chill wind this morning and he was grateful; the cold would preserve the body well; reduce the usual swelling and keep some of the insects away, it would make his job a little less disgusting. He hated this part, seeing someone lying still and cold on the ground, someone's child or parent or lover. There was often a wailing woman around but today he hoped he would have the place almost to himself; it would help his concentration.

They reached the woods fairly quickly and headed straight for the mound. There was a healthy fire burning nearby with two men huddled next to it; they looked chilled to the bone and understandably pleased to see the Keeper. In his profession that expression was not one he got to see very often.

"Where is the body Reeve? Let us get this done, and then maybe we can think about getting some food." The Reeve merely pointed to the mound, unwilling to look on the body again, he could still see that frozen expression, every time he closed his eyes. The Keeper squatted next to the body, looking closely at the face, eyes cloudy but frozen open. He sighed, it was always a little sad to have to see a dead body but he must stay focused; he did not want to miss anything important.

"Reeve," he called out, "has this body been touched since it was found?"

Reluctantly the Reeve stepped forward; he glanced towards the two men by the fire, silently repeating the question. They both shook their heads vigorously, disgusted at the mere thought of touching it.

"No, Sir, not that I know of, why?"

"Come here, look at it, does it look any different to you?"

Steeling himself with a deep breath the Reeve peered over the Keeper's shoulder and looked at Roger's body, fearful of what he may see.

Hugely relieved the Reeve stepped back again, "No sir, it looks just as it did before."

"You did not mention the fingers last night, why?"

"Well, it was animals, the hand was sticking out of the mound, foxes must have got to it; I did not think it was important." The Reeve was slightly put out by the Keeper's question, it seemed obvious to him, what was the Keeper trying to get at?

"Not all of these fingers have been eaten away Reeve, look again. See? If this had been an animal there would be claw marks on the hand, the edges would be rough and torn, as they are here, see? There are no scratches here; these fingers have been cut away by a sharp blade. This was intentional mutilation and I would guess it happened before this man died."

The Reeve was appalled and confused. If a man was going to kill someone, surely that was it, why start cutting him up, before or after the deed?

Ralph had turned Roger's body over, letting the blanket that covered him fall away. There were large purple blotches on the back of Roger's legs and his buttocks where the blood had pooled just after he had died. The Ralph noted that he had probably been sitting up when he had died and then moved after death; probably straight here to this grave. Then sometime over the last couple of days a small animal had dug up the hand, attracted by the scent of blood on the hand where the two fingers had been cut away. That would be how the hand had come to be sticking out of the grave. The shallowness of it told the Keeper that whoever had buried Roger had either been short of time or was not concerned about the body being discovered; or both.

"There are no other injuries or marks on the body, apart from his throat. He was strangled to death." Turning to the two men huddled by the fire he ordered them to take the body and arrange for it to be buried. The Reeve was standing stock still, trying to make sense of what the Keeper had just told him.

"Reeve?" The Keeper was speaking to him, he roused himself and looked up, realising that he had been staring at Roger's body.

"Do you have any idea who may have killed this man?"

"Absolutely not, I do not even understand why they," he hesitated, "no, I do not."

Ralph felt sorry for the Reeve; the poor man clearly was not used to this. Ralph was not sure he was either but his experience as the Keeper had taught him to be able to detach from all the emotions that attached to such an event. Calmly he spoke to the Reeve.

"Well, he was strangled, probably did not even see his attacker coming, there are no defensive wounds on his hands or arms. He is naked, which is odd, people who commit crimes of anger do not normally stop to undress their victim before burying them. Then there are the missing fingers, deliberately cut away."

Ralph waited for the penny to drop with the Reeve, after a few seconds he continued. "That suggests some kind of ritual to me." Again he paused, waiting for the Reeve to catch his drift, in fact any kind of reaction would be welcome; the man seemed to have turned to stone right before him. He would clearly have to be more plain.

"Reeve, are all of the villeins in this hundred good Christians?" The Reeve stared back, confusion furrowing his brow. Ralph's patience was running out.

"Do you think you might have a witch in your midst?"

Chapter 17

Breakfast was quiet and thoughtful in Catherine's hall. Catherine could not stop thinking about the events of the last two days. It was all so strange to her and she could not work out what was going on. It seemed as if something had begun but she did not know what. First there were the churches being desecrated, and then Hugh's home was robbed. Yesterday some boys from the hundred had found Roger's body and people were accuse him of robbing his master's house yet none of the stolen items had been found and it seemed that Roger had been killed and buried. None of it made any sense to her. It was tempting to try and link all these things together but she could see no common theme or pattern. The effort was threatening to give her a headache. Perhaps it was just an unfortunate rash of random events, coincidence that they all seemed to happen around the same time.

As Catherine looked around the table this morning she saw similar expressions and guessed that they were all struggling with the same thing. Aelfric broke the silence, saying he wanted to discuss herbs with her today and she found herself trying to imagine why. The only answer she could come up with was salves and tonics with healing properties. Catherine was far too distracted, having the Keeper around was never a good thing and the possibility that the murderer was someone from the village chilled her to the bone.

Michael had not come to the hall to eat yet. Catherine turned to Arthur and asked where he was, curiously missing his company. They had not spent much time together since Aelfric had arrived, she had been so caught up with all that had happened before and swept along with all that had happened since. Catherine was still immersed in her own bubble but today she felt, was the first time she had managed to surface long enough to notice the people around her, long enough to notice her friends.

"He went to check on Hugh, make sure he is coping all right," replied Arthur, "he will be back soon my Lady."

Sure enough, less than half an hour later Michael strode into the hall, to be greeted with a warm smile from his mistress. It was a pleasant surprise and took the edge off his morning so far.

"How is Hugh?" she asked.

"Not too bad, considering he seems to be the prime suspect in Roger's murder. He is the only one with any reason to kill him, however slight that reason may be. The Keeper arrived just as I was about to leave, wanted to search the house for some kind of evidence. The Reeve says, "Michael reconsidered the gory detail he had been about to divulge "says Roger was strangled." He would fill Arthur and John in on the other details later; he did not want to give Catherine any more concerns than she already had. Catherine rose from her seat, "I should visit Hugh and his wife, and let them know that they have my support. I just cannot believe Hugh capable of such a thing. He has always been so gentle and quiet; I have never known him even to fight. He must be distraught."

Michael had expected this from Catherine and was pleased to see that despite all her troubles lately she had not lost her compassion, not lost herself completely. He and Arthur would ride with her to Hugh's home to make sure she was safe.

"Robert is preparing your horse now my Lady."

She smiled; it was a great comfort to her to know their bond of friendship was still intact.

It felt strange to Catherine to be leaving the house and grounds. She could not help but remember the last time she had left, with Roland. This time was different though, this time she had her two best friends with her. The temperature had dropped still further and most of the leaves had fallen from the trees now, leaving the world around the manor looking very bleak and unforgiving. Catherine pulled her cloak tighter around her to keep out as much of the wind as she could but it still nipped at her neck and fingers.

The ride to Hugh's farmhouse was short and uneventful. They arrived just as the Keeper was leaving. Ralph nodded to them as he hurried by and Catherine returned his genial smile. The Reeve followed a few paces behind looking far less genial. Catherine noted that he looked as if he had not slept in days. He looked rumpled and tired, as if he was about to run out of patience. Michael called to him.

"Reeve, what is going on?" Stopping at the sound of his name, the Reeve looked up. At the sight of them his face seemed to lift slightly.

"Michael, back again? The Keeper still has some questions for Hugh but we have got to go, there is a fire over at Thomas' place. We are going to see if we can help."

"What on earth is going on round here?" Catherine was beginning to feel as it her world was starting to spiral out of control.

Michael and Arthur looked across at each other and Arthur nodded.

"I will ride over to Thomas' and give them a hand. See you back at the house." Arthur whirled his horse around and cantered off after the Keeper and the Reeve.

Catherine turned to Michael, unnerved but determined to show no fear.

"Shall we go in and see Hugh my Lady?" His smile was easy and confident and it calmed her nerves. They dismounted and went into the house. Hugh was being brave but was mortified that anyone thought he may have killed Roger. His wife was stretched out on a cot in the far corner of the single room. It was not a large building and the one room served the whole family. It had a food store, a fire place, water bucket and beds. There was also a table and a few stools scattered around. They slept here and ate here when they were not working the land or tending to the animals. Today, Hugh told them, his wife had head all she could take and had cried herself to sleep. It was hard on the while family but she was suffering the most apparently. Catherine and Michael did not stay long, leaving Hugh to care for his poor wife.

On the ride home Michael was as preoccupied as Catherine, but his thoughts leaned in a different direction. His tactical mind was trained to consider what the enemy had done already and what they might do next. There was a lot going on around him at the moment and there seemed to be some links but it was all very confusing. It was possible, he supposed, that there was only one person or group behind all this but he could not think why. What did anyone have to gain from all of this? Michael just could not convince himself that there was only one motive in play here, or that these were random events. He could not put all the pieces together yet but he was sure this was not over.

Back in the stable yard Catherine handed the reins to Robert and walked quickly into the house, rubbing her hands to warm them. Rachel took her cloak from her and she made her way to the hall where there would be a roaring fire to warm her. The warmth of the room and the glow of the fire mingled with the gentle crackle of the burning logs helped to ease her mind as she settled into her chair to mull over the weirdness that had taken hold of the hundred. She no longer felt isolated by events, this was affecting everyone now and oddly that made her feel a little better, a little easier. She had been living with mild paranoia for some time now and it was strangely comforting to realise that whatever was going on was not just about her.

Catherine wondered if this could be a random string of events, a spate of bad luck going back to her father's death but as optimistic as she tried to be she knew it was highly unlikely. Besides, she could tell Michael was concerned about it, more so than Arthur and John. He seemed to be suspicious of everything lately and as for Aelfric, he was being just a little too brave in the face of each new crisis for it to be entirely natural. Having said that, he was a stranger to this place, he did not know the people like she did. He had no connection to them so it would affect him less. Then she recalled something he had said to her, something about good magic and evil magic and choosing a path. Perhaps someone from the hundred had taken the wrong path lost control and gone mad. That might account for some of what had happened. It did not account for Roland, or her father's death, if that was even a part of this mess. As she recalled her father's passing she felt a sharp pang and a single tear fell to her cheek and trace a quick path down to her chin.

Catherine was snapped back to the present by the sound of the door opening behind her, prompting her to brush a hand across her cheek and sit up straight.

"My child, you have returned" said Aelfric, moving to stand near the fire. "I trust Hugh is as well as can be expected?"

"He is upset, of course, and his wife is frantic with worry that he will be sent to the gaol but they are unharmed and I do not believe anyone can really think him guilty, in their heart."

"You do not believe he killed that man then?"

"Aelfric, I have never heard him so much as raise his voice let alone strike anyone. No, I do not believe he did it for a second, certainly not for a few candles and a trinket."

Arthur rode quickly towards the village, his horse panting, ears pricked up. As he rounded a bend he saw a blur up ahead, low to the ground, darting into his path. Realising quickly that it was a child playing in the rough cart track, he guided his horse around and urged her on.

He soon came to Thomas' house and he saw the orange glow before he noticed most of the men from the village. Some were still relaying buckets of water in a line to try and quench the flames but Arthur had seen enough fires to realise there was no saving this house.

The keeper was already there and Arthur was pleasantly surprised to see that both he and his servants had rolled up their sleeves and pitched in to help. His horse was unsettled by the noise and bustle and Arthur dismounted and held her head to calm her. He called to a burley man standing nearby, "Smith, what happened?"

The Smith was a large, powerful man, blackened by soot and dirt. He stood, shaking his head slowly, his strong arms folded across his barrel chest.

"It is a terrible business Arthur; we only managed to save a few of his things before it got too bad. There is no hope for the house now. Poor Thomas will have to start again from scratch and with the new baby too. It is lucky they were not all home."

The Smith looked back toward the blazing timbers as they crackled and fell, shaking his head slowly again. Arthur stepped a little closer to him, "Does anyone know how it started?"

Without looking away from the house the Smith answered him, "Miller's oldest son says he saw two people running from behind the house right before it went up. Then young Cedric says he saw two men sneaking about just a little while before that. Neither got a look at their faces but then they were not expecting the house to burn and to have to point anyone out."

Arthur was shocked. Thomas was a popular man with a lovely wife. They were cottagers on Catherine's estate and it was unlikely they had upset anyone so badly they would want to burn down their home, and in winter too. With two separate witnesses it seemed certain it was arson but it still did not make sense, there was no obvious motive.

It did not take Arthur long to find Thomas' wife and child. They stood well back from the crowd, crying, the woman grieved at her loss, the child cold and scared from the noise. He made sure she was safe and warm and had somewhere to stay until they could rebuild, before pressing a couple of coins into her hand. She looked up at him, her wide eyes full of sadness, disbelief and gratitude for his kindness. He smiled at her before swinging himself back up into the saddle and returning to the manor.

Arthur was also disturbed by the chain of events of late. Obviously someone wanted to cause trouble and hardship in this hundred but to what end? There did not seem to be any gain in any of the acts. Churches, homes, damage, theft and fire, they seemed to be getting worse, more serious each time but where was the link? And where did Roger's death fit in? Perhaps he had caught the criminal red handed and been silenced to protect their identity but they seemed to be getting careless. Two people had seen them today. If they continued they would no doubt be recognised and punished. In the meantime the Keeper would be losing count of the fines he would need to issue to punish the moral degradation he must think he could see all around him.

Back at the house Catherine was desperate for distraction and so was glad when Aelfric suggested taking up their lessons once more in her solar.

"The other day we talked a little about herb lore, how much do you recall?" he had asked, keen to press on with her training. He felt a tide of evil heading their way and could see the daily evidence of the devastation in its wake. They had already had some discussion about herbs and other plants and she had seemed to recognise many of the plants she would need to use. The next step would be learning to blend them in the correct way to get the desired results. Each plant had its own properties and when mixed with another it could alter its effect. Catherine would need to pay attention; mistakes in content or quantity could be costly and dangerous.

"I think I could recognise most of the plants we talked about, but why do I need to learn this? What would I use it for? I have a cook and she is very good at what she does."

Aelfric considered for a second before answering.

"I believe your mother was able to blend plants to make ointments and creams and the like, and these assisted her greatly in," he paused briefly "in helping people." As he spoke he caught a glimpse of the stone around Catherine's neck and recalled the chest she had mentioned three or four days ago. Perhaps now was the time to ask.

"You mentioned a chest, where you found the stone." He gestured gently towards the pendent. "Was there anything else in there?"

Catherine was immediately on her guard. She knew she trusted Aelfric but this was a part of her parents, she was not sure she was ready to share it yet. But that was not the only reason, she could not put her finger on it but something, perhaps it was instinct, told her she should keep the chest and its contents to herself. She recalled the contents of the chest. There had been the pendent, another small box, the letter from her father, the recipes and pots. The recipes. Perhaps they were what Aelfric was hoping to discover. They certainly seemed relevant to their lesson.

"There was some parchment, it looked like recipes but I did not read them properly, it was dark and I was, tired. Wait, I will get them."

Catherine rose and left the room, apprehensive about opening the chest again. She was still not sure if what she remembered had been part of the dream or a part of the reality of that night. Fervently hoping that it was a dream she opened the door to her father's chamber, entered and quietly closed the door behind her. The chest stood on the floor, precisely where she had left it, with the lid closed.

Shaking off the first stirrings of anxiety she crossed the room and knelt in front of the chest.

'Stop being so silly' she thought. 'There is nothing in there that is going to leap out and hurt you.' Holding that thought at the front of her mind, repeating it slowly, she placed her hands on the chest and gently lifted the lid. Once it was all the way up she dared to open her eyes. There was no hum this time and everything was just as it had been before, the candles, mortar and pestle, crystals, herbs, the jars and the bowl, the boxes and the parchment. Reaching in Catherine took up the parchment and closed the lid, hugely relieved that nothing odd happened while the chest had been open.

Getting to her feet she glanced at the parchment in her hand. She had thought these may have belonged to her father but now it seemed that they, along with everything else in the chest, had been her mother's. Catherine absently stroked the words on the parchment with her finger, her heart aching for the mother she had never known. She sighed heavily, recalling where she was and made her way back to Aelfric. He seemed very pleased with them, in fact they were more than he had hoped for. He looked up at Catherine who had settled herself back in front of the fire.

"These have been excellently preserved," He began leafing through the sheets, pulling one out and handing it to Catherine.

"This is a healing balm, it will rapidly speed recovery from cuts and scrapes." Aelfric was more animated than she had seen him before, almost excited and it was a little infectious. She looked at the recipe in her hand. The ingredients all looked familiar; she would be able to find them all but she had never imagined they could be used to heal. It was a shame she had not known this several days ago, she thought with a wry smile. Aelfric was still reading.

"This one," he said, handing her the sheet, "will increase vigour and concentration, while the one below will induce sleep."

Aelfric was indeed pleased with the parchments, they were the beginnings of a potion book that Catherine could learn from and add to. It was a great place to begin their lessons and a perfect way for her to start to feel more connected to her parents, especially her mother. Growing up without a mother's guidance must have left a huge hole in Catherine's life, although it was obvious her father had loved her very much.

Aelfric would start by teaching her the properties of each herb and how they might be blended. This way she could understand these potions and would in time be able to create new ones of her own.

As Aelfric began his instruction Arthur arrived back at the house. Once he had tended to his horse he sought out Michael, eager to discuss what he had heard. He caught up with Michael as he made his way towards the hall. Michael was still not entirely sure he trusted Aelfric and had decided to spend some time sitting with Aelfric and Catherine in the hopes of catching some of their conversation and either putting his mind at ease or confirming his unformed suspicions about the man. He heard footsteps behind him and turned to see who was following him. He was pleased to see Arthur. Michael could tell from Arthur's expression that he had important news and was eager to hear it.

"How is Thomas?" he began. "Could the house be saved?"

"Only a few belongings and nobody was injured. I saw the whole family, they are naturally shaken and distraught but otherwise healthy" replied Arthur.

"How did it start? An ember from the fire?" Michael probed, hoping for an innocent answer but suspecting foul play.

"No accident Michael. Firstly the wife had been with her parents, had not built a new fire yet, so it could not have been that. Secondly two of the boys from the village say they saw two strangers sneaking around the house just before the fire started."

"Definitely arson then." Michael considered this for a moment then looked at Arthur. "What do your instincts tell you?"

"I think we have two people spreading trouble. I think it is very likely they are the ones responsible for the churches, Hugh's home and Roger. He was more than likely silenced as a witness."

Michael frowned. "But why? What possible motive can they have?" he asked, unable to accept Arthur's explanation without a good reason for the crimes.

"They are probably heretics, no doubt driven from their own village for their lack of faith. They have probably become a little mad being on the run and quite desperate for food. Now they see a village that has enough to survive on, with God fearing people and they have decided to attack it out of jealousy, envy or hate, take your pick." Arthur seemed convinced in his own mind, and it did seem entirely plausible, except that theirs was not the only church that had been ransacked. If they were travelling through the area why would they still be here? Why not cause their mischief and keep moving to avoid capture. Surely they knew that if they were caught, then as heretics they would certainly burn.

"I do not know Arthur, I cannot help thinking that there is a piece of this puzzle that we are missing, if not several pieces. As much sense as your explanation makes I cannot quite get it all to fit together as it should. Still, this may be enough to clear Hugh, now he is not the only Cottager to have trouble. Goodness only knows what the Keeper must make of all this." Michael sighed heavily, still not comfortable with this puzzle and together he and Arthur made their way into the hall hoping to join Catherine and Aelfric.

Chapter 18

The following day the village was a mass of activity. Most of the men had collected their tools and begun to rebuild Thomas' home. Some went to the woods to find timber and others started to clear ash and debris from the site of the old house. Two of the women had been through the village begging pieces of fabric and blankets and several more were now gathered in the Miller's large, warm room cutting and sewing to clothe Thomas and his family. The sense of community was at the highest the villeins had ever seen it, even more so than the early days of the last crop failure. Of course, as the hunger had worsened, people had held on tight to whatever they had, fiercely guarding their meagre and secret supplies lest a neighbour should discover it and try to steal from them.

Now though, the threat was different, it was not nature, it was mankind and any one of them could be next. They wanted to help Thomas but it went much deeper than that, they needed to know their neighbours would help them too, should the worst happen.

Catherine had given as much as she could and promised to buy more fabric at the next market to assist. This was almost the worst time for something like this to happen. Winter was upon them, warmth was hard to come by in most homes at the best of times but with no home at all you had to rely entirely on family and neighbours. It had been a small miracle that Thomas' food store had been separate from the house and had been saved. He had meant to build a store within the house but had not got around to it yet, in the struggle to collect all the food before the frosts destroyed it.

At the manor Catherine's lessons continued and her confidence grew. Only now did all her father's strange nagging make sense to her, why the herb garden was her responsibility and why she had to learn to read and write.

Later that afternoon Aelfric had decided it was time for a practical lesson, he had always believed that too much study from books alone dulled the spirit and prevented the mind from really learning.

"Can we evict your cook from her kitchen for a while? I would like to teach you how to make a simple potion this afternoon and for that we need a pot, a fire and something to crush the plants with."

Catherine's mind was suddenly wide awake. A million thoughts tumbled around her head, colliding and fogging, and then one would bounce to the front of her mind and become startlingly clear but just for a second, then the jumble returned.

It was fantastically exciting to think that she would be following in her mother's footsteps, she was also a little nervous. Reading and reciting was all very well but what if she was hopeless at actually making this potion? Then it occurred to her that a potion was probably only a small step away from an actual spell. Her next clear thought chilled her. Learning the craft and understanding its history was one thing, actually practising witchcraft was a completely different matter. A brief vision of flames licking around her ankles assailed her mind, vivid and almost painful. She recalled the stories she had heard of heretics being burned alive and, wait, how many of them had been burned for practising as opposed to merely knowing or even just being suspected? She could not think of a single one. Apparently it did not matter to the authorities. So, really, she had already taken that deciding step, she was already in harm's way and had been almost since Aelfric had arrived. No, before then, from the moment she had discovered the chest. As the fear ebbed away it was replaced with a determination to continue, although she really did not know where it came from.

She raised her eyes towards Aelfric. He had apparently been watching her and on his face was an expression of recognition, she wondered if he had been able to read every thought as it had crossed her mind or perhaps he had himself reached this crossroads and understood how she felt.

They could not go to the kitchen. Cook was just too nosey, she would have to know what Catherine was making and why she was doing it herself. She would want to help. They would have to go somewhere more private and her solar was the most secluded place. It was on the other side of the house from the kitchen and bake house, where most of the servants would be gathered, where it was warm from the ovens and fires. Now, how could she sneak pots out of the kitchen without anyone noticing? After a few seconds of thought, of considering a large cloak and trying to create a distraction outside, which may or may not attract everyone, she finally realised what the obvious solution was. There was already a fire in her solar and in the chest was a ready made potions kit. She smiled, resisting the urge to slap herself on the forehead for not thinking of it before.

From the look on his face Aelfric was becoming concerned at her lengthy silence.

"Meet me in my solar, I will collect the things we need and be there shortly."

Aelfric smiled and rose from his seat. A minute or two after he had left the room Catherine rose and left the hall too. She went through the Dias and up into her father's bedchamber. Closing the door softly behind her she felt the drop in temperature and shivered. There was no fire here and it was very cold, despite the shutters being closed and a heavy tapestry being drawn tightly across them. With the shutters closed it was also very dark and she needed to wait a few seconds more for her eyes to adjust to the gloom. When they had, she took a blanket from the bed and knelt before the chest, lifting the lid carefully. Still no strange hum, she was grateful for that. She reached into the chest and removed the mortar and pestle, the bowl and the herbs together with some of the jars, placed them all on the blanket and began to wrap hem carefully so that she could carry them.

When she was done she leaned forward to close the lid of the chest. As she did so a brief glow caught her eye. It seemed unnatural in the darkness and she started away from it, rocking back on her heels. The light faded considerably but she could still see a very feint glow and it was very close to her. Slowly she leaned forward again and this time she saw it. It was her own pendent, pulsing a strange, eerie glow in the darkness of the room and it seemed to grow brighter the closer she got to the chest. Fear gripped her as she recalled why the pendent had shone before. She closed the lid and moved away from the chest, noticing that the glow had now disappeared. But what could be evil about her mother's things? Aelfric had told her that her mother had been a good witch. The stone must be mistaken.

Not wishing to investigate further while the room was so dark, she gathered up the blanket and its contents and left. The Dias was empty and she moved unseen into her solar where Aelfric sat waiting for her.

"This is the potion I would like to begin with" he said. "The, uh, vigour and slumber potion. You will note that they are basically the same recipe but with one or two small variations."

Catherine read through the list of ingredients, most of them were here in the bundle of things she had brought from the chest, one she would need to get from the larder. There was one she did not recognise though.

"What is this one Aelfric, Ginger?"

"Oh, you will call it Billings Root, although I have a feeling the name 'ginger' will catch on. It has quite a ring to it, do you not think?"

Catherine smiled. Aelfric took pleasure in the simplest things and she envied that. She had once been much lighter hearted than she felt now, until the day she had been forced to grow up. She had thought of herself as an adult for some years now but until recently she had not realised just how innocent she had been. It made her wonder if she had any innocence left to lose, wonder if there were any more horrors out there for her to face.

"In that case I only have one more ingredient to fetch and we can begin."

By the time Catherine returned to her solar Aelfric had rigged up a wooden frame by the fire. It was ingenious really. It held her metal pot and had a tall arm that could swing to and fro so that she could move the pot over the fire for heat or swing it back out to add things without having to lean over the flames. This would make life much easier.

A further glance at the paper showed that this was going to be a little more involved than simply dropping leaves in a pot. The ingredient at the top of the list was a root and it required grinding to a paste. Catherine selected the root and held it up in front of her, unclear as to how to begin.

"Preparation is everything," piped up Aelfric, "if just one of the ingredients is not quite right the rest will not bind with it correctly and then you will not get the even distribution you need for the potion to work correctly."

Catherine looked again at the root in her hand and guessed that her plan of dropping a rock on it was not going to satisfy Aelfric's need for perfection. It felt like a tough little thing and she could not imagine how she was supposed to grind it carefully. Then the small bowl and tiny cudgel caught her eye.

She raised an eyebrow slightly at the prospect of these two tools being her means of preparation.

Sensing her reluctance Aelfric felt he needed to reinforce the point before bad habits set in.

"Try to imagine that you are mixing a potion to heal and you do not take the time to crush one of the herbs fully. It does not spread through the mixture as it should because the pieces are too large. The wound you want to heal is bad and may result in death if you cannot stop the bleeding. You apply the balm and wait. However, because the balm has not mixed well it is not as strong as it should be and the wound fails to heal. The victim could be left crippled, disfigured at best, or may even die."

The thought hung in the silence for a minute before Catherine asked Aelfric the best way to crush a root.

First Aelfric showed her how to cut it to the right size, and then he showed her how to slice it and gently to mash it into a paste. That then went into the pot over the fire, along with a small amount of milk. These needed to be left to warm together slowly for a short while, in fact, just about the time it took to prepare the next ingredient on the list. In it went, then the next and lastly some chopped herbs, including valerian. It needed only to heat enough to barely begin to boil and then be removed from the heat.

As Catherine leaned forward to check the temperature of the steaming liquid Aelfric put a hand gently on her arm.

"Take care not to breathe the steam, remember, this is a tonic to induce sleep."

Catherine looked at the pot; there was steam everywhere around it. How on earth did he expect her to not to breathe that noxious air? It did not smell good from here. She could not believe it would get any better if she got closer. She would just have to hold her breath. As she drew closer to the fire she instinctively brought her sleeve to her face to block the smell and made a mental note to create a fabric mask she could wear over her nose and mouth the next time she did some cooking. She swung the arm towards her taking the pot from the flames just as it began to boil.

"You see Catherine, how the potion was about to boil? This is its most potent time. Take it out of the fire too soon and it does not acquire its full strength, too late and it is ruined. All the goodness burned away."

Catherine stared at Aelfric for a few moments. He seemed overly excited by this, it was just a sleeping aid after all. His eyes were wide and bright as he gazed into the cooling potion, carefully searching it for signs of an uneven texture, colour or distribution of herbs.

"Now that the potion has cooled a little you can put it into these phials. You must take care to get it sealed in the jars before it is cold. It must still be warm so that it can continue to ferment."

Aelfric handed Catherine several small earthenware jars. She held four in the palm of her hand, each one just large enough to hold a spoonful or two of liquid. They all had their own earthenware stoppers held on with twine that had been coated in wax to ensure an airtight seal. She had never seen anything so tiny and was impressed with their quality.

The pot had stopped steaming and she moved towards it with the phials and a spoon. As she began to spoon the mixture out of the pot and into the small phials she turned to Aelfric.

"Where on earth did you find these Aelfric? They are so small; I have never seen anything so small."

As she spoke she spooned mixture and found it hard to be accurate with her pouring and some spilled onto her fingers. It was very hot working so close to the fire and she found it uncomfortable as she worked.

Aelfric looked up from the sheets of parchment to answer her. "I made them. A skill I will teach you in time."

Catherine looked again at the phials and doubted hers would ever look as good. She saw many hours of practice ahead of her.

All four phials were now full and stopped up and with a sigh of relief she stepped away from the fire. Her face felt hot and a little damp, she imagined she looked quite flushed and raised her hand to wipe away the moisture.

"Catherine? Catherine."

Aelfric sounded a little frustrated as he spoke to her but she could not imagine why. She had done all that he had asked so far. The potion was cooked and she had got it into the phials without breaking anything. Potion. When had Aelfric stopped using the word tonic and started saying potion? He was still calling her name. Now someone was touching her face and she awoke with a start.

Catherine found herself on the floor, with Aelfric standing over her, a damp cloth in his hand. She tried to sit up and clutched at her forehead as a brief stab of pain shot through it.

"Ahhhhh, what happened?"

Aelfric gave a wry smile. "My guess is that you spilled some of the sleeping potion and then put your hand up to your face. You have been down there for nearly half an hour. Your head will stop hurting in an hour or so and perhaps you will be more careful next time?"

As the pain in her head ebbed Catherine very slowly got to her feet and went to her chair at the fire side and settled herself there. This potion must be incredibly strong if just that small amount was enough to knock her out. She wondered how long a whole phial would last.

"How would I take this if I needed it?" She asked. "Would I take a few drops in some water?"

Aelfric settled himself in the chair opposite her and laced his fingers together, resting his elbows on the chair arms, and his hand against his chest, looking at her solemnly.

"It depends what you want to use it for but I would not suggest you take it at all." After a small pause he continued.

"You should treat it more as a defence than a tonic to aid sleep. As you are now well aware the vapours can knock out an adult quite effectively, giving you time to think or act in safety. The more you use the more people it will affect. Alternatively, you could use it in liquid to put someone to sleep but it is very powerful, you would only need a few drops for one person and that would put them out of action for several hours. You must take care though, too much and you will not induce sleep, you will invite death."

Catherine did not have time to be stunned by the revelation as a knock at the door announced a visitor to her solar and she panicked at the prospect of discovery. Glancing around she realised with a huge sense of relief that Aelfric had used the time she had spent sleeping much more wisely than she had.

"Come in."

It was Arthur and he looked grave.

"My Lady, Michael and John have been called away. The Hue and Cry has been raised again, another farm has been raided and a servant girl is missing. I can protect you better from here, if I may join you?"

"Of course, have a seat. Do you have any theories?"

"No, but we may know more later."

A heavy silence settled over the small group as they each considered the implications of this latest piece of news. None could fail to be struck by the recent string of events. To Catherine it felt like something evil was surrounding the area and slowly pecking them to death. First the churches, it had been easy to assume that pagans and heretics were responsible for that but now homes too. Someone was trying to destroy their community, spread fear and unrest, but she could not understand why. There was no apparent link, no one person was being targeted, no single place or group or trade. And it was far more than just mischief, the fire demonstrated that much on its own but there were people missing, two now, and Roger was dead.

Aelfric sat very quietly, trying hard to keep emotion from his face. He thought he knew what was going on, suspected what the root of this evil might be. Aelfric knew the warlock would come, the dark stranger who had murdered Edric in the cathedral. Aelfric had hoped he would have had more time to teach Catherine, she was still so innocent, still so new to the craft; she would not be able to fight him as she was. Aelfric was faced with an awful decision. Did he stay quiet and tell no-one what he knew or did he share his knowledge and suspicions with Catherine and Arthur?

If he kept his silence he may have more time to teach her while she was still reasonably calm, panic would inhibit her performance and may put her in more danger than she already faced. It seemed to him that whoever was behind these raids was looking for something or someone. Aelfric believed it was the warlock and that he was searching for the Guardian. If Catherine panicked she could draw attention to herself and present the warlock with an obvious target.

His other option was to tell all. Yes, she might panic, but she might not. The news might focus her more; give her a good reason to study hard while they still had time. She deserved to know what was hunting her and this knowledge would almost certainly make her more cautious, keep her safer for longer.

Aelfric was torn over his choices. He wanted to tell her, felt she deserved to know it all but worried that this knowledge might saddle her with fear that would make her vulnerable to the warlock. Every time he looked at her he felt a stab of guilt for the possible consequences of either choice, the consequences of a decision he had not yet made. Feeling a need for solitude Aelfric excused himself and went to his cot in the stable block to think.

Arthur also suspected some method behind the attacks. There had to be something driving whoever it was, something very important to make them risk capture and that risk increased every time they raided a house or set a fire. He did not know what might be driving these people but he felt certain it was not religion. He was also convinced that there was more than one person involved. Not only was this a lot of chaos for one person to cause alone, two men had been seen on the day of the fire.

Arthur and Catherine settled down to wait for Michael and John to return with more news.

Chapter 19

Catherine awoke with a start. It was already morning and it was bitterly cold. She lay still as she became accustomed to the weak light in the room and watched her breath form a thin mist in front of her face as she breathed. The ale pot she had taken to bed with her last night now had a thin layer of ice across the top of the liquid and she assumed that it had been much colder outside, where the wind found its way into even the tiniest gap. She briefly though of Aelfric bedded down in the stables but had been assured that it could get very warm amongst the hay. Then she thought of Michael and Arthur, who often put their mats down in the hall. They would no doubt have been very warm by the large fire. Even though she had a lovely bed, covered in blankets and furs she may still have been the coldest in the night, especially when she had first crawled inside and had to wait for the blankets to take her warmth into themselves. Until then the blankets were as cold as the room and she would shiver for several minutes.

Snow would follow soon; she could almost smell it in the air. In the meantime the harsh frost overnight would have damaged or killed any of the seasonal vegetables not yet harvested. She was glad she had gathered all of her herbs and roots in already.

Michael and John had not returned by the time she had retired last night although she had sat up very late with Arthur. Aelfric had returned to them some hours later seemingly having dealt with the troubles that had bothered him earlier.

Catherine was anxious to know if they had found the missing servant girl and started to sit up in bed, bracing herself against the cold air of the room as her blankets fell away from her.

A banging sound from downstairs startled her. Someone was hammering on the door and perhaps that was what had woken her. She went to the shutters and opened them. Peering carefully out she could see a number of the villagers there, armed with axes, knives and various farming tools. The hue and cry? Surely they were not still looking for that poor girl, if she had spent the night outside she must surely have frozen to death by now. Perhaps they had found her, that is why they had come here looking for men.

Catherine could make out voices below, one of them belonged to Arthur.

"How long has it been burning?"

"For some time now, burned almost to the ground by the time we left."

"Was anyone inside?" Arthur asked, his voice anxious.

"Seems the whole family were in there, cottager wife and two young lads. Probably died in their sleep, at least nobody heard them call out."

Catherine gasped in horror and hot tears filled her eyes as she listened to the men talk. Another fire and people dead this time. Why? Why was someone doing this to these people? They were simple decent folk, who had harmed no-one. She heard Arthur's voice call out.

"Michael!"

Down at the front door Arthur waited as he heard footsteps jogging towards the group. Michael appeared with concern etched on his features. He was beginning to wonder if he had ever been relaxed, he had felt tense and alert for so long now. He walked the last steps towards the group at the door, waiting for Arthur to speak.

"There has been a fire, another of the estate's cottagers up on the hill side." Arthur pointed in the direction of the hill and Michael could see a column of thick black smoke weaving an unsteady course up into the sky, breaking and kinking as small gusts of wind caught at it and played with it.

Arthur lowered his voice and continued.

"We should go and search for the godless monsters that did this." His throat tightened as he spoke and he paused, squaring his jaw before going on.

"They all died Michael, mother, father and two small boys, all perished in the house as it burned. Someone will have to see justice for this."

Michael nodded gravely, stung by the news of the deaths. "You are sure it was deliberate? It was not just a hearth that got out of control?" Michael searched for some hope, some sign that his fears were unfounded.

"No, it was deliberate. The Keeper is still in the village, he was one of the first there, says he saw footprints in the frost on the grass around the house and a dead torch just away from the place. That was when he raised the hue and cry. John has gone to fetch the horses. Michael, any news from last night? Did they find her?"

It was a few seconds before Michael could answer, he was finding it impossible to make sense of all this, he could not see a reason but he suspected this was not as simple as most people thought. The general feeling in the village was that there was one group behind this, either pagans or witches and they just needed to be hunted down and tried for their crimes. Michael could not see a pattern in it all. They started by raiding churches but essentially causing no damage, if destruction was not their reason then what? They did not steal from churches, although there was little there to steal in the first place. Then they start stealing from homes and people are going missing, the monk, still not found. Roger was found dead and then the servant girl. Now they were burning homes down with no care for the souls inside. There had to be a reason, he just could not see it. Yet.

He wondered if perhaps he was looking too deep, perhaps he was so certain he would find a pattern, some plan or reason behind all of this madness, that he was missing the truth. Arthur and John were convinced it was all the work of a small band of people, two or maybe three of them who had gone quite mad. They could easily be witches, Michael had heard that their dealings with demons robbed them of their sense and reason, not to mention the risk of possession. In many ways this was worse than Michael's own, still jumbled theory. A small group of men who were mad or even possessed would be wildly unpredictable, there was no telling where they would strike next, even they may not know and they may never know why.

"Yes, Arthur, we found her. Nothing was taken from the house but it was a mess, someone had a good look around that it sure enough. We found the girl in a shallow grave in the woods, barely covered, just like Roger, and missing some fingers. The strangest thing though, the Keeper says she looked like she had been there for days but her master said he saw her just yesterday morning."

Arthur's face only hardened further.

"This must stop, now." Arthur's voice was chillingly calm and measured but his eyes glittered with a fury that Michael had never seen there before. Of course they should go, whoever had done this cannot have got far yet, this would be the best chance of catching them.

John appeared with Robert, leading three horses between them. Michael turned to his friend.

"Arthur, we cannot all go, you know that. Someone must stay with Catherine, we cannot leave her defenceless." Michael was surprised that Arthur intended all three soldiers to leave the house together and his expression said that just as clearly as his words, despite his efforts to keep his tone calm and matter of fact.

Arthur's anger flared anyway, his fuse was dangerously short today. Arthur had also been tense lately, keeping watch at all hours, watching for danger everywhere, not to mention the day Catherine was abducted. That had been a nightmare in itself but combined with the underlying tension at the house and these recent attacks, it had taken its toll on him. He was in need of a vent for his tension and the news of this senseless slaughter of a family had brought it all to a head. He had to act now. Arthur was acting on instinct alone now. His voice was a low angry growl, reflecting the rage he was keeping barely contained inside.

"And what about everyone else? Michael, six people have lost their lives, maybe seven. Thomas and his family are homeless. Are they any less worthwhile? What about whoever might be next if we do nothing? Are they less deserving of our efforts? We have to do this Michael, and we have to do it now. It has been almost two weeks with no sign of trouble here. She will be safe enough in the house with Robert."

Michael flinched a little under the onslaught. This was a side of Arthur he had never even suspected existed.

Catherine dressed as quickly as she could without waiting for Rachel to help her. Her mind raced, trying to make sense of what she had heard. The cottager had said the whole family had perished in the fire. Was it possible that it had been an accident? But why had the hue and cry been raised when the fire was almost out? Perhaps it was just until the Keeper could be called to confirm it an accident. Catherine had been unable to hear any more of the conversation after Arthur had called for Michael. She needed to do something, she needed to be active and busy. Perhaps there was something she could do to help.

That was when the reality of the situation hit her and she sat down heavily on the end of her bed.

She would not be able to help because there was no-one left to help. They were all dead, even the two boys. Tears began to flow freely now and a deep feeling of hopelessness filled her. How could these people fight something they could not see? Whoever was behind all of this was too quick to be caught if they were too quick even to be seen.

As she sat and thought she stared blankly at the floor of her chamber and the first tinglings of desperation began to creep into her heart. What was yet to come? Could she be next? That thought sparked her natural instinct for survival and it suddenly gave her a strong boost of adrenalin. Strong enough to propel her to her feet and through the door of her chamber before she was aware of what she was doing or even where she was going.

'Aelfric, he will know what to do,' she thought as she hurried towards the hall to find him. She was only vaguely aware of how much she had come to rely on Aelfric since he had arrived. It had been a quick but subconscious shift within her that had crept up on her to the point where she felt she would struggle without him.

Just inside the tree line on the hillside overlooking the manor and down to the village, three men mounted on horseback sat in silence. They had only arrived there a short time ago, less than an hour. The short, fat man had arrived first, then the other two, younger men, had joined him a little while later.

The three men watched the group of villagers arrive at the manor house, apparently armed for a war. They waited while the hue and cry presumably explained what had happened that morning. They looked at each other as the group of armed men in the valley below had hurried away from the house. They had smiled as they watched three men on horseback follow the group.

The short man turned to his companions. "Now remember, I do not want her so badly hurt that I cannot marry her, just do enough to get her and bring her back. Try not to bruise the face. You should have about an hour before anyone comes back and starts looking for her. I do not care about the servants."

"Yes, Mr Preece." One of the younger men nodded curtly as they both urged their horses out from the cover of the trees and rode carefully down the steep hillside towards the house. Thy did not hurry, there was no need, nobody was around to see them coming now that everyone was off investigating the fire and chasing all over the countryside trying to find the villains responsible. The two men had to admit that their master seemed to have hit on a genius plan this time. The way was clear for them now, it was all so simple. A few minutes later they were almost at the gates and Matthew Preece, watching them from the trees smiled as he turned his horse's head and started the short ride home to await his prize.

Catherine found Aelfric in the hall settled by a roaring fire. She rushed into the room at such an uncharacteristic pace that Aelfric immediately turned to look at her in surprise. He leapt from his seat when he saw the look of panic on Catherine's ashen face. Had the warlock found them? Was he coming? Aelfric instinctively looked over Catherine's shoulder, half expecting to see some kind of demon chasing her but she appeared to be alone.

"What on earth is the matter my child?" he blurted, quite startled by her anxious appearance.

"There has been another fire, they are all dead, and they have gone to look but..." Catherine ran out of breath and had to stop for a second to recover a little before she could explain her agitation more clearly.

"Someone has set fire to another of my cottager's homes. He was inside with his wife and children, they were probably asleep. The hue and cry came a little while ago to get help for the search."

Aelfric's first reaction was to relax, greatly, and was surprised at how tense he had become so quickly. Once he felt his muscles starting to ease and his pulse slow, he began to comprehend just what Catherine was telling him. He had been crossing the hall to assist Catherine but stopped in his tracks now, his habit flowing around his ankles as their momentum continued for a second longer. He was confused.

"All dead you say, in a fire?" He had to check what Catherine had just said. It had all happened so quickly, perhaps he had misheard.

"Yes." The word was barely more than a breath as Catherine herself began to unwind a little from her adrenalin rush. She felt drained and hollow, still quite scared but guilty also. Guilty that fear for her own safety was more important to her than those people. She searched through her void but could initially find nothing for those poor souls and that briefly troubled her but it soon passed and she was left with her own emptiness once again. It was as if she had been wrapped in a cloak made entirely from fear and those parts of her it did not touch were numb.

She walked slowly to the fire and took a seat, staring at the floor, unable to look into the flames, afraid of the images she might see dancing there, images that would surely return to haunt her dreams.

Collecting himself Aelfric returned to his own seat. This was not the work of the warlock, he was sure now. True, there were demons in this world that thrived on death and destruction, it was all they existed for and he could believe this of them. But this warlock was very different. He was far more sophisticated and focused. This warlock was almost certainly using demons to achieve his goal but he was searching for something very specific. He would not waste time in this way. That meant that there was more than one evil at work in this place, more than one enemy to guard against. What this new evil wanted to achieve beyond chaos and fear was a mystery to Aelfric but it could only help the warlock by causing confusion and diverting people's attention away from him.

Despite the large fire burning richly at his side Aelfric felt chilled to the bone. He knew he would need to gather his wits quickly. Catherine's lessons had only just begun and she was clearly in no fit state mentally to battle a warlock of his power and skill.

A loud crash sounding through the house brought both Catherine and Aelfric to their senses and both sat up straight. The crash was followed quickly by the sound of men shouting.

"What is going on?" Aelfric asked the question of no-one in particular and was fairly sure he did not want to know the answer. Until now he had been brave and focused, secure in the knowledge that he was fulfilling his own destiny and moulding a Guardian to protect this world from evil. He had been sure that when the time came he would be ready to face anything and lay down his life if he needed to. But now that moment was upon him he discovered he was not ready at all. His destiny had not been completed; the warrior he was supposed to be grooming was little more than a frightened child. Aelfric felt lost and panicked, sitting frozen in his chair he did not have a clue what to do.

In complete contrast Catherine sprang into action. Her survival instinct once again fired through her and she pushed herself out of her seat, stepping quietly away from potential obstacles like the chairs. Turning to the door to check how much time they had she found her voice and startled Aelfric out of his trance-like state.

"We need to get out of here, get somewhere safe. Follow me." She gathered a handful of skirt, lifting it from the floor and ran to her solar. Aelfric was puffing in his efforts to keep up with her astonishing pace. As soon as Aelfric came through the door to the solar Catherine pushed it shut and turned to find anything she could use to wedge it shut long enough for them to find another way out or wait for rescue.

As she cast her gaze around the room she spotted a small wooden box on a bench by the wall. She stared at it knowing it was important but not immediately knowing why.

'Come on Catherine, think about it. It is the potion box with the herbs inside. What could I use from in there? Think, think. What else is in the box?"

Suddenly it was as if someone had pulled back the curtains and let in a ray of bright sunlight. She knew what to do and ran to the box.

"Stay here Aelfric, you should be safe. You must keep the door shut after I have gone." Catherine heard the confidence in her voice but did not know where it came from. It felt like someone else speaking through her. She opened the box and took several phials out.

"I am not staying on my own, I will come with you." Aelfric sounded as scared as he felt and as much as he feared what was on the other side of that door, he was more scared of waiting in the solar alone, not knowing what fate had befallen Catherine or anyone else in the house.

"Very well, but stay behind me." Catherine did not have time to argue. She closed the box lid and moved quickly to the door, listening carefully for any sounds outside. It was all quiet so she opened the door and moved into the Dias. It was empty but she could hear the muffled sounds of shouts and metal clashing against metal and stone coming from somewhere nearby.

She ran into the hall. At the far end she saw three men fighting. Two were facing her, she had never seen them before and they both seemed to be attacking the third man whose back was to her. She would recognise that back anywhere. It was Michael and he was fighting well but he would not last long against two men. Instinctively taking brief stock of the entire room, Catherine made sure there was no-one else there waiting to ambush her and then ran swiftly towards the three men. As she made her move one of the attackers spotted her and peeled away from the other two men. Quickly changing direction Catherine ran to the side of the hall, drawing the man away from the other two. She had to give Michael a fighting chance and one man each would be easier for them both to deal with.

The man came at her quickly and when she was just a few yards from him she stopped and threw one of the phials at his chest. It smashed into a thousand shards instantly and some of the liquid splashed his face while a barely perceptible cloud rose from the stain on his jacket. As he kept coming Catherine darted left, out of his path and back towards Michael. As she came at the two fighting men she threw a second phial and sent a small prayer along with it. Stopping abruptly she turned to see where the other man was and saw with an enormous sense of relief that he was sprawled on the floor behind her. As she looked at him she heard a thud and a clatter of metal on the stone floor and turned to see Michael and the other man falling to the ground.

A very pale and shaken Aelfric entered the hall, looking at all the bodies in horror.

"Aelfric run to the stables, fetch something we can use to tie them up. I will stay and keep watch." Aelfric did not seem to be moving.

"Aelfric hurry, they could wake up at any moment."

Aelfric ran then, as fast as his legs could carry him and returned with several lengths of rope. Between them Catherine and Aelfric managed to securely truss up the two strangers and carry Michael to the fireside where he continued to sleep. Only then could Catherine begin to relax and she stopped to take a look around the hall. That was when she began to laugh. It was quiet at first, hardly more than a smile but it soon bubbled out of her in gentle waves.

Aelfric stood in stunned silence and he stared at the woman in front of him, a frightened child no more it seemed. At some point in the last hour their roles had changed. She had grown in strength and she had found her courage and intelligence where Aelfric had discovered the depths of his cowardice and impotence in the face of fear. He still had much to teach her but he felt the shift in their relationship. She would learn things very quickly now and Aelfric suspected she had found within her what she needed to embrace who she was.

Aelfric, did you see what happened?" she paused and looked at her friend. He looked really much shaken. "I did this, I can hardly believe it but I did. It was as if someone else took control of me and I was not scared anymore." There were a few seconds of silence as an unpleasant thought occurred to her.

"Aelfric you do not think someone or something else did take control of me, do you?" Her voice held a hint of worry again and Aelfric was able to shake himself back into his mentor role to answer her.

"No, Catherine, it was all you. This is who you were born to be, it is your destiny. You were thinking and moving faster and with more intelligence. You seemed to be thinking far ahead of your actions. It was very impressive to watch." Aelfric hung his head a little. "And I am ashamed that I only barely had the courage to watch and none to help you."

Catherine moved towards Aelfric and hugged him in silence before taking a step back, holding his arms.

"You will still teach me, will you not?" she asked quietly.

Aelfric smiled weakly and nodded. A small groan made them both jump a little and they turned to find Michael waking up. Catherine bent to his side, gently brushing his hair from his face with her fingers, as he opened his eyes.

"Are you all right?"

"My head hurts." Michael looked up at her and seemed genuinely surprised to see her there. "You are all right? They did not hurt you? How did you get away?" He groaned again as another flash of pain seared through his head.

"I am fine Michael, do not worry. We heard the shouting and came to see what was going on. One of the men you were fighting got behind you and knocked you down. He did not see me coming up behind him with a piece of wood and Aelfric took the other man by surprise. We managed to overpower them and get them tied up."

Michael struggled to sit up, clutching at his head and rested against a chair before trying to get to his feet.

"I do not understand, I thought the other man got by me and out into the Dias, he was not going behind me." He looked around him, at the swords and the two men tied up and slumped against the wall. "What did you hit him with?"

"Oh, something I grabbed on my way in I think. I do not really remember, it all happened so fast. I think Aelfric must have taken it back. Rest now Michael, we are all safe." She helped him into the chair and fetched him some wine, sitting with him until his head cleared, sympathising with every twinge he felt, having felt it herself not so long ago.

The other two men woke shortly before Arthur, John and Robert returned and Catherine was obliged to explain once more, her version of events. Arthur felt awful, not only had they not discovered the killers but he had left Catherine and Michael vulnerable and they were attacked. It could all have turned out so differently, so badly. Michael was on his feet by now and pacing the floor trying to walk off what remained of his headache. As he crossed the floor again he noticed some small shards of pottery on the floor and bent to examine them more carefully.

"Where did these come from?" he asked the room in general.

"That was me," said Catherine quickly "Aelfric has been teaching me how to make some old healing remedies and I was bottling balm when I heard all the noise in here. I must have had some small phials with me and when I ran in and grabbed the wood I must have dropped them."

Her answer was easy, simple and natural but still Michael had doubts about what had happened. He just could not remember being hit and he could recall every hit he had ever taken. Something did not quite fit but he could not decide what, although he doubted he would answer that question, at least not today. Instead he turned his attention to the two men while Robert rode for the Keeper.

It was not long before Robert returned. He brought with him the Keeper and the Reeve, who was looking exceptionally harassed these days and was truly tired of following the Keeper from one disaster to the next. The Keeper himself was starting to despair of ever bringing order to this place and getting back to his wife. He had to admit that for a small place that had never come to his notice before, it had made a deep and lasting impression on him now.

Ralph had been here in his capacity as Keeper only four days but it felt more like a month. Since he had arrived he had seen six deaths, two fires and a robbery. He would never have believed so much trouble was possible in such a small place, and he was no nearer to solving it all, until now. As he entered the hall behind Robert the first thing he noticed were the two men sitting against the wall, secured with rope. The hall was reasonably large and there appeared to be an upper floor. Ralph was impressed, it was a fine building. Pacing in front of them was a tall, dark haired man that Ralph recognised as Michael, one of the soldiers here. Michael was rubbing his temples and judging from his face he was in some pain, probably a headache. The next thing Ralph noticed was the striking young woman sitting by the fire. He guessed this must be the Lady Catherine. He knew this was her estate and had intended to pay his respects when he had a few free hours, but not under these circumstances.

In a seat opposite Catherine by the fire Ralph spotted a monk he had not seen before. Just then Arthur stepped forward to greet the Keeper.

"Arthur, we meet again. I see you have a monk here; I take it he is not the missing monk?"

Arthur glanced across at Aelfric. "No, Keeper, this monk came from Worcester to visit the late Lord and seems to have decided to stay, for the time being."

"Was this recent?" Asked Ralph.

"Yes, about two weeks ago."

"Before all this trouble began?" Ralph probed further. Arthur guessed where the question was leading.

"Yes, but I do not believe he has left the grounds in all that time. He and Lady Catherine have become quite close and spend much of their time together. I do not think you need to worry about him."

Ralph was naturally curious about most people and made a mental note of this information.

Next he made his way to the fire to introduce himself to Catherine. She looked up as he approached and smiled.

"My Lady, I am Ralph, Keeper of the King's Peace. I understand you have had some trouble here today. Can you tell me what happened?"

Catherine appraised the older man standing in front of her. He was not particularly tall, he certainly did not have the height of Michael or Arthur but he was solidly built. He appeared to be able to look after himself. She could tell that he was strong and muscular but he also carried the paunch that was common to the wealthier men of his age. He had an air of authority and a calm, weathered face, full of knowledge and experience of the world. She imagined that each line on that face had a story to tell and many long evenings could be pleasantly whiled away listening to them all. Despite her initial feelings of trust she was also very wary of this man. He was here to discover the truth and she was about to tell him a lie, the same lie she had already told Michael. She knew Michael was not convinced and she had years of trust on her side there. This man knew nothing of her character and was used to having people lie to him. She was almost sure he would catch her out and could not begin to worry about the consequences for her if the truth were even suspected.

Ralph made Catherine go through her story twice before asking to see the wood she had used as a weapon. She floundered for a second.

"You want to see what I used to hit the man?"

"Yes, my Lady, just a quick look if you do not mind."

Catherine started to panic. He doubted her story, had he caught her in her lie? Her pulse quickened and she was aware of her heart beating hard. She had cleared away the phials a short while ago but was alarmed that she did not have a weapon to produce for inspection.

A voice at her side made her jump. It was Aelfric.

"Keeper, I am Brother Aelfric, I believe this is the item you were asking for."

Aelfric produced a small log from the wood basket near the fire and Ralph took it briefly and looked it over, running his hand across it before handing it back to Aelfric with a small nod.

"I hope you did not get a splinter my Lady."

Catherine felt herself flush under the pressure of his gaze. "I hardly noticed. I do not believe so." For effect she looked down at her hands, turning them over. "No, it would appear I have been lucky."

"You have indeed my Lady, you have been very lucky today. Now, I have detained you long enough. My men and I will relieve you of your guests. It would not surprise me if you have caught our trouble makers. I hope this hundred can see some peace now."

Ralph rose fluidly from his seat and spoke briefly with his men who hauled the two trussed men to their feet and bundled them out into the cold and into custody where the Keeper could question them in privacy before delivering them to the magistrate for punishment.

Catherine watched the men leave and as the door closed behind them she felt an enormous rush of relief. It was all she could do not to cry as she became overwhelmed with emotion. For a few minutes she sat silent and still, staring at her hands as they lay trembling in her lap.

She reflected on what had happened over the last few hours and could hardly believe it had been her. She hardly knew herself. Two very long weeks ago she had been a child, naïve and, in hindsight, carefree. Now she had grown up, discovered she had this…. was it a gift or a curse? She guessed time would tell, either way she had a talent she had never known about before. She apparently had instincts and reflexes that had saved the day. Where had they come from? Catherine had never noticed that she could think so quickly and act so decisively before, but then she had never faced a situation like that before. Her father had dealt with everything, protected and sheltered her. Until today she had thanked him for that, for making her life simple and easy. Now she was not so sure it had been the best thing for her. She was facing a time when she would need skills that she had not yet learned. Not for the first time recently, Catherine was afraid, for herself and for the future. Movement caught her eye and she raised her head, seeing Michael still pacing the floor.

Michael was too wrapped up in his thoughts to notice anyone else's troubles just now. He knew he should be relieved; they had caught the men responsible for all the death and destruction. The hundred could now begin to mourn and heal, yet he could not settle his mind. Things still did not add up. There seemed to be too much going on for it to be only two men acting alone. Certainly these two were working for someone and Michael had his suspicions but not a clear reason for it yet. But why work in such different ways? Usually when a man set himself on a path of violence he had a favoured technique but here there were murders and thefts, then there were fires. Could there be more than one evil at work here? Michael sighed heavily and slumped on the nearest bench. Perhaps chaos was the only method here but those two men were experienced soldiers. They knew how to handle their weapons and themselves. Michael had struggled to hold them as long as he had and yet a young woman and a monk managed to overpower and restrain them.

Michael glanced over at Catherine. She was watching him and their eyes met. She was very pale and looked shaken and scared. She was also keeping something from him, something important, and he felt sure the monk knew what that was. He smiled at her and she managed a weak smile in return. Michael tried to imagine why she felt she could not trust him with her secret when she had always been so open before. It must be something big. He softened a little, his feelings for her did not give him the right to know all her secrets and perhaps he was better off not knowing, for now.

Chapter 20

Autumn had passed and winter was taking hold. Most of the trees stood bare while some still clung to a few leaves and this bleak, skeletal landscape was broken only by the vivid green of a fir tree here and there. The grass had died and colour had been largely drained from the world, leaving only shades of grey and brown. Children played outside less and less, adults hurried about their tasks and rarely stopped to chat as they passed on roads and tracks. Migratory birds had long since left. Hibernating animals were already slumbering in their holes and nests. Life had become a dull, muffled version of itself with the arrival of the bitter north winds.

Catherine woke from a disturbed and fitful sleep. Strange and frightening dreams had plagued her as she slept and when she had woken to escape them she had been tortured with thoughts of her reality. She lay still for a while, considering staying in bed all day where it was warm and quiet, where she would not have to face people and answer difficult questions. She was too hungry, she would have to venture downstairs for some breakfast, it would be hard to avoid Michael and she could see a hundred questions in his eyes last night. He may have more by now. Perhaps she should tell him, he deserved to know the truth, to know who and what he was protecting. But did she really know the answer to that herself yet? How could she begin to explain what she barely understood herself? Of course there was always the risk that he would leave. He might be so disgusted at what she had become that he would not be able to stay. It never occurred to her that he might betray her secret, no, Michael would not do that to her, he was, if nothing else, an honourable man.

As Catherine climbed out of her bed she immediately felt the pinch of the cold at her feet and hands, then her arms and legs. She hurried to dress but was pre-occupied with thoughts of the previous day. She recalled what she had done, how she had taken on those two soldiers and how she had won. She had made a potion, it had worked and she had saved Michael, Aelfric and herself from whatever fate the men had in mind for them. Whatever it may have been, their swords had made it clear that it could not have been a good one.

A small smile emerged on her lips as she remembered charging across the hall, thinking so fast, moving so quickly, the skill of her aim. She had been thinking like a trained soldier, tactics, outcomes, fluid movements. A small bubble of pride formed inside her and as it popped it dispersed a warm comforting feeling all through her body.

If she could do that with a small potion phial, what else was she capable of? Aelfric said she was a witch; would she be able to cast spells? Suddenly Catherine's despair was replaced with curiosity and a growing sense of urgency to learn all she could as soon as possible. She needed to feel prepared without knowing or suspecting what for.

Having finished dressing and braiding her hair she made her way downstairs feeling a lot more positive and confident than when she had woken this morning. As she entered the hall a wave of warmth hit her from the fire that crackled and spat on the other side of the room. She felt her spirit lift and walked towards her usual seat. There was no sign of the normal evidence of breakfast. Either she was earlier than she thought or it was closer to midday than she suspected. Apart from sounds of the fire the room was quiet and she was alone for several minutes.

Rachel was the next person to enter the hall. She came from the kitchen, her arms full of plates and bread.

"Morning, my Lady. You are up early, I did not think anyone else had risen yet, except Michael, he was up before the birds. I will have the rest of the breakfast things out in a minute or two." Rachel smiled warmly at her mistress. Catherine envied her ignorance, a small part of her wished she still knew nothing of this new world of hers but mostly she was keen to know more about her craft.

Aelfric was the next person to arrive. Catherine was helping herself to bread, cheese and meats from the table when the door opened. She turned, saw him and smiled. As he closed the door she spoke.

"Good morning Aelfric. I was hoping we could continue with our lessons today. I thought maybe we could work on some more potions after breakfast and then perhaps some spells this afternoon?"

Aelfric had been quite shaken following the attack the day before and Catherine was not sure how he would react. He may have changed his mind and decided to leave. She hoped not, she had come to rely on him for his wisdom and belief in her. What she saw in his face now surprised her. It was relief.

"I am so glad you want to continue. I had thought, well wondered anyway, if yesterday had frightened you too much; maybe put you off knowing any more because you wanted to avoid any more, uh, encounters."

"No, if anything, it made me determined to know more. Look what I achieved with the little knowledge I have. I want to be prepared in case I need to protect myself, or others, again. I just have this nagging feeling that yesterday will not be the last time I need to protect myself."

Aelfric was glad that she was not going to run away from her gift, but he was also scared and he did not like to admit it. He had spent many a restless hour during the night fighting the urge to run away, back to Worcester, to the relative safety of the cathedral. It had been thoughts of Edric and what had to be protected that had sealed his resolve. Although, he suspected that he may have more doubts and weakness before this was all over.

"Of course," he said, "we will begin straight after breakfast." He was still questioning his decision not to tell her about the warlock. She seemed to be embracing her destiny and there was no doubt of her natural abilities but might this be a step too far, too soon? To want to protect yourself from a possible danger at some time in the future was a very different thing from needing to protect yourself from a superior foe. Aelfric knew that it was a foe who was definitely coming, and soon. Then there was her Guardianship. Was this the right time to tell her what she was protecting? He suspected not and turned his thoughts towards potions, considering which ones may help her most in the coming days or weeks.

With renewed respect and determination Catherine applied herself to the potions lessons. She had underestimated the sleeping potion as some kind of herbal remedy. Now she recognised it as a defensive weapon as well. As she worked on the vigour potion she bore this in mind and worked at it very carefully. Being very similar to the sleeping draught, with just a few key ingredients substituted, she found it fairly easy to make. As it heated over the fire she took great pains to stay away from the fumes, much to Aelfric's amusement. Apparently this potion you drank, as quickly as possible. She had to admit, it smelt truly foul.

By the time the midday meal was due Catherine had mastered the vigour potion along with one to create light. Aelfric said it burned in the phial like a torch and she also made one to heal wounds and Aelfric assured her that this would even work on a slashing wound from a sword.

During the afternoon they spent hours locked away in her solar learning the art of spells. How to construct them, timing, pronunciation, precise wording to get the desired result and the risk of backfire if any of these were not quite right. They finished the day with a short chant to control the air in her immediate vicinity. Aelfric was not entirely sure of its usefulness beyond its brevity and simplicity but felt sure it would be worth knowing, otherwise why would it have been with her mother's things?

Catherine was exhausted by the time Rachel came to announce that supper was ready. As much as she enjoyed what she had learned, she welcomed the break and the opportunity to see other people. When they entered the hall she found Michael had returned but still looked serious and pensive. Arthur and John also joined them at the table. Michael had been with the Keeper most of the day, questioning the two men they had caught of the day before. It had taken several hours but finally the two men had given in and admitted who they had been working for. They were only prepared to admit to two fires, both at the cottager's homes and denied knowing there were people inside the second but it seemed certain that Preece was behind this. Of course, the Keeper had not believed them, he was sure they were responsible for most, if not all the crimes of late but neither he nor Michael could work out why they would admit to the murder a family sleeping in their beds but not to Roger or the servant girl.

Michael was not as sure as the Keeper regarding the extent of their guilt. He still could not shake the feeling that there was more than one agenda at work here.

At least they would have peace from Preece's torments for a while. He would of course be relieved of two of his men, which would certainly cause unrest among the others, and the Keeper would be paying him a visit next. Michael was sure that Preece would be brought before the magistrate the following week and they would have peace until then at least. Even if he was not punished he would probably lay low for a while, allow the dust to settle, the gossips to find a new interest.

"You should be pleased Catherine, you can finally relax, for a while anyway. Perhaps we all can." He said.

Michael smiled at her, it was a sincere, warm smile that seemed to reach out to her across the table, but his eyes told her that he was still worried about something. She smiled back and it was equally warm. She had come to rely on Aelfric for his knowledge and wisdom but she relied on Michael for his strength and skill, she realised that now. Catherine also realised that she missed him. They had not spent much time together over the last few weeks and she missed his easy company, the sense of safety he engendered. It was true of Arthur too and she missed him, not less, but differently. She could not pinpoint where the distinction was but she knew she felt very differently for these two men.

The following day she practised her four potions and bottled them up, making sure she marked each phial carefully so that she would recognise each one, if she needed them in future. Aelfric had taken some time to make some more phials and today they were ready to use.

The day after that they went over the spells again, making sure she knew the first one before learning another. This new one was longer and a little more complex, although understanding how it was constructed helped her to learn most of it. Aelfric had explained that this was a defensive spell like the first and would shield her. Aelfric felt it was strong enough to protect against objects and would probably block some spells too, in case she encountered someone who might know something of magic and seek to harm her with a spell of their own.

In the evenings Catherine made an effort to sit in the hall with Michael, Arthur and John, talking and telling stories. She had begun to feel isolated from her previous life, from normality and she felt a strong desire to reconnect with it. The more she delved into Aelfric's world the more she felt a need to keep herself grounded in her own world and Michael and Arthur were the best way she could think of to do that. Neither man knew her secret and as far as she knew, neither one knew anything of magic either.

As she sat that evening and thought about how her life had changed, it occurred to her how much she had changed too, she felt it. The knowledge that Aelfric brought had made sense of some of her past, it seemed to give her a sense of purpose for the future and it filled a large hole in her present. Perhaps she was using it to compensate for the loss of her father, she still missed him so much. Or perhaps there was more to it, maybe there had always been something missing and now she had found it. Catherine certainly felt more alive and confident than she ever had and that was a good thing. She was not the only one to notice either.

On the other side of the fire Michael reclined in his chair, watching her. He had known Catherine for years now, watched her grow into a woman. He knew her habits, her moods, had become accustomed to the way her mind worked. He had watched her develop into that person over the years. It had been slow and gentle but he had seen her alter more over the last few weeks than in the last two yeas together. Since Aelfric had arrived, in fact. She had been naïve, sheltered and open and she had the fear of a child. It was a vulnerability that he had thought was lost to the world in these harsh times of struggle and suffering. Michael looked at her now and saw the same gentle woman but the vulnerability seemed almost gone. He saw a more determined and confident woman, one who had learned to lie. Michael was sure of that now, her story about how she had overpowered the two men who had broken in the other day, was good. She had nearly got away with it, until the Keeper had come and asked to see the weapon. Michael had seen the briefest flutter of panic cross her features and at that moment had caught her in the lie.

Michael was now more suspicious of Aelfric than ever. He was as sure as he could be that Aelfric was not involved in any part of the recent crime wave but he had been part of Catherine's lie. If he could bring her to that what else might he be introducing her to in all those hours they spent together? Michael resolved to watch them much more closely, to find out what was going on and with Preece and his men out of the way for a few days at least, he would have time to do just that.

A loud hollow banging sounded through the house and brought Michael out of his thoughts and back to reality. He glanced across to Arthur, who met his gaze and together they rose to answer the door.

Michael pulled back the bolts and put his hand on the door to pull it open, his other hand on the hilt of his sword. Arthur stood behind him, similarly ready to draw his weapon if necessary. Michael pulled open the door and was surprised to see the Miller standing before him, with a crowd of men standing some way back armed with burning torches and various farm tools.

"Miller, what on earth is going on? Someone has raised the hue and cry?"

The Miller nodded gravely. "Yes, Michael, that Tanner's house has been ransacked, bits of furniture and pots all over the place, a right old mess." The Miller lowered his head and shifted his substantial weight from one foot to the other.

"What is it Miller, what else has happened?" Michael could see the man before him was troubled by something much worse than broken pots. Slowly the Miller drew in a large breath, raised his head, his gaze meeting Michael's before answering.

"It is young Meg, Tanner's girl, she is missing. No–one has seen her since this morning and she has never strayed in her life. We need to raise a search for her and anyone else that might be up to no good. There is talk, well, some of us think, maybe it is the monk."

Michael immediately thought of Aelfric and for a second was afraid that these men were here to siege the house and take Aelfric away for questioning. The monk may be guilty of something but Michael did not think he was capable of this, nor had he had the opportunity, as far as Michael knew.

The Miller saw the concern in Michael's face and mistook it for confusion.

"You remember? The monk from the church, three weeks ago? He has not been seen since." His voice became quiet then. "Not like the others. People are saying maybe it is him raiding homes and killing folk, that maybe he has gone mad. Keeper says those other two are still denying all but the fires and he is starting to believe them. Reckon the monk is the most obvious one, probably hiding out in the woods."

Michael thought this unlikely but was relieved that he would not have to defend the house from these men today.

"Let me get John and we will come with you Miller."

Michael turned to Arthur, who was standing quietly behind him still.

"Do not worry Michael, I will look after things here."

It was not long before Michael and John were mounted on their horses and riding out with the other villagers. Michael was baffled. Even he had been tempted by the idea that Preece and his men were responsible for everything that had happened. It was a wish that had quite probably been fuelled by the hope of peaceful times to come with them in custody. He suspected that the monk the Miller had spoken of was probably lying in a shallow grave, like the others they had found, just somewhere they had not searched yet. His heart sank as he thought of the girl. Everyone knew Meg. She was a friendly vibrant girl that anyone who met her was instantly fond of. Michael was afraid that he was riding out tonight to recover a body though he fervently hoped that there would be another reason for her disappearance. Perhaps a village boy had tempted her away, she might return at any moment, or maybe she had ….. but Michael was unable to think of a positive ending for that possibility. Feeling sick to his stomach he admitted to himself that his first fear was the most likely.

The night was cold and clear, with a bright moon high in the sky providing some natural light for the men to see by. As he rode Michael could see his horse's breath puffing out in a cloud around its head as it snorted in the chilled air. He could feel the cold biting at his skin and thought again how unlikely it was that the monk would be hiding out in the woods at this time of the year. True, monks tended to live mean and spartan lives but he had yet to meet one that was built for the elements. In Michael's opinion they spent so much of their lives closeted away studying and praying that they became weaker, less hardy than the normal folk that surrounded him now.

The sound of voices calling out for Meg became fainter, more distant as the group spread out for the search and as Michael and John headed into the woods. The moon could barely penetrate the branches here, even though most of the leaves had now fallen. Michael and John found it increasingly difficult to see and relied on the tiny circle of light afforded by their torches. They rode in silence, sometimes catching a brief glimpse of the glow of an animal's eyes as it stared at them, before it darted deeper into the wood, startled by these strangers.

After several hours of fruitless search Michael and John rode back to the village. They went straight to Tanner's home to see if Meg had returned or been found. Tanner's wife was there. As soon as she heard the men outside she hurried out, her anxious face full of hope and fear. Hope that the nightmare might be over and fear that the news would be the worst. Michael did not bother asking how the search had gone elsewhere; her face told him all he needed to know.

People were starting to return now, stiff and numb from the cold, tired after a long day and unsure whether to be relieved that no-one had found a body or worried that she was still missing. Mostly people seemed to be clinging to the hope that she would return on her own shortly and that the absence of any evidence to the contrary was good news. Naturally these sentiments did nothing to comfort Tanner or his wife and Michael suspected that they would not be sleeping much for the foreseeable future.

Michael and John began their ride home.

"John, what is your view of our house guest?"

"You mean Aelfric? I am not sure, I have hardly spent any time with him, you would need to speak to the Lady about that, they seem inseparable."

"Exactly, does it not seem odd to you? One minute he is a complete stranger, the next he is part of the family. And why is he staying so long?" Michael paused, trying to answer his own questions, then continued.

"What do you think they do in all those hours they are shut away together?"

John took in a heavy breath before answering. "I do not know, Rachel says they talk a great deal, although she has never caught any of what they say, they keep pretty quiet. She did mention there was an odd smell in the solar the other day, thought someone had been cooking something over the fire. I cannot imagine why though." John fell silent. He did not seem concerned about Aelfric or about the changes in Catherine. This comforted Michael a little. Perhaps he was too used to looking for trouble. He was seeing it where it did not exist now.

They made the rest of their short trip home in silence, both men looking forward to being near the great fire.

Arthur greeted them at the gate.

"Any news?" he asked.

"No, nobody found any sign of her. At the moment we have to assume that is good news."

"And what of the monk?"

"No sign of him either, although most people seem to be assuming he has been involved in these troubles of late. Tanner seems to think he knew Meg, that they got on quite well. Even the Keeper is suggesting that the two of them may have run off together. I suppose it is possible that the monk has been robbing homes to collect everything they might need and now they have enough she has followed him. But I do not believe it. If it is true, why the killing? Even if he got caught stealing, it does not make sense. You know Meg, she would never be involved with someone capable of killing. There has to be something else, something we are not seeing."

Michael and John handed the horses to Robert and went inside to warm up.

It was well past midnight by the time the three men were back beside the fire in the hall. Catherine and Aelfric had gone to bed a little while before, having waited up until they were both dozing where they sat. Unable to settle themselves, the three men sat talking quietly, trying to find a link or a pattern in these crimes, trying to make sense of the apparent chaos that surrounded them. Eventually they too were overcome with tiredness and went to their beds.

Chapter 21

After the cloudless night, the following day dawned early and brightly. Birds sang, animals foraged and the first people started to emerge to begin their day.

The Keeper awoke with the birds. He was not usually such an early riser but this place had changed him. He was kept busy constantly, never quite completing one investigation before he had to begin another. It was as if the hundred were cursed, even though he did not strictly believe in such things, but it was beginning to look like the best explanation. This morning he was awake early, unable to silence his thoughts. He felt entirely pre-occupied with sights, sounds, words and feelings, all the evidence he had collected since he had arrived here. Mostly he was able to maintain some clarity but when his guard was down, like now and late at night, his thoughts became jumbled and confused.

Ralph had spent the previous day questioning his latest prisoner. In all that time he had only managed to ascertain some very basic facts whilst developing a strong dislike and a stronger distrust of Matthew Preece. The only thing he could say for sure, the only thing Preece had admitted to, was that the other two men did work for him. Preece had denied all knowledge of their actions and angrily refuted having ordered fires. Ralph did not believe a word the man said but unfortunately that would not be enough to convince the magistrate and so until he had more evidence he would have to release Preece, allow him to return home. It did not sit well with the Keeper but he had no choice, his best hope now was in letting the man go.

In the Keeper's experience people like Preece were reasonably predictable. Of course he may be wrong but he suspected that on being released Preece would believe he had beaten the Keeper, that he had won a battle of wits. He would get cocky and would more than likely pick up where he had left off with whatever his plan was. Give the man enough rope and he would hang himself.

Ralph had spoken to enough of the locals to know what Preece was up to and if this was the case then Preece had not yet accomplished his goal and would keep trying to persuade Lady Catherine that she wanted to marry him. Now Ralph could see clearly why she kept soldiers at the house, the only wonder, having met Preece, was why she did not have more.

Despite the potential benefits of his plan it was still something that left a bad taste in his mouth and he resolved to get it over with as soon as possible. So, before he had even had his morning meal Ralph fetched the Reeve and together they went to where Preece was being held.

Preece grunted as he awoke at the sound of the two men approaching. He was bleary eyed and puffy from sleep as he looked up at the Keeper standing before him.

"More questions Keeper? You are persistent, I will give you that." He spat the words at Ralph, who ignored him, turning to the Reeve.

"Let him go, I do not have any more questions for him at the moment. I will let you know if that changes." He turned then and started walking away, trying to ignore the voice that followed him out.

"So, that is it? No apology? You keep me locked up like an animal with no evidence, question me until I am exhausted and now you are letting me go, just like that. What is it Keeper cannot admit that you are wrong?"

Ralph kept walking, grinding his teeth to keep himself from turning around and telling Preece exactly what he thought of him and his guilt. But he knew that would not help, he needed

Preece in exactly the mood he was in if this was going to work. Soon enough he was out of earshot of Preece and he started to calm down. A pot of ale would help, then he could think about eating in a civilised manner.

Preece made his way straight home as quickly as his stiff and sore body could carry him. He dreaded to think what awaited him there, had his servants looted his property? Did he still have servants? The thought of what he might find there quickly eroded his triumphant mood, leaving him achy and extremely irritable as he arrived at the house.

To his annoyance nobody was waiting at the door for him, he had to open it himself. Similarly there was no manservant there to meet him as he entered the house. Sigar should have been here by now. Perhaps he was already fetching food and ale in anticipation of his master's needs. Preece doubted that, although Sigar was about as good a servant as he could hope for.

"Sigar! Get here man, I need ale and food." Preece bellowed across the hall. Still there was no answer and Preece's anger flared still further.

The house remained silent as he made his way to his bedchamber to change his rumpled clothes. He was beginning to think he really was alone in the house and this muted his anger, replacing it with a hint of worry. How would he cope without people to do things for him? As he made his way through the house he noted with a spark of satisfaction that his belongings appeared to be in their place, so he had not been robbed then.

In fresher clothes now he made his way back to his hall, increasingly disturbed by the silence of the house. The hall was still empty but this time Preece noticed the fire burning in the grate, confirming that someone had been here, recently at least. Moving nearer he noticed that a pot of ale and some bread and meats had appeared on the table since he had arrived. Someone was definitely here, and they had heard him calling out earlier. His relief was great as he settled into a chair and began eating.

Some time later he finally finished his meal and pushed his plate away. Not long after that he drained his pot dry and belched loudly. He still felt thirsty though and could not understand why Sigar had not yet been in to check on him.

"Sigar," he bellowed again, "Sigar, more ale. Where are you man?"

Preece turned back to the fire warming his toes slowly, glad to be home, which reminded him how angry he was with the Keeper. Holding him with no proof, the gall of the man, did he not realise how important Matthew Preece was?

It was a few seconds before Preece registered that there had been no answer to his calls and he could not hear footsteps running to his hall. Incensed at the dereliction of duty he was witnessing, Preece flung his flagon at the wall where it smashed and fell to the ground in a hundred pieces, littering the floor with sharp shards and leaving a damp mark where it had struck. Still there was no sound. Preece heaved himself out of his seat and lumbered towards the door. He would not stand for this, he would find the man and beat him.

As he reached the hallway he roared again.

"Sigar! Get here you insolent son of a whore."

Just before he reached the kitchen Preece was faced with a woman he did not recognise. He stopped in his tracks and glared at her. She was very pale and visibly trembled in fear before her irate master. Standing in front of her and trying to hide in her skirts was a small boy with a dirty face. Gently the woman reached down and took the child by the shoulders, and then she shoved him forwards towards Preece, at the same time taking a defensive step backwards. The boy started to cry and turned to his mother. She gestured at him to turn back, a look of urgency on her face.

"What on earth is going on here" bellowed Preece. He was not fond of children at the best of times but this one was getting in his way. The boy finally opened his mouth and spoke. It was a small, timid voice.

"Please, sir, Sigar's gone, we have not seen him since last night, he is missing, sir."

Having relayed his message the boy turned and fled back into the kitchen, nearly knocking down his mother on the way. She was holding a flagon of mead out towards Preece, at arm's length, as if she thought he were a wild animal and might bite her hand off if she got too close.

Only slightly appeased by this gesture Preece snatched the flagon from the woman and growled at her.

"Find him and send him to me."

Then he turned and lumbered back to his hall to drink his mead. He was having an awful day, and now his manservant, the selfish little worm, was gone too. It had taken Preece years to train the man to do things just the way he liked and he did not relish the idea of having to start again with someone new. It just was not what he needed to be doing at his time of life.

It was almost midday when the latch on the kitchen door lifted and the door swung open. The small boy seemed to have recovered from his ordeal and was engrossed in herding a small black beetle around in front of the hearth. His mother stood close by, stirring a steaming pot of stew that hung over the fire, nearby a loaf of bread lay browning on a stone. Despite the cold wind outside it was sweltering in the kitchen, with the fire and the steaming pot and as she stirred she lifted an arm to her forehead to wipe away the drops of sweat that had formed there. Her face glowed pink in the heat and her feet ached but she would not be able to rest until the midday meal was over.

She heard the door opening, as it scraped over the hard stone floor and turned to see who had entered.

"Sigar!" she exclaimed, "where have you been? The Master has been going crazy calling for you. You will be lucky if he does not flog you."

Sigar did not respond immediately but stood still in the doorway, gingerly rubbing the back of his head and staring at his feet.

"Sigar, what is wrong? Come in and sit down." She bustled over to him, a look of concern filling her kind face. Closing the door behind him she took his arm and guided him to a chair by the fire, shooing away her son, who was not at all pleased at having to let the beetle go. Once she had seen Sigar settled in the chair she crouched before him, looking up into his face.

"Sigar you look awful, what happened?"

He looked up at her and spoke, slowly and deliberately.

"I am not really sure, I think I was hit on the head and I fell but I do not remember anything after. Everything is so, so, vague."

"Did you see who hit you?" she asked, concerned at his answer. Until now she had been trying to convince herself that he had been drunk and fallen asleep somewhere. This was very different though. Sigar liked his ale but he was a gentle, patient man, putting up with all kinds of abuse from their Master. He just was not the type to get into a fight. She was hugely relieved that he had returned, too many had disappeared under suspicious circumstances recently.

"No," he mumbled, "I do not remember seeing anyone, I do not remember much at all. I remember that I work here, the Master, who could forget him! I do remember you, but I have not got your name in my head and I do not know that I could find my way home." With that his head drooped and he ran both hands through his greasy, unkempt hair.

The woman's mouth had dropped open at this news. She had seen men fight before and take hard blows to the head, and they had been disconcerted for a while but this was far worse.

"I am Margaret, remember? And this is little Tom."

She was interrupted by a roar from the hall, a sound she both knew and dreaded.

"Master has run out of mead again. You must take him more Sigar, and be quick about it; he is already after your hide for being so late." As she spoke she hurried into the buttery and fetched a flagon of mead, then returning to the fireplace she held it out to Sigar. "Here you go, go, hurry."

Sigar looked gratefully up at her and rising from his seat he took the mead from her hand.

"Thank you Margaret." He smiled weakly and moved towards the door and onward toward the hall, watched all the way by a frowning Margaret.

Preece was building himself up into a thunderous temper by the time Sigar entered the room armed with the flagon of mead.

Sigar put his head around the door and felt rather than heard the ale pot whistle past his ear before smashing against the wall. He stopped to look at the fragments on the floor beside him before looking back up into the room and at his master. Sigar raised an eyebrow as he appraised the irate man before him with something like mild amusement. Having paused for only a few seconds Sigar continued into the room and placed the flagon on the table next to Preece.

"Is there anything else I can get for you, master?"

Preece looked up at his manservant. Sigar seemed different to him today, less jumpy perhaps, more confident? Preece could not put his finger on quite what it was. Only briefly distracted from his rage Preece now wanted to know why Sigar had kept him waiting for so long.

"I have been calling you, why did you not come immediately?" His tone was milder than his mood called for, softened by a substantial dose of suspicion and curiosity. "Well? Answer me man!"

"I was attacked; someone knocked me out last night. I woke up in a hedge a little while ago and my memory is still a coming back to me, Sir."

Preece considered this information for a minute or two and satisfied that Sigar had not been up to anything Preece would want to know about and that the man would soon return to his normal cowering self, he demanded his midday meal and sent Sigar from the room.

Sigar left quietly, closing the door softy behind him. He looked towards the kitchen and then turned towards the back of the house. Once he had reached the rear rooms he paused, looking quickly around him and entered Preece's bedchamber. There was a chest in the far corner and Sigar went directly to it. He opened the lid, felt below the blankets and withdrew his hand before closing the lid again. Crouching beside the chest he looked around the room again before hurrying towards a plain wooden box that rested on the floor beside the bed. It was small enough that Sigar could just hold it in one hand. The lid fitted tightly and Sigar had to work at it for a few seconds before it came loose. Breathing deeply now Sigar put the lid to one side and looked into the box. Inside he saw the glint of metal as a glimmer of light caught at the jewellery inside. The room was dark and gloomy and Sigar carried the box to the window to inspect the contents more closely. As he pulled back the tapestry that covered the window he could see that there were several pieces of jewellery in the box and he began to lift them out, peering at each of them closely.

Sigar's face was a study in focus and concentration, so intent was he on the task in hand. The first piece was a fine bronze ladies circlet that had been skilfully shaped and decorated. He held it up to the light, turning it around and around before tossing it onto the bed and taking out the next item. This was a bracelet, also wrought of bronze and inlaid with stones. Again Sigar held the piece up to the light and examined it closely before throwing it aside as he had the circlet before it.

As he reached into the box once more a sound brought his head up and he froze, holding his breath, waiting for the next sound. A few seconds later his patience was rewarded. It was the sound of straw rustling, the sound of someone in the corridor. Someone was coming. Stealthily, with barely a sound, Sigar allowed the tapestry to fall back into place and moved to the bed, quickly placing the circlet and bracelet back into the box with the other pieces as he moved around the bed to the box lid. A further rustling sound told him that whoever it was out there was now a step or two closer and still coming. He had just put the box back in its place when a face appeared around the door.

Composing himself Sigar turned slowly and rose to his feet. As he saw the face he appeared to be startled.

"Tom, what are you doing creeping around the house? You made me jump." As he said the words he smiled at the boy, although it looked a little strained.

"Mama sent me, the midday meal is ready and I am hiding from master. He has been so angry today; I do not want to get another hiding."

Tom glanced around the room, his eyes wide, his face alert as if he were expecting Preece to appear at any second and catch him around the head with a fist. With his message delivered successfully Tom turned and skipped down the corridor, apparently no longer concerned with creeping about the house.

Sigar looked back at the box for a second or two, as if considering resuming his inspection and then stepped towards the door and down the corridor to the front of the house.

In the kitchen Margaret was looking very red faced and harassed. The weather outside had turned cold but inside the fire blasted out heat and working so close to it made her very hot. It was Preece that made her flustered. He was worse than normal today and she had no wish to risk his wrath by having the meal ready late. On a table Sigar could see plates of meat, cheese, bread and butter together with a large jug of ale and a steaming bowl of stew. Margaret suddenly stopped her bustling and stared at him.

"Sigar, what are you doing? Do not just stand there, get these plates into the master, before he has all our hides."

Sigar seemed to hesitate.

"Now, Sigar!" Margaret snapped at him and he seemed to come to his senses. He moved across the room and collected several pieces before heading for the hall to serve the food. As he left the room Margaret looked across at Tom.

"Poor man, if he does not snap out of this soon Preece will do for him." She handed a tray of bread to the boy. "Here, take this through for him." Tom looked terrified by his mother's request and she took pity on him. "You can wait at the door, you do not have to go in."

Tom looked hugely relieved and trotted off towards the hall with the bread. Margaret collected the remaining plates and followed him.

Preece had been sitting in the hall alone with his thoughts trying to make sense of things and find a way forward, but he was no clearer than when he had started. He had been so sure that his plan had been foolproof, that he would have a wife by now. Instead, not only did he not have a wife, he had lost two paid soldiers, spent a night in the small gaol and would be lucky not to have to face the magistrate. His only comfort was that the soldiers had not identified him as being behind the fires. Yet. Preece had no confidence that this loyalty would last, especially when the two faced the magistrate, charged with a long list of crimes that Preece suspected they were not entirely responsible for.

He heard Sigar enter the room, heard him place plates on the table but continued to stare into the fire, engrossed in his own thoughts. With a great sigh he forced himself to accept that he would have to put his plans for Catherine on hold for a short while. The Keeper would be watching him closely for a time, hoping to catch him out and besides, Preece no longer had any men to help him. Two were in the gaol still and the others appeared to have left while he had been there himself. At least they had not robbed him blind before they had gone.

Preece turned towards the table as Sigar finished laying down the plates and knives and was turning to leave.

"Where do you think you are going? Get back in here and serve me." Preece shuffled to the table and seated himself in his usual chair, waiting for Sigar to bring food to him.

For the rest of the day Preece barked out orders and kept Sigar busy fetching and carrying, stoking the fire, bringing in more wood and keeping his ale pot full. The more Sigar fidgeted and seemed to want to be gone, the more pleasure Preece derived from finding more jobs for him to do. In this way Preece managed to while away a reasonably happy afternoon, until the evening meal arrived and the cycle began again. By the middle of the evening Preece had drunk so much ale and mead that his lack of sleep from the night before caught up with him and enveloped him in a haze of exhaustion. With a long and noisy yawn he announced he was going to bed and shuffled slowly away to his bedchamber.

Slumping in a chair near the fire he had stoked many times that day, Sigar sighed and muttered quietly to himself.

"Finally, some peace." It had been a long, hard day and there had been no other opportunity to get back upstairs for Sigar. "Try again tomorrow." He muttered, his eyes closed, enjoying the warmth of the fire on his body.

"Try what again tomorrow?" Margaret was standing near the door and Sigar jumped at the unexpected company.

"Oh, to remember what happened to me, it still has not all come back." He smiled at Margaret and she smiled back at him.

"I am surprised the master has gone up to bed so early, he normally sleeps by the fire for a good while first. I would love to know where he spent last night, I have not known him spend a night away before, would probably explain the temper this morning." Margaret stopped and looked back at Sigar. "Will you be all right? Getting home I mean?"

Sigar seemed a little surprised by the question but smiled at her.

"Oh, do not worry about me, I know what I am doing. I am just going to sit here for a while first." He closed his eyes and rested his head on the chair back.

Margaret closed the door softly behind her as she left.

Still with eyes closed Sigar stretched his stiff and aching limbs and shivered a little. He opened his eyes slowly. The hall was gloomy but there was enough light creeping in for Sigar to determine that the fire had gone out and that morning had arrived. Realising he had fallen asleep by the fire Sigar put his hands up and rubbed his face vigorously. He had woken by himself so Preece was clearly still asleep, that was something at least. For now the first order of the day was heat and food so he set about re-laying the fire in the hall. Once that was done he made his way to the kitchen to find food.

When Sigar returned to the hall the fire was burning strongly in the grate and warmth was starting to infuse the room. He stopped by the door, hands on hips and surveyed the place. There was the table and several chairs arranged around it with some by the fire. There was also a bench against the wall. He moved to the table first and bending down he checked the underside, then he tipped over each of the chairs in turn looking them over carefully before putting them back in their place. The bench was also thoroughly investigated in a like manner. Sitting on the bench Sigar appraised the room once more. He could see no recesses in the walls, no loose flags on the floor. Just to make sure he lifted all the rugs and was relaying the last one when he spotted the seat under the window. It had been built as a bench seat where one could sit in the summer and look out of the small windows. It was also a roomy chest when the cushion was removed and the top lifted away.

Sigar went to the bench, removed the covering and lifted the lid. It appeared that this was where many of the tapestries that now covered the windows were kept when the weather allowed. A small, well worn tapestry remained, folded in the corner. Sigar moved to close the lid when something caught his eye. Barely showing under the edge of the tapestry was a small wooden box. Sigar grabbed at it, lifting it out of the chest. He took a deep breath and licked his lips as if in anticipation before opening the box. Inside was quite a collection of coins. It appeared that Matthew Preece liked to keep his wealth hidden in small boxes. It seemed sensible, after all, if he was robbed the chances of the thieves finding all his money and jewels was significantly reduced and in these increasingly lawless times, when even nobility were fighting each other tooth and nail, robbery was an ever increasing risk.

Sigar let out his breath in a long stream and bent to replace the box. He paused half way, his face thoughtful, and then emptied the money into his own, purse before replacing the box under the tapestry and closing the bench lid.

Turning back to face the room once more he glanced around again. Apparently satisfied that there was nowhere left to search, Sigar made his way towards the door. From above him there was a hoarse bellow that rang around the house, announcing the rising of Matthew Preece. Sigar looked up, wincing slightly at the implications and continued out of the room. Margaret had arrived by this time and was nearly finished putting together the breakfast food.

"Morning Sigar" she said brightly as he entered the kitchen, "I hear master is up." Margaret gave Sigar a sympathetic look as she said it.

Sigar nodded silently, helped himself to a piece of bread and sat down by the fire. Margaret stopped what she was doing and stared at him for a moment.

"Sigar, is everything alright?"

Sigar looked up at her, "of course" he said, remaining in his chair. Seeing that he was making no sign of moving from his seat Margaret tried again.

"Master is up, do you not think you had better hurry? I would rather he was not in that temper again, if you do not mind."

"Sorry Margaret, I suppose I am still trying to remember everything. Where should I hurry?" Sigar looked so lost again and Margaret felt really sorry for him.

"To the master's room, to dress him. I would do it but we both know he will not let anyone but you near him. Seems for all his bluster you are the only one who does things right."

"Right, of course, thank you, ah, Margaret." With that Sigar rose and left the room. Margaret worried about him. He barely recalled her name just now and they had been friends for years, he was certainly not himself. Having to learn everything again would be hard enough but learning it to Preece's standards and with him constantly shouting must be awful. She went then to set out the food in the hall for Sigar.

With Preece dressed and settled in the hall feeding his hunger, Sigar had a chance to go back to Preece's bedchamber and continue his search. This time he went directly to the small box by the bed and emptied the contents out onto the blankets. He put the circlet and bracelet back in the box and went to examining the other pieces. There were a few pendants of various metals and a couple of rings but nothing that seemed to take Sigar's fancy, certainly not worth pocketing. They all went back into the box. He lifted the palliase and found nothing underneath, checked under a stool and checked the floor for loose stones that might afford a potential hiding place for treasures. Apparently frustrated in his search Sigar left the room.

"I do not have time for this" he hissed as he made his way to the food store. Inside he began searching the pots and barrels. After a while he found a jar that held not food but a purse full of coins. These he returned to the pot and continued with his search. As his frustration grew he became more careless and before too long one of the pots toppled from the shelf and crashed to the floor. A layer of straw there muffled the sound but it seemed to bring him to his senses and he stopped to hide the mess before completing his search in relative silence. He left this room empty handed too.

Chapter 22

The midday meal was almost over and Michael was determined to put his plan into action. Catherine and Aelfric had been shut away all that morning in her solar. From time to time Michael had gone to the door, half hoping to hear something that would confirm his suspicions of Aelfric. He was looking for something that would give him a perfect excuse to charge in, bring Catherine to her senses and eject Aelfric from the house, thus bringing life back to normal. Michael missed things the way they had been, when Catherine had been a normal, sociable woman who had relied on him. On his third trip to the door he realised that his problem with Aelfric may be nothing more sinister than that. He was simply jealous. Michael had got used to Catherine relying on him, coming to him for strength and protection. Now Aelfric was here and suddenly Catherine did not need him anymore. She had her own strength and if the other day was anything to go by she no longer needed his protection.

Now as they were all eating together Michael was prepared to admit that this may be true, but he had to be sure. There were a lot of bad people out there who would think nothing of taking advantage of Catherine, Preece being a prime example. Michael had to be sure of Aelfric's motives before he could let this go. So, as the meal was drawing to an end Michael took the opportunity and spoke up.

"My Lady, it is a fine day. With Preece no longer a threat and the two men responsible for these crimes in custody I wondered if you wanted to ride out this afternoon. I would be happy to ride with you. You have been in the house for so long now. Would you like Robert to ready your horse?"

He had sounded light and casual but inside he was tense, waiting for her response, expecting her to turn him down in favour of time spent with Aelfric. As he had expected her first response was to look to Aelfric, as if for approval and that stirred his anger. But, to his great surprise Aelfric had smiled at her and nodded without hesitation.

"You should go, my child. It would do you good to get out, Michael is quite right and of course, he knows best when it comes to your safety."

Catherine smiled broadly at Michael.

"I would love to, thank you Michael. Do you really think it is finally safe? It has been hard being stuck inside day after day."

"Yes," Michael replied, "it will be safe. I will ask Robert to ready the horses now but you will need your cloak, it is fine but still very cold."

Within half an hour the two of them were riding out through the gates. Catherine breathed in deeply and lifted her face to the bright, clear blue sky.

"Thank you Michael. It feels so good to be outside again, it makes me feel almost free again. I have been feeling so trapped lately."

Michael took his chance.

"You have been shut away for a long time. I assume Aelfric is good company? You have spent many hours together since he arrived." He looked directly at her, hoping to discover as much as he could from her answers and her reactions. She responded quickly and clearly, no hint of hesitation or any attempt to hide anything.

"He is Michael, it is almost like having another father. I miss my father very much and Aelfric fills a small part of that gap for me. He is very wise and he knows so much, so many different things. He has helped me come to terms with my loss and to see that there is so much more worth living for."

Her answer seemed genuine and although not what Michael was expecting it was encouraging.

"It must be a great comfort to have someone like that at a time like this." Michael was immediately aware of how churlish his comment had sounded, as if he felt put out by her preference of Aelfric. Whilst that might be true to a degree he did not want their conversation to be diverted by it.

"Oh yes. You and Arthur have been so busy lately, I would have been very lost otherwise, I think."

For a few minutes neither said anything but then Catherine spoke again.

"You cannot know what it means to me to have someone be so protective of me Michael, thank you. You do not need to be concerned about Aelfric though. He is open and very honest, he has never said or done anything improper. I trust him. He has given me such confidence and encouraged me to learn more of life. For all that I am indebted to him."

Michael was a little stung by her perception. He believed he had concealed his lack of trust in Aelfric well. Any further probing on this subject was out of the question now, her gentle rebuke had made her feelings clear.

"Very well, my Lady. While you trust him so do I, just promise me that if ever that changes you will tell me immediately?"

"I promise Michael." She looked across at Michael, her expression warm and friendly again. "Race you to the trees." Urging her horse forward she savoured the sensation of the wind whipping her hair around her face and shoulders. She felt the power of her horse, the solidness of its hooves pounding on the ground. She saw flecks of grass and clots of earth being thrown up as the horse sped towards the trees. She heard the air whistle by, heard the heavy breaths and snorts of the animal as it worked. For only the second time in her life Catherine felt fully awake and alive, felt her worries fading, scoured away by the wind.

Michael and Catherine reached the edge of the woods at the same time and slowed their horses to a walk among the trees. The ground seemed softer here. Under the cover of the trees it was damp and mossy, muffling the sound of the horses. Birds chirruped in the trees above them, deer foraged deeper in the trees and Catherine was very much aware of how much had changed here and that life had been carrying on without her. She realised how isolated she had felt lately.

As they rode further into the wood the ground became less even, scattered rocks, exposed tree roots and fallen branches all required the horses to slow down and take greater care with their footing. Still, occasionally one of the horses stumbled slightly as they made their way.

"Perhaps we should go back towards the edge of the woods, where the ground is more even." Michael suggested. Catherine nodded her agreement and they turned their horse's heads to cut across the woods and emerge at a point further down the tree line.

Catherine looked ahead but could still see only trees, and then her eye was caught by a flash of blue from above. She looked up at the fleck of sky that was briefly visible through the canopy as the breeze caught it. Suddenly she realised that the lilting motion of the horse had changed and she was being pitched forward as her horse caught its foot and stumbled over a large root. With a thump she landed on her backside, in front of her horse. Falling backwards from there and bumping her head slightly· Catherine felt as it all the air had been knocked from her lungs and was aware of some pain where she had landed heavily.

Opening her eyes slowly she groaned, not quite sure what had just happened she lay still and looked around. Her horse was nuzzling at the ground very close to her ear, so close that Catherine could reach out and touch her nose. On the other side Michael crouched beside her.

"Are you all right?" he asked, just barely hiding a smirk.

"Oh, very funny Michael, I could have been killed you know." She put her arm out for him to help her up and he took it, carefully pulling to ease her up to a sitting position.

"I do not think you were in too much danger. The ground is soft here." He pushed the earth next to her to demonstrate his point.

"Actually, it is very soft, much more than I would expect for this time of year."

As Catherine sat up straight Michael was able to see much more of the area where she had fallen.

"It looks like it has been disturbed recently," he continued, "here, let me help you up." Michael stood and helped Catherine to her feet. She stood aside brushing earth and twigs from her clothes as Michael looked closer.

"There is something here." Michael seemed almost to be talking to himself now as he bent to his knees again and gently brushed at spot on the ground.

"What is it Michael?" Having finished cleaning the dirt from her skirt, Catherine leaned over Michael's shoulder to see what he had found. "Is that fur?"

As Michael brushed at the earth it became clear that it was not fur they had found. A few seconds later Catherine was able to make out what remained of an ear, a human ear. She was too stunned even to gasp in shock and Michael immediately stopped brushing at the dirt. He stood then and guided Catherine to her horse.

"One of us has to get the Keeper. I will stay if you are happy to ride to him. I am sure you will be safe but ride quickly. Go to the Reeve, he will know where to find him. Let me help you up."

Michael kept his tone calm and even and took care not to let her have time to think about what she was doing.

Once she was mounted he spoke again. "Hurry, it will be dark soon and it will be much harder to find your way back." With that he patted the horse on its flank and sent her on her way.

Catherine rode as quickly as she could, managing to dodge most of the low twigs and branches until she was out in the open. Michael was right; although it was fine and clear the light was starting to fade now. Once in the open she urged her horse on and rode quickly to the Reeve. Ralph and his men were with him and within an hour they were all with Michael and gathered around the body. Between the five men they soon managed to uncover the rest of the body. Ralph knelt beside it.

"Well, he is not stiff anymore and he is swollen and bloated. I would say he has been here several days. It looks like this ear has been chewed by an animal but these fingers were removed cleanly. See how sharp that cut is?"

Michael looked at the body. He had seen dead bodies before but never stopped to look at them this closely. The skin was very pale with a slight purple tinge to it and the veins were very well defined in death where they would normally be invisible in life. The eyes were frozen open and bloodshot, the pupils were cloudy and there were strange small dark spots around the face. Looking lower Michael could see an ugly red mark around the neck. It looked almost raw with ragged edges; this man had been strangled to death. Along the man's side Michael could see several large dark patches.

"Keeper, what are these?" asked Michael.

"I have seen these before. It would be my guess that this man was not killed here. He was moved to this spot. These patches, I believe, indicate how the body was lying when he died, he would have been lying on his side. You see here? The shoulder, upper arm, ribs, hip and thigh are all much darker than the rest of the body. Also, I would expect to find blood around the cut hand. There is none." Ralph sighed, this was an unpleasant job at any time but he was glad of the cold weather today. "Does anyone recognise him?"

Michael spoke, "Yes, he was a servant of Matthew Preece. His name is Sigar."

"Are you sure? His appearance is altered and he is not wearing any identifying clothes." Ralph wanted to be completely sure before he went to Preece with the news. It was a visit Ralph did not want to make, unless of course Preece was guilty of the man's murder, and by implication the others too. It would be extremely satisfying to be able to lock Preece up, solve the crimes and go home. He thought for a minute or two. All the victims that had been found all seemed to have died the same way, a thin, rough cord pulled tight around the throat. Each of the victims then had two fingers removed, probably before death. Ralph was not sure he ever wanted to know why.

"Right, let us go. Reeve, fetch the men and send a couple of them here to bring the body back to the village. Bring the rest with you and meet me outside Preece's house."

He rose to his feet as the Reeve hurried away.

"Lady Catherine, how are you? It would appear that you are not having much luck lately."

"Thank you Keeper, but I am all right. I will admit that it was shocking at first but regrettably this is not the first death in these parts and it will not be the last, what with taxes, wet summers and hard winters. These have been hard times for us all. May I go home now?"

"Of course my Lady. We will ride with you and then pay a visit to your neighbour. I would like to borrow Michael and Arthur if I may? I am aware that Preece had paid soldiers of his own but I do not know if any of them are still there. I do not expect any trouble but I would like to be prepared, just in case."

"Certainly Keeper, especially if it helps to stop all this trouble and allows the village to return to some kind of normality." With a shiver Catherine allowed Michael to help her back onto her horse and together they rode back to the manor.

Once Michael was sure Catherine was safely in the grounds with Robert and John he collected Arthur and the men rode on to meet the Reeve. He was waiting for them outside Preece's house with a number of villagers, all armed with various tools and implements. Ralph went to the door and pounded on it. After a short while of silence Ralph pounded again. From within he heard footsteps, moving towards the door accompanied by a bellow from the bowels of the house, which he took to be Preece.

Slowly the door swung open and there before them was a reasonably tall man. He had dark hair and a worn face, the face of a man who had suffered daily to survive. Michael drew in a sharp breath and Arthur muttered "dear God" under his breath. Ralph turned to look at them, concerned at their strange tone.

"What is it?" he asked, thrown a little by their expressions.

From behind the servant came a voice. "Who is it?" As the words reached the men at the door Preece came into view. "Well, Sigar? Who is it? I do not want visitors" said Preece.

Ralph's head spun back to the servant before him, his mouth open, his eyes widened, struggling to understand what was happening here. With a great effort he managed to speak.

"You are Sigar?" He turned back to Michael for an explanation, "But the body Michael, how can it be? Were you mistaken?"

Hearing these words the man before them gritted his teeth in frustration, reached into a small pouch on his belt and brought out a dark powdery substance, which he threw down between him and the Keeper with some force. Preece stepped closer to Sigar, trying to work out why half the village had appeared on his doorstep. He saw the Keeper looking confused, he saw Sigar thrown down a powder and then he would later swear that he had seen the flash of a flame dart from the end of Sigar's finger just before the powder sparked and caught fire, throwing everything into chaos. As soon as the flames leapt up between Sigar and the Keeper, Sigar had turned towards Preece and run right at him. Momentarily afraid for his life as the larger man had charged at him, Preece tried to stumble out of the way but was knocked from his feet as Sigar barged past and out through the kitchen.

Michael quickly realised that the man in the doorway was running and leapt through the flames to chase after him. Preece was still on the floor, dazed and stunned into silence as Michael rushed by, sliding a little on the loose straw covering the ground. As Michael came through the door into the kitchen he was aware of a woman huddling against the far wall, clutching a small child to her. She looked terrified but pointed towards the outside door as Michael ran through. He burst out through the door into the gardens and was just in time to see a foot disappearing over the wall. Michael ran to the wall and was joined by Arthur, who had come around the side of the house. They jumped at the wall and looked over the top but could see no sign of their quarry in any direction.

Thwarted they made their way back into the house. The smell of smoke had become very strong and Michael and Arthur could hear people beating at the flames around the door. Grabbing at a large pot by the fire Michael noted that it was almost full of water. He carried it to the front door and doused the main body of the growing fire while the others beat back the remaining flames. Once he was sure the fire was out he returned to the kitchen with the pot. Preece was still sprawled on the floor but Michael did not stop to help him. Back in the kitchen he approached the woman.

"Are you all right?" he asked, as calmly as he could in the circumstances.

She nodded, looking at the floor, tears sliding down her cheeks.

"Do you know where Sigar might have gone?"

Margaret raised her face and looked at Michael.

"Sir, I have known Sigar for years, we have been friends for most of them. He has not been right lately, acting odd. He was here with me when we heard the door and he did not look… well. Then he ran back through….." she paused, tears streaming, nose running and sniffed. "Those were his clothes, but that was not Sigar."

Michael was confused. "What do you mean? You said he was just here talking to you."

"I did, and he was, but when he ran back through here, he looked over at me and he was, he was different. It was a different man."

"You mean he was behaving differently than normal?" Michael asked.

"No," said Margaret, becoming increasingly upset, "I mean he was literally another man, bigger, darker, longer hair. It was another man in Sigar's clothes. I would swear to it."

Unable to make sense of what he had just seen and heard Michael made his way back to the front of the house. Once more he passed Preece and again he left him lying on the ground.

Chapter 23

Night had fallen and clouds had rolled in to obscure a large part of the moonlit sky. While the clouds afforded a little insulation against the bitter cold they also blotted out much of the available light, leaving the night as black as soot. Every now and then a small break in the clouds allowed a brief glimpse of a deep blue sky, studded with tiny specks of bright light. During these short interludes the moonlight managed to dart through the gap and illuminate a swathe of the landscape like a giant spotlight before the clouds closed in once more. Beneath the cover of the trees it was gloomier still, so dark in fact, that it was hard to see more than a few paces ahead.

Deep in the woods a fox emerged from its den, foraging for food. It crept forwards in short, timid bursts, stopping to sniff the air, ears pricked, listening for the sounds of approaching danger. Gradually it moved away from the warm, safe hole, sniffing at the ground, still occasionally raising its snout into the frosty air. Catching a tempting scent the fox trotted forward to investigate. Finding something good to eat the animal snatched it up into its jaws. As he chewed his head snapped up, ears forward, nose in the air. A muffled sound wafted through the undergrowth and the fox's ears flattened against its head, a further sound and the fox darted straight back to the safety of its den.

A few hundred paces from the den a large black horse stood sniffing the ground, hoping to find something, anything, to eat. A few paces further on from the horse a tiny white light emerged from the darkness, slowly growing in brightness. There was no visible hint of colour, no flicker of flames. The light was star bright and the purest white. Gradually the luminescence became bright enough that the horse was clearly visible and so too was the man holding the stone bowl that cradled the light.

Roland sat cross-legged on a blanket outside a small natural cave in the side of a small wooded hillock. His free hand gently roamed across his face.

"Well, Saracen, I have not found what I am looking for. It must be there somewhere." He slammed his fist into the ground as anger and frustration sparked within him.

Slowly Roland calmed himself and was able to think more clearly.

"It would appear that they have found the body. That is going to make searching the rest of the house much harder. They may not have worked out what is happening yet but they will certainly be suspicious of everyone now. Damn!! It has to be there Saracen. The man is hungry for power, even though he does not have a clue how to use meagre power he already has. Preece is arrogant enough, or desperate enough, to hunt for it, if he discovered its existence somehow. Clearly though, he has no idea how to use it, that at least is in my favour."

Saracen raised his head and looked directly at his master before snorting reproachfully and resuming his search for food.

"You are right, in our favour, I am sorry."

Roland was frustrated. He had been travelling for years in search of his prize. Recently he had been approached by one of the King's aides. It seemed the King had long ago learned of its existence from his father. Roland had seen an opportunity to forward his own agenda and had secured the financial support of the King in the process. Now he could afford to sleep on a bed and eat decent food, at least he could if he had not become so conspicuous in these parts. Of course he had no intention of handing it over to the King when he did find it. If the King was naïve enough to trust him, or stupid enough to think Roland would not or could not use it, then so much the better for Roland, in his opinion.

His plans had run into some snags though, meaning that his face was well known and generally unwelcome. He could live with that for now though, a little discomfort would not deter him when he was so close, and once it was his he would never have to be uncomfortable again. Things would change then. He had great plans and it was his dream for the future that kept him going. It was his desire to harness great power for himself that fuelled those dreams.

Back in control of his frustration, Roland carefully placed the stone bowl on a rock beside him and leaned towards the firewood stack in front of him. He extended his arm towards the small pile of wood, pointed at it and whispered "ignitio". As he finished the word a small orange spark flew from his index finger and ignited the kindling at the centre of the fire. Slowly at first the flame took hold but within minutes it was hungrily consuming the wood and reaching out to grasp each and every stick.

Saracen raised his head and gazed at his master, his ears flicking forward, his large intelligent eyes questioning.

"Yes, Saracen, I am tired and I need to rest. These searches have drained me more than I expected. The last one took far too long. I will eat now and then rest to regain my strength."

Under the watchful gaze of his companion Roland cooked some meat broth and ate that with some bread he had stolen, before settling back into the cave under a blanket and falling asleep.

The morning dawned with a sharp frost covering the ground, transforming everything it touched, making everything crisp and brittle, white and glistening in the sun. During the night the clouds had drifted away, allowing the temperature to plummet. The air was cold and seemed to bite wherever it touched, sounds were sharper, travelling further and clearer.

Catherine woke early and hurried down to her hall. Michael and Arthur had returned quite late the night before and Arthur had gone to his bed almost immediately. Although Michael had settled himself in the hall by the fire he had made it clear that he did not want to discuss their trip to see Matthew Preece. Despite her insistent probing he would give her no clue and eventually he asked Catherine to stop questioning him about it. After that he had been silent and withdrawn, staring into the heart of the fire but not really seeing it. His face wore a concerned frown, his eyes appeared troubled and deeply thoughtful.

Catherine was concerned by this behaviour. For her it meant that there was more trouble coming and he did not want to tell her for some reason. That or something awful had already happened and he was keeping from her. Either way it worried her that she did not know and could not prepare for what was coming. It did not occur to her that perhaps Michael was not telling her because he did not know, or did not understand what had happened.

Michael had spent a large part of the night trying to make sense of what he had seen and heard that day. He had discovered the body of a man he knew well, a body the Keeper had said had been in its grave for several days. Then he had come face to face with that same man when they had knocked on Preece's door. He could find no way of explaining how Sigar may have gone from the grave to the house before Michael had travelled that distance. Even if that was possible, Michael had seen the wounds, the bloated body, seen the discolouration of the skin. The man at the house had two complete ears and all his fingers, that man was a normal, healthy colour. The rest was even harder to make sense of. Sigar knew Michael, they had spoken many times, why run then? And Margaret, she had sworn that Sigar had been sitting with her for some time before he had arrived and then changed almost before her eyes into a stranger. This stranger had managed to outrun Michael and Arthur and apparently disappear. Although Michael was bothered greatly by all of this, the thing that bothered him the most, what kept him awake much of the night, was Margaret's description of the stranger.

It was morning now and Michael was back in the hall having slept only a few hours. Arthur was with him.

"Arthur, have you been able to make any sense of what you saw yesterday?"

Arthur sighed before looking up at his friend.

"You did not sleep either then? No, Michael, none of it makes any sense. The only explanation is that there were two different people, three if we are to believe Margaret. There is no way Sigar could have risen from that grave. I agree with you, that was definitely Sigar there. So that leaves us with a question. Who was that at the door? He was clearly the impostor, too tall to be Sigar. I have not been able to adequately explain how he looked so much like Sigar though, not unless we are willing to accept that witchcraft is not only real but being practiced. Here!"

Several minutes of silence passed while each man went over the events again.

"Arthur, do you think all these murders are linked? All connected to this one man? And why have we not found Meg yet?"

"I suppose it is possible, but we will not know until we find him, and we cannot do that until we know who he is."

Michael was about to speak when the door opened and Catherine entered.

"Good morning," she said brightly, moving to a chair at the table where the two men sat. She looked at each man expectantly, both men met her gaze briefly and then looked down at their hands. All three knew what her question was but neither man had an answer for her, at least not one that would make any sense, or even sound in any way reasonable.

"Is no-one going to tell me what happened yesterday after you brought me home?"

The silence that hung in the room was heavy with expectancy and anticipation, fraught with confusion and resistance. It was Arthur who spoke first.

"My Lady, if we had answers we would give them to you but," he glanced at Michael who was still studying his hands, "honestly, we do not know what happened ourselves."

The door opened then and Aelfric entered, followed by Rachel, laden with plates of food. Catherine had been denied answers, she felt frustrated both by not knowing what was going on and by her own inability to get information from either Arthur or Michael. Now that Aelfric and Rachel had joined them she felt unable to express her frustration and anxiety and had to bury them for the time being.

Aelfric greeted them all brightly and proceeded to discuss the weather with no-one in particular, hypothesising on what it might bring over the coming days. Catherine stared at him in disbelief, infuriated by his ability to make idle conversation. As she watched him she began to wonder if he even cared. He knew they had found Sigar's body the day before, he knew Arthur and Michael had gone with the Reeve to Preece's house. He knew because she had told him but he did not seem interested in what had happened next nor did he seem to notice how quiet Michael and Arthur were this morning.

With very little conversation around the table the meal was over quickly and Michael and Arthur excused themselves, closing the door behind them.

"Aaaarrgh!" blurted Catherine, unable to contain her frustration any longer. Aelfric looked up, surprised at her outburst. She was sitting at the table still, her arms lay across the table top and her head rested on them.

"Catherine what is wrong?" Asked Aelfric quietly, sensing her frustration more now than he had when he had entered the room earlier and it had been obvious then. After a short while she raised her head, her expression had something of defeat about it now.

"I know something happened last night but neither Arthur nor Michael will tell me what. They are both very distracted by it so it must have been bad but all they will say is that they would give me answers if they had any."

Aelfric considered what she had said and then responded.

"Perhaps that is the truth."

Catherine furrowed her brow in despair. "They were there, they must know what happened."

"True, but have you considered that perhaps they do not understand what happened?" Seeing that this answer did not placate her, Aelfric elaborated. "Michael and Arthur are both very logical men, not given to accepting on faith, they need solid answers that make sense. Maybe something happened yesterday that they do not yet understand, they know you will question them where they cannot answer so feel that they should wait until they do have answers. Or maybe they are simply upset. I understand they both knew the man who died."

"I suppose it is possible," Catherine conceded, "but I do not believe it. I am sure something bad is coming and they do not want to tell me."

"Is that something they have done before? Keep you in the dark to protect you?" Aelfric's voice was calm and even, trying to soothe her nerves. He needed to remove or at least reduce this distraction so that she could concentrate of her lessons.

Catherine thought about his question. All through the madness with Preece they had always told her where the danger was. Aelfric's explanation did seem to make sense. She let out a long and heavy sigh, expelling much of her nervous tension along with it.

"Very well, I will accept your theory as slightly more likely than my own." She smiled at him, a cheeky, girlish smile that told him she knew she had over–reacted and was feeling more balanced now. "What are we learning today?"

Aelfric chuckled at the irony. "Actually I had planned to teach you a charm today, to protect yourself, but I do not want to encourage your anxieties."

Catherine smiled. "It will not Aelfric, honestly, teach me."

They went straight to her solar and sat near the fire that Rachel had set there ready for them.

"You have the basics of potions now, and we can build on that with time but I want you to start learning more about spells. They are the incantations that use your own power and draw on the natural magic that is all around us to make something happen, to change something or to prevent something. For example, the spell we learned to thicken the air. You could use it to stop something from falling if you did not want it to break or you could protect yourself if you needed to."

"What do you mean by 'my own power'?" Catherine asked, captivated by the potential of what Aelfric said.

"Well, you know that there is magic all around us, all the time, and that it can be used for good or evil, depending on the intentions of the person working the magic. This can only be done by one already gifted with the ability to channel the magic.

You have that gift and you have a certain amount of magic within you too, that is the catalyst that gets the whole thing started."

"Have I always been able to do this? Why have I never noticed before?"

"You have always had the gift and the magic you inherited from your mother when she passed away. You never noticed before because it did not become active until very recently."

"When my father died?" asked Catherine.

"No, my child. Your father was gifted in other ways. He was blessed with great strength and courage and with a sharp mind." Aelfric paused briefly, choosing his words carefully. "Your father was also a Guardian, one who devoted himself to good magic and when he died, magic sensed his loss. From time to time there comes a master in magic. A master is someone very powerful who can not only channel magic but harness it, trap it within an object that can magnify and focus the power of the master. Eventually they die and the object passes to another, but it holds the bias of its creator. If it was created for good then it will always be good and evil can never use it, and vice versa. When good magic sensed the passing of your father it reached out to the new Guardian, to you."

Catherine's eyes were wide with wonder, her expression one of almost surprise. Aelfric continued.

"Tell me, Catherine, how did you find your necklace?"

Catherine's hand went to her throat and rested on the cool stone, her fingers running around its edges as she recalled that night in her father's room.

"I had a dream. In it there was a sound coming from my father's bedchamber and I went to see what it was. I woke up in my bed and it all felt so real that I had to go and see if it was true. The chest was there, just like in my dream and that is when I found the stone. Are you saying the stone gave me that dream?"

"Not the stone exactly, but magic did, yes. Your necklace was crafted by a master to channel good magic and you are now its Guardian." Aelfric stopped there. It seemed the ideal time to tell her what else she was harbouring but he decided against it, still fearing that it would prove too much of a distraction when she needed to be concentrating on her defence.

"Do you remember what we discussed about constructing spells?"

"Yes."

"Good. A charm is a type of spell and it is intended to be entirely defensive, for your protection. Charms are not weapons but you need to be able to use them before you learn anything more aggressive. It is very important that you can defend yourself, otherwise you may not have an opportunity of launching any kind of counter-attack. Michael will tell you, I am sure, that good defensive skills are the first thing he learnt as a soldier."

Catherine was starting to look a little alarmed by this but Aelfric could not afford to protect her from the truth for much longer. He suspected the warlock could arrive any day now and she needed to be prepared to meet a far superior opponent.

"I do not mean to alarm you my child, but as a Guardian you may sometimes be called upon to defend that which you protect." Aelfric paused for a short while to allow her to calm down and she did seem comforted by his brief explanation.

"Are you ready to go on?" Catherine nodded, her expression grave now. Aelfric sensed a change in her in that moment, as if someone had placed an invisible mantle of responsibility on her shoulders, a mantle that she had accepted and chosen to carry. He felt pity for her then. When he had arrived here she had been cloaked in grief but still inside, she shone with the light of innocence, now, as he looked at her, that innocence was almost all gone. Sometimes though, he thought he could still see some sparks in the embers and prayed that she would soon rise to her potential as a strong, vibrant woman.

"Which is better? The man who lays down his life to defend what he believes in, or the man who recognises defeat as the outcome and walks away?"

Catherine was surprised, this was such an easy question. "This first man."

"Really? Perhaps he will be remembered as a hero or a martyr but when all is said and done he is still dead. His enemy has won and there is nothing more he can do about it. The second man is wise enough to see that he cannot win this fight, strong enough to put aside his pride and lives to fight another day, with a better plan. Do you understand?"

Catherine sat for a second, absorbing what Aelfric had said. It made perfect sense and she could see how that applied to her.

"Yes Aelfric. You are saying that I need to be wise enough to know which battles I cannot win and defend myself when I need to so that I can retreat, live and try again when I am stronger, better prepared, on my terms not theirs." She raised her head and looked Aelfric in the eye. "Do you think I will ever feel like myself again? Am I changed forever?"

Aelfric felt a sharp burst of pain in his heart, felt his throat constrict. Edric had not warned him about this part of his duty and he felt responsible for robbing her of her innocence, guilty for temporarily obscuring her hopes and dreams. A small part of him wanted to tell her everything would be all right, that there was nothing to worry about, until he remembered the reason he was here. The warlock was coming regardless of what Aelfric did or did not do, it was up to him to give her the best chance of survival, hope for a brighter future. He knew she could do it, he just had to remember the day those two men had broken in and how she had acted instinctively to deal with it, to prove it to himself. Once he could trust his voice again he answered her.

"What you are in essence, what you have always been, has not changed. Your beliefs, your ideals and morals, your likes, dislikes and desires, they are all the same and will surface again. This all feels very overwhelming now, I know, but it will not last for long. But, saying that, you cannot avoid being changed at least a little bit by all this. It is vastly different than your old life but from what I know of your character, I believe it will be a change for the better."

Slowly Catherine managed a smile, it was weak and forced to begin with but was gradually replaced by a gentle, natural smile.

"So," said Catherine, "retreat is a good thing, knowing my strengths and limits is an excellent thing and being able to defend myself is absolutely essential. Got it. Teach me the charm."

Aelfric was hugely relieved. For a while that conversation could have gone either way but her strength had won through.

"Very well. You will need to commit this to memory, if you need it you will not have time to read it from a parchment. You begin by addressing the relevant forces and then tell them what you need. Brevity is important here, it could make all the difference, but you need to speak clearly. Try it: arma ab adluvio et aerius"

Catherine repeated the first part after Aelfric.

"Next part, accedo me" Again Catherine repeated.

"Good, your pronunciation is very good. The last part then. Custodis ab magicus ista adsecula defendo."

Catherine repeated the last part out loud and then ran over it a couple of times in her head to make sure she had it.

"Right," said Aelfric "try the whole thing now but this time stand up in the middle of the room and touch your stone while you speak."

Catherine stood and walked to the middle of the room, turning to face Aelfric, who had also risen from his chair and was draining his pot of ale.

"When you are ready" he said.

Reaching up with her left hand, Catherine wrapped her fingers around the stone at her throat, closed her eyes and began to speak.

"Arma ab adluvio et aerius, accedo me
custodis ab magicus ista adsecula defendo"

Holding her breath she waited for something to happen. She felt a little warmer than she had before but that was all, and she put that down to feeling a little bit silly.

"Catherine!" At the sound of her name being called she opened her eyes and looked at Aelfric. He stood a good five strides away from her, with his arm raised above his head, ale pot still in his hand. As she watched he launched the pot at her with as much force as he could muster. The pot came flying across the room at an alarming speed and Catherine flinched, shrieking aloud, expecting it to hit her at any moment. She heard it smash and the sound made her jump. She heard the pieces fall to the floor but she felt nothing. Expecting to find blood on her face she raised her hand to her head and looked down at the floor. The pieces of the pot lay scattered on the floor two strides away from her and there was not a drop of blood on her face. She looked up at Aelfric in amazement and although he was grinning at her he looked as surprised as she was.

With a crash the door flew open and Michael rushed in.

"My Lady, are you all right?" When he saw that she appeared to be unharmed and that Aelfric was on the other side of the room he stopped where he was, his hand on the hilt of his sword.

Startled by his arrival Catherine turned towards him, momentarily struggling for words to explain what had happened.

"I heard you cry out and then something smashed," Michael eyed the shards of pottery on the floor, "are you injured?"

"No, Michael, I am fine, I promise you. Aelfric tripped and dropped his pot. I thought it might have been full and I am afraid I shouted without thinking. I am sorry to have worried you." Looking down at the broken pot Catherine added "I should call Rachel, we should clear this up."

"I will find her. Excuse me." Michael bowed and left the room. Her explanation made sense but her reaction was too much for a broken pot. She had appeared really startled by something in that room and he was sure it had not been him.

Michael found Rachel in the kitchen and sent her to the solar. Arthur was in the buttery. Michael explained what he had seen.

"Something is going on Arthur, something not right. Why would they hide it otherwise? I do not trust that man and Catherine has changed, have you noticed?"

Arthur finished filling two pots of ale and handed one to Michael.

"Yes, I have noticed and maybe there is something going on but have you considered what she has been through lately? Her father died in her arms, she was kidnapped and we may never know what Roland did to her in those woods, not to mention all the death and destruction going on around us all. I think that might change most people in some way. Perhaps Aelfric is trying to help her make sense of it all and she does not want the whole house to know about it."

Michael sighed in frustration and looked up at his friend.

"Michael, you promised her you would not interfere and she promised she would tell you if she needed help. Until you have solid evidence to the contrary you will have to leave it at that."

"I know Arthur, I am so used to being in control, I suppose it is hard to let go sometimes."

"I understand, but she is not a child anymore, I know you have noticed that! Things will get back to normal soon, and besides, the monk will not stay forever, surely he will have to go back to Worcester at some point."

Arthur was right, of course, and Michael was calmed by his reasoning.

Arthur stepped closer to Michael. "We will keep an eye on the monk together." Clapping his hand on Michael's back Arthur left the room.

Chapter 24

It was late the following day when Roland awoke and for several hours he was groggy from his long sleep. Saracen was nowhere to be seen but Roland was not concerned. The horse could take care of himself, he was probably off searching for food. After a while he started to feel stronger and set about lighting a fire to cook some more broth. The fire was crackling strongly when Roland became aware of movement away to his right. He stared intently into the trees, tracking the movement of a dark shadow as it drew near.

He passed his hand over the top of the fire and as he did so the flames died down to embers, his other hand went to the sword lying by his side. The shadow came into view then and Saracen whinnied a greeting to his master. Roland passed his hand over the fire once more and the flames sprang back up, as lively as ever.

"Welcome back my friend. I do not suppose you have had any brilliant ideas to get me into that house to finish the search?" Saracen snorted gently.

"Having said that, I cannot think where else to look." Roland sat for a while in silence, stirring his broth, considering his options.

"Perhaps it is not in the house, in which case a further search would be pointless. But if not in that house then where? Another house? There are not many left un–searched and I still believe Preece has it. Perhaps I could enchant Preece, make him trust me and tell me where to find it but that would take time and I would need to catch Preece alone in order to work the enchantment on him."

Roland fell silent again, continuing to think, continuing to stir. The stew was ready and Roland lifted the pot from the fire to eat his meal.

"Let us say I can get myself into the house, where would it be? Where would I keep something so precious? Well, that is easy enough, if it were mine I would not let it out of my sight."

The answer came to him in a flash and he nearly spilt his broth.

"That is the answer Saracen. It was not found because it was not there. Preece had it with him the whole time. Well, perhaps he is not the idiot I took him for. If the legends are true then it would certainly be small enough to hide on his body or in his clothing. That makes life a little easier, no enchantments necessary, just a good old fashioned ambush the next time he is out."

Satisfied that he was close to having a good plan Roland tucked into his meal and settled down for more rest.

****

At Withington Manor conversation had turned to Catherine's gift. Catherine and Aelfric had spent much of the day practising the protection charm and the thickening spell she had learned. Then Aelfric had taught her a disarming spell, one that would knock a person hard enough to make them drop anything they held, giving her time to take action or run away.

As she expanded her knowledge and increased her options, so her confidence grew and as it did her mood lightened and she did not feel quite as oppressed by her new destiny as she had done. Their lessons had ended for the day and now they talked before going to the hall for the evening meal.

"You seem much happier today Catherine, do you know why? Aelfric was pleased to see this change in her, it was encouraging, it meant that she was more at ease with her gifts.

The more comfortable she was the more successful she was likely to be.

"I am not sure, but I think it has something to do with knowing more of my ... gift. What you said yesterday, about my parents and the necklace, it made me feel that I was chosen somehow. Having this gift means I still share something with my father and I have a piece of my mother. It is hard to describe but I feel I belong now."

"Why do you say 'chosen'? What do you mean?"

"The dream. It was so real Aelfric, I thought I was awake and then when I did wake up I felt drawn to the chest, it was like I was being called by the stone and I was the only one who could hear. It led me to the chest and the first time I put it on it felt warm and, well, it was an odd sensation."

"That seems quite normal, the warmth, but you were going to say something else then, were you not? Did the stone do anything else?"

Catherine hesitated, worried that she had imagined the rest but as she thought about it, she had come to accept much lately, much that had been hard to believe. Why then should she doubt this?

"I thought that it glowed a little as I lifted it out of the box and put it on."

She had all of Aelfric's attention now, this was not normal and he struggled to recall what Edric had told him of the stone, many years ago.

"Do you know, has it glowed since?"

Catherine tensed, every muscle and tendon in her body taught and ready to flee. Aelfric was asking her to revisit a memory that she had worked hard to bury deep in the back of her mind. It was a memory that would bring her pain, one that she associated with fear and hate. When she spoke, her voice was quiet, barely audible, her eyes cast down, her face sombre.

"Yes."

Aelfric waited for her to elaborate but when it became clear that she would not, he prompted her.

"Catherine? When did you see it glow?" Despite his eagerness to know, he tried to keep his voice calm and low, soothing. He wanted her to feel comfortable enough to tell him, this could be very important.

Eventually she spoke again, in hushed tones.

"It has glowed twice since and both times I believe it was warning me. When we fist met you asked me what it told me about you." Catherine raised her head and looked at Aelfric. "It told me nothing, so I knew I was not in danger from you."

"Tell me of the dangers you faced when the stone glowed." He could see how reluctant she was to relive those memories but he needed to know. It was a struggle to keep calm but he stayed quiet.

"The day you arrived.... my neighbour wants my lands and he sent a man to kidnap me so that he could force me to marry him and take everything I have. When he laid his hands on me the stone vibrated and glowed."

She fell quiet then and Aelfric felt he had to prompt her once again.

"And the other time?"

Catherine looked into the flames, afraid that if she looked at Aelfric she may lose control and she did not want to cry.

"The man who took me held me in the woods but I escaped and managed to hide from him. There was a time when he came very close to discovering my hiding place. The stone glowed again then, to warn me of the danger. It may have glowed one more time, just a little earlier the same day, but I cannot be sure."

Aelfric allowed her the silence this time. He was deeply troubled by this news, having now recalled what Edric had told him. He knew the stone had been crafted by good magic. He knew that it was a powerful conduit and that it would protect its Guardian where it could. The stone had responded to the closeness of the same man on two occasions, Aelfric had heard Catherine speak of him and name him as Roland of Langley.

Catherine had almost been correct in her reasoning, except that it was not danger that it sought to warn her of. It was great evil.

That could only mean that Roland of Langley was the warlock. He had been here, in this house, he had captured the Guardian but somehow let her go.

Aelfric was briefly confused about why the warlock had been here and not seized it for his own, why he had not killed the Guardian when he had the chance? He cannot have known. It all became clear to Aelfric now. All the churches and homes that had been ransacked, the warlock had been here all the time, searching for it but never knowing exactly where to look. Those poor people must have caught him during his searches, or maybe they had been enchanted to search for him. The Keeper held the men responsible for the fires but the warlock was responsible for the rest. Catherine had said she had escaped but Aelfric suspected that if, this Roland, had known who he had captured she would never have had an opportunity to escape. An experienced Guardian is a significant threat to evil but a novice Guardian, one who was barely aware of her powers, would have seemed like a gift. It was a miracle that Catherine was still alive.

Panic rose in Aelfric as he realised the position they were in, the very real danger they were all in. He was the only one who knew. Aelfric recalled that Catherine had said the stone had glowed over the chest when she had first found it. That must be where it was hidden, in her father's chest. Catherine's home was almost the only house in the area that had not been searched, it was just a matter of time before the warlock returned here. Despite days of teaching Catherine, of witnessing her natural talent; despite the knowledge that she had changed and grown, Aelfric was afraid. He had never been a courageous man and now he lost his nerve. He knew what was coming and it terrified him so much that he doubted they could defend the house against it.

They had to leave. He needed to get Catherine and that which she guarded away from this place, out of harm's way. He could take her back to Worcester, they might be safe at the cathedral, after all, the warlock had already looked for it there. He cleared his throat.

"I have been here almost three weeks now." Catherine continued to stare into the flames, seemingly unaware that he was speaking to her. "My Abbot allowed me one month's leave to come here and it will take several days to travel back to Worcester." Still she stared at the fire, motionless except for the slow regular movement of her eyelids. He tried again.

"Catherine, I must leave, soon." Now he had her attention. Slowly she turned her head towards him, her expression pained.

"You are leaving? How long will you be gone?" There was something of the child in her voice again and his heart went out to her.

"I had thought that perhaps you could come with me, continue your studies at the cathedral for a while. I can teach you just as well there. What do you think? It might be easier to learn away from the troubles and distractions here."

Catherine stared at him for a few seconds. "I do not know Aelfric, it will be hard to leave all that is familiar at a time like this. I still need to feel close to my father. I need time to think about it." She rose from her chair then. "It is nearly time for the meal, we should go to the hall and sit with the others." Quietly she glided to the door and left the room.

It was not the rousing 'yes' he had hoped for. A delay could be very costly but he recognised that she could not be rushed, that would almost certainly earn him a definite 'no'. He thought his best chance lay in securing the support of Michael and Arthur but he knew that would be more than difficult. Neither of the soldiers trusted him, that was clear. He would need to be cunning to succeed, appeal to their love for Catherine, their concern for her welfare.

Aelfric stood and followed Catherine to the hall. Michael and Arthur were already there and seated at the table. Aelfric watched them as he settled himself in a chair, they seemed serious and sombre tonight, it was unlikely this would help his cause. Perhaps a direct approach would be best. It had worked with Catherine and Michael seemed to be a straightforward and up front man. As he thought about it, it occurred to Aelfric that perhaps Michael did not trust him because he did not know him. They had not had a chance to speak, what with Catherine's intensive lessons. That was probably it, all the time spent closeted away with Catherine, it must seem very secretive, largely because it was and with good reason, but Michael would not know that. Decided on his course Aelfric waited for an appropriate point in the conversation. Just as soon as a conversation began.

After a full five minutes of silence while the others ate, Aelfric took the plunge.

"Michael, I thought it would be nice if we talked, got to know each other a little better." He was rewarded with a surprised sideways glance from Michael but nothing more. Not to be deterred Aelfric continued.

"I am aware you do not trust me and I would like to know how I might put your mind at ease."

This time he was rewarded with Michael's complete attention. In fact Catherine, Arthur and John had also stopped eating and were looking at Aelfric apprehensively. He quailed a little under the scrutiny but was determined and continued to smile at Michael.

"That is right Aelfric, I do not trust you." Michael was equally direct with his answer, somewhat more so than Aelfric had been prepared for.

"May I ask why?" Aelfric's voice had lost some of its vigour and brightness and his smile was fading.

"Michael!" Catherine's tone was sharp, letting the whole room know that she was concerned with the way this conversation was going. Michael appeared not to have heard.

Aelfric waved his hand dismissing her worries. "No, no, I asked and he answered. I appreciate your candour Michael. Do you believe me to be responsible for or involved in any of the tragedies that have occurred here?"

The tension in the room increased tangibly as the stakes of the conversation rose. No-one had yet resumed their meal, gripped by the drama enfolding before them.

"No, I do not believe I would go that far. Perhaps your timing was merely unfortunate. Since you ask though," Michael glanced at Catherine, believing himself released from his promise, "what concerns me most is the secrecy you appear to encourage. I cannot believe it can be healthy. If you have nothing to hide why exclude yourself from the rest of the house for so much of the time?"

Aelfric knew he should have seen that coming and been more prepared for it, but he was not. He looked from Michael to Catherine. She stared back, her eyes pleading. He could not tell Michael the truth but he could not lie either, at least not convincingly enough to fool the soldier. It was time to fall back on the stock answer.

"As a monk I am sometimes party to privileged information. The things people tell me are often in confidence, if you like, discretion is my trade. What Lady Catherine has shared with me of her feelings and beliefs was in confidence and must go with me to the grave. I can tell you, however, that anything that has been said or done, has been strictly within the confines of my duties as a monk, in accordance with the Lord's will, as my Abbot and I understand it to be."

Proud of his speech Aelfric looked back at Michael. His eyes were narrow and he seemed to be studying Aelfric very closely. After what seemed an age Michael spoke.

"Well said, Aelfric. If my Lady is happy that nothing is amiss then so am I."

It was as if someone had sucked all the air from the room and now suddenly it came rushing back in. Catherine realised that she had been holding her breath and let it out in a long, shaky sigh.

Relieved that they would not have to break up a fight, with a monk no less, Arthur and John went back to their meal.

Michael and Aelfric held each other's stare for a few seconds longer before Aelfric broke the link. They both turned their attention back to their plates. Aelfric was hugely relieved that it was over. He felt he had made some headway here tonight and briefly considered raising the subject of an immediate removal to Worcester. On reflection though, he felt it best not to push his luck. Perhaps tomorrow would be better.

Chapter 25

Matthew Preece sat in his hall, trying to eat his breakfast. Loss of appetite was unusual and it bothered him. He wondered if it might be a sign that he was ill. Illness would ruin his plans, or at least set them back quite significantly. Of course, it could all be Sigar's fault. Preece was not sure he understood all that had happened the previous day. He recalled being in a bad mood and then half the village had turned up at his door, led by the Keeper. Sigar seemed to have been panicked by it all and run out of the house, knocking Preece off his feet in the process. Preece was considering having him flogged just for that, it had hurt. He had struggled to get up again and of all the people at his door not a single one of them had stopped to help him.

The next thing he knew, another man had rushed by him, so quickly that he had not seen his face. Worse than that he discovered his house was on fire. Fires in wooden structures were terrifying things, they spread at an incredible rate and consumed everything. The men at the door had eventually put it out but none of them would admit to having started it, no matter how loud he had shouted. While he had been standing at his door berating the peasants around him he had seen two men from Withington Manor come from around the back of his house and approach the Keeper. After a few seconds of whispering, the Keeper had then come to him, asking for a moment of his time.

Preece had been expecting an offer of compensation for the fire damage and had been prepared to negotiate the price up as high as possible. At the very least he wanted an apology. Instead the Keeper had sat down in his hall and told him they had found a body, Sigar's body, no less. Well, that was just ridiculous, clearly Sigar was not dead because Preece had just seen him. Obviously the Keeper was quite mad but he had somehow managed to convince all the others around him.

After a few minutes of listening to this utter nonsense Preece had asked the Keeper to leave. The Keeper had persisted, even inviting him to visit the body, then when he had declined the Keeper almost demanded that he go. He had been forced to tell the Keeper that he would see the body today just to get him out of his house. Of course, he had no intention of going.

Sigar had failed to return and Preece blamed the Keeper entirely. He had hounded his servant out of his house for no good reason leaving Preece at the mercy of the mouse-like woman who seemed to live in his kitchen. He thought that she may have been there for years but Preece had no idea what her name might be, he had never needed to know before.

There had been some good news the previous day. Word had spread that the Keeper had released Preece and the remnants of his armed guard returned. Three swarthy men had appeared at his door just in time to eat his food. Preece was not naïve enough to believe that the men had returned out of loyalty, they were only there because he paid them, but he did not mind. This was the start of his own private army, the army that would make him lord of these lands and indispensable to the Barons. It also meant that his plans for the Lady Catherine could begin again.

Now, this morning, Preece sat at his table, picking at his meal. Sigar had still not returned and Preece was beginning to wonder if perhaps the Keeper was not mad after all. Preece had to admit, even though Sigar had been his servant for years he had never paid him that much attention. He supposed that it was possible that the man in his house yesterday could have been an impostor. Preece absently shook his head. If the Keeper was right about that then maybe he should visit the body, settle it once and for all. No, that would serve no purpose, if he could not recognise an impostor in his own home then he would not be able to identify the real Sigar after several days in a shallow grave. Preece could think of nothing more disgusting. It was settled then, there would be no trip to the village and the woman in the kitchen would just have to find another manservant. Preece thought he recalled seeing a child around the house recently that might be trained to do the job but quickly discounted the idea, children irritated him.

The only thing that continued to bother Preece was this talk of an impostor. If there even was one! Preece was unsure why anyone would want to trick their way into his home. Certainly he was wealthy compared to the villeins around him but compared to the Barons he was poor. A purse of money was missing but he suspected that had been his soldiers. One day soon he would be rich and then perhaps he would be worth robbing but even Preece admitted quietly, to himself, that he owned only trinkets that he had inherited from his mother.

Unable to find an immediate answer Preece let it go and returned to his wedding plans. He had tried to kidnap her, and that had failed. He had sent Roland in to get her, much good that had done him, the man had lost her in the woods and then disappeared. Incompetent. Preece was glad he had not paid the man in advance. Then he had tried luring her soldiers away with the fires and that brilliant plan had not only lost him two soldiers but earned him a night in the gaol. His next plan would have to be far more cunning.

How did other men do it? How did they get married? It seemed to be happening all around him, all the time, but he had not the first idea where to start. It was time for some research. He pushed himself up from his chair and lumbered out into the kitchen, catching Margaret off guard. She turned to find him standing there in the doorway and jumped.

"Can I help you Sir?" she stammered.

"How does a man get a wife?" he blurted. He suspected that there would normally be some form of small talk before a question like that but he had never done that in his life and he did not know how. Taken aback by the directness of his question and the strangeness of the subject, Margaret was initially lost for words. She quickly found her tongue, very keen not to trigger one of his rages.

"Well, Sir, a man would normally ask the woman he wanted to marry if she wants to marry him and she more often than not says yes. That is it, really."

She stood still, wringing her hands, suddenly very afraid that he was about to ask her.

"They just ask?" Preece was surprised by the simplicity of it, "and they say yes?"

"Usually, Sir, yes." Margaret's voice shook a little and her palms were sweating. Her master had never engaged her in conversation before and she was at a loss to know how to behave. Did she look at him when she spoke, or look away? Did he want honest answers or should she be trying to work out what he wanted to hear? She wished he would go away, very soon.

"Right" he said. Margaret hoped it might be over but he did not leave.

"You will need to find another manservant for me. Make sure they know what I need." At last it seemed he was finished talking and he started to turn away. Margaret began to relax but then he stopped and seemed to be thinking. She was about to ask if there was anything else he needed when he spoke, without looking at her.

"What is your name?"

Startled and confused by his question Margaret managed to stammer out her name. Finally then, he left. Relieved she went to a stool and sat down, trembling.

Preece went back to his hall to consider what he had learned. He had not considered simply asking her before, he had merely assumed she would oppose the idea and immediately embarked on more aggressive tactics. This was all very complicated and confusing. His parents had not thought to educate him about such matters early and before it became an issue they had died. Without them he grew more and more reclusive, less able to function in social circles and increasingly dependent on Sigar for the necessary day to day interactions.

He was, however, experienced enough to know that he would not be welcome at her door now and that it would be her soldiers who would invite him to remove himself. He would not even get a glimpse of her. He knew he would need to placate the men to get access to her, perhaps a peace offering, a deer maybe, to show that his intentions were good. It was settled then, after the midday meal he and his men would ride out on a hunt for deer. The woods around Withington had not yet been proclaimed a Royal Reserve for the King's hunting pleasure alone, making it a safe place to hunt, without consequence but that would only last as long as the King was unaware of the large supply of deer there.

Feeling far more settled he returned to his meal and looked forward to a bit of sport and then the positive response to his proposition that Margaret had assured him he could expect.

He passed the morning pleasantly enough, dozing in his chair by the fire, waking only occasionally to shout for more ale.

****

Catherine had spent the morning working hard at her lessons with Aelfric and was now hiding away the equipment they had used. She had a box seat in her solar that sat beneath a window and she taken to storing the tools of her craft there. It was not as obvious as a box as it was covered by a large embroidered cloth, richly coloured, over which cushions were scattered for comfort. As she put the last of the pots away and re-arranged the cloth there was a soft tap at the door. Hurrying to replace the cushions and sit down she called out.

"Come in."

The door opened and Aelfric stepped into the room. He glanced around, checking for anything out of place and satisfied that all was as it should be he returned to his usual seat near the fire before speaking.

"Catherine, have you thought any more about my suggestion?" he ventured.

She sighed and moved to her own seat. She looked at him, her eyes almost pleading with him. After a few seconds she spoke.

"Aelfric, this is a big decision for me. You are asking me to leave everything I know at a turbulent time. Surely I am stronger here. Besides, I have never been from home before, never travelled further than the market, with my father. I know you mean well and you want what is best for me, but I do not think I am ready. Please, allow me more time to consider this?"

Aelfric nodded quietly, at the last second remembering to smile to hide how he felt but Catherine could still see the disappointment in his downcast eyes and his weak smile. He was not entirely surprised at her answer, after all, she did not know all that he knew and perhaps her answer would have been different if she did. He did not want to panic her, although he was disappointed and more than a little afraid. He had hardly slept last night, listening for the smallest sound that might give away an intruder out in the yard. Inevitably, in a wooden framed building there were many noises throughout the night and each and every one had sent a chill down his back, leaving him frozen where he was, unable to move for fear of alerting an intruder to his presence and bringing them to him. Holding his breath he lay, waiting for a further creeping sound but he would hear only silence. Then the logical part of his mind would dismiss the noise as something innocuous and he would eventually start to doze before another crack would rouse him and set the cycle in motion again.

Sitting in the warm solar he was not sure how long he could survive with this level of tension hanging over him. He could not argue with Catherine though, could not try to bully her because he still suspected that would earn him a flat refusal.

****

In Chedworth, the midday meal was completed and Preece set out with his three men to hunt some deer. They rode out through his gates and on towards the woods at a leisurely pace. The day was cloudy but did not threaten rain. The air was chilled and still tinged by the lingering scent of autumnal decay. As the men breathed, puffs of fine mist blew out ahead of them and they pulled their jackets a little tighter around their throats. Preece had chosen to wear some of his best clothes for the occasion and had put on his finest red cloak, sure that this would impress Lady Catherine.

It did not take them long to reach the woods and soon they were enveloped within the cover of the trees. Among the skeletal trees it was dim and what light there was, was patchy, seeping through the canopy in sporadic bursts. It was warmer here though, out of the bitter wind and Preece felt sure they would find some deer taking shelter here.

His three men were all armed with a bow and arrows instead of their swords, which were no use in a fast hunt, and that was what they were hoping for. Speaking only in hushed tones the men rode in almost silence for some time, getting ever deeper into the trees. This way they hoped to catch sight of their prey before they startled it with unnecessary noise. For long periods the only sounds were the horse's hooves snapping dead twigs on the ground, rustling through dead leaves, thudding gently on the hardened ground, occasionally snorting warm air from their nostrils.

They had been riding in this way for almost two hours and Preece was rapidly coming to the end of his patience. His rear was beginning to feel bruised from the motion of the horse. It had been some time since he had been in the saddle and he was out of practice and out of rhythm with the horse. This did not help his mood, and left him feeling sore and irritable.

He was about to suggest they give up and return home when one of his men made a low, quiet whistling sound. It was barely audible over the horses but being out of place here, it stood out. Everyone stopped and looked in the direction that he was pointing. About thirty strides away, through the trees, stood a magnificent stag with two smaller does, grazing on the ground. Preece's mood lifted immediately.

If they could return with all three deer he could make a gift of one of them, preferably the smallest, then take the other two home for his own table. He held his horse steady where it stood while his men spread out to move in on the deer. One went twenty strides to the left while another went a similar distance to the right, leaving the third to move forward in a straight line. After moving forward about ten strides the men halted their horses and carefully reached over their shoulders for their curved wooden bows, silently fitting an arrow. When they were ready each man drew his bow back in a fluid movement, rotating it at the same time from horizontal to vertical. Strings were pulled taught, left arms straight and firm, no hint of a tremor, right arms drawn back, fingers barely holding the strings. To succeed they would need to loose their arrows at the same instant and they would need to do it in silence. The smallest sound out of place could startle the deer, they would be quick to run and extremely hard o catch on horseback in this densely wooded area. This would be their best and possibly only chance today.

Breathing slowly and deeply each man steadied himself. The two flank men kept half an eye on the middle man, waiting for his signal. When it came they would each have time for one more deep breath and then as the last of the air was released from their lungs they would all shoot. They had hunted together many times before, they knew the plan, each one knew what to do.

The signal man sat on his horse a few paces ahead of the others, making him easier to see. It was his task to pick the best time to strike, too soon and the prey may not be fully exposed and harder to hit, too late and they may be startled and run. He sat, watching carefully, his arrow drawn, his arm steady. He would have to strike soon, the stag had become aware of at least one of the horses and was eyeing it warily.

The signal came and all three men drew in one more deep breath and began to exhale ready to loose the arrow at the end, when the body is at its steadiest.

Without warning a sudden sharp crack echoed among the trees making it almost impossible to know where it had come from. The man on the left loosed his arrow as he jumped and it sailed through the air, high of its mark. At the same instant all three deer heard the noise and leapt into the undergrowth, accelerating to an incredible speed in no time at all. Before the sound had died down they were gone. Seeing their prey disappearing the three men slung their bows over their shoulders and urged their horses forward, chasing the deer. Before Preece had quite registered what was happening he was sitting quite alone in the woods. He looked around, wanting to shout at someone but having no–one to shout at. For the first time in years Preece felt alone, isolated in the silence of the trees. He could not even hear the call or flutter of a bird. Unsure what to do next he briefly considered his options. He could chase after his men but doubted he would be able to find them now. He could wait and hope his men would return to him at this spot, or he could try to find his way home. This seemed the best option so he turned his horse's head and started walking back the way they had come.

He had only been riding for a few minutes when he thought he heard a twig snap not far off to his left. Stopping his horse he turned to peer through the trees, looking for his men returning but he could not make out any sign of movement. It was still deadly quiet around him, no sign of birds or other wildlife. Preece noted it was starting to get dark but not enough for birds to have roosted already. Feeling a little vulnerable now, Preece nudged his horse onwards again. They walked quietly for a few minutes more and Preece was beginning to feel foolish, a grown man afraid to be alone in the daylight, he knew he would scorn anyone else who felt that way.

SNAP!

Preece jumped and his horse whinnied gently, upset by the strange noise. It seemed very close but Preece could not see what could have caused it. Once again all around him was silent, no birds, no other animals. No longer feeling foolish, all sense of shame gone, Preece was now acutely aware of the unnatural silence in the wood around him, as if every living thing had run away to hide.

His horse refused to stand still, eyes wide and glaringly white in the gloom, ears laid back against its head and nostrils flared. It did not need to be asked twice to head for home at a faster pace. Preece was no longer sure which direction would lead him out of the trees but was more concerned with just getting away from this place. He bumped along on his horse for another few minutes, eyes darting all around; occasionally glancing over his shoulder; letting the horse steer them both, trusting its sense of direction.

Light was fading fast now and Preece was anxious to be back out in the open, to find people, any people. He did not want to be alone anymore. Without warning a bright light flared up in front of him. It dazzled him, and made it very hard to see but at that instant he thought he could hear something fizz and crackle just up ahead. The sudden blast of light panicked his horse and it shied away in fright, rearing up on its hind legs and crying out a pitiful sound. Preece was startled and disorientated, unable to keep a grip and he tumbled off the back of his horse, hitting the ground hard. All the air was knocked from his lungs and he felt a burst of pain tear through his back. Gasping for air he opened his eyes, blinking quickly, trying to see what was there. He caught a glimpse of his horse running away through the trees.

He knew he could not afford to lose his horse now. That was his best chance of getting out of the wood but as he struggled to get to his feet he knew that he did not have a hope of catching it. Staggering now, trying to balance, he lurched in the same direction his horse had just bolted. He was dazed and confused but instinct told him he had to keep moving to survive. It was almost dark under the cover of the trees and it was very cold but Preece hardly noticed. He focused on putting one foot in front of the other and staying upright. As he got his wind back each step became a little easier and his sight was a little clearer but he was unable to keep the panic at bay.

His breathing was coming in short, quick gasps, his pupils were fully dilated and his pulse raced as he lumbered forwards. Feelings became indistinct as every part of his body laboured to keep him moving as quickly as possible. A loud, sharp crack close to his left grabbed his attention and he veered to his right, away from it but he could still not see what might have caused it. Five paces on, now ten, Preece was utterly convinced that there was something there with him and a lone voice in his head screamed at him to keep running.

He dodged around a thorny little bush, snagging his tunic as he ran, then around a tree trunk, narrowly missing its raised roots. He was looking ahead only a few feet at a time, willing himself to reach that point and then choosing a new goal to aim for. This time it was a large gnarled old oak tree with a wide trunk. Ten paces, five, two, he was there. His lungs burned and his heavy legs endured stabbing pains with every step but he knew he could not stop, not even to rest against this trunk. As he passed it he was struck hard from his right, knocking him clear off his feet. He fell to the ground and rolled on to his stomach. Terror gripped him as he registered the body blow. Pushing up onto his elbows he looked quickly around, unable to see what had hit him. He was scared for his life, tormented and hunted, desperate for it to be over but mortally afraid of what he might find if he stopped running. Tears flowed freely down his cheeks, his lower lip quivered and he found himself softly calling for his parents. Got to keep running, must not stop, cannot let it catch him. His mind raced, telling him what to do and he clambered to his feet and stumbled on, completely lost.

Blood was pumping fast now and his lungs struggled to meet the oxygen demand but Preece knew he had to keep moving, he had to believe that he would reach the edge of the trees soon, as long as he could just keep moving.

Wham!

Preece was thrown backwards as a large solid force hit him head on. He felt like he had run straight into a wall but there was not even a tree directly in front of him. He curled up on his side and squeezed his eyes tightly shut, terrified that he might see his end coming. He was sobbing freely now but he could still hear the awful sound of soft footsteps coming nearer and each step seemed to speak of his doom. The footsteps stopped and the wood fell silent around Preece.

"Please," he whimpered, "please do not hurt me."

He said the words over and over, begging, pleading for his life. Still unable to open his eyes he was certain that the reality would be far worse than his wildest imaginings.

As he lay there, holding himself and crying he felt a small tremor in the earth below him. It steadily increased, stunning him into silence. The very second he stopped crying so the tremor ceased and he held his breath in anticipation of what might happen next, still sensing a presence looming over him.

Unable to bear the suspense any longer and more terrified by the horrors in his imaginings than the possibility of what the reality held Preece flicked his eyes open. He glanced around his limited field of view. Almost immediately he saw a large black shadow on the ground. As he traced the lines of the dark shape upwards he could make out a tall, cloaked and hooded figure standing no more than four paces from him. He opened his mouth but no sound came out. Swallowing hard he tried to lubricate his throat and forced his mouth to speak.

"Wh… wh…. What do you…..want?" His voice was barely audible and it cracked and broke as he used it. The figure seemed to have heard him though because it began to lean toward him, looming even larger. He waited, hardly daring to breathe or move, waiting for it to speak.

The sound that issued from the figure was unlike anything Preece had ever heard. It was deep and low, a rich, wet and venomous growl that quickly built into a roar and somewhere, threaded deep inside it, Preece could almost make out a thin, shrill scream.

Every cell in Preece's body shied away from it and he let out a hellish scream of his own that was cut abruptly short by a constricting pain that ripped across his chest. There was no air he could breathe, and he gasped like a fish, clutching at his chest as his heart nearly exploded under the stress of Preece's horror. It gave one last quivering pulse and then stopped.

Preece lay on the ground, his arms wrapped around him, his eyes wide open, his face contorted into a fearful scream. The dark figure straightened and stood silently over the lifeless body for a few seconds before it began to laugh. The voice was deep and smooth, almost human now. An arm reached up and slowly drew back the hood.

"Well, Mr Preece, it is time you gave me what I have been searching for."

Roland bent to Preece's side and began searching the body, through every fold of cloth, gently at first. When he did not find what he was looking for he began to tear at the clothes, feeling for thongs or small purses where it might be hidden. It soon became apparent that it was not there. He raised himself to his full height and let out a wolfish growl. His anger and frustration boiled over and he shouted out into the night, spittle flying from his mouth, his eyes narrow, his fists clenched, a vein throbbing in his forehead.

"Arghhhhhh, where is it?"

He received no answer from the otherwise silent wood and began to calm himself as he realised there was only one place left that it could be, only one place left he had not yet searched.

"Saracen, come!"

Roland called to his horse to follow and set off into the trees, quickly disappearing into the inky blackness.

Chapter 26

Almost as soon as dawn broke the next morning Roland was up, sitting beside a small fire. He held his hands up, cupped in front of his face as he muttered strange words under his breath. As he finished speaking he scattered a number of little objects onto a small patch of cleared earth in front of him. There were small stones and some small animal bones, each one bearing a unique mark. He studied them for some time, their position on the ground, their orientation, how they had fallen in relation to the other pieces. All this told him something. These were Roland's runes and he had been using them for many years. He was practised in reading them now but when he had first begun he had found them difficult and confusing. Once he had mastered them he found them to be a useful tool and still more effective when used with a spell.

Today they all told him that what he sought was still near. It had not moved since he last checked, which meant that whoever had it either did not know what they had and what was coming or they were supremely confident in their ability to defend it.

Roland was now as sure as he could be that it was at Withington Manor, it was the only place with any kind of status that he had not already searched. It galled him that he had been in the house already and not thought to search it then, but this was no time for regret. The only thing that confused him, that did not fit, was Catherine. He had been so close to her on several occasions but never sensed any magic in her. It was unlikely then that she was a Guardian, which ruled out the possibility of supreme confidence keeping her here. She could not know. Roland was sure of it now. When they had talked, before he had captured her, she had been so absorbed with what Preece was doing to her that she had not seen his attack coming.

If she had known about it and its power she would have been far more wary of him. Roland wondered if he could be so lucky a second time, to encounter her while she was completely unaware of the power she had at her fingertips. If she had discovered it she would be harder to fight and defeat. His planning would need to be faultless, he would need rest first. Wrapping himself in a thick blanket he settled down to sleep.

Several miles away, in the village, the Reeve was up and about early. The two men he was holding in gaol for the Keeper had been very vocal over the last couple of days, calling for food, calling to talk, demanding to know why Preece had not been fetched to vouch for them. They had kept him awake half the night and today they seemed to have risen with the larks and were just as noisy.

The Reeve was quick to note that the Keeper did not seem bothered by all the noise. As soon as the two soldiers had started with their rowdy behaviour the Keeper had chosen not to stay with the Reeve any longer and he and his men had taken up a room at the inn. The Reeve was feeling particularly hard done by. At least when the Keeper had been under his roof he had had some idea what as going on, he might have the odd opportunity to assist or encourage the Keeper to be lenient with his fines. Now all he could do was sit and wait. He did not even have the Keeper's men to help him keep his prisoners quiet.

He was desperate for this all to be over, for life to return to some kind of normality but at the same time he dreaded it. That would mean the Keeper leaving and before he went he would levy the fines that would be due for all these crimes. The Reeve did not have the first idea where the payment would come from. As a community they had precious little in the first place. He did not even know how much they would be, it might be a sum beyond anything they could even pay, a debt their children would inherit.

He stood by the brook, staring into the water as it bubbled and gurgled past. Sighing with heavy resignation he bent towards the water and filled the bucket he carried. Then he trudged back to the gaol and stood before the two prisoners. From the dark looks he had been thrown on his way back, the two men had not taken a breath since he left. Raising the bucket he threw the contents over them and listened as they squealed when the icy water hit them.

"Now Shut Up!" bellowed the Reeve, he had no sympathy for them, as far as he was concerned they deserved everything they got. The sooner they saw the magistrate and received their punishment the better. It worked. The two men stood shivering in a corner, stunned into silence and a little afraid of what the harassed Reeve might do next.

Leaving the gaol, the satisfied Reeve headed back towards his bed to catch up on some lost sleep. He could hear shouting and calling not far off and after several seconds spent wondering if he could pretend he had not heard and get away with it, he changed course and headed in the direction of the noise. He soon came across a small group of villeins, gathered around something and that was apparently what had upset them so much. As he neared the group someone spotted him and called to him to join them.

It quickly became apparent to the Reeve that there was some scuffling going on in the middle of the group and as he reached them he cold see that two of the villeins were holding a struggling man. Able to get a closer look now the Reeve could see the man was dressed in a long, rough brown garment and fraying, simple shoes. His head was shaven in a circle at the back, the traditional tonsure worn by monks. Surprised that the villeins had reached the point where they could treat a monk this way, he called out to them.

"Hey! What are you doing? This man is a monk, can you not see that?"

Hearing the Reeve's voice behind them the two villeins holding the monk turned him around.

"Dear Lord," breathed the Reeve, "you there, fetch the Keeper. Now!"

He carefully appraised over the man in front of him. He seemed thin and pale and looked as if he had been sleeping rough lately, judging from the stains and grass on his habit. His hair was dirty and full of dirt and moss and his eyes were red rimmed from a lack of sleep. Without taking his eyes off the monk he addressed the others.

"Where did you find him?"

"He just walked into the village Reeve, bold as you like, as if he had done nothing wrong" answered one of the men.

"That is because I have done nothing wrong. Unhand me!" spat the monk, wrestling with his captors.

"Well, we will just see about that, as soon as the Keeper gets here" the Reeve said.

The monk seemed genuinely surprised and stopped wrestling for a second. "The Keeper is here? Already?"

A shout from behind the Reeve made him take his eyes off the monk to turn to see what was going on. It was the Tanner, followed by the lad the Reeve had sent to get the Keeper.

"Where is my girl you monster, what have you done with her?" Tanner seemed to be somewhere between rage and desperation, his face red, nostrils flaring and fists clenched, but with tears welling in his eyes. He was bearing down on the group at quite a pace and the Reeve suspected that fists may fly if he did not at least slow the much larger man down. Placing himself firmly between the monk and Tanner the Reeve drew himself up to his full height and puffed out his chest.

"Now, Tanner, we do not know for a fact that the monk has done anything yet. Let the Keeper question him first, do not do anything you might regret."

It seemed to work, and Tanner stopped just in front of the Reeve, his expression and posture unchanged.

"Keeper is on his way Tanner," said the Reeve much more gently, "right?" he threw a scathing glance at the young lad who merely nodded and sidled out of arm's reach of the Reeve. Thankfully it was not long before Ralph arrived, on foot and puffing a little, with his men following behind.

"What is this Reeve? What is going on?" asked Ralph, walking up to the group.

"Keeper, this is the monk we told you about, the first man to go missing, when all this trouble started."

"I see." Ralph understood that the monk had become the chief suspect in the eyes of the villeins, largely because they hoped their fines would lessen if they caught the culprit responsible. He knew it was important to deal with this quickly and firmly to avoid a lynching. Many of the events of the past few weeks did seem to point to him but it was all circumstantial as far as Ralph could see.

"Take him to your place, Reeve, we will question him there." He waited for the Reeve to walk away with the monk and then addressed the remaining villeins. "You must leave this with me now, allow me time to investigate this properly. I will not tolerate mob behaviour." Then he turned to the Tanner. "Tanner, I understand, I do, but you need to let me handle this my way."

Tanner said nothing, he simply nodded curtly and walked away, face still red, fists still clenched by his side. Taking a deep breath Ralph made his way to the Reeve's home to speak to the monk.

Ralph sat down in front of the monk. He sat in silence for a while staring at him with his arms folded across his chest, eyes slightly narrowed, head tipped a little to the left. He could see the monk was feeling uncomfortable and thought he would let him stew for a minute longer, before taking in a deep contemplative breath through his nose. When he spoke his voice was calm and quiet.

"What is your name?"

Relieved that the silence had been broken, the monk sputtered out his name.

"Brother Willan, Sir."

"And you left after your church was ransacked, is that correct?"

"Yes, Sir. Mine was not the first church to be defiled so I left to get help. I did not know someone had already gone for you."

Willan seemed scared and confused, wondering why he was here being questioned by a Keeper of the King's Peace but Ralph had met men before who could lie very convincingly and he was not ready to believe everything the monk said just yet.

"Tell me, Brother Willan, when you left, where did you go?"

"To Worcester, to consult with the Abbot or his aides. I was not sure what to do."

"Why did you tell no-one where you were going? The people here were worried, they thought you had been killed."

"Killed? Why would they think that? Oh, because of the mess at the church, yes, I see. Well, I was quite disturbed by what had happened. I did not feel safe to stay at the church and I had not intended to be away for so long."

"Really? When did you intend coming back?"

"I had hoped to see the Abbot or his men straight away and then come back immediately, but I was detained."

"So, Willan, tell me, what have you been doing for the past few weeks? You seem to have been spending a lot of time out of doors lately." Ralph indicated the state of Willan's clothes with a sweep of his hand.

"I have been travelling Keeper, regrettably not every door is open to a stranger these days, not even a monk."

Ralph smiled at Willan in rueful recognition of the sad state of affairs around the country today. He nodded then,

"I know, I find this general suspicion and lack of trust to be very saddening. It is a moral decline I had hoped never to see."

Seeing that he was starting to win Willan's trust, Ralph watched as Willan pursed his lips and slowly shook his head. Ralph continued with his questions.

"You said you were detained, for how long?"

"It was about five days after I arrived at the cathedral that I was able to consult with the aides. Several days after that I was sent on an errand, which took me until now."

"And what was that errand Willan?"

Willan seemed reluctant to answer the question and was clearly choosing his words carefully.

"I had to deliver a message from the Abbot."

Ralph was not at all satisfied with this answer, suspecting there was much more to tell. So he left the monk in silence for a while longer, knowing it to be a technique that worked. It was not long before Willan felt so uncomfortable that he began to volunteer information.

"I was only supposed to be there for a day or two but I had to wait for the .... person to come back."

Ralph merely nodded, maintaining the pressure of silence on Willan, and again it worked.

"That is all I have to say. I went to Worcester the day my church was defiled, I stayed there almost a week to see the aides. They sent me with a message but the Baron was away when I arrived. I stayed there until two days ago and now I am returned. Why am I being held? You can clearly see I am alive and well."

Ralph was intrigued and a little disturbed by this news. A message had been sent to the Baron. He wondered what it had said and why the Abbot had chosen to go direct to the Baron and not send for the Keeper, this was unusual. The Baron would not normally want to be involved in these kinds of matters, he would be far too busy with much grander things. These had been turbulent times; times that had seen many struggles and battles for power, on a countrywide scale. A couple of church robberies, which is all it was when the monk had left, would fall well below the notice and interest of the Baron. This piqued Ralph's curiosity even further. There had to be something bigger going on, something much more serious than Ralph knew of. Perhaps he could get Willan to tell him without realising it. He would need to be subtle with his questioning.

"You are being held because shortly after you left people started to disappear."

"And what? You think I took them with me? You think I know where they are?"

"No." Willan was surprised by the Keeper's blunt answer and frowned, perplexed.

"We do not think you took them with you to Worcester, because we found them," Ralph paused for the maximum impact, "they were dead." It had the desired effect and provoked a response from Willan, albeit a silent one. His mouth sagged open, his eyes were wide and he slumped against the back of his chair. Eventually he found his voice but it was weak, barely more than a whisper.

"You think I killed them? I am a monk!" Willan's voice was so thin and quiet that the depth of his outrage was completely lost. Ralph decided it was time for the killer question.

"Where is Meg? Hers is the only body we have not found."

Willan seemed initially shocked at this question but recovered far too quickly for Ralph's liking. The monk knew where Meg was, Ralph was sure of it. He was not sure about Willan's involvement in the rest of this nightmare though. Ralph grudgingly had to admit that Willan's story was temptingly believable, right up to the point where Willan paid a visit to the Baron. That part needed further probing.

"Well, where is she? You clearly know." Ralph's voice was calm and low, yet firm. He did not want to scare Willan so much he stopped talking in an attempt to protect himself, but he did want Willan to believe that this was very serious and that he would not stand for deceit. He wanted Willan to be considering the penalties for murder in the hope that they might loosen his tongue.

As Ralph looked at him Willan seemed to change, the open vulnerability was gone, hidden, as if he had closed the shutters to protect against bad weather coming. This would make things harder, it was time for a new tactic.

"So, how is the Baron these days Willan? You left him well I hope." Now Ralph's voice was lighter, almost friendly.

Caught off guard by this abrupt change of subject and demeanour Willan was unsure of what the Keeper was up to but felt that he was on safer ground talking about the Baron than about Meg although he was still wary about where this might lead.

"Decidedly hale, life would seem to be treating him well at present."

"Good, good. It has been a while since I saw him, it would be nice to see him again. I thought I might take a trip up there, while I am in the area, perhaps in the next few days, as you say he is at home now."

"Oh, no, he will be away from home by now, when I left he was going to …." Willan's voice trailed off as he realised how he had almost been tricked. Drawing himself up to sit straight he closed his mouth and met the Keeper's stare. Ralph rose from his seat and began to pace the room.

"That is all right Willan, you keep your secrets." Ralph was not ready to give up yet although he had to admit that the monk was stronger that he had anticipated. "Did you see the large man earlier, the one who was shouting and called you a monster?" He waited long enough to get a nod from Willan. "That was Meg's father, did you know that? How do you imagine he feels? He has seen people go missing then heard that their cold, dead body has been found. Then he discovers that his only daughter has gone missing, but no body. You were missing, and no body. Tanner may be a simple man but he connected you to Meg very quickly and he believes that you know where she is, he thinks you may have killed her."

Ralph let that thought hang in the air for a moment, until he was sure he had absolutely all of Willan's attention.

"We both know that you know where she is. This hundred already believes that you are responsible for all the deaths here so how can it hurt you to tell me where she is?"

His speech appeared to be having an effect, Willan looked scared and he looked at Ralph with wide, shocked eyes, his lips parted in a silent gasp.

"WILLAN!"

The monk jumped as Ralph shouted his name and he appeared truly shaken.

"I……I…..have not……k….killed…….anyone. Meg is not dead."

Slowly Ralph sat back down and leaned towards Willan, his elbows resting on his knees, hands clasped in front of him.

"Where is she Willan?"

"I promised not to tell, she told me in confidence." Willan's voice was thin and weak, like a scolded child pleading for lenience. Ralph left him in silence, knowing that he could not stand it. He did not have to wait very long for Willan to start talking again.

"She fell in love with a boy, a cottager's son. He lives about two hour's walk from here. She met him at the market and they have been meeting in secret since the spring. Meg told me that her father would not understand, that he would not allow her to marry this boy, so she was planning to run away to be with him. I am sure you will find her there." His voice trailed away, ashamed of betraying a trust.

Ralph nodded to one of his men who immediately stepped forward. "Go, find her; bring her back if you can, even if only long enough to show everyone she is healthy. Willan, tell him where to go." After receiving directions from Willan, the man left to fetch his horse. If Willan was telling the truth then his man could be back with her in two or three hour's time.

"Good Willan, you are doing very well. Now you are going to tell me about the message you took to the Baron, and do not leave out any of the good parts." Ralph leaned back in his chair and folded his arms across his chest, his expression making it clear that he would not take no for an answer.

"I do not know what the message was." Willan sounded defeated, his eyes were cast down towards the ground, his shoulders sagging. Ralph suspected that he was getting the truth now.

"Then tell me *exactly* what you were told."

"The aides told me I had to go to the Baron, tell him I was sent by them and where I came from, I mean, where my church is. I was to tell him "the one may need his assistance" and that he would know what the message was about."

"The one? What is that?"

Willan shrugged. "I do not know, honestly." He sighed heavily, watching as he worked his hands in his lap. "The Baron asked me what I knew of what had happened and then said I was to return and he would join me shortly to find out what was going on."

"The Baron is coming here?" Willan nodded. "With his men?" Willan nodded again but did not look up from his hands.

Ralph did not like the sound of this. In his experience when the Baron and his men descended on a place to quash trouble, his actions tended to be swift and brutal. These people were not to blame for what had happened, Ralph was sure of that but he had no confidence that the Baron would stop to ask questions before exacting his own brand of justice on the hundred. Leaving the monk in the care of the Reeve, Ralph went in search of ale and peace. This may be the calm before the storm and he needed to make sure he was prepared for what was coming.

Around three hours later, as he had expected, Ralph's man returned, with a pretty young woman on the back of his horse.

Before he had a chance to speak Ralph heard a cry from behind him.

"Meg! My Meg, you are all right, thank the Lord." Tanner came rushing forward with his distraught wife running in his wake. The girl jumped down from the horse and was almost smothered in an embrace from both her parents.

Ralph's sense of relief was almost tangible, finally something good had happened. Perhaps the tide had turned here, perhaps there was reason to hope after all. Having no desire to intrude on a personal moment for the family, Ralph turned away and made his way back toward the Reeve's home to speak further with Willan. As he neared the place he raised his gaze from the track and looked ahead. There on the track were maybe twenty men, all on horseback with swords glinting, making their way into the village. Instantly on edge Ralph recognised the man at the head of the group as the Baron.

"Here we go!" he muttered to himself.

Chapter 27

Aelfric was suffering today. A second night of sleeplessness had left him feeling drained and irritable. His limbs were stiff and heavy, he had struggled to rise to say prayers at the time when his fellow monks would be at Prime. His eyelids felt weighed down and his mind was sluggish. Aelfric knew that he had a choice to make, very soon. He had lied to Catherine about having to return to Worcester at this time. He would either have to leave as threatened and hope that it provoked a change of heart, or he would have to tell her he had decided to stay with her, help her with her studies and bear his punishment when he returned to Worcester.

The first option was most tempting. Aelfric had no desire to stay here and die at the hands of a warlock. If he could make it back to Worcester cathedral he felt sure he would be safe, felt more confident that he could keep Catherine safe there. They would of course need to take what the warlock sought with them, which would bring danger but frightened as he was, Aelfric knew that the warlock could not succeed, if he did nobody would be safe. Every fibre of his body told him to run away and hide. His heart though, told him to stay with Catherine. She needed all that he could teach her in the little time they had left. She was learning quickly and he was both impressed by and thankful for it.

This morning Aelfric sat huddled in a chair near the fire in the hall waiting for the rest of the house to rise and come in to break their fast. He let his heavy lids droop down over his red eyes, his lashes settling on the smaller, lower lids, dark and puffy, ringed from a lack of rest. He was pale and appeared to have aged in the night. About an hour later Michael pushed open the door and went to the fire to warm himself. The morning was bitterly cold and his fingers were numb. Once he started feeling warmer he turned towards the table to take a seat there and noticed the monk. At first Michael thought he might have died in the chair, he was so still and quiet and he had not looked at all well the day before. Stepping a little closer Michael could see Aelfric's chest gently rising and falling as he slept and was a little surprised at the relief he felt.

Arthur was the next to arrive and still Aelfric did not wake. Arthur nodded to Michael.

"Have you heard the news from the village?"

"Good morning Arthur. Yes, Robert told me. Can this possibly be good news?"

"It is doubtful, although......" Arthur stopped as the door opened once more and Catherine entered.

"Good morning. Winter is certainly here now, it was quite cold in the night." She walked to the table and sat down.

"It was cold my Lady, there has been a heavy frost in the night, I would not be surprised if we saw snow soon." Michael looked across the table at Catherine and smiled. She was not wearing a wimple today and her long, silky hair hung loose. It covered her shoulders in a fine, dark veil and framed her face, contrasting with her fair skin, making her appear almost to glow as the firelight caught her delicate face. Michael recalled how cold it had been last night and wondered how much warmer it would have been if he had been holding her in his arms.

The door pushed open and Michael was shaken from his dream-like state, realising he had been staring at Catherine the whole time. As his mind rushed back to reality he saw that she was gazing back at him, from beneath dark lashes, blushing slightly. Embarrassed at his lapse he smiled briefly and looked away, missing the warm smile he got in return. He had told himself that he would banish these thoughts, that he was happy to accept the relationship they had as the best that they could have.

Rachel bustled in and started laying plates of food on the table.

"Has anyone seen Aelfric? He is not normally late for a meal."

"He is here my Lady," said Arthur from his place near the fire, "but he does not look well."

Concern furrowing her smooth forehead Catherine rose from her seat and went to the chair that Arthur had indicated. Aelfric was still fast asleep, looking frail and sickly.

"He seemed fatigued yesterday but I did not think much of it, he looks much worse today. Do you think we should wake him to eat?" She glanced over at Arthur as she spoke, her brow arched, questioning.

"No, he is best sleeping. He will wake when he gets hungry enough."

Arthur sounded very sure of his advice and so she left Aelfric where he slept and went to the table. Once all three of them were seated Catherine looked up and spoke.

"I wanted to ask your advice, both of you. Aelfric has told me that he must return to Worcester very soon." Pausing, she took a second to gather her words.

Michael's head snapped up, this was good news, finally Catherine would be free of the monk's influence and Michael would be able to see that she was all right. Surely once he was gone her behaviour would return to what it had been previously.

"You should certainly allow him to leave, he has been away from his home for some time now. He must have duties to attend to there, he must be missed."

"Oh, I know Michael, and I will. It is not that simple though. He has asked me to travel there with him, to stay for a while.

There may be much I can learn of the world while I am with the monks." She fell quiet, seeing the concern on both men's faces. Michael had stopped eating, his hand still halfway to his mouth holding a piece of bread. It was Arthur who asked the obvious question.

"Have you said you will go with him?" he asked.

"No," her answer was subdued, sensing the discomfort from Michael and Arthur, "I have not, but I was giving it thought. To begin with the idea of leaving my home was just too much, but now I begin to think it may be good for me."

Michael and Arthur looked at each other, each recognising that there was a very good reason for her to go at this time. They were both well aware that whoever, or whatever, it was that they had found at Preece's house five days ago, was still out there somewhere. After this long without a sign it may be that he, or it, had left the area, moved on, or could just be waiting for an opportunity to cause more trouble, for who knew what reason. There was always a risk travelling but they could travel with her, protect her.

Today, though, they both had a better reason to advise against this trip. Arthur, looking at Michael, raised his eyebrows, encouraging his friend to explain it to Catherine. Putting down his bread Michael searched for the right words, not wishing to be entirely negative in his answer. Catherine sat still in her seat, looking expectantly from one to the other.

"My Lady," said Michael, "we believe it would be a good thing for you to travel and wherever you choose to go, Arthur and I will travel with you to ensure your safety." He paused briefly, wanting to be sure of his tone before he continued, but seeing the smile emerging on her face he knew that he must go on, quickly.

"However," the smile immediately faded, "we have received news today that casts a different light on things. We do not believe that now is the right time to be away from home."

"What has happened?" she asked, almost afraid to hear the answer.

"There has been some good news, Meg has been found safe and well, it seems she decided to marry a lad she met at market, in secret. Also, Brother Willan has returned to us." Michael paused for all this to sink in. "It appears that after his church was defiled the good brother went to his superiors for advice. They thought it best to alert a higher authority and yesterday, the Baron arrived with some of his men."

Catherine nodded slowly, holding Michael's gaze. She was not so naïve that she did not realise the implications. Her father had always told her that the Baron was a good man, a fair man but he also had rights and a lot of power. If she were to be found away from home he might consider her home abandoned and try to seize it for himself. Even if she stayed she might encounter problems. Under the law of the land she owned this estate, it had passed to her upon the death of her father. She was unmarried though. There was every chance that the Baron may put her under a lot of pressure to marry one of his own men to gain control of the estate that way. Preece may turn out to be the least of her troubles. With the Baron here the wisest option would be to keep a low profile, not attract his attention, but be there to meet it head on if his attention should turn in her direction anyway.

"Then it is settled. I will stay and Aelfric may leave as soon as he is well again. I hope it is not a serious ailment."

"I do not believe so," said Arthur, "there are no signs of lesions or welts, or swellings that I can see. He merely looks tired, perhaps he is not sleeping well. In any case he is best left where he is, rest can only do him good."

Catherine nodded and continued with her meal with much less enthusiasm that before. Presently she spoke again.

"Would you really travel with me if I went?" she hardly dared look at Michael in case he glimpsed inside her and saw how she felt. A little confused by the question Michael looked at her. He had thought it obvious that he and Arthur would follow her anywhere. Of course, that is why her father had taken them on in the first place, but there was more to it now, they were her friends. Michael was surprised that she had not assumed that they would go with her and was touched by the feeling in her question.

"Of course we would, we could not allow you to come to harm, wherever you are." Said Michael as lightly as he could.

They were all saved from the awkward silence that followed by a loud grunt from Aelfric. Still he did not wake. Catherine could not help but laugh quietly. The room had been so tense up to that moment, the laughter was a more than welcome relief. Michael and Arthur smiled with her and went back to their meals.

A short while after the meal Michael came to Catherine in her solar. She sat alone near the fire with her needlepoint in her lap.

"My Lady, Aelfric still sleeps, heavily. Arthur and I laid him out on a bench with a blanket, he seems much more comfortable now. I am going out to see if I can find a boar for the pantry. I will not be gone long." He turned to leave and hesitated. "I am sorry if I was a little harsh this morning," he turned back to face her, "it is my duty to protect you and I truly believe you would be safer here at present."

His duty? Catherine was taken aback by these words, she had thought there had been something between them earlier; clearly she had been mistaken.

"No, not at all, I quite understand. You were quite right. It is better that I stay here. Good luck with your hunt." She smiled briefly and picked up her needlepoint. Michael left and went directly to the stables to saddle his horse. Moving at a brisk pace he rode towards the woods to search for boar that would still be around, looking for food.

Once inside the cover of the trees he slowed to a walk to reduce the noise they made.

****

Roland was becoming very frustrated. He had been so patient for so long and he was very close to getting everything he wanted now but was being thwarted at every turn he took. Still, he had narrowed his search and was sure that his prize was somewhere on Catherine's estate. He had been unable to decide if Preece had been pursuing Catherine for her obvious attributes, for her lands, or both, or if Preece knew something much more precious was there. As ignorant as Preece had shown himself to be he was not a complete imbecile, and there had been some hunger about the man. Perhaps that was why Roland had been drawn to him in the first place.

Now he needed to get into that house but he was not sure how. What servants she had seemed to live there and nobody travelled about alone anymore. The house never seemed to be empty either, so his best chance may lie in sneaking in at night when they were all asleep and trying to search for it then. His next challenge was to work out the best way to get in. For that he would need both inspiration and some first hand knowledge. He would need another look at the place, which meant coming out of the safety of the woods for a short time. It was not ideal in the current climate of unrest, a climate he had admittedly created himself but nevertheless, people would be watching for anyone unusual. He would need to be careful. He let out a low whistle and Saracen came to him.

Slowly they rode through the woods aiming to emerge at a slightly elevated point where the house would be visible. Once there Roland sat for a while, assessing the wall, the house and gardens. With Saracen's help the wall should not present much of a problem, then there was a small door at the side of the house, possibly a kitchen entrance that may be best in case he made a noise breaking in. The stable building was probably far enough away that no-one would be disturbed. There was an upper level, Roland guessed Catherine slept there, she would be easy enough to overpower in her sleep. He would start with the ground floor and then the upper level, and he would do it tonight.

Taking a last lingering look at the layout, committing it to memory, Roland turned Saracen's head to ride back into the woods until nightfall. As they turned Roland looked down on the village and was intrigued to see a number of men there, armed and mounted on horseback. They appeared to be an organised group. Roland felt sure that this could not be good for him and rode a short distance along the tree line to get a better look. He counted nine riders but noted other horses tethered at various places. He did not have to wait long before a tall man strode out from one of the buildings followed by a man that Roland recognised as the Keeper. The armed men gathered around the tall, well dressed man. Roland had been correct, this would not be good for him. A small army of men following a wealthy man, who was not the Keeper, could only mean that someone had gone for the governing Baron.

Roland knew that the Baron would seek to eradicate trouble swiftly, wherever and whatever it was. Allowing trouble and lawlessness to continue or spread would throw into question his ability to control his lands. The man's own pride would not accept that but it would also send a signal to his rivals that he had become distracted or vulnerable. These men were here to search for Roland and it would not be long before they went looking for him in the woods.

"Damn! I only needed one more day. Come Saracen, we will need to find somewhere else to stay, but we will be back, as soon as the Baron leaves." Turning the animal's head he headed back into the woods to collect his belongings.

Michael had not had any luck finding boar today so he had decided to go home and try again the next day. As he rode out from the tree line movement down in the village caught his eye and he glanced to his left. He guessed that the Baron was organising his first search party and decided to hurry in case they chose to pay a visit to the manor. As he looked, another movement caught his eye. It was further up, level with him on the tree line, a man on a horse, a tall man on a black horse. The horse turned and Michael could see the man's face in profile. It was Roland of Langley. A burning hatred rose in Michael, his first instinct was to charge at him and inflict as much pain as possible. His second thought was to attract the attention of the search party, get their help to capture Roland, but he could not do that without also alerting Roland to his presence. He would have to act quickly, Roland was already into the trees. Michael decided. He would follow Roland himself, catch him unawares and if necessary deal out some swift justice.

Michael turned his horse's head back into the trees and started to follow Roland at a distance, watching carefully to see where he might be going.

They rode this way for some time and Michael began to wonder if he had made the right decision. The air had turned colder as the day wore on, the canopy grew thicker above them and filtered out more and more of the weak sunlight. The ground was damp and as his horse disturbed the soil and moss with its hooves Michael could smell the heavy odour of winter decay, late coming in this sheltered place. It was too late to change his mind now, it would take far too long to return for help and then try to track Roland this far. Once or twice Michael lost sight of Roland through the trees and thought he may have lost him altogether but both times Roland had re-appeared, having changed his course slightly to avoid an obstacle.

The silent ride gave Michael an opportunity to consider what he was doing. He had made an emotional decision and acted on impulse. Michael knew that this alone would put him at a disadvantage. When they reached Roland's lair he would have to plan better, think smarter. Roland clearly knew this area of the woods, he would also know the terrain of his lair, may even have set traps and warning signals around it to alert him to approaching trouble. As time went on Michael became concerned that they may come right out the other side of the woods. In the open it would be almost impossible to follow Roland without being seen.

If Roland's lair was not in the woods, then where? Michael had not considered an alternative before, surely Roland would not be living in the open, among people. As Michael considered these new alternatives he realised he had lost sight of Roland again. For a large man on a horse he was hard to follow. He rode on a few steps but still could not spot Roland in the trees ahead. Michael brought his horse to a halt and stared hard into the foliage hoping to catch even the slightest hint of movement. Nothing. Frustrated with himself even more now Michael sat, looking ahead, knowing that he had lost Roland.

To his left a bird fluttered in the branches and Michael instinctively turned his head to look for it. It had been some time since he had seen other life in these trees.

There! A movement, not a bird, too big. Michael squinted. It was Roland, he had changed course again. He looked for the landmark that Roland must have seen and saw a large white stone on the ground. It appeared to have been bleached in the sun and Michael was surprised to see no moss or lichen growing on its surface. Turning his horse's head he set off after Roland again.

Not much farther on Michael noticed a clear rise in ground level where it formed a small hillock directly ahead. To the left the ground dropped away reasonably sharply, while to the right it sloped gently upward. Here the trees thinned a little and were replaced by small but robust looking bushes full of thorns and prickles. Instead of riding straight ahead, Roland steered his horse around to the side of the hill. Michael did not want to follow Roland around a blind bend and possibly straight into an ambush. Instead he struck out at an angle to get a better look at what was around that corner and if Roland did suspect he was being followed then Michael may have the upper hand in not coming from a direction Roland would expect.

Michael had only ridden for a few strides when he saw the black horse standing still, apparently alone, nuzzling the ground. Pulling up his own horse, Michael stopped where he was and slid quietly to the ground. He could still not see Roland from here but the man could not have gone far. Gripping the hilt of his sword Michael crept forward, bending low so as not to be seen. He stopped, he could still not see Roland from this point. Moving around further he could see more of the hillock and it seemed to end abruptly in a sheer face. Immediately in front of the sheer face was an area of flat ground but beyond that it sloped up and away to meet the raised level of the ground there.

It was not high, perhaps the height of a small hut and it was bulky and littered with rocks of different shapes and sizes. Michael could see trees and bushes growing on the higher level where the difference had not been obvious before.

Moving around still further, he was presented with a much better vantage point. Now he could see that this end of the outcrop formed a small, crude cave. On the ground at the entrance he could see the evidence of a camp fire. It was not clear how deep the cave was, Roland may only be a couple of paces inside or he may have travelled some distance in. Michael crouched by a bush assessing his options. It would be very dangerous to storm the cave, there was no way of knowing where Roland was, if he was armed, even if he was alone. For all Michael knew there may be twenty men hidden in the unknown depths of the cave. He would be better served staying where he was for now and watching to see what Roland did. Perhaps now he knew where the lair was Michael would be wise to go back and find help.

Michael's nerves were on edge as he crouched on the ground watching and waiting. He heard every sound around him, saw every twig sway in the breeze, felt its gentle touch on his skin as it blew silently by. His muscles were tense and his heart pounded in his chest waiting for the moment when he would leap into action.

Suddenly Michael saw movement at the mouth of the cave and Roland stepped out. He was carrying something, possibly a large bag or a sack. He placed it on the ground, squatted down and began placing things carefully inside it. Michael realised what he was doing then. Roland was packing his things, he was leaving. Michael guessed that Roland must have seen the Baron's men and decided to run before he got caught. This would be Michael's only chance, he no longer had the option of going for assistance. Leaving the bag Roland ducked back into the cave. Seizing his chance, Michael ran back the way he had come, back to the other side of the rise. Once there he crept up the slope to kneel on the roof of the cave near the entrance.

From here he would be able to see Roland and have the element of surprise.

He crouched low, waiting, every nerve tingling, every sense feeding messages to his brain at an incredible rate. From here he could see small bones littering the floor around the remains of the fire. He could also see a little wooden bowl on the ground with what looked to be pebbles inside. Next to that was the sack, bulky now. A scuffling sound from below alerted him to movement, Roland would come out at any moment and Michael was ready.

Michael saw the dark curly hair on his head first as it emerged from the cave. When he was two or three paces clear of the entrance Michael took his chance, he took a deep breath and leapt at Roland's back. Time seemed to slow down for Michael and he imagined himself slamming into the man's back, knocking him to the floor, stunned and hopefully winded allowing Michael to draw his sword and attack. As he sailed through the air Michael watched as Roland suddenly twisted and ducked to the side. He looked across at Michael as he fell to the ground.

Michael hit the ground very hard feet first and his ankle twisted beneath him sending a shot of pain up the length of his leg. He heard himself grunt as the pain reached its peak. As his body hit the ground he felt the air rush harshly from his lungs in an involuntary gasp.

Once the initial shock had passed Michael's instincts took over and he rolled once, twice, to take his body away from the enemy. Using the momentum of his movement he sprang to his feet, his eyes darting around, getting his bearings, seeking out Roland. Michael was alarmed that he could no longer see him anywhere. Suddenly he was acutely aware of the pain in his ankle again and felt it give way beneath him. Desperate to stay upright Michael stumbled forward, hoping to keep moving by reducing the time he had his weight on the foot.

How did this all go so wrong? Roland must have known he had been there but how long had he known?

Michael swung his leg forward, he needed to retreat, to get back to his horse. As his foot touched the floor Michael felt the burn of pain flare up again. He gritted his teeth and completed the step, putting his weight on the foot. A wave of nausea swept through him and for one horrifying second Michael thought he might pass out. Swinging his good foot forward he planted all his weight on it. The sickness passed and his vision cleared. Taking a deep breath he braced himself for another step. The next wave of pain took his breath away but he had to keep moving. He could see his horse now and focused on getting to it.

He barely registered the crack of broken twigs. Slowly he lifted his damaged foot and started to swing it forward, anticipating the burst of pain that would come. Suddenly something soft was clamped firmly over his nose and mouth. He panicked and tried to take a step back, away from it, but he stepped back into a solid object. Michael's hands flew up to his face trying to remove whatever it was, desperately fighting for air. His nose and lungs quickly filled with an acrid stench, bitter and unfamiliar. The rough cloth scratched at his skin and released tiny fibres into his mouth.

Michael's hands grasped at the obstruction, finding fingers and a hand holding it in a vice–like grip. There was a man standing behind him and his other arm was now holding Michael tightly across the chest.

Michael's arms flailed wildly as he gasped for air but he was quickly overcome by the fumes on the cloth covering his face. He heard a rushing, whooshing sound in his ears as it became steadily louder. He saw bright sparks flying across his vision.

At the same moment he realised that it was Roland holding him everything went black and Michael collapsed onto the ground.

Chapter 28

Dusk was creeping across the countryside. Its progress was slow and gentle and silent, like a mother pulling a blanket over her sleeping infant. As the light failed, shadows started to lengthen, creating patterns and designs where none had been before. Some were large and shapeless, others were tiny and intricate, leaping about as the icy north wind played with twigs and leaves. Children would torment their friends, telling stories of devils that inhabited the dancing shadows, devils who would occasionally reach out to grab at children's feet if they strayed too close.

Shutters were closed and tapestries hung across the window spaces to keep out the draughts as much as possible. The fires, crackling and spitting in their grates did the rest. Catherine huddled by her fire as she sat in the hall. Aelfric had finally woken a short time before the midday meal and he looked much better. His colour had returned, he seemed brighter, his eyes no longer looked red and sore. He had eaten an astonishing amount during the meal and subsequently required a short nap to recover himself. Michael had not returned in time to eat with them, it was not particularly unusual but Catherine had felt strangely disappointed not to have seen him.

The afternoon had been spent in lessons with Aelfric and she was feeling quietly confident in her limited abilities. Catherine realised that she knew very little but what she did know she knew very well and she had a good understanding of the basics, upon which she could build and improve her knowledge of spells and potions. It was now just past the middle of the afternoon and it was starting to get dark. Catherine and Aelfric had decided to take a short break from their studies and had returned to the hall for refreshment. As she stared into the flicking flames of the fire Catherine recited incantations in her head to make sure she knew them by heart, but as time went on she was finding it easier to learn, easier to understand. Catherine was not sure if it was because she enjoyed her studies so much or that she had a gift for it. She knew what Aelfric would say, he would tell her that it was all a part of her gift, the talent for magic.

As she sat musing, the door opened and Arthur entered the room. Catherine only needed a brief glance at his face to know that something was wrong. She immediately sat up straight.

"Arthur? What is it? What is wrong?"

"Nothing my Lady, John and I are just a little concerned that Michael has not yet returned from his hunting trip."

He had her attention but she was not yet worried.

"When did you expect him back?"

Arthur looked briefly down at his feet and then up at Catherine.

"He was going to be back in time for the midday meal. We will give him a little while longer and then go out to look for him."

Now she was worried. The meal had been more than three hours ago, but she trusted in Arthur's judgement and tried to curb her concern for Michael. She glanced across at Aelfric, hoping to borrow some calm from his placid demeanour. Aelfric sat on the edge of his seat, staring at Arthur, his eyes wide, lips parted, completely still, as if he had been frozen to the spot. Catherine was concerned that he had been taken ill again.

"Aelfric, are you all right? Is something ailing you?" she asked gently.

Aelfric jumped a little, startled by the sound of his name, and he turned his head to look at Catherine. It was not illness she had read in his face, it was fear. Something had really frightened him. Catherine glanced back, in the direction that

Aelfric had been staring, in case he had seen something, but she saw only Arthur. She looked back at Aelfric. He now sat with his hands resting in his lap, they were open with the palms facing up; eyes cast down, seemingly staring at his hands.

"Aelfric?" she prompted, hoping he might respond, but he said nothing. She looked back at Arthur, truly puzzled by Aelfric's reaction, not knowing what he had reacted to. Arthur looked as confused as she felt. He stood, staring at Aelfric, frowning slightly. He looked at Catherine and shrugged.

"I will let you know if Michael returns or if we decide to go out looking for him." Arthur nodded his head to Catherine, turned and left the room.

Suddenly Aelfric became animated, every part of him seemed to move in a tiny way. He raised his head and looked at Catherine, his expression intense and a little wild, a little desperate.

"Aelfric tell me, what on earth is the matter?" He was really beginning to scare her now.

"I know. I know what is happening, in this place. I guessed it two days ago. It is why I have not been able to sleep. I cannot keep it from you any longer. I should not have kept it from you for so long. I hope you can forgive me, one day"

Catherine was really very alarmed now, she had not seen Aelfric this way before. He had always seemed very calm and serene, able to cope with anything. Catherine had relied on that strength and yet here he was, babbling, almost incoherent, clearly very scared of something. He was no longer speaking but she knew more was to come, suspected that she would not like what she was about to hear. She could see Aelfric struggling with himself, trying to find the right words or possibly he had the words but was just trying to find the courage to say them.

"You must hear me," he said, "you must promise to hear me to the end." His voice was a little desperate but hard and commanding. She nodded her head in agreement.

"I believe Michael is not lost but captured and I believe I know who has him." He paused, Catherine's face gave a reflective expression to some of the emotions churning round inside her. She opened her mouth to speak. Aelfric cut her off sharply. "You promised! Let me finish." Catherine reluctantly closed her mouth, trapping inside a hundred different questions.

"I came here because I believed something was coming and I needed to warn your father. Finding him gone I knew I had to stay, to guide you and teach you."

Catherine's eyes were wide, her face pale, almost translucent. He could see that he had alarmed her but she had to know now. There was no longer any benefit in keeping this terrible knowledge to himself.

"Before I travelled here I lived in Worcester, at the cathedral, with Brother Edric." Aelfric paused again, saddened by the memory of his friend. "I had known Edric for many years, he was a very good friend. We worked together, also." As he spoke Aelfric felt a surge of anger well up within him, it bubbled over into his features. "I was in the crypt the day it happened."

Catherine watched the rush of emotions as they washed over Aelfric's face. She saw as a deep sadness settled over him, a grief that etched lines across his face, adding years to him. That was quickly replaced by a smouldering anger. His eyes darkened, his voice lowered through almost gritted teeth. Aelfric seemed darker, dangerous, and for the first time since she had met him, Catherine was afraid of what he might be capable of.

"I heard a sound and came up the stairs. Before I reached the top I heard Edric's voice. He sounded frightened, I had only heard him that way once before but I recognised it immediately. He was talking to someone and like the coward that I am I crept to the top of the stairs to watch. I did not go to him. I should have gone to him, to protect him from the stranger who came. He was a big man, very tall and broad. I could not see his face beneath his dark hood. He was looking for something he thought Edric had but Edric would not tell him where it was."

Aelfric paused as he remembered the day, as clearly as if it had been just yesterday. He could hear Edric's voice in his mind, strong and clear. 'It is safe, evil will not use it again.' Edric had held up his cross then, certain that his faith would protect him. 'Out demon! You will not get the tool of the devil from me.' Aelfric flinched as he recalled the flash of the blade, heard Edric's cry of pain, saw the hot red blood pouring from his friend. Tears flowed freely down Aelfric's face as he felt the shame of his cowardice. He had done nothing to assist Edric, he had stayed hidden, afraid for his own life, until it was too late. Gradually the memory passed and he became aware of his surroundings again. Catherine had left her seat and was kneeling on the cold floor in front of him, holding his hands. Her deep concern was clear in her face, her eyes pleading for some explanation. Aelfric sniffed, wiping his face with his sleeve.

"I watched while my best friend was murdered. I did nothing to help him until the monster was gone and then it was too late. Edric was already gone." Aelfric's voice was strained and speaking was clearly difficult but he continued.

"I knew what the stranger was. I knew what he was looking for. I consulted with the Abbot and he sent me to you, to teach you." His voice was quiet now, weak, haunted. "It was my duty to prepare you. It should have been Edric who came."

Aelfric fell silent then, but Catherine could not keep her promise any longer.

"What are you saying? That it is my destiny to find this thing before the murderer does? You are training me in case I have to fight this man?"

Aelfric shook his head. "You do not understand. He is not just a man. He is a powerful warlock. He is evil and he has been hunting it for years. He will not stop until he has it. The magic I have taught you so far, will be insignificant to him. He is coming, Catherine, and we cannot win. We must go, go now. Gather your things and come with me. We will be safe at the cathedral, for a while at least. Please, hurry, there is no time." As he spoke Aelfric became more and more agitated, fidgeting in his seat, his expression almost wild with fear.

Catherine was overwhelmed by all this new information. Aelfric was obviously very afraid of this man, with good reason, clearly, but it still did not make sense to her.

"Wait, Aelfric, I do not understand." Taking back her hands she raised one to her head to try and steady the dizziness she felt. So many things spinning around in her mind, so many gaps, things she did not know.

"Why is he coming here? And where is Michael?"

"I will tell you everything on the way, please, we must go now." Aelfric was on his feet, desperate to leave, to get away from the warlock. Catherine suddenly felt as if a candle had been lit within her, things became simpler, clearer. She could not run away, not while Michael was missing. She had to know it all, Aelfric had to finish his story, now. Slowly, absolutely determined, Catherine raised her head and looked at Aelfric.

"No." It was calm and firm, short, simple and very effective. Aelfric stopped in his tracks, turning back to look at her. Catherine had risen to her feet and stared at him, a picture of strength and composure.

"I am not leaving this place until I know Michael is safe. You need to sit back down and tell me everything."

Stunned by this abrupt change in Catherine's mood and demeanour Aelfric stood still, staring at her.

"Aelfric! Tell me, you are still hiding things. I have to know." Her voice was so firm and commanding that he hardly believed it had come from the same woman he had met three weeks ago. He moved back to his chair and sat down. Catherine moved her own chair closer and sat too.

"Why is the warlock coming here?"

Feeling utterly defeated and hopeless now, Aelfric answered her.

"He is not coming. He is already here. He has been here for some time. He certainly arrived before I did, although I did not realise it until two days ago. It is the warlock who has been killing in his search. It is he who has caused most of the evil and trouble in this place. I say most, because I believe the fires were ordered by Preece, set by the men the Keeper rightly holds. I suspect he was taking advantage of the unrest to lure your protection away."

Aelfric's words certainly seemed to make sense. All that had happened over the last month was easily explained by this. Catherine began to understand.

"The warlock has been making an orderly search of any places he thought might be harbouring his prize. I suspect he may have killed people who discovered him while he was searching. This is the only house he has not yet searched. I believe he will try to remove any obstacles before he attempts to come in."

"You think the warlock has Michael?" Catherine was deeply concerned about this. Aelfric had already suggested that the warlock had no qualms about killing.

"Yes," Aelfric's voice was almost a whisper and his head dropped, "he may have been able to lure Michael into a trap to capture him or……."

"No, not Michael, he is a good soldier. He would know better than to walk into a trap." Catherine refused to entertain the possibility that Michael may be dead.

"That is true, but suppose Michael thought he knew the man? Catherine, I believe the warlock to be Roland of Langley."

Catherine's head snapped up at that name, she reeled from the shock. Roland had been here, in this house, had captured her, had. …….he was going to give her to Preece. How, then, had she survived? Why had he not searched her house when he had the chance? Aelfric could easily guess the theme of the torrent of thoughts flowing through her mind just then.

"I do not believe he knew what you were then. It was before you knew so he could not have sensed it fully. I think he was merely looking for sport, activity or possibly just money. That may be the only reason you are alive today, the reason yours was the last home he considered searching. And I believe Michael may have sufficient provocation to walk into any trap Roland may have set."

Catherine allowed herself a minute to absorb this new information before asking her next question.

"That is still not everything. What does Roland, this warlock, think I have?" Her voice betrayed her emotions. As she said his name she felt hatred and disgust, she felt the pain and humiliation he had given her, remembered the fear she had felt because of him. She was angry, vengeful, a cold hard determination to end all of this suffering took hold of her and it made her strong. She felt power within her, as she waited for Aelfric's answer.

"The Shadow."

"The what?"

"The Shadow. Do you remember a few days ago, we spoke about your pendent?"

"He is looking for my necklace? My necklace is the Shadow?" Catherine was a little disturbed by that thought.

"No, not your necklace. Do you recall we talked about how it was created by a master, to channel good magic?"

"Yes."

"Well, there are also masters of dark magic and from time to time one of them will create a conduit for dark magic, for evil. A very long time ago one of those masters created the Shadow. It is not widely known that it exists, its age means that it appears in only a handful of ancient texts and only one of those tells of its form. It is possible that the warlock does not know exactly what form he seeks but he will be well aware of the power it could give him. It is said that if a man who possesses the Shadow is hungry enough for power, the Shadow can feed on that hunger, it is what it desires. In return it will give the keeper as much power, wealth and protection as they could dream of."

"But I do not know where it is. I do not have such a thing here."

"The warlock has been tracking its essence for years and he had narrowed it down to this place, this house."

Catherine's mind raced. She knew every object in the house, had grown up with most of them. She could not think of a single one of them that might hold an evil power. Surely her own pendent would have reacted to it if she had been near it recently? But it had not …….. wait, it had. The chest, it had reacted to something in the chest. There was still a small box in there, a box she had not brought herself to open yet.

"It is here Catherine, your father was its Guardian for years. Do you have any idea where it is?"

"Yes, I know."

"You should get it now. We must leave. If we can get to the cathedral we can consult with the scholars and perhaps find a way to destroy it. It was not attempted while it was still safe, it seemed we had plenty of time to find just the right way. But it is surely worth the risk now."

"Risk?" Catherine was feeling her head begin to spin again. Aelfric was becoming increasingly frustrated at these delays, he was acutely aware of time slipping away from them.

"Catherine, please, we can discuss this later, when we are safe."

Catherine looked at him steadily, her determination clearly written on her face.

"No, Aelfric. The time for running is long past. You said it yourself, he is already here, and he has Michael. I will not leave without Michael."

Aelfric became angry now, his frustration boiling over.

"You asked about the risk? If we get the Shadow to Worcester we may be able to find a way to destroy it without releasing the Shadow itself. If that happens, it will be a terrible plague on the world. There will be famine, the likes of which man has not seen. There will be disease, pain and suffering. We may never be able to trap it again. If we do not get it away from this house, if the warlock gets it, he may use it to gain power, start wars, plunge the country, the world, into poverty. He would revel in the pain and strife. Or he may release it himself and subjugate himself to it. It is very sad that Michael is gone and in all probability he is already dead, but he is one man, we must protect the thousands who *will* suffer and die if we do not act *now*!"

Catherine was stung by these words but it only fuelled her determination to stay and search for the warlock and for Michael.

"You are suggesting we run, and keep running. Every time he comes close to finding it we run away again. I do not want that life. I do not want to be always looking over my shoulder, wondering where he is, when he will come for me. No! We stay, we fight. Better still, we take the fight to him. You said it yourself, he does not suspect what I am, what I have become. He will expect us to run and hide. If he can track, then so can we. We find him and we fight him, it is the only chance we have to succeed. Hit him quickly and hard, before he is ready."

She glared at Aelfric, blood pumping quickly through her, breathing hard, eyes bright and alive.

"Are you staying? Will you help me?"

Aelfric was torn between his desire to run from the warlock to the comparative safety of the cathedral, and his sworn duty to guide Catherine, teach her. He felt the two sides battling within him. He was very afraid but he wanted to be brave enough to stay. He saw her determination, felt her power but he knew the warlock was more skilful, more experienced.

"That will be his downfall." Catherine's voice was suddenly soft, assured. "His own confidence, all his experience, he will expect us to behave a certain way. But we are making this up as we go, how can he defend against that?"

Aelfric was quite sure he had not spoken his thoughts aloud and yet she seemed to know them. He had underestimated her power, misjudged her.

"I will stay."

"Good. Now I want to see what I am harbouring."

She walked quickly across the room.

"Are you coming?" she called back to Aelfric without breaking her stride. His first response was an emphatic 'no'. He did not want to be anywhere near the Shadow. Being in the same house was close enough. But his curiosity overcame his fears and he trotted after her.

Catherine paused outside the door to her father's chamber. She wanted to see what was so special about this Shadow for herself, needed to see it, to give it proper perspective. At the moment she imagined something non–corporeal, mist–like and large, but she could not equate that image with what she had already seen. Taking a deep steadying breath she opened the door and went in, just as Aelfric caught up with her. He lingered at the door, watching as Catherine knelt before a large chest.

Catherine laid both hands on the top of the chest, half expecting to feel heat or some kind of movement. Relieved, she felt neither. Slowly she began to lift, she was tense and ready to jump away should anything leap out at her. When nothing happened she opened the lid all the way and let out the breath she had been holding since she had knelt before the chest. She looked inside. It was almost empty now. The parchment, bowls and herbs she had already taken to her solar, now there were only the two wooden boxes.

One lay open. It was the small carved box in which she had found the pendent she now wore. The other box was also small but quite crudely carved and plain, with no thought to decoration. She reached into the chest as she would reach for a viper, afraid that it would strike at her and bite. It did not strike. As her fingers neared the box she felt a strong jolt at her throat. Her pendent had literally leapt by its own will, pulling against the thong. It felt hot and continued to vibrate vigorously. Acutely conscious of the warning it sought to give her Catherine lay her fingers on the box, ready to snatch them away at the slightest sign of life. She carefully took hold of it and began to lift the box. As she did so she felt a wave of nausea wash over her and a kind of tightness inside her head. Catherine sagged forward a little, distracted by the discomfort.

Aelfric stepped forward, worried.

"Are you all right?" he asked.

"It is hurting me, I feel sick to my stomach and my head hurts."

"You are reacting to the evil, revulsion is probably the best word to describe it. Perhaps you should put the box back?"

"No, it is passing, give me a second." Catherine sat up again and took several long shaky breaths. When the sensation had passed she looked again at the box in her hand. It looked so small and inoffensive.

"Is this it? Does this box contain the Shadow?" she asked. "You said that one of the ancient texts described its form."

"No," replied Aelfric, "the Shadow's cage is very small, of metal and gem stone."

Catherine took the small box in both hands and carefully opened the lid. Her heart was pounding quickly, she felt scared but more alive than she had ever been before. Nothing leapt at her from the box, there were no strange sounds. There was a strange odour though. It smelt very odd, a little mouldy perhaps. She looked inside. There were several things there, some small bones that appeared to have been decorated with brightly coloured symbols. There were also two small, brown feathers, one white feather and some dried herb stems. In the centre of the box there was another object. Hardly larger than an arrowhead it looked small and insignificant at first glance. Looking closer she could see that there was a delicately carved metal plate, covered in symbols or patterns that she had never seen before. In the middle of the plate was some kind of stone, as Aelfric had said. It appeared to be a deep red in colour and it was perfectly flawless. She could not see a chip or spot in it anywhere. The base was flat, where it met the plate, but the top surface was rounded. As she looked it seemed almost to glow.

"Aelfric, is this it?" Her voice was hushed as if afraid of waking the spirit that resided within the stone. Aelfric cautiously stepped forward, peering into the box.

"Yes." His voice was also low, almost awestruck.

"What are these other things for?" She indicated the bones, feathers and herbs.

"They are charms that the scholars put with it to suppress its essence. The brown feathers are from an owl, they represent the watchers. The white feather is from a dove, for peace. The bones and herbs are charms to hide it from anyone who may seek it. Perhaps over the years they have lost some of their potency, or perhaps the scholars did not anticipate the warlock's power and persistence."

"Aelfric, have you seen this before?" Catherine stared at him intently.

"Yes. It is a long story that I will tell you one day, suffice it to say, I helped to liberate it from its previous owner."

Satisfied, Catherine closed the lid of the box and stood up.

"We will either need to take this with us or hide it well until we can return. Can we use the protection spell to shield it?"

"I think we may be able to modify it, yes."

"Good, then let us go to my solar and start to plan. We will cast a charm on this first, after that we will find out where the warlock is holding Michael."

Aelfric simply nodded and followed her back to her solar. Once there they set about hiding the box. Catherine lifted one of the mats covering the floor and cleared straw from one of the stone slabs there.

"Here, help me lift this."

Eventually, between them, they managed to move the stone, dig a small hole and bury the box. They then replaced the stone and the floor coverings over it. Kneeling over the spot Catherine began to chant.

"ventis me, arma ab adluvio et aerius
cis malum occulto, custodies ab magicus"

Satisfied now that the Shadow would be safer, for a while at least, Catherine turned her mind to finding the warlock and Michael.

"How do we find them?"

"There is a seeing potion I can make, it is quite simple. It will help you to see their location in your mind's eye." Aelfric rummaged through the chest for the ingredients he would need. "Please fetch me a small pot of water." Pleased to have something constructive to do, Aelfric threw himself into the task. It did not take him long to prepare the mixture and pour it into a pot for Catherine to drink.

"Try to drink it all, as quickly as you can. I do not imagine it will taste good" he added apologetically.

Sitting cross legged on the floor in the centre of the room, Catherine took the cup and drank the contents. It was truly foul stuff and she had to fight the sudden urge to be sick. The feeling passed quickly and she began to feel drowsy. Her eyes flickered shut and she felt incredibly sleepy, while knowing her body was still alert. It was hard to grasp, how she could be in two very different states at once, but before she had a chance to examine it further she was startled by a picture. It was in her mind and it rushed upon her, large and bright. She instinctively leaned back to avoid being hit and felt Aelfric's hands on her back, preventing her from falling.

In her vision she was slowly rising from the ground, she could see it getting further and further away. Her feet hung limp in the air and she was hovering above her own stable yard. She felt so light and free. Remembering what she was looking for she suddenly found herself moving forward, as if she had willed herself to move. Now she could see tree tops below her, she was flying quite high now. The trees started to rush by.

Catherine found she was able to look around and saw her own house disappearing into the distance behind her. Very soon she could see an area of grassland rushing toward her beyond the line of the trees, a little way on from that there was a tiny hut and outside was a fire. One man sat by the fire with a steaming pot over it. She looked closer and saw the man's face. Catherine jumped again as she recognised Roland's face. Recovering quickly she looked around again. The picture was fading fast before her. 'No'. She had not seen Michael. To the side of the hut was a pile of bags or cloth, it moved, there was a foot. It must be Michael and he was alive.

Just as suddenly as it had arrived the picture rushed away from her again and once more she was awake in her solar, with a very concerned Aelfric kneeling beside her.

Chapter 29

It was dark when Michael woke. Dark and bitterly cold, he began to shiver before he even opened his eyes. His head was pounding; it felt like someone was beating on his temples with a stone. The next sensation he felt was a dull throbbing pain in his foot. He lay still, waiting for his head to clear a little more before he could think about what had happened. Slowly the various pains in his body began to subside until they remained a constant background noise in his mind, secondary to the confusion that dominated. He tried to remember how he had come to be lying on the hard, frozen ground. Had he fallen from his horse and hit his head? It was a total blank. He tried to remember further back, to when he had woken up that morning. It was foggy, but encouragingly still there. Michael concentrated on that and slowly it began to focus into a solid memory. Although he was unsure how much of it was imagination or true memory from this morning.

Michael recalled that he had woken early and gone out to perform some chores. Then he had gone to the hall for some food. Then what? Aelfric. That was right, Aelfric had been fast asleep in the chair, looking like he was at death's door. This was good, it set this memory apart from every other morning in the last six years. He was making progress. Eventually he and Arthur had moved the monk to a bench where he would be more comfortable. Then, yes, then he had decided to go hunting for boar while the weather was still reasonably good. He had saddled his horse and ridden into the woods. Michael could not remember finding any boar. That was it. He could not recall anything else and trying to force the images only made his head hurt more so he gave up. Resolved to try again later.

Finally Michael opened his eyes and tentatively looked around him. It was clearly night and he was lying on the ground. There was something over him, covering his body. To his left was some kind of hut, it appeared to be small but from where he lay, Michael's field of view was small, it was hard to tell. He could not see any trees nearby, although it was very dark, he guessed that he was probably not in the woods anymore. There was a sharp, icy breeze blowing about his head, it seemed fairly constant, unbroken by trees, making it more likely that he was on open ground. Above the sound of the wind he could hear a gentle crackle, it was a sound he knew but he could not immediately place it. Smoke, he could also smell smoke. Then it was a small fire he could hear.

Considering his current condition Michael thought it very unlikely that he could have built the fire himself and even if he had, why would he then take himself away from its warmth to lie down? He was therefore, more than probably not alone. Perhaps if he called out they would come to help him. No, if they had his welfare at heart he would surely be closer to that fire. It was time to properly assess his injuries, carefully, quietly. Michael tried to move his hands. They were tied tightly together. He had thought his situation was bad, now he knew it was worse. He was being held captive, but by who and why?

Just then Michael heard a rustling sound behind him and he froze, pretending to be unconscious still. Then he heard slow and heavy footsteps, coming closer, until they stopped just in front of his face. The figure crouched down beside him.

"So, you are finally awake."

Roland! Now Michael remembered all that had happened. He remembered following Roland through the woods, the ambush and his ankle. Finally he remembered Roland smothering him until he had passed out. He must have been unconscious when Roland had moved him. They could be anywhere by now. Michael was just beginning to wonder why he was not dead when a hand roughly grabbed the cloth at the back of his neck. Suddenly Michael was being dragged roughly across the hard ground, his limp foot bouncing over every frozen bump.

"Aaaarrgh!" Michael cried out in pain as these new and raw sensations tore up his leg. He was not dragged far before he was dropped on his side next to the fire. Michael was glad of the instant warmth, it momentarily distracted him from the pain in his foot. Roland went back to the other side of the fire and sat down.

"Do not flatter yourself that I have brought you to my fire for your benefit. I want to watch you now that you are awake and I do not want to be cold while I am doing it. And I do not want this to boil dry." He indicated the pot hanging over the fire. Now that he was closer Michael could see it steaming and could smell a strangely sweet odour that he guessed must be coming from the boiling contents. As he lay still the pain began to ebb away once more and again Michael began to wonder why he was still alive. He watched Roland closely as he tended to whatever it was he was cooking.

"Come on Michael, you have questions, go ahead, ask away. You may as well."

Michael was surprised at the polite invitation. He had never known a captor to be so...chatty. That was the only way he could describe it. Michael was concerned by the last part of the invitation but chose not to pursue that just then. Roland was right though. Michael did have a lot of questions that he wanted answers to. The only problem was which one to ask first.

"Why are you still here? After what you did, why did you stay?"

"Be more specific Michael, what did I do?"

"When you took Lady Catherine, and hurt her." Michael felt his anger rising again and struggled to subdue it, he was, after all, in no position to do anything about it.

"I had other business in the area. Still do, actually." Michael could not believe how casual Roland sounded in his answers, it was almost as if they were discussing a recent trip rather than the awful things he had done. He persevered through his disgust.

"Business with Preece?"

"No, I am finished with him. I am impressed, I did not think you had recognised me that day." Roland's tone was light and easy, conversational. It displayed an arrogance that disgusted Michael still further.

"How did you do it?" Michael asked. "How did you change your appearance, to look like Sigar? That is what you did?"

"Excellent! Well done. I was right, you are a bit brighter than the rest. You asked a good question, because this answer will also answer your next question. Why you are still alive."

Michael was initially surprised that Roland seemed to have known his thoughts but then if Roland was a tactical man, if their positions were reversed he may have asked the same thing of Michael.

"I did it with a potion, much like this one in fact. You see, I am looking for something and I know it is there somewhere, I am just not sure exactly where, at least I was not until very recently. Now, obviously, I am easily recognisable, and people would notice a stranger in their home. So I simply take one of their own, borrow a couple of fingers to add to my potion and then simmer for a while. When it is ready I drink it and take on the appearance of that person. It gives me the freedom to come and go as I please and search almost at my leisure. I stayed too long at Preece's house and it wore off. A bit inconvenient, as you saw."

Michael thought about this for a few seconds and suddenly so many things made sense.

"That is why there were always reports of someone having seen the dead person just before the body was discovered, when the body was clearly days old."

"Right, now I have only one place left to search. I was going to do it tonight, just creep in, but then I noticed the small army running around the village. It is a little frustrating, I was hoping to have finished and been on my way by now. These potions take so long to make and you have to do it just right, otherwise, well, you will just have to trust me, it is not pretty."

Michael was struggling to follow the conversation. It sounded like Roland was talking about some kind of, well, magic. Surely he was wrong.

"What are you?"

"Shame, and you were doing so well. I am a warlock of course, and yes, I am talking of magic. It is what I do and I do it very well." He paused briefly to stir the contents of the pot. "You are key to my plans because I need to get back into your Lady's house, and I know she trusts you. I saw the way she looks at you. I wonder if she will look at me the same way." He shot a glance at Michael and was gratified to see the intense anger in his face. He laughed "Oh, calm down, I no longer have the patience for such games. I have already wasted enough time coming out here to avoid being disturbed in the woods. It was just a matter of time before those men went looking for me there." Roland fell silent then for a while, but there was still something Michael was not clear on.

"So, you have me to 'borrow' my fingers." Roland smiled and nodded. "Why have you not already taken them? Surely they would be easier to carry than an unconscious and injured man?"

"Because the flesh has to be alive when it goes into the potion. Dead flesh is no good." Again Roland spoke as if they were swapping old family recipes for stew and Michael found it hard to believe.

He wondered if he were dreaming all of this. Magic and warlocks, talking about his impending death with a man he detested as casually as they would about livestock. This had to be a fever induced hallucination, a dream at least, made stranger because he had knocked his head. The trouble with that theory was the pain in his foot, which was very, very real. He had to be awake.

* * * *

Catherine stayed where she was, sitting on the floor for a few more minutes, until the disorientation was gone and she felt she could stand without falling.

"That was absolutely incredible. I felt like I was flying and I could look all around me."

"What did you see?" asked Aelfric, still a little bit worried about her.

"I went from here and flew over the woods. I travelled all the way to the other side. There is some grassland there and a small hut. Roland was there, he was sitting by a small fire, and Michael was there too. He was lying down near the hut but I am sure I saw him move. I believe he is still alive."

Catherine was elated by her experience and felt a thrill of emotions flowing through her body. It was almost as if she was still floating.

"And what was Roland doing?" Aelfric could see her attention wavering and tried to bring her back to reality.

"He was sitting by the fire. Wait, there was something hanging over the fire, a pot. He was cooking, some kind of broth maybe?"

"Or a potion perhaps?"

Catherine quickly caught what Aelfric was getting at. They had no more time to marvel over the vision, Michael might not have much time. She got to her feet and rushed from the room.

"Arthur, Arthur." She called as loudly as she could and he met her in the hall.

"What is it my Lady? What is wrong?"

"I know where Michael is. I cannot tell you how I know, I just need you to trust me and come with me to rescue him."

"Rescue? Then you believe he is in trouble?" Arthur was becoming more and more concerned about his friend.

"Yes, I do. Will you come?"

"Of course." Arthur's reply was instant. He would risk his life for Michael. Arthur also had his suspicions about what Catherine had been doing these past few weeks, how she knew where he was. If she said she knew, he believed her.

"Please ready three horses, Aelfric will be riding with us. I need to find Rachel." With that she hurried off leaving Arthur to see to the horses.

It was not long before she returned to the solar. Aelfric was sitting by the fire fretting about what might happen next.

"Arthur is readying three horses. I have spoken to Rachel. If the Baron's men come to the house she is to tell them there is disease here and they should not enter." She hurried to the chest.

"And she believed you? Who is sick?" Catherine stopped for a second.

"You are." She turned to look at him. "You looked really ill this morning, she saw that. Do not worry, it will work. Now, please help me to collect the things I might need."

Aelfric moved to her side and began collecting phials and herbs and placing them carefully in a small cloth bag with a long handle that Catherine could wear over her shoulder.

"Who is the third horse for?" Aelfric was afraid to ask and added hopefully, "is John going too?"

"No, Aelfric, you are coming. I am going to need you, by my side."

He did not speak, did not even acknowledge what she had said, until he felt her hand on his shoulder.

"Aelfric, please, I cannot do this without you."

He looked at her then and nodded, collecting a few more phials and secreting them in his robes. Then she really took him by surprise.

"Thank you" she said and threw her arms around him, hugging him hard.

By the time they had put on warm cloaks and got to the courtyard Arthur was ready with the horses. He helped Catherine to mount and then watched in mild amusement as Aelfric tried to mount his horse. Arthur turned to Catherine.

"Are you sure you would not rather have John come with us?"

Catherine smiled, "No. Please help him, we may need him before this is over."

Finally all three were mounted and ready to go. Arthur indicated that she should lead the group as she was the only one of them who knew where to go. She nodded in silence and urged her horse forward. As soon as she had cleared the gates she urged her mare to a canter and headed straight for the woods. Arthur followed in silence. Aelfric watched them go, slightly concerned that he would not be able to keep up. Fortunately his horse had other ideas and cantered off after the other two, almost unseating Aelfric. He clamped his legs to the horse's sides as best he could and grabbed a handful of mane, uttering a quick prayer for his deliverance. Once they reached the tree line Catherine had to slow to a brisk trot but was unwilling to go any slower while she could maintain this pace. She was well aware that time was running out.

The woods were very dark and although the moon had risen a short time ago, very little light penetrated through the mesh of branches and leaves. Smaller plants were hard to pick out and exposed roots almost impossible. She had to trust her horse to pick its way through these obstacles for both of them. For the most part her mare did very well, finding safe ground almost instinctively but once in a while she would catch a hoof and stumble. Catherine had to hold on tight to avoid falling. In some places the foliage was so thick they had no option but to slow to a walk.

As they travelled through the wood Catherine was constantly caught by twigs and overhanging branches. It felt as if she were being clawed and pulled at by unseen creatures. Her hair was braided today but as she rode and twigs caught at her she felt wisps being pulled free, falling around her face. As she put a hand up to push them aside she felt something wet on her temple. Clearly one of the twigs had done more than simply scratch. This was not the time to stop and deal with trivial injuries. Only a few minutes later she was nearly caught out by a low hanging branch, noticing it just in time to duck underneath. She called softly to her companions but still heard a muffled cry as Aelfric's head connected with the branch.

Eventually they came to the far edge of the woods, the trees thinned and light found its way in. Catherine sensed rather than saw open ground ahead and she raised her left hand and stopped her horse. Aelfric stopped behind and Arthur rode up beside her.

"What do you see?" he asked in a hushed voice.

"Nothing yet, but I think we are at the edge of the woods now, I do not want to ride out into the open and give our presence away." She looked across at Arthur. "Hold my horse, I will go and have a better look."

She handed the reins to Arthur and slipped from her horse's back. Dry leaves and small twigs crunched under her feet and she cringed a little, knowing she would need to be almost silent from now on. From her vision she did not think the hut was very far from the tree line. Catherine crept forward slowly, trying to step on clear ground where she could, trying not to make sudden moves that might give her away if Roland was looking out for a rescue party. After a couple of minutes in this manner she made it to the very edge of the trees and stopped behind one of the trunks, peering out across the open ground.

After a few seconds of allowing her eyes to adjust to the extra light, Catherine looked out into the night. Some way off she could just see the orange flicker of fire and even in the moonlight she was barely able to make out the small hut nearby. She was not close enough to get a good view of Roland or Michael. Catherine crept along the inside of the tree line, moving around to the back of the hut, putting it directly between her and Roland. She was a little closer now and it occurred to her that this may be the best way to approach the fire. It was the only cover once beyond the comparative safety of the trees. The wind was icy here and, it seemed to cut through the gaps in her cloak with ease. She pulled it closer around her and made her cautious way back to Arthur and Aelfric.

Arthur was beginning to worry about her when he saw movement ahead and left of their position. To his credit Aelfric had sat in complete silence while they waited. Arthur suspected that this was probably because the monk was consumed with fear. He had no idea why Catherine had insisted on bringing him, he just hoped that when it counted Aelfric would be able to rise above his fear and play his part, whatever that may turn out to be. Catherine was now back with them and spoke quietly with Arthur for some time. Aelfric watched as they whispered earnestly, sometimes Catherine pointed and Arthur looked, other times Arthur pointed and Catherine followed the direction of his finger. There was much shaking of heads and then finally both nodded. Apparently some agreement had been reached. They continued to whisper for a few minutes longer and then Catherine moved towards Arthur to embrace him. He immediately returned the embrace and they stayed that way for a few seconds.

Aelfric had always loved to watch the people around him, fascinated by their differences. Michael and Arthur for instance, they were both strong, decent men. Both had a lot of respect for Catherine and her father and clearly both cared deeply for Catherine but they expressed it in very different ways. Michael was reluctant to express openly how he felt and chose instead to show it by being strong and practical, protective and valiant. Arthur on the other hand, while no less of a man for it, was more able to express how he felt. He was comfortable with her embrace and readily returned it. He laughed more, seemed more relaxed in general.

Aelfric was also surprised at how easily Arthur had followed Catherine. They all lived in a heavily male dominated society, and Arthur was a trained soldier, a natural leader, with far more experience in combat than Catherine. In fact Catherine had virtually no experience and yet Arthur followed her into the woods, sat patiently while she assessed the area and then discussed plans with her on an equal basis. Aelfric wondered if Michael would have followed her with that degree of faith.

Catherine stepped towards Aelfric. "Time to go Aelfric, we are on foot from now on. Arthur will tether your horse here with the others." Her tone was gentle but confident and commanding and Aelfric slid from his horse the best he could. Glad to have his feet on safe and solid ground again he set off after Catherine. They travelled within the tree line for a while, crouched low, moving slowly but surely back to the spot Catherine had picked out earlier. Then she stopped. Aelfric crouched beside her and looked over his shoulder.

"Catherine, I think we lost Arthur, he may not be able to find us while we hide down here."

"He is not coming Aelfric, this part we do alone." Catherine continued to stare intently out across the dark grassland towards the spot of orange light. Aelfric was surprised at this apparent show of over-confidence. Catherine had brought an experienced and trained soldier with her and chosen to leave him in the woods while she confronted the warlock alone. This only served to increase Aelfric's fear. In an effort to distract himself he looked around them and out across the grassland.

"Is that where Roland is?" whispered Aelfric.

"Yes. Do you see the hut Aelfric? When I say 'go', we need to get to that hut as quickly and quietly as we can. We will be very close to Roland then so you cannot make a sound. We will also be very exposed so make sure you keep the hut between you and the fire. Are you ready?" She glanced at him, her eyes steely and bright, her face grim and determined. Aelfric swallowed hard, his mouth suddenly dry, his palms sweaty. He was nowhere near ready for this but he felt he had no choice now.

"Yes. What do you need me to do?"

"Do you have a sleeping phial?"

"Yes."

"If it looks like I am in trouble, throw it. Shout some warning so I can cover my face but be quick, do not hesitate. Do you also have a healing potion?"

"Yes." Aelfric was feeling more terrified by the second and doubted his ability to do the right thing when it came to it.

"If you get a chance, get to Michael, he may be injured. Otherwise, stay out of sight behind the hut. Is that clear?"

"Yes." Aelfric's voice was barely audible. Noticing this Catherine turned to him and squeezed his arm gently.

"I am terrified too Aelfric, but we have to do this, and not just for Michael."

Feeling strangely comforted Aelfric nodded and Catherine went back to her watching. Suddenly her gaze seemed to be caught by a movement to her right and she looked towards it. Aelfric followed her eyes and could just make out a man on a horse riding out from the tree line. He stopped briefly and then launched his horse towards the fire at a hard gallop.

"Now, Aelfric. Run!"

Still crouching low Aelfric and Catherine ran toward the hut. It was much colder out in the open but neither of them noticed as they made their way across the hard ground.

As they ran they had an excellent view of Arthur charging at the small camp. He sat bolt upright, riding with confidence, a drawn bow in his hands, his left arm lifted and straight. As he drew level with the fire he loosed his arrow and immediately threw his bow aside, taking up the reins once more and galloping on in a fluid and practised movement. As they neared the hut Catherine and Aelfric could both make out the sounds of scuffling on the other side. There was no turning back now, Roland was aware of their attack and was probably preparing himself for battle. They reached the back wall of the hut to the sound of hooves thundering towards them again from the other direction. Apparently Arthur was coming back for a second attack at Roland. Aelfric crouched low to the ground, thankful that he had made it this far and having no desire to move again. Catherine cautiously peeped around the corner of the hut.

Arthur made another pass at the camp, this time his sword was drawn and as he rode past the camp fire he took a long broad swing at someone, Catherine could not see who but she assumed it must be Roland. As Arthur's sword came scything swiftly down at its target Catherine heard a low, smooth voice. It was horribly familiar, a voice she would never forget as long as she lived and she knew that Roland was there. At the same instant she realised that he was chanting. Arthur was in danger. Arthur's sword started to swing up the other side of its arc, back up at its target as the chanting finished with an emphatic final word and Catherine watched as Arthur was thrown from his horse. The horse kept running in the direction of the trees and Catherine was able to see Arthur as his body slammed into the ground. She watched closely, her heart in her mouth but he did not move straight away. Her anger flared and she reached into her little cloth bag and took out a small phial marked with a symbol for vigour. She uncapped it and swallowed the contents, gagging on the awful taste.

A second later Arthur was leaping back to his feet, agile and strong, his sword still in his hand. He was running almost as soon as he was upright and he let out a bloodthirsty battle cry as he ran towards Roland, his sword arm raised above his head. At the same time Catherine burst out from behind the hut, a dagger in her right hand, raised in the air, charging towards Roland.

Roland was chanting again and as he completed the words he waved his arm into the air in a grand sweeping gesture. The spell he had cast knocked Arthur's sword from his hand and another sweep of his other arm knocked Arthur off his feet, throwing him backwards at least five strides. As he hit the ground this time his head snapped back hard against the cold earth and he lay limp and unmoving.

Catherine saw this as she ran, as if time had been slowed around her, but she could not worry about Arthur now. She was only a few paces from Roland, her dagger raised and pointed at a spot between his shoulder blades. She was aware of her pendent glowing and vibrating at her neck, reacting violently to the evil ahead of her. Three paces, two. Roland spun to face her, it was too late to stop running or change direction now. She saw his eyes, they seemed to gleam in the dark, an orange glow that could no longer be a reflection from the fire behind him. He was already chanting under his breath as he turned and she saw his hand coming up. There was an arrow lodged in his shoulder but it did not seem to be slowing him down at all.

She watched as his hand waved through the air, lifting her from the ground, throwing her to the side as if she were a child's toy. She barely had time to register the sensation before she hit the ground, shoulder first. All the air was forced from her lungs, a sharp pain pulsed across her shoulder and back. Then her hips hit the ground, sending a further shock through her battered body. She opened her eyes, alert to the danger that faced her. Roland was some ten paces away, walking towards the fire. He bent low and lifted something from the ground, it was Arthur's sword. Then he turned and started walking back towards Catherine.

She knew she had to get up, if she stayed where she was she was as good as dead. Using her good arm she pushed herself up and turned to face him. He was striding towards her, supremely confident in his superior power, murder written clearly across his features. He raised his sword arm and started to swing it in her direction.

"Arma ab aerius, congrego adeo;
obicio ab nubilis accedo prope;
exarmo cis malefactor, defendo tua adsecula"

Catherine chanted the words as quickly as she was able, closing her eyes as she said the last words, flinching away from the sword as it swung down on her. When it did not hit her she opened her eyes again, Roland stood a couple of paces from her, his expression one of shock, he was looking towards the sword that now lay ten or more paces away from them.

It had worked! Catherine was amazed and her confidence was significantly boosted by the look of complete surprise on Roland's face. However, she was smart enough to realise she only got that once, from now on he would throw everything he had at her. Taking advantage of his pause, Catherine started moving away from him, staggering a little as she forced her bruised hips into motion again.

Roland was looking at her again. His expression was murderous and he had begun chanting under his breath. She was under no illusions, this spell might kill her, and she needed to be quick in casting her shield charm.

"Arma ab adluvio et aerius ventis me;
tua adsecula defendo, custodies ab magicus."

They finished chanting at the same instant and she felt something knock her back a step or two as his spell hit her shield. Having no desire to see what he might throw at her next Catherine started to run as fast as she was able, heading for the cover of the trees, thrusting her dagger back into the cloth bag.

From somewhere not far behind her she heard a feral growl followed by a roar, the likes of which she had never heard before and prayed she would never hear again. Too afraid to look back she kept running, praying that her shield charm was travelling with her.

Roland unleashed his wrath, he had never before been so angry. He had been momentarily taken by surprise at the power this child had found since they had last met. He was not prepared to be beaten by her again, he was too close to reaching his goal to let her get in his way. Leaving the potion over the fire he strode after her. He would not be needing that any longer, once he had killed her there would be no need for a disguise, he would enter her house freely.

Aelfric heard the roar from his hiding place behind the hut. It sent chills through his whole body and he curled up in fright, praying silently, begging for protection from this hellish evil. Gradually he heard footsteps moving away from the camp on the other side of the hut and summoned the courage to sneak a look around the side where he saw Roland striding towards the woods. Just beyond he saw the small figure of Catherine running into the woods, in a second she was gone and Aelfric sent a prayer after her.

Slowly he crawled around the hut and towards the figure lying on the floor by the fire. It was Michael, he looked bad. There were beads of sweat on his brow and he appeared to be unconscious. A little way beyond the fire he saw another figure and hurried to it. It was Arthur, he was also unconscious having had a blow to the back of his head. Aelfric dug into his robes, looking for the healing balms and began to tend to the two soldiers. It was the only way he knew how to help Catherine right now. If he could get one or both soldiers back on their feet they may be able to go to her aid.

Feeling less exposed in the darkness of the woods Catherine's first instinct was to run for the horses and get away and she set off in that direction. As she hurried through the undergrowth she thought of the three men she had left behind at the camp. Leading Roland to the horses may rob them of a means of escape. She stopped, looking around, desperate for an escape route. Then her own words came back to her.

'No! We stay, we fight. Better still, we take the fight to him. He will expect us to behave a certain way. But we are making this up as we go, how can he defend against that?'

Those words had certainly made sense when she had said them before. She knew that she was doing exactly what he would expect, running like a frightened child, out of her depth.

'What can I do that he will not expect? I need to get close to him without him seeing me.' Then it struck her. She knew a way. She could hear him coming, crashing through the bushes, stamping on the undergrowth. She would have to do this quickly. Catherine began chanting under her breath.

"Arma ab adluvio et aerius, accedo me;
tua adsecula occulto, custodis ab magicus"

She held her hands out in front of her and watched as they began to fade. She was not becoming invisible, just dim, harder for evil to find. She had adapted the spell she had used to cloak the Shadow to cloak herself and it seemed to be working.

Next she put her hand carefully into her bag and pulled out a few phials. Selecting the one she needed she put the others back. She grasped it and gave it a gentle shake and as she did it began to emit a soft glow. She began chanting again.

"Phasma ab aerius audiere me nutus;
congrego adeo, cis locus substantia tribuo;
pareo me nutus – transporto"

As she watched, the phial in her hands began to float in front of her. Thrilled at her success and hugely thankful for her diligence in her lessons Catherine pointed at the phial and as she waggled her finger so the phial moved. She sent it off into the trees, weaving a little to miss the trunks she could see. She did not want it to go too far from her, unsure of how far her spell would reach from her.

Roland was close now, maybe five strides from where she stood. He stopped suddenly and for a terrifying moment she thought he had seen her. Then the light caught his eye and he turned, running towards it.

It was working, he was falling for her plan. This would be the hardest part though. With shaking hands she began to guide the tiny phial back towards her. As it floated gently in her direction, with Roland fast gaining on it, she started another whispered chant.

"Phasma ab aerius audiere me nutus;

congrego adeo, cis locus substantia tribuo;

pareo me nutus – profundus"

Roland was beginning to suspect a trap. The light he was following did not seem to be going in any particular direction and now it seemed to be returning to the spot where he had first seen it. There was no noise as it moved and he could not see any of the vegetation being disturbed. He needed to think, work out where she had gone. He did not think she would be going back to the house; that would be too obvious.

Thunk!

He ran into what felt like a wall. He expected to bounce back from it but instead he was stuck, as if he were caught in thick mud. He struggled against it for a second and then began to chant the counter-spell for such a trap.

"Clever little witch. I was not expecting that, but your light gives you away, I see you now." His voice was deep and menacing. Catherine wondered if it might be a trick, in the hope that she would run and give herself away. She looked down at her hands and was horrified to see that as the light phial had returned to her it had cast a feint glow around her, showing the outline of her figure.

Roland was gradually freeing himself from her charm, her concealment charm was wearing off and she felt the last effects of her vigour potion sapping away. It was time to run again. She managed to get a small head start before he freed himself entirely from the spell and she ran as hard as she could, back into the woods, hoping that the thicker undergrowth would hide her from him.

He fought everything she tried, she was no longer strong and powerful. She had no more vigour potions, if she threw a sleeping potion at this range she would probably knock herself out too, and he would certainly wake up first. Roland was storming after her. She had made him incredibly angry and now she was out of ideas. Her only option was to keep running. She dodged past the trunks, hopped over small bushes, darted around small trees, running as quickly as she could, oblivious to the scratches that she suffered in her flight.

She glanced over her shoulder, needing to know if she had gained any distance on him at all. There he was, only a few steps behind her. Panic flared as she pushed herself harder still. Her feet flew over the ground until her toe caught on a knotted root and sent her flying forward onto the ground. Roland was immediately upon her and slammed his fist into the side of her head. Dazed and confused she tried to get up, but he was on her and she could not move. There was only one thing she could do and she prayed it worked. She started to chant under her breath.

"Arma ab adluvio et aerius ventis me;"

He heard her and wrapped his hands around her throat.

"Try chanting when you cannot breathe witch!" He tightened his grip and she felt her head begin to spin. Her hands flew to her throat, grabbing and clawing trying to prize his fingers away but they were too strong for her. Suddenly she felt her pendent, burning hot and strong and she grasped it, her voice was thin and hoarse but she knew she had to finish the spell.

"tua adsecula defendo, custodis ab magicus."

Instantly the huge weight was lifted from her chest and the grip around her throat was gone. Gasping for air she lifted her head a little and saw Roland flung backwards through the air, crashing into a tree trunk. He looked winded. She knew from experience that she would not have long before he was on his feet again and she needed to get back on her own feet and run for her life.

Struggling to get her breath she clambered back up and began to stagger onwards. She had nothing like the speed she had had before, she was in pain and everything hurt. She tried to take deep breaths but it was agony. Her throat was tight and sore, her head thumped from lack of oxygen, her legs were heavy and she knew she would not be able to outrun him. From behind her she heard him roar again. He was coming, he was going to kill her. Desperate and hopeless Catherine began to cry. This was not how she had seen her life ending. She had only just found her new life, barely even begun to realise her destiny and already it was all over. She recalled Aelfric's lecture about the wise man retreating and wished she had run away to Worcester when he had asked her to.

She stumbled on for a few more steps before she tripped and fell once more. As she hit the ground she felt her strength sap even further. This was it. This was how she would die, alone in a wood. Lying on her side she could see Roland rushing at her and instinct took over. She began to mumble the words of a spell without really knowing what she was doing.

"Phasma ab aerius audiere me nutus;
congrego adeo, cis locus substantia tribuo;
pareo me nutus – profundus"

She knew he had fallen for it once and it was unlikely to work again but it may give her a few seconds longer. A barrier of thickened air sprang up between them and Roland was instantly caught in it as he lunged towards her. Somehow this time it seemed stronger, he seemed less able to fight it and that gave her a small glimmer of hope. She had no idea which potions she had left in her bag, perhaps she could try a sleeping potion. She dug her hand into her bag to find a phial.

"Argh!" She cried out as her hand ran down the blade of her dagger, slicing it open, blood flowing freely. Instinctively she pulled her hand out of the bag to protect it. Perhaps she had one more option after all.

The binding spell started to wear off and Roland was lunging at her again, faster and faster. She reached back to her side and grabbed the cloth bag in both hands. Rolling onto her back she thrust it up as far as she could, as hard as she could, letting out an anguished cry as she did so.

Chapter 30

Aelfric had succeeded in rousing Arthur and together they tended to Michael. Arthur supported his head and helped him to sip some water, while Aelfric applied some of the healing balm to his ankle. It would not heal it immediately, but the balm might allow him to walk on it far enough to get back to the horses. Further applications of the balm later would help it to heal far faster than it would do alone. Arthur rubbed his head gently. Aelfric was unable to do much about his headache, that would have to pass on its own, and it would, but slowly.

As Michael started to come round he began to look about him and saw Aelfric crouched at his feet.

"Where is he? Where is Roland?" His voice was hoarse and strained and he winced as he spoke. It was Arthur who answered him.

"He is gone, for now. Can you sit up, we need to get you away from here?"

"Arthur, is that you? How did you find me?"

"We had some help. I will explain it to you later, if I can. Please try to sit up." With Arthur's help Michael managed to get himself sat upright and looked into the flames of the fire, fighting the urge to be sick. He looked around, trying to make sense of what was going on.

"Aelfric? How do you come to be here?"

"He came to help rescue you. Can you stand? Try Michael." Between them they managed to raise Michael to his feet. Aelfric quickly gathered his things, kicked the pot over, spilling its contents, and took Michael's arm around his shoulders.

"Arthur go, I will get him to the horses, you must help her." Arthur nodded and started to jog towards the trees, collecting his sword on the way. He had not gone more than twenty paces when the air was split with a terrible cry. It was full of pain and anguish, tortured and afraid. It sounded like the final battle-cry of a soldier in the field, only worse. It was the cry of a woman. Arthur stopped, frozen in horror. Michael and Aelfric halted too, both looking up towards the tops of the trees, half expecting to see some unearthly creature rising from the depths of the woods.

"What the hell was that?" Michael whispered.

Unable to move, paralysed with grief, Aelfric could barely find a voice to answer Michael. Tears slid down his cheek as he summoned the strength to say the word.

"Catherine."

Michael looked across at him, incredulous. He must have heard Aelfric wrong. He cannot have said her name. There was no way that awful sound had come from her. She would not even be out here. Arthur would never have let her come with them. She was at home with John, that sound had to have come from something else. Then he recalled Aelfric's last words before Arthur had run on ahead.

'Arthur go, I will get him to the horses, you must help her.'

"No, it was not Catherine. It cannot be."

Aelfric, still crying turned to him, his eyes full of grief.

"He will be coming now, we have to go."

Michael looked towards Arthur for confirmation. He was standing stock still some way ahead of them, fixed to the spot. As he watched he saw a glimpse of a movement up by the trees. Dawn was barely upon them and light was beginning to seep across the grassland. There it was again, a small movement just this side of the tree line. Arthur had seen it too and he sprang into life, running towards the spot.

Gripped with fear, Aelfric started dragging Michael towards the trees to their right. The monster would be coming, they had to get away; they would have to find their way back by some other path. Michael stopped him.

"Aelfric, it is not Roland. See?" Aelfric dared to look and true enough it did appear that the figure was not Roland. It was small and slight in build. Could it be? Could it possibly be Catherine?

As Arthur ran towards the figure he turned and shouted over his shoulder.

"It is Catherine, Aelfric bring your medicine, quickly."

As they watched the small figure collapsed onto the ground, exhausted beyond measure. As Arthur reached her he saw that she was smothered with blood and his first thought was that she had been stabbed.

"Catherine, where are you injured, can you tell me?"

Her eyelids flickered open as she recognised his voice. Her own voice was tiny and weak.

"Everywhere, it hurts everywhere. I do not think t is my blood." Unable to speak further Catherine passed out and lay limp in Arthur's strong arms.

It was not long before Aelfric and Michael arrived and Aelfric immediately began to administer aid to her. After some extremely tense minutes he turned to the two men.

"She will be fine. She has some bad bruises and some nasty scratches, but they will all heal. For now she needs rest. We need to get her home."

"I will fetch the horses." Arthur ran to the trees leaving Michael and Aelfric to care for Catherine.

Chapter 31

Catherine felt herself lift from her sleep, as if she were slowly floating upwards. Sounds were the first thing to reach in to her cocoon. She could hear birds and feint footsteps fading into the distance. She could also pick out the delicate patter of rain outside.

Feelings were next. She felt a soft bed beneath her, a pillow under her head. There were blankets too and the roughness of them tickled her skin, but for now she did not want to move. Then her body swamped her with aches and twinges. Her head throbbed gently and her shoulder felt very stiff. She suspected now that it had not been a dream.

Finally she opened her eyes. She could tell that it was daylight outside. A movement to her side startled her and she twisted her head to see what it was.

"Do not worry, it is only me. How do you feel?"

It was Aelfric, his kindly face beaming down at her, she relaxed again and tried to find her voice. It was scratchy to begin with and Aelfric helped her to sit up and sip some water. After a little while she felt able to speak.

"I feel like I have been trampled by a herd of cattle. Do I look as bad?"

"You look fine. The healing balm you made is doing wonders. Well done."

She smiled but it faded as she recalled why she felt so bad.

"Is it really over?"

"Yes, Arthur found his body when he went to get the horses. He is dead and you saved us all."

Aelfric spoke as if she should feel triumphant of what she had done, as if she should be proud. She did not feel triumphant. She felt tired and somewhat jaded by her experience.

"How long have I been asleep?"

"Since yesterday morning, it is now almost time for the midday meal. Do you feel like you could eat at all? You should if you can."

She smiled at him and nodded. Aelfric left to fetch Rachel to help her dress.

It was almost an hour before she made it down to the hall and she was met with a very warm welcome. Both Michael and Arthur came to her straight away. Arthur reached her first and hugged her tightly. She groaned a little as her shoulder protested under the pressure but she did not push him away. Behind him, Michael limped to her side and smiled warmly. For a second they just looked at each other, knowing what the other was saying, not needing to speak the words out loud. Then she reached out to him and wrapped her arms around his neck, it was suddenly all worth it to know that he was safe. At first he stood still, uncomfortable, not quite knowing how to react to her embrace, but then slowly he lifted his arms and tentatively held her. At the feel of his arms around her she squeezed him even tighter and they stood that way for a few seconds longer. When she finally released him Michael looked a little embarrassed and took a hasty step back, guiding her towards a chair near the fire.

"How do you feel?" It was Arthur who had spoken, his voice quiet and gentle.

Catherine was silent, not sure how to answer him. She had thought of nothing else since she had awoken. She felt terrible, beaten and bruised, and everything ached. Worse than that she had killed a man. Until that moment, she had never even considered the possibility that one day she might kill someone, and if she had, she would never have believed herself capable.

It all felt like a nightmare that she could not wake up from. When she had been asleep she had been plagued with dark and sinister dreams, when she had finally woken, those feelings were still there. There was no escape for her.

The only thing that stood between her and insanity, that prevented an unbearable degree of personal torture, was the knowledge that Roland was evil. He was a bad man who had done despicable things and would have done much worse had he been allowed the opportunity. Strangely it did not comfort her that when it had come down to it, it had been an act of self-defence. She suspected this was because some part of her had gone out last night intending to destroy Roland if she could. Some part of her had been looking for revenge. Catherine was greatly disturbed by what she had learned about herself, what she was capable of. She was saddened by the very real possibility that this might not be the last time she would be faced with that choice. Would she choose to kill again, or would she be able to find a better solution?

Catherine was torn between her desire to be surrounded by warm, loving people and a consuming need to be alone, to adjust to the changes going on inside her, to learn how to control these new powers, ensure she never became as dangerous as Roland. For now her desires won the battle, she would have plenty of time for reflection over the coming days as she healed physically.

"I am going to be fine." She told Arthur. She turned then to Michael.

"How are you, will your foot heal?"

"I do not know what Aelfric put on it last night but it has worked wonders. As you see I can just walk on it today. Yesterday I was sure it was broken and that I may never walk again. It is incredible."

Catherine had to admit he did look much better today and she had to bite back the urge to tell him that she had made that potion. It was a topic she did not want to explore with him just now. She was only just coming to terms with its enormity herself, she was not yet ready to share it with another. Besides, to do so would be to make them both vulnerable, the smallest slip of the tongue to the wrong person could see them both sent to the stake. No, she was not ready to burden Michael with that yet. Perhaps one day, but not today.

As she sat thinking, Michael watched her. He and Arthur had been talking that morning about the events of the previous morning. They had both tiptoed around the subject for a while, until Michael could stand it no longer and had asked Arthur if he had seen anything, felt anything, unnatural. Initially a little afraid to admit it Arthur had eventually talked about being thrown through the air by an unseen blow. Michael had himself seen Catherine apparently disarm Roland with a wave of her arm before his pain had overcome him. Together they had reached some chilling conclusions about who Roland was and what Catherine may now be. Both knew the penalties involved for her and anyone who protected her and they recognised that there was a critical decision to be made. Each man had to decide if he was prepared to keep her secret and he needed to make it now.

Within a few minutes of the recognition both men had committed to protect her, to protect what she was and keep her secret. Michael had turned to Arthur then.

"And if she faces this kind if situation again? If she finds herself in harm's way some time in the future? What then?"

Arthur had not needed time to consider his answer.

"Then we stand by her side and fight, again. You saw what Roland was; saw what he was capable of. He was evil and she stood up and fought him, as far as I am concerned that makes her good and I will always fight for that."

There was a pause while they both considered how much their lives had changed in the last day. Two days ago life was simple, there were good people and bad people but they were all just trying to get through life the best they could. Today they found themselves living in a whole new world of good and evil, magic and spells. The possibilities were beyond their imagining. It would take a lot of getting used to.

"Do we tell her we know? She would probably be glad of the support, perhaps relieved that she would not have to keep such a big secret from us anymore." asked Arthur.

"No, whatever her reasons are for not telling us I am sure they are good. She will tell us when she is ready."

The door to the hall swung open and Michael was brought back to the present as John walked in. Of course John had wanted to know what had happened to them all two nights ago. They had come home very late, and in a bad way. Michael had told him the truth, just not the whole truth. He had explained that Roland had been behind all the deaths in the hundred and that he had also been working with Preece to gain control of Catherine's land and property. He went on to say that Roland had ambushed him in the woods to remove some of Catherine's protection and that when Arthur had realised that he was missing. They had managed to work out what was happening and gone to his rescue. John had seemed to accept this, in the most part. For the rest he had seemed to accept that he would not be told the whole story.

This morning John had travelled into the village to speak with the Keeper and let him know that Roland of Langley's body could be found in the woods and that he had confessed to committing all the murders in the process of trying to rob homes.

He had just returned from that errand and it appeared from his expression that he had brought news from the Keeper.

"John" Michael nodded in greeting. "What news from the Keeper, has he sent his men out to bring Roland's body back?"

"He has. He also told me that the Baron's men had already been into the woods searching for Roland and anyone else who might be hiding from justice there. They found a body just before dark the evening you were ambushed."

Michael was surprised by this news. He was not aware that anyone else was missing.

"Who was it, do they know?"

"Oh, yes, he was recognised by the Reeve." John glanced across at Catherine, unsure how his news would be received. "It seems that our friend Mr Preece passed away a few days ago. His body was in the woods, Reeve said it looked like he had died of fright. I suppose we will never know how that happened."

Catherine was a little lost. She was unsure how she felt about this news. In some respects it was a relief to know that he was gone and she would not have to worry about his plots any longer. On the other hand it was disturbing to know that anyone could have died in such a way and she thought she could guess at how he had died.

John continued.

"The Baron found out about Preece almost immediately. He has already seized the house and lands for his own and made arrangements to install his own man there to run the estate."

Arthur sighed in resignation, apparently unconcerned at the news of Preece's death.

"That could go either way. It is hard to imagine anyone could be worse than Preece but only time will tell how much the Baron will want his man to get involved in local affairs from now on."

Chapter 32

Later that afternoon Catherine was resting in her solar. The Baron had arrived shortly after the midday meal to introduce himself and she had found it very tiring recounting a heavily edited version of the awful events leading to Roland's death.

Now she was sitting in her chair by a warm fire enjoying the silence, trying to make sense of her thoughts and feelings, trying to adjust to the consequences of her gift. There was a gentle tap on the door.

"Come in" she called. The door opened and Aelfric's kindly face peered through the gap.

"Can I come in, I would like to talk with you?"

"Of course. Come in, sit down."

Aelfric moved into the room and pulled a chair closer to the fire where he could speak quietly with Catherine.

"How do you feel, you look tired?" he asked.

"A little, but I will be fine. I am sure I will feel much better in a few days. What did you want to talk about? Have you come to say goodbye?"

"No, I have to ask your forgiveness on that point. I do not have to leave to return to Worcester, I lied to you in an effort to get you away from the house, to a place I believed would be safe."

"You are forgiven Aelfric."

"Some time ago I told you about my Order, what we stand for, what we do. I told you that your mother and father worked with us in the battle against evil as Guardians. "

"Yes Aelfric, I remember. Now that Roland is gone we will need to find a way to destroy the Shadow and then we can all go back to our lives. In the meantime I believe it is safely hidden."

Aelfric lowered his head for a second, seemingly unable to meet Catherine's gaze. It was clear that there was something weighing heavily on him still and she suddenly realised what that might be.

"It is not over is it?" she asked. "There are more like Roland out there."

Aelfric raised his head and looked at her now.

"Yes. There are. There are also things much worse than him in the world, and there are artefacts just as powerful as the Shadow too. Members of my Order spend their lives travelling the world, finding them, bringing them to a safe place where they can be guarded until the threat is gone, one way or another. I spent some time doing this myself, until I was sent to you." Aelfric paused, allowing Catherine time to understand what he was saying, allowing himself the time to raise enough courage to continue.

"Catherine, you have a gift, you know that you are very strong and capable of great acts." He paused to take in a long and shaky breath. "The world is plagued with a lot of evil but there are many more good people, people who do not realise the depths of the world they live in. These people need protection, they need someone who can fight for them so that they can sleep at night. So they can live in peace, free from the horrors that the souls of this hundred have witnessed. Will you help us, will you be a Guardian for good?"

Catherine sat perfectly still, her gaze firm and steady on the flickering orange and yellow flames. On the outside she was a picture of peace and serene confidence. Inside she was in turmoil. She did have a gift and she felt very strongly about it. She had enjoyed all her lessons, had looked forward to learning more. She had even felt a great thrill from using her powers to defeat Roland, despite the pain and injury that followed. But Aelfric was asking her to put her life at risk on a regular basis, asking her to witness the wickedness of man, deal out justice to the purveyors of pain and destruction. He was asking her to throw herself into a nightmare world that would in all probability change her forever. All the dreams she had as a child were gone now, husband, home, children. How could that be possible for her now?

She knew what her answer had to be and she knew that Aelfric must be tormented waiting for it. She raised her eyes to meet Aelfric's and her voice was quiet yet firm.

"Yes."

THE END

ISBN 1425109993